THE
KAT
TRAP

Dear Reader:

There is only one word to describe this book: Hot! Cairo has exploded onto the scene with one of the hottest, engaging, realistic, street novels to date. Kat is an assassin but she is also a complex woman. Having been raised by a single mother, she learned early that her "cat" was the only thing men were truly interested in. So she decided to use it to her advantage and now she makes her living killing men at the exact moment that most men would yearn to die: while inside of her "Kat Trap."

The sex scenes in this book are on fire, the storyline is incredible, and the relationships between Kat, her mother, her aunts, her friends, and her lovers are all clearly drawn out. You will not be able to put this book down. Cairo is the writer to be watched and the next book, entitled *The Man Handler* is coming your way soon.

Thanks for supporting one of my many authors under Strebor Books. I appreciate the love. Make sure you join us on www.planetzane.net or visit me on the web at www.eroticanoir.com.

Peace and Many Blessings,

Zane

Publisher
Strebor Books International
www.simonandschuster.com/streborbooks

ZANE PRESENTS

THE KAT TRAP

A NOVEL BY
CAIRO

SBI

STREBOR BOOKS

NEW YORK LONDON TORONTO SYDNEY

Strebor Books
P.O. Box 6505
Largo, MD 20792
http://www.streborbooks.com

© 2009 by Cairo

ISBN-13 978-1-59309-228-3
ISBN-10   1-59309-228-8
LCCN 2009924321

First Strebor Books trade paperback edition May 2009

Cover design: www.mariondesigns.com
Cover photograph: © Keith Saunders/Marion Designs

10 9 8 7 6 5 4 3 2 1

Manufactured in the United States of America

For information regarding special discounts for bulk purchases, please contact Simon & Schuster Special Sales at 1-866-506-1949 or business@simonandschuster.com

The Simon & Schuster Speakers Bureau can bring authors to your live event. For more information or to book an event, contact the Simon & Schuster Speakers Bureau at 1-866-248-3049 or visit our website at www.simonspeakers.com.

THIS BOOK IS DEDICATED TO NAKEA MURRAY—
my literary sister, supporter and friend, who planted the seed
and nourished the process, bringing life to a wonderful creation.
The Kat Trap wouldn't exist if it weren't for you challenging
me to step outside of my box and pushing me along the way.
Thank you for being you! I am forever grateful for
your undying support and encouragement.

ACKNOWLEDGMENTS

All praises to the Almighty, who continues to forgive me and love me in spite of all of my shortcomings. It is through HIS grace and mercy that I am still evolving, still growing and still learning how to be better than the day before, one step at a time.

I'd like to thank the following special people who helped make *The Kat Trap* a reality:

My agent, Sara Camilli; my publisher, Zane; Charmaine Parker, Navorn—editor extraordinaire, and a very special thanks to my publicist, Yona Deshommes. I appreciate all of you for being a part of this literary adventure.

My literary friends, who shared their thoughts during the early stages of this writing project and listened to me whine about Nakea daring me to leave my comfort zone: Anna J and Tu-Shonda L. Whitaker. Thanks a million, for the laughs and the support!

And lastly to the readers, I thank you in advance for your support. Without you, this journey would be senseless. I truly appreciate you, and hope you enjoy reading *The Kat Trap* just as much as I enjoyed writing it!

Cairo

CHAPTER ONE

They say the closest ones to ya are the same ones who'll sneak up behind ya and stick the knife through ya. Sleepin' on me is your biggest mistake. Close ya eyes, and ya'll find ya'self in a river of blood. One for the money, one for the nut, one bullet to the skull...nigga, what?!

My name is Katrina, Kat for short. Voluptuous, vivacious, and vicious—at five-feet-eight, a buck-twenty-five, I'm *that* bitch. Be clear. Fine, fly, and fabulous with a wicked brain game and a fat, wet, deep pussy so good it makes a nigga shake the minute I wrap my walls around his dick. I'm that chick with the small waist and the Hottentot Venus ass: big, round, and juicy. The kinda ass that makes a nigga's jaw drop and his neck snap every time I walk past. Niggas love it when I make my bootie bounce, shake, and clap for 'em. With my cinnamon skin, shoulder-length hair, thick lashes wrapped around chinky eyes, I am a hood goddess. I'm that chick the bitches bow down to, and niggas worship. I was born and bred in Brooklyn, a product of one of the most notorious housing projects known for drugs and murders. If you're an uninvited or unwanted guest, beware. You might get in, but you comin' out either slashed up, beat down, or bodied.

I'ma keep it real cute for ya. Ain't shit sweet 'bout life on the compound—the hood, the concrete jungle. It's ruthless. Game recognizes game. And ya either learn to play hard or get played. Ya either eat or be eaten. It's that simple. Make no mistake: The hood don't give a fuck 'bout you or the next chick. And it definitely ain't beat for what the next nigga's into. You either handle ya business or get handled. Ain't no way 'round it. I ain't tryna make excuses. It is what it is. I learned how to handle mine without sellin' my ass, or suckin' a string of dicks in alleyways or up on somebody's rooftop. I studied the game, watched its playas, and mastered the rules without stuntin' on the next bitch, or hustlin' a nigga off his grip. I ain't have to claw or scheme my way up to nobody's top. I'm from Brooklyn, baby! I kicked open the muh-fuckin' door of opportunity, smashed out its windows, and fuckin' snatched my spot 'cause I'm *that* bitch.

So, if ya lookin' to hear me spit some whack-ass story 'bout some fast-assed little ho from the hood stretched out on a pissy mattress in shit-stained panties, eating dry-ass cereal out of a dirty-assed plastic bowl watching cartoons on a busted-ass black-and-white TV while counting roaches, then you got the wrong one. If ya wanna hear 'bout a bitch goin' hungry 'cause her moms sold her food stamps to get high, nope…not gonna get it. If ya lookin' to hear 'bout some young chick who got her ass beat with extension cords, razor straps, and switches because she was too hot in the ass, then ya might as well step now, 'cause that ain't what I'm here to serve ya. Yeah, we had roaches, okay…who didn't? But I never got my ass beat, always had food to eat, and I ain't never laid around on no pissy-assed mattress.

Uh, yeah, a bitch was born poor. Yeah, my moms was clockin' welfare, and? Her ass still worked, though. And she gave me what she thought I needed, which—outside of food and a roof over my head—was close to nothin'. Fuck what I wanted. No, she wasn't on crack or dope or a fuckin' drunk. Maybe she shoulda been. But I can't give ya no fucked-up tales of watchin' her smoke up, shoot up, or snort up. And I can't tell ya jack 'bout no tricks or johns runnin' up in her pussy all hours of the day and night. Sellin' her ass wasn't her thing. Yeah, she went through men like water, and moved one in after the other...okay, and? That's her story, not mine. She did her thing, and I learned to do mine.

Yeah, I knew...uh, I mean, *know*, who the fuck my father was/is, so? It ain't like the nigga ever did anything for me. Besides hustlin' and robbin' niggas, the only good thing he ever did was donate his nut to my moms, a half-Spanish, half-black chick who spit me outta her hairy pussy when she was sixteen. Other than that, goin' in and out of prison and breakin' my mom's heart was the only thing his sorry ass was good for. Be clear. I ain't hatin' on dude. He was a street nigga who tried to get in where he fit in. From breakin' into cars to burglaries to drug dealin' to numerous parole violations to runnin' with known felons to fuckin' any unsuspectin' trick willin' to spread open her legs and her wallet, he was a rebel, down for whateva.

The hood raised him. Bitches praised him. And the streets and pussy were what turned their backs on him when his black ass got popped fifteen years ago. Now he was on lock for another ten years for an aggravated assault he didn't commit, and drug charges for shit that wasn't his. But the nigga ain't a snitch. Turnin' state's evidence on his niggas was outta the question. That's the code he lived by, and one he'd proudly die by. That's how the real niggas get down. So fuck what ya heard 'bout me needin' him. A bitch can't miss what she never had! Other than sharin' the same DNA, the only thing dude and I will ever have in common is our love for the benjamins. Believe that!

So, you wanna know what's really good with a bitch like me? Then I'll tell ya. I'ma give it to ya straight, no chaser—as real and as raw as it gets. I fuck for sport. But I murder for business. And because most muhfuckas are so driven by lust and the desire for good pussy and a slow, wet dick suck, it doesn't take much for me to lure 'em into their own death traps. My mission is simple: Wet a nigga's dick, then put a bullet in his skull, or in his chest, just before he cracks his nut. That's right. Send his ass to his grave with his eyes rolled up in his head and a smile on his face before he ever knows what hit his ass.

Make no mistake. This shit ain't 'bout love. It ain't 'bout revenge. And it surely ain't personal. In this business, there's no time for compassion or sympathy. And there's no room for regret. It's 'bout clockin' that paper. And a bitch like me gets paid by the body. Welcome to the Kat Trap, muhfuckas…it's 'bout to get poppin'!

CHAPTER TWO

"Lay back, nigga, and let me wet your dick with my pussy," I said, mountin' my target for the night, then slammin' my hot, wet snatch down on his long, black cock. I leaned forward, brushin' my perfectly rounded titties with their Hershey kiss nipples against his lips as I galloped up and down on his brick-hard dick, positionin' myself so that the shaft of his pole stroked my clit while I rode him down into the hotel mattress. I slowly lifted up, used my pussy muscles to milk the head of his dick, then slammed back down. I repeated it. Up. Down. Up. Down. Bounced and twirled my hips, buryin' e'ery thick inch of him deep inside me until I had the nigga beggin' me, until I had him practically slurrin' his words.

"You like this wet pussy, nigga? You like this pussy grabbin' ya dick?"

"Uh…uh…Oh, fuck yeah! Oh, shit! Ride that dick, baby."

I glanced over at the digital clock on the oak wood nightstand. It read 11:42. I had been fuckin' dude for almost forty minutes and was determined to cum for the third time before I sealed his fate. Murder made me no never mind. I didn't ask no questions, didn't want no answers. The less I knew, the better. The only thing I needed to know was: when, where, and who.

Easy cum, easy go, I thought as I took in my target's face. The nigga had the nerve to be fuckin' fine. Deep, dark chocolate-coated, broad-shouldered nigga with waves that spun so deep a bitch could get seasick just starin' at 'em. His eyes were slits of lust, his face slick with sweat as he thrust upward, matchin' my rhythm stroke for stroke, stabbin' my pussy, stokin' the fire that ignited inside me. Damn! And the nigga had some good dick. Too bad that in another few minutes it'd be a wrap for his ass. I didn't give a fuck. Wasn't shit I could do about it, even if I wanted to. His time on this earth was limited. The mother-fucka was on borrowed time, and didn't even know it. Oh, well.

The clock ticked in my head. His life meant nothing to me. I didn't give a fuck whether or not he had a wife and kids, and I definitely didn't give a fuck how his family's world would be after tonight. The only thing I cared about was gettin' my fuck on, bustin' a nut, and puttin' this snitch-ass nigga outta his misery. My pussy got hotter and wetter just thinkin' about my next move. "You ready to nut for me, big daddy?" I asked, clampin' my pussy around his throbbin' dick.

"Damn, ma, you got some killa pussy. Ah…uh. Shit. This pussy is mad tight. Yeah, baby. Just like that. Got my dick wetta than a muhfucka," he said in between his moans, grunts, and groans.

If you only knew, I thought, smilin'. "That's right, make my pussy cum, nigga," I whispered into his left ear. "Fuck this pussy. Give me that nut, daddy. Yeah, nigga, just like that…fuck this pussy…Mmmm, give me that nut." The lower I spoke, the harder he jabbed his dick in me. "Oh, yes," I moaned. I sucked on his ear lobe, then stuck the tip of my tongue into his ear. "Oooh, daddy, this dick feels so good. You ready to give me that hot nut?"

"Yeah, baby, I'm 'bout to spit. Oh, shit. Damn, girl."

I cut my eyes over at the clock again: 11:52. I quickly gazed down at the unsuspectin' victim beneath me. He was 'bout to bust his dick milk. I smiled. And in one swift move, I reached up under the pillow and pulled out my shiny black silencer gun.

"Oh, shit! Oh, shit! I'm cuuuuming, baaa—" *Theessrrpp!* Before he could finish, before he could get his nut off, I shot him dead center in his forehead. *Mission complete*, I thought, pullin' myself up off this dead nigga's still stiff dick.

I stared at his lifeless body, silently admired his perfectly chiseled abs and his big, black dick, then yanked off the condom and dropped it into a Ziploc baggie. I licked my lips, watchin' his nut spurt and run outta the tip of his dick. I shook off the thought of lickin' it up from 'round his big, hairy balls, diggin' into my Gucci satchel and pullin' out a bottle of rubbin' alcohol and a pack of wipes. I started wipin' him down. Leavin' a trail of clues that could potentially lead back to me was not an option. I was a stickler for details and there was no room for bein' sloppy, which is why I *always* did my dirt solo.

When I finished wipin' all the evidence off the corpse sprawled out in the middle of the bed with his dick slick from his own juices, I pulled the sheets from underneath him, rolled them up in a tight ball, then stuffed them in a bag. I glanced at the nigga lyin' on the bare mattress one last time before pickin' the spread up from off the floor, then tossin' it over his body. I had seen enough, and needed to get the hell outta there. I had about twenty minutes before the "clean-up" crew came through to dispose of the body, or do whatever the fuck else it is they did. I just knew I wasn't trustin' no niggas I didn't know or hadn't seen before to make sure my fingaprints and pussy juice wasn't still lingerin' all over the place.

I went into the bathroom, wiped my soakin' wet pussy with some tissue, then used several baby wipes to give myself a whore bath. When I was done, I quickly dressed, slipped on my white gloves, then slid my feet into my Jimmy Choo mules. I straightened my burgundy wig, then applied a fresh coat of burgundy-wine lipstick to my full, soft, made-for-dick-suckin' lips. Satisfied that everything was dusted off and in place, I shut off the bathroom light, then strutted toward the door. On my way out, I caught my reflection in the mirror and almost didn't like what I saw starin' back at me: the slanted, eyes of a cold-blooded killa. I shook the image from my mind, and pressed out the door and toward the elevators.

Growin' up, a bitch had dreams. I dreamed dreams of bein' rich. And baggin' a fine-ass hood nigga with a big black dick and fat pockets who would love me, and fuck me, and get me far the fuck away from the roaches that crawled all over the walls and from all the dirty dishes that overflowed in the sink 'cause my moms was too motherfuckin' stressed 'bout life and no-good muhfuckas to ever give a fuck 'bout what I was doin'. I dreamed dreams of being loved and wanted and needed 'cause a bitch was special. But then I woke the fuck up and realized that dreams ain't real, and that love won't always love you back, and that the only way to keep the dirty-ass nigga with his nasty-ass fingers and grimy-ass hands off ya ass and titties, the only way to keep the duck-ass nigga from smackin' ya moms up, was to stretch his ass.

Yeah, a bitch had dreams. Bein' a murderer was never one of 'em. But it quickly became my reality the night I sucked a young nigga on the come up's dick and gave him some pussy as payment for a gun to kill my mother's sorry-ass nigga because I was tired of him creepin' into my room, suckin' on my titties, and eatin' my pussy. I guess I should be grateful that the old nigga just jerked his long, black dick while lickin' my clit instead of tryna run it up in me. But I knew it was only a matter of time before he'd want to feel my young, tight, hairy pussy wrapped around his dick. And I swore I'd never let that happen. So, I snuffed his ass. And fuckin' that young nigga and lettin' him bust this pussy open was far better than lettin' some nasty-assed nigga steal the little string of innocence I had left.

Say what ya want. In my mind, the payoff was well worth it. I got what I wanted, and dude got himself a taste of some virgin twat. But after it was all said and done, I promised myself that I would never, *ever*, again, suck another nigga's dick or give up my pussy to get shit again. And I meant that! If I fuck or suck a nigga it's 'cause I *want* to, not 'cause I need to.

Anyway, I'ma tell ya some foul shit. A part of me thinks my moms knew what time it was, but she wanted to act like she was stuck on stupid or some shit and ignore it. Sometimes I thought I saw it in her eyes when she looked at me. Guilt. The fact that she was tryna pimp me, her only child. Maybe it was regret I saw. Maybe it was just my fucked-up imagination. Well, whether or not there was ever any truth to it—not that she would ever admit it—is neither here nor there. I handled the nigga my way by lurin' his ass into a darkened stairwell for some pussy, then shootin' him in his head. His eyes were wide open and filled with shock and panic when his brains splattered against the cement wall. I looked down at his lifeless ass with a smirk on my face, then left him lyin' in a pool of blood. I was fifteen. At that moment, some-thin' in me changed. It opened my eyes to the power of pussy, and showed me just how far a nigga—young or old—would go to feel it, taste it, and try to possess it. And a bullet to his head is the only thing that would stop his muhfuckin' ass from tryna claim it.

So, hell the fuck no! I didn't choose this life—this muhfuckin' life chose me. I was pushed into this shit. As a result, it has become my callin', a way of life that has evolved into a way of bein' for a bitch like me. Don't get it twisted. I ain't makin' no excuses, and I ain't lookin' for no sympathy. I accept life for what it is: unfair, with a set of fucked-up rules you either live or die by. And no matter how many dreams a bitch dreams, ain't shit comin' true unless ya get on ya grind and make shit happen 'cause life don't give a fuck 'bout you or no whack-ass fairy tales.

I stepped off the elevator, strutted through the lobby of the Marriott, then quietly slid out the revolvin' glass doors, unheard and unnoticed. When I reached my rental—a blue Ford Taurus— and was safely behind the steerin' wheel, I pulled off my wig, took out the blue contact lenses, then flipped open my cell, pressed speed dial, and waited for the voice on the other end.

"Yo, what's good?"

"I know why the caged bird sings," I stated, startin' the car, then pullin' out of the parkin' lot and onto the highway. It was the code I used to let him know when a job had been completed.

"That's what it is. I'll get at you."

"Same spot?"

"No doubt. One."

Click. I pressed the END button and disconnected the call, along with my emotions.

I drove in silence. I didn't wanna hear shit. The only thing I wanted was a hot shower, some sleep, and to be back on that plane first thing in the mornin', headin' to Jersey. I couldn't wait to get home to collect the remainin' half of the hundred gees I had comin' to me for smokin' that nigga back at the hotel. *Not bad for a day's work*, I thought, headin' to my hotel suite on the other side of town. *Murkin' these crab-ass niggas is as easy as snatchin' candy from a baby.*

The followin' afternoon, I was home chillin' in my two-story condo in the suburbs of Jersey, standin' at the mahogany island in the middle of my walk-in closet, waitin' for the whir of the countin' machine to finish totalin' my money. Snoop Dogg's "For All My Niggaz & Bitches" blared through my Bose surround sound system. *Oh, hell naw. Somethin' ain't right*, I thought. But I knew what I saw. It totaled my paper at forty thousand dollars. I knew shit wasn't wrong with the machine, but I recounted my money anyway. Nothin' changed. I stormed outta the closet, snatchin' up the cell on my nightstand. I punched in his number and waited. The deep voice answered on the third ring. "What's good?"

"My motherfuckin' money, nigga!" I snapped, turnin' down my stereo. "That's what the fuck's good. Now where's the rest of my shit?"

"Yo, chill, ma," he said, lowerin' his voice. "I got you."

"Nigga, chill my ass. I want my motherfuckin' shit. And I want it today. And I want another ten for you tryna finger-fuck me."

"Whoa, whoa," he said, soundin' like he was ready to raise up. "You buggin' for real, ma. I said I got you. And that's what it is."

"Buggin' hell, muhfucka! I tell you what, bring me my shit and the extra or we got problems. And *that's* what it is. This is like the third time you tried some bitch shit on me, and I'm not the one. So, you betta buy a vowel and get a fuckin' clue. Now what's it gonna be, 'cause another body don't mean shit to me."

"Aye, yo. You tryna write a check you ain't gonna be able to cash, baby girl. So watch how you come at me. I said I got you."

I wasn't tryna hear shit he had to say. I paced the floor, burnin' a hole in my white Persian rug while clenchin' my fist. On the real, this nigga really had me swole. My mind was made up. If this fat, black muthafucka didn't have my money by day's end, I was gonna stretch his ass. I didn't give a fuck how many goons he had in his camp. I'd just lie in wait until the right time—I didn't give a fuck if it took weeks or years. I would smoke his ass, real talk. There were two things you didn't fuck over: my money, and my pussy. Try it if you want, and you got hell to pay.

I screamed on his ass. "No, nigga! You watch how you handle ya business. I ain't one of them sucka-ass bitches you fuck with. My name ain't Wonder Bread, and ain't shit soft on me but my ass. Now, like I *said*, I want my shit…*today!*"

"Hold da fuck on," he snapped. I pulled in a deep breath, then counted to ten. I heard muffled sounds in the background as he attempted to cover the mouthpiece of the phone. I welcomed the momentary silence. I knew the nigga really didn't wanna beef with me. I was the best thing on his squad. Bein' the only female on his team, as far as I was concerned I was his most valuable asset. And one of the baddest killers he had. Not only was I sexy as hell, I was reliable, dependable, and with the promise of a good fuck and dick suck, I seductively lured my marks into the Kat Trap, then served them the heat—clean and swift. Of course the fuckin' was a perk he acted like he wasn't aware of because he'd never confronted me about it. But I knew he knew what time it was. Bottom line, no one suspected a chick like me was capable of slumpin' muhfuckas. But I was. And I had no problem killin' again, so dude had better play his position real quick, or he'd be next on the list to get earthed.

This fat, black, six-foot-three, three-hundred-and-thirty pound grizzly bear's name is Cash. I met his ass at that spot the Brooklyn Café back in '03. The nigga approached me after peepin' me mop a bitch's ass across the dance floor for tryna shine on me in front of some niggas. Wrong move!

He was sittin' at the bar when I walked over to order me a drink.

Fightin' that ho had a bitch's throat dry. "Yo, ma, I dug how you handled ya'self out there," he had said, eyein' me real hard, lickin' his lips like he was tryna suck my panty liner.

"Oh word," I responded real easy-like. But in the back of my mind I was thinkin': *Why the fuck is this crusty, black muhfucka lickin' his lips at me? I know this beast don't think he's L.L. or some shit.*

He smiled, showin' a top row of big teeth and big red gums. I yanked my neck back, tryna check my frown. "Yeah. You stomped chick's back in."

"Next time I'ma slice the bitch's throat," I snapped, tossin' my fresh-to-death wrap—compliments of this Dominican spot up in the Bronx—and lookin' him dead in his frog eyes. "Ain't no bitch gonna talk greasy 'n shit, then think shit's sweet. I got somethin' for that ass."

I really wasn't beat for all the chit-chat. I just wanted to wet my throat, get my dance back on, and chill with my girls. But, he insisted on tryna lean in my ear. "I hear ya, ma," he replied, rubbin' his chin. "I've been checkin' ya all night. You seem like a real thorough chick. Where you rest?"

"Brooklyn," I said with much 'tude. "Why?"

"How 'bout I buy you a drink, and we find us a spot to politic."

I twisted my lips. "Nigga, I know you ain't thinkin' a drink is gonna get ya black ass some pussy."

He laughed. "Chill, ma. I ain't on it like that. Don't get me wrong, you some real eye candy and I'd love to tap that ass inside out and all. But this is on some strictly legit shit." I twisted my lips. He flagged the bartender. "Get this beauty whatever she's drinkin'."

I smiled. Obviously, the nigga didn't know just how deep my throat was. I ordered me two double-shots of Rèemy, peeped my girls gettin' their drop 'n pop on out on the dance floor, then followed dude to a corner table. As soon as we sat down, he got right to the point.

"Dig, how you feel 'bout makin' some real cheddar?"

I tossed my drink back. Although I was already sittin' on cake thanks to a sudden windfall, a bitch was still boostin'. It was cute and it kept me laced, but that shit wasn't pullin' in no real paper. I wanted more. A chick like me, bein' an opportunist, needed to step her game up and stack some real cheese, but pushin' or holdin' or transportin' somebody's weight wasn't ever gonna be it.

"What ya talkin'?" I had asked, raisin' my naturally arched eyebrow.

He leaned in real close, wrapped his thick arm around the back of my seat, then spoke into my ear. He said again he was diggin' my style, then told me 'bout a "work-for-hire" operation he ran, and how he was lookin' for a thorough chick to be on his team.

"Hmmm," I said, takin' my second drink to the head. I studied dude's swagger. He was ugly as fuck, but was dipped and paid. The nigga smelled like real money. And I wanted in. I peeped his Rolex, smilin'. "Order me another round, then let me sleep on it. A bitch don't like to make any decisions when I'm gettin' my drink and smoke on."

He grinned. "Yeah, you definitely the real deal. Here's my card. Hit me when you ready." He slid me his business card, then turned to step. He turned back around. "Yo, ma, you gotta name?"

"Katrina," I said. "Kat for short. And you?"

"Kashmir. But the streets know me as Cash."

When the bartender returned with my drink, I smiled, liftin' my glass. "I'll get at ya."

"Do that," he replied, walkin' off. I watched him give a few niggas pounds, then disappear out the door.

A week later, I called his ass and we spoke briefly. Then, the next day, we met for dinner at Junior's in Brooklyn to discuss and finalize his offer. The paper was right, and it sounded sweet. Now, here I am, four years later, still fuckin' with his slimy ass. Usually he was on point, but lately the nigga had been slippin' and I really wasn't feelin' it. I didn't give a fuck who he was, or how he got down for his. As far as I was concerned, the muh-fucka could get it, too.

There were fifteen of us on this nigga's money clip, and he received anywhere from five to twenty contracts a month, some-times more. And he got paid *well* for the delivery of services; services that we carried out. The blood from my work was on my hands, not his. He had better recognize who kept him sittin' his stankin' ass up on his throne.

The longer he kept me on hold, the more heated I got. Dude was caked the fuck up and was on some real bitch shit tryna pinch corners with my paper. I'm sorry, but I was not diggin' it at all! I was gonna have to make a major move, and soon, before I ended up shuttin' his lights out.

"Yo," he said, yankin' me from my thoughts, "I'ma have that for ya in 'bout an hour. You know where to go."

"Yeah, muhfucka," I said, suckin' my teeth.

"Oh, and check this out. The next time you come at me like that, I'ma forget I don't put my hands on bitches and knock ya fronts out, ya heard?"

"Don't fuck with my money, then," I warned.

"You heard what I said," he said, lowerin' his voice. It almost sounded like his nasty ass had his hand down in his pants playin' with his shit. The thought made me sick to my stomach. "Watch how the fuck you come at me. You work for *me*, not the other way around. Don't get the game fucked up."

I knew I was playin' with dynamite comin' at his neck like that.

This muhfucka was a real shiesty-type nigga. I knew that the moment I jumped on his team. I also knew he could be real shady if pressed, and had no problem settin' that ass up lovely if he felt disrespected or played. But, at the moment, I didn't give a fuck!

"And I'm the one out here puttin' heat to these muhfuckas, so don't hit me with that bullshit. I ain't the one. Play ya position, cowboy, and have my shit. I deliver ya bodies on time, and I expect my paper delivered on time, in full. And I ain't tryna hear shit else. So *don't* try 'n dry-fuck me."

"I done warned you," he snapped, "and you still yappin' ya fuckin' jaws. You'se a crazy bitch."

"Whatever, nigga," I said, snappin' the phone shut on his ass. "I'll be glad when I've stacked enough money to get the fuck outta this shit once and for all," I said out loud, slippin' into a pair of sweats and a hooded shirt. *I need a fuckin' blunt*, I thought, searchin' for my stash. *Fat muhfucka got my nerves rattled*. I lit the blunt, then took a long drag, inhalin' deep, allowin' the smoke to flow through my nose and mouth simultaneously. *I really hate fuckin' wit' these snake niggas*, I thought, takin' another deep, long pull before puttin' it out. *I'll smoke the rest of this shit later*. I grabbed my purse and headed out the house to collect my loot.

Forty minutes later, I was back in the same spot I'd started out from, watching the money counter count and total the rest of my money. Twenty thousand. I smiled, placin' it in the floor-to-ceiling safe with the rest of my paper. It was like Bank of America up in this bitch. And I was lovin' it. I stood there and stared at the rows of bills neatly stacked. The smell made my snatch tingle. I just wanted to fuck, and rub my pussy over every single bill. I pinched my clit, then clamped my legs shut before slidin' my hand between my legs and slowly rubbin' my pussy. A bitch was in heat. I needed to be fucked, deep, long, and hard. But there wasn't one nigga on my roster who I wanted to come through and slay me. I wanted some new dick. I sucked my teeth, then walked into a smaller walk-in closet and opened up a chest full of sex toys. I pulled out a ten-inch dildo, then climbed up on my king-sized bed, spread open my legs, and slid it in and out of my hungry hole, deep-fuckin' myself until my cum-soaked pussy dripped a stream of hot, sticky juice down the crack of my ass. My pussy lips flapped around the width of my manual dick as I used my other hand to press on my swollen clit, pullin' the dildo out of me e'ery so often to lick and suck my sweet cum juice off my rubber companion. I want some dick! I screamed in my head. "Fuck me! Fuck me! Fuck me!" is the last thing I remember chantin' and screamin', before I closed my eyes and fucked myself into a deep, well-needed sleep.

CHAPTER THREE

> *If ya tryna play a bitch like me, ya better be ready to rock. Let me catch ya sleepin', and ya gonna find ya'self knocked. Crabs in a barrel gonna try 'n steal yo shine, hatin'-ass hoes gonna try 'n steal ya spot… fuck what ya heard…a bitch like me will blast ya ass with somethin' hot…before I ever let a muhfucka snatch me off top …*

T he shrill sound of my cell pulled me outta my sleep. The sound of the ring tone told me who it was, and which cell line it was. I glanced over at the digital clock on my nightstand, rollin' my eyes.

"Shit," I groaned, jumpin' out of bed and diggin' through my purse for my phone. I glanced at the number. Sure enough it was my moms. "Hello."

"Is there any reason why you haven't called me?" she asked with 'tude. No "hello." No "it's good to hear ya voice," nothin' except her fuckin' attitude. I swear the older she gets the more evil she gets. The conversation hadn't even gotten started and I was already ready to snap my phone shut on her ass.

I sighed. "Well, hello to you, too," I said. "And to answer ya question, I haven't called 'cause I've been busy."

"Humph. Doin' what? Are you workin'?"

"Yeah, I'm workin'. And before ya start tryna get all up in what I do, save it. As long as I'm not askin' you to dig in ya pockets, what I do to make my paper is none of ya concern. Now, who pissed in ya Cheerios today?"

"Ain't nobody piss in nothin' of mine. I haven't heard from you in almost two months, and I shouldn't have to be the one to call you."

"Uh, and why not?" I asked, sittin' on the edge of my king-sized poster bed. The fuckin' nerve of her!

"Because I'm your mother, that's why. *You* should be callin' and checkin' on me."

I rolled my eyes. "Really? Well, thanks for that news bulletin. I woulda thought as a mother *you* would wanna pick up a phone to see how ya only child is doin'. You know how to reach me. Anyway, now that ya got me, what's been happenin'? Anything new goin' on in ya life?"

"Nope," she said, a bit too quick if ya ask me. "You know I don't mess with too many people. Ever since I got my money these phony bitches 'round here always smilin' and whatnot and tryna be up in my face. I'm like, 'bitch, please, I ain't got no time for it.'"

"Hmm. I hear ya. How's Grandma?"

"You'd know that if ya ass picked up a phone and called her sometimes."

I sucked my teeth. I really wasn't in the mood for her shit. *Beeeep!* The call waitin' tone signaled in my ear. *Good.* "Listen, I gotta go. I have another call comin' in. I'll be over next Saturday or Sunday."

"That's what ya ass said two months ago, and I still haven't seen you."

Beeeep!

"Alright," I said, gettin' agitated. "I'll see ya on Sunday. 'Bye."

"Well—"

I pressed the TALK button, disconnectin' her ass. "Hello?"

"Damn, baby," the nigga said in his silky voice. "Your voice got my shit on brick. When you gonna let a nigga see you?" It was Raynard, this cat from Long Island I had met when I was out in Vegas for All-Star Weekend in February. Humph. I knew I shoulda never given this nigga my digits.

The first night I met him was at the party P. Diddy was hostin' at the Ice House Lounge. I was up in that piece lookin' fabulous in a sexy Christian Dior white slip dress with a cutout back and plungin' neckline that showed off my perfectly shaped ass, titties, and legs, and rockin' a bangin'-ass pair of white beaded Gucci stilettos. *Yes*, a bitch slayed 'em in all white. I had the niggas droolin' and every hatin'-ass bitch in that piece gaggin'.

Anyway, I was up in the VIP lounge standin' out on the patio drinkin' a flute of champagne when dude stepped to me tryna get his mack on. I ain't gonna front, he was a dark-chocolate cutie—six-three, sexy brown eyes, nice thick lips, neatly trimmed mustache and goatee, with a beautiful bald head. The nigga was dipped in a fly-ass black Hugo Boss suit and it was somethin' 'bout his swagger that made my pussy jump. But I kept it cute. I let him get his rap on, then sweetly smiled and bounced on his ass.

The next night, I bumped into him again when I was walkin' through Caesar's headin' toward the Forum Shops. As I walked past him and his boys—there was like six or seven of them niggas— he stopped me and tried to get his shine on in front of his mans while them vultures swarmed around me like they were ready to eat me alive. I wasn't pressed, though.

"Listen," I had said. "I'd love to stand here and let you and your boys gawk at me, but I got shoppin' to do."

"Anything I can help you with, beautiful?"

I looked his ass up and down real easy-like, then smirked, starin' into his eyes. "Nope," I said, "'cause I ain't shoppin' for dick."

He grinned. And his boys started laughin'. "Oh word. Well, let me get your digits then, so I can hit you up later on tonight."

"Wrong answer," I replied.

"Do you believe in fate?" he asked, smilin'.

"Why?"

"'Cause this is the second time I done ran into you. Outta all these heads out here, I spot you again. You dipped on me last night, but I ain't letting you off that easy this time."

I smiled. "So, you believe in fate, I take it?"

"Most def."

"Good. Well, they say three's a charm so if we happen to run into each other again, then I'll give you my number. If not"—I shrugged—"then it wasn't meant to be."

I looked at him, then over at his boys. "You boys enjoy the rest of your stay. I'm out."

He threw his big hand up over his chest, like he was clutchin' his heart. "Damn, ma. I'm heartbroken. How you gonna leave me hanging like this?"

I grinned. "Easy," I said, gettin' ready to step off. But I stopped dead in my tracks when I heard one of his boys say: "Yo, Ray, I wouldn't even waste my time on a stuck-up bitch like her. I can tell she'd be a fuckin' headache tryna get some pussy from."

I turned to face his wide-nosed, big-lipped ass, then let that ass have it. "Nigga, what the fuck did you just say?" I asked, steppin' up in his face. I could tell the nigga was lit. He smelled like he'd been drinkin' all night. But I didn't give a fuck. Drunk or not, that nigga stepped outta pocket. In a split second I was 'bout to bring my blade to his face. "I know you didn't just disrespect me.

Muhfucka, I don't know what type of bitch you think you talkin' to, but I ain't *that* bitch. How dare you try to come at me and you got the fuckin' audacity to look like a muthafuckin' cross-eyed gorilla!"

"Yo, you better go 'head 'fore you get hurt in here."

"Go 'head nothin'. Fuck you, you crusty muhfucka. You probably the only duck-ass nigga outta ya crew who ain't gettin' no real pussy unless you beggin' for it, or trickin' ya money up for it. You done fucked with the wrong one, nigga. I'll have ya muthafuckin' lights smashed out before the sun comes up, fake-ass baller." I knew if my girls were with me, we woulda tore that casino up and been hauled off to jail for stompin' his ass.

"Yo, tell this bitch to step the fuck off before—"

"Before you what, nigga?" I said, cuttin' him off while reachin' into my bag to get my shit. Fuck splittin' his shit with my blade, I was gonna ram my ice pick in his thick gut. If he kept pressin', it'd be a bullet instead.

Dude stepped in between us, pushin' his boy back with his forearm. "Yo, nigga, shut ya drunk ass the fuck up. Yo, ma, don't pay his dumb ass no mind. He's fucked up."

I stared the drunk nigga down, then turned my attention to him. "And he's about to get really fucked up 'cause he done came at the wrong bitch."

"Yo, y'all take this dumb nigga outta here," he said to two of his boys. They snatched his ass up real quick and got him the fuck away from me before I put a slug in his skull.

"Don't no nigga talk slick and think shit's sweet."

"I hear you. That was some real foul shit. I apologize for how he came at you, but I'ma check him on it."

"Yeah, you do that. But, please be clear. If I run into that crab-ass nigga again, he had better be in a position to apologize for how he came at me, otherwise you and the rest of ya crew gonna be goin' to a funeral."

"I feel you, ma. So, I guess tryna get ya number is definitely out now?" he asked, flashin' me a beautiful smile.

"You got that right," I said, leavin' him starin' at my ass.

Oh my God! It was live and poppin' in Vegas that weekend and every fuckin' night the strip was filled to capacity with niggas and bitches tryna shine in their wears. Even the white bitches were tryna get it in. But none of them pasty, weave-wearin', frontin'-ass tramps could rock with me. And I was slayin' them hoes every night at every damn party in all the ill shit. Long story short, I ran into this nigga in the airport, and wouldn't you know he stepped to me, holdin' open his BlackBerry, ready for me to program my number into his phone. And the nigga has been callin' me ever since. Now I wish I woulda gave his ass a wrong number.

Anyway, I had to pull the phone from my ear for a minute. *I swear I don't know why I gave this nigga my fuckin' number*, I thought, rollin' my eyes. "Nigga, you must be smokin' dust or eatin' mufuckin' paint chips to come at me like that. I don't know you like that. And to answer ya question, never. Now do me a favor and delete my number 'cause I ain't feelin' ya ass like that."

He laughed. "Damn, ma, why you gotta be so hard on a brotha. I'm only fucking with ya sexy ass. I know you ain't that type of chick."

I sucked my teeth. "Whatever. You still might as well delete my number 'cause I ain't givin' you no pussy." The Kat line started ringin' off the hook. And I was glad. "Listen, I gotta go. Don't call me anymore."

"Yeah, aiight. I'ma keep callin' 'til you stop answerin'," he said. "There's somethin' 'bout ya evil ass that turns me the fuck on."

Click. I hung up on his ass, pressin' the TALK button on my other cell. "Yeah."

"We still beefin'?" Cash asked, soundin' like Barry White.

"Nah," I said, "we straight." *For now, muhfucka*, I thought, rollin' my eyes.

"Good. I got some gigs for you. You wit' it?"

"When?" I asked, ploppin' down on my bed. I ran my hand through my ultra-silky hair, then twirled the ends through my fingers. "And where?"

"Everything needs to be wrapped up within a week."

I let out a sigh of relief. I was glad I had a few days to chill. "Where?" I asked.

"Atlanta and Chicago," he stated.

"Give me two days."

"I'll have everything ready for you."

"Cool. Oh, and don't try that shit you pulled on that last gig. I want seventy-five percent of my paper before I start."

"Now, you know how we do. Half now, the rest later."

"No," I stated flatly. "That's how we *used* to do up until you tried to stunt me."

"Come on, ma. Why you tryna bust a nigga's balls?"

"'Cause a nigga can't be trusted," I replied. "And, besides, I like it when I got a handful of balls in my hands, squeezin' the nut outta it. Now, like I said, I want seventy-five percent now and the rest when I touch down." My mental calculator started churnin' in my head. That meant a hundred-and-fifty thousand for the price of two bodies upfront. I smiled.

"I got you," he said, soundin' real tight. I didn't give a fuck. *Play me, get played, sucka!* He musta read my mind because he said, "You know I'd never game you."

"Yeah, that's what your mouth says," I said, hangin' up.

Later on that evenin', I was in my kitchen heatin' up some left-overs from the Cheesecake Factory, smokin' a blunt, with the stereo blarin' Nas's *Hip Hop Is Dead* CD throughout the house. And I had the flat-screen TV on with the volume down. I wasn't big on watchin' TV 'n shit, but every now and then a bitch liked to peep the news to stay up on the comin's and goin's of the crazy-ass niggas and silly bitches in this fucked-up world. So while the six o'clock CBS news was on, I was just standin' in the middle of my kitchen waitin' for the microwave to stop, listenin' to Nas spit his lyrics and gazin' at the TV when a special news report flashed across the screen. I ain't gonna front, a bitch got real curious when this Asian-lookin' reporter chick was standin' in front of the Delano Hotel in South Beach. The same fuckin' spot I was a few weeks ago. And when the face of the nigga I bodied appeared, I almost fainted. I ran across the kitchen to grab the stereo remote to turn that shit down. I caught what the chick was sayin' in mid-sentence.

"...Prominent criminal defense attorney Lyndon Blair Holmes was last seen at this world-class urban resort nestled here in the heart of South Beach three and a half weeks ago. Although the details regarding his disappearance are sketchy, hotel staff state the multimillionaire had been served at the Rose Bar around nine p.m., and was sitting alone. At ten-thirty that evening, he called housekeeping from his room for fresh towels. No one has seen or heard from him since. All of his personal items were still in his suite and his 2006 Lamborghini remained in the parking garage. His wife alerted authorities when she had not heard from her husband in two days, and he hadn't returned any of her calls. Authorities urge potential witnesses to come forward. A one-million-dollar reward is being offered by the family to anyone with information that will lead investigators to his whereabouts. Currently there are no leads..."

'Cause his ass is dead, bitch!

His wife, a cute brown-skinned chick dipped in jewels, was sobbin' and talkin' into the camera. I turned that shit off. I wasn't beat to hear her beggin' and pleadin' for his safe return home. I didn't wanna hear jack 'bout her missin' him, and how much she loved him, especially when the bitch probably had somethin' to do with his ass bein' slumped. A bitch was through. I put my food on a plate, then took my ass downstairs into my theater room to spark a Dutch, eat, and watch *Perfect Stranger* with Halle Berry.

➤➤➤

At nine p.m. my phone rang. I glanced at the caller ID, then picked up. It was my girl Chanel. "Whaddup, ho?"

"Hey, hooker, what's good?"

"Shit," I said, holdin' the phone in the crook of my neck while I spun the chamber of my revolver, making sure it was packed with a full load of heat. I placed the safety latch on it, then laid it back in its case and closed the drawer. "What's poppin' tonight?"

"This baller nigga, from Newark, Thug Gee, is havin' a party tonight at Studio 9. Word has it it's gonna be packed with long dollars and thick dick."

"Hmmph," I grunted. "And a bunch of dick-thirsty Wal-Mart bitches," I said, rollin' my eyes up in my head. I really wasn't in the mood for bein' around a bunch of hatin'-ass hoes, especially them Jersey bitches, 'cause I already knew that the first one who eyeballed me recklessly or said somethin' slick outta the side of her neck, I'd have to slide her ass. But I also knew them bitches didn't really want it.

Although me and Chanel were restin' across the dirty-ass Hudson here in Jersey while Tamia and Iris still parlayed in Brooklyn, it had been a minute since me and my girls all chilled together. Although Tamia and Iris were my girls, Chanel and I had been friends since second grade and I'd only been friends with Tamia and Iris since junior high. So my history with them bitches was a little different from the one with Chanel. Granted, Chanel was much tighter with them than I was, but I must say, for the last six or seven years, the four of us were thick as thieves and had a rep of rockin' the hottest wears, pushin' the slick-ass whips, fuckin' the finest niggas, and turnin' a club out. However, on some real shit, it was all an illusion 'cause along with that rep came some extra shit for a few of these hoes. But I ain't gonna pull any cards right now. So, I'ma keep it cute, and keep it movin'.

Anyway, after thinkin' 'bout it, it was a Friday night, and I really did feel like poppin' and droppin' it a bit. *What the fuck*, I thought. "Okay, trick, what time we rollin'?"

"Eleven," she said. "Tamia and Iris are already here chillin' at my spot. You want us to come through and scoop you?"

I looked down at my diamond bezel timepiece. It was ten after nine. "Nah, I'm drivin'," I replied, shiftin' the cordless phone from one ear to the other, walkin' into my elaborate walk-in closet laced with all the illest shit from Chanel, Emilio Pucci, Vera Wang, Gucci, Louis Vuitton, and Hèrmes. "I'll be there quarter of. Make sure you hoes are ready."

"Yeah, yeah, yeah...*whatever!*"

"And you cock suckas ain't smokin' in my shit either."

"Love you, too," she said, laughin'.

"See ya asses in a minute," I said, laughin' to myself before hangin' up. I stared at my enormous designer collection, then, after ten minutes of shufflin' and rustlin' through shit, I decided to rock a black, knee-grazin' Gucci wrap dress and a pair of Gucci stilettos. *Yeah, give them broke bitches somethin' to hate*, my mind snapped as I headed toward my bathroom, thinkin' about gettin' my two-step on.

An hour later, I was standin' in my full-length mirror, fully dressed, puttin' my two-carat studs in my ears and makin' sure my hair and face were on point. "This is why I'm hot, dammit," I said, admirin' the way my fifteen-hundred-dollar dress clung to my curves, lettin' muhfuckas know just what I was workin' with and revealin' an ample amount of cleavage—just enough to let 'em know my titty game was right. I grabbed my black Gucci hobo bag and made my way to my garage, then opened the door to my metallic silver S550. I slid inside the butter-soft gray leather interior, pressed the garage door button, then turned on the CD player. Lil' Kim's "Kitty Box" blared from the speakers as I made my way to pick up my crew.

When we finally pulled into the parkin' area, it was packed. The niggas and bitches were pilin' outta luxury cars in droves. The thought of grindin' my ass up against a nigga's dick made my pussy twitch. I pulled into a parkin' space next to a sweet-ass bronze-colored Bentley. The shit was bangin'. *I wonder who's pushin' that whip?* I thought, flippin' down my visor. We all checked our faces and hair to make sure shit was regulated.

"What I tell ya'll bitches?" Chanel announced all excited 'n shit in between pulls of her blunt. "I told ya'll hoes this shit was gonna be live tonight. We 'bout to work the hell outta this spot."

"I don't know 'bout the rest of ya'll, but I'm tryna run deep in a nigga's pockets tonight. Drinks all night on his ass," Iris replied, applyin' a fresh coat of lip liner to her neatly painted lips.

"I heard that," Tamia said, chucklin'. "And not that cheap shit either."

I rolled my eyes. "I have my own paper," I said, tossin' my hair to the side. Bitches hated the fact that I didn't need a weave or extensions or a perm. My shit was all natural, and I shitted on these chicks every time I let 'em know that with the toss of my head.

"And?" Iris asked, tiltin' her head as if I'd said somethin' foreign to her.

"*And,*" I said with much 'tude, "I can buy my own drinks. I'm not one of you hard-pressed bitches, lookin' for a nigga to buy me drinks 'cause your asses are pinchin' pennies."

"Fuck you, trick," Chanel said, takin' another deep toke from the blunt, then passin' it to Iris. She exhaled a thick cloud of smoke. Iris took two pulls, then offered it to Tamia.

"Nah, bitch, I'm good," Tamia said. Iris handed it back to Chanel who took another hard pull, holdin' the smoke in her lungs.

"No, tramp," I said, closin' my sunroof, then openin' the door. "I'ma fuck you if you burn my seats back there, trick-ass hoes. Now, let's roll." Tamia and Chanel started laughin' and chokin', but I was serious as hell. That's my girl and all, but I'd ram a blade in her ass real quick if need be.

There were three lines to get into the club, and each one was practically wrapped around the damn building. Around the back there was some sort of tent that led into another entrance, and that was overflowin' and packed with niggas and bitches. Ain't no way a bitch like me was standin' in some busted-ass line.

"I hope one of you bitches is fuckin' one of the bouncers 'cause I ain't beat to be standin' out here all night," I said, scannin' the area. I spotted a few thugged cuties, but nothin' to write home 'bout. I peeped a group of low-budget bitches cuttin' their eyes over at us, tryna take in our wears. Humph.

"No," Iris said, grinnin'. "But I am fuckin' one of the deejays."

The rest of us looked at her, dumbfounded. "Bitch, then why is we standin' out in this crab-ass line?" Chanel snapped, suckin' her teeth.

"You know this ho gets brain-dead after she smokes a few trees," I said, rollin' my eyes at her simple ass. Iris had already found her first prey of the night and was standin' to the side of us, spittin' game to this nigga who was gazin' into her eyes like a star-struck junkie. Hell, why wouldn't he? On the outside lookin' in, we were four fly bitches laced in the hottest shit, and didn't fuck with no broke niggas, so it is what it is. I knew if his paper was long and he was spendin', she would probably fuck him after the club, unless someone else came along with deeper pockets or a bigger dick.

Say what ya want. But, personally, I ain't fuckin' no nigga on the first or second night. Well, not a nigga who's gonna live to tell about it. Let's be clear. Yeah, I gets it in like the next bitch, but the niggas I waste don't count 'cause ain't none of 'em alive to kiss 'n tell shit about fuckin' me. So I can fuck and suck and do whatever I want with 'em and never have to worry 'bout some chump-ass muhfucka tryna play me close. But if I'm straight fuckin' a nigga on the bricks, it damn sure ain't gonna be on the first night. I don't care how wet my pussy gets, or how thick his dick gets. It ain't gonna happen.

I glanced back over at Iris, then rolled my eyes. If a bitch wanna play herself, then...oh well.

"Fuck ya'll," Iris said, catchin' the eye of one of the bouncers, a tall, caramel-coated nigga with a bald head and thick arms, lips, and what looked like big hands. He smiled over at her. "Hey, Len," she said, wavin'. "Is my name on the guest list?"

"You already know," he said, wavin' us to come up to the front of the line. We followed Iris up the ramp, and heard teeth suckin' and agitated grumblin's. I looked back and smirked at the common bitches, then stepped inside the club where the beats were rockin'.

All night long, niggas were tryna get at us. Tamia and Chanel took a few numbers, but none of them niggas appealed to me. I wasn't beat. Iris was up in the deejay's booth with her new man toy. "I'm going over to the bar," I yelled over the music. "You want anything?" I asked Chanel.

"Yeah, a shot of Ketel One and an apple martini," she said. Tamia was on the dance floor, shakin' her ass up on some buffed nigga rockin' shoulder-length locks. The music was tight. Fabolous's "Make Me Better" was pulsin' through the huge speakers. I smiled at my girl slayin' her dance partner on the floor as I made my way to the bar. I knew she wouldn't be wantin' any more drinks since she already sucked down her six-drink max. And I knew the bitch was lit the way she was bouncin' and grindin' her ass all up on dude's dick.

While I waited for my order, I felt someone towerin' over me, but paid it no mind. "Yo, ma, what you drinkin'?" a voice asked, leanin' into my ear. His warm breath against my ear and the scent of his expensive cologne made my nipples harden. I slowly turned to face the nigga with the deep, panty-wettin' voice in back of me, and parted a sly smile. The nigga was *fine*. He had smooth, cocoa-brown skin, big brown eyes, a thick nose, and nice, full, pussy-eatin' lips. And when he smiled, he had straight white teeth and a sexy-ass dimple in his left cheek. I peeped the shine around his neck and wrist, and the rocks in his lobes. Yeah, the nigga was blingin'…just how I like 'em.

"Why, you payin'?"

"No doubt," he said, grinnin'.

"Thanks, but no thanks. I got it, but I'll buy *you* a drink," I said, real sexy-like.

He smiled wider. "Nah, baby, I'm good."

I licked my lips, roamin' every inch of his body before lockin' my eyes on the bulge in his pants. Although there wasn't much light to really see what was good, there was something 'bout the way he stood that told me he was hangin' just right. I smiled, stickin' the tip of my tongue outta the side of my mouth. "I bet you are," I said, brushin' past him, leavin' him with his tongue waggin' as I headed back over to Chanel. Tamia was now sittin' at the table, sippin' on a drink.

"Bitch, where you been all this time?" Tamia asked, smilin'.

"In that long-ass line tryna get these drinks," I said, handin' Chanel her order.

"Thanks," Chanel said, takin' the shot straight to the head.

"Then this fine-ass nigga was tryna get his rap game on, but I gave him no play."

Tamia rolled her eyes all dramatic and whatnot. "You are so fuckin' tired with that bullshit. You're gonna end up an old-ass maid with a dried-up, dusty-ass pussy if you don't stop tryna be so stuck the fuck up. How the hell you think you're gonna get some dick, actin' all stank anytime a nigga tries to get at you?"

I flipped her the finga. "For your information, ho, I gets dick, trust. I don't let you vultures know 'bout it." Well, what I said really wasn't a lie. I mean, I was fuckin'. I was killin' the niggas afterward. Still, I was gettin' dick, and that's all that mattered.

Chanel giggled. "Yeah, you fuckin' alright. Fuckin' the skin off them damn fingas." Tamia fell out laughin'. Just then, the nigga from the bar was comin' toward our table, grinnin'.

"Who the fuck is that fine-ass muhfucka right there?" Chanel questioned, tossin' her head in his direction, then sittin' up in her seat. "My God, that nigga looks like he's paid out the ass. I'd fuck him on the spot."

I smirked. "I know your nasty, trick ass would. He's the nigga who was at the bar. And I'm—"

He stepped up in our space and locked his gaze on me. "How you ladies doin'?" he asked, lockin' his gaze on me. Everyone said their hellos, practically ready to suck and fuck him, then zoomed in on me. *All eyes on me, bitches*, I thought. "So can I at least get a dance since I couldn't buy you a drink?"

I grinned, eyein' his ass down. "That depends." I licked my lips. "On?"

"Whether or not you can move."

He rubbed his chin, flashin' his beautiful teeth again. I was one of the few bitches who hated niggas who had their grill fronts all chromed and iced out. That shit looked so nasty and country to me. And a nigga with a mouth full of teeth that looked like piano keys, or like he's been gnawin' on bricks, was a no-no. "I guess you'll have to find out for yourself."

"Then I guess I will," I said, gettin' up from my seat and fol-lowin' him to the dance floor. I looked back at Chanel and Tamia, then stuck my tongue out. We found a spot on the floor and started doin' the damn thing to Beyoncé's "Get Me Bodied." Before I knew it, I was poppin' my hips and droppin' down real low, lettin' this nigga know what time it was. It had been so long since I'd been out that I almost forgot how good it felt to be out shakin' my ass.

I worked up a nice sweat and when that sexy-ass Nas's voice came over the speakers with "Let There Be Light," I spun around real slow, then twirled my hips into his crotch and pressed my

Yeah, okay, I thought. *This fat, nasty nigga did this shit on purpose, tryna be funny.* "What the fuck's so funny?" I snapped.

"You," he said. "I wish I coulda been a fly on ya wall when you peeped his flick. I know that shit was priceless."

"Whatever," I said. "You ain't funny. So you know, now what?"

"Do what you do best. I promise to make it worth your while."

"So why you send this shit to me instead of one of ya dudes on the squad?"

"'Cause I wanted to line ya pockets with a little extra somethin'."

I sighed. "Yeah, right. That's what ya mouth says."

He busted out laughin' again. "And I wanted to see how you'd handle this nigga since he ain't fuckable."

"Fuck you, Cash. I'm glad you think this shit is funny. How long have you known?"

"For 'bout a year now," he said. "At first, when the crew was findin' all the niggas you slumped naked, I didn't pay the shit no mind. But, then I peeped how every time you went on an assignment the muhfuckas would be butt-ass naked and the sheets would be removed. Shit wasn't addin' up. Then it hit me, and that's when I put shit together. Like I said, I thought the freaky shit was fiyah. And the only reason I kept it on the low is 'cause at the end of the day you real thorough. And I really don't give a fuck how you handle yours. So, you got this one or what?"

"How much you tryna line my pockets with?" I asked, usin' the photo to fan myself.

"An extra twenty-five gees," he said.

"Fuck that," I snapped. Now that I knew this nigga knew, he'd be tryna clown me every chance he got if I let him. I ain't the one. The only way to shut a nigga like him down—other than puttin' a bullet in his skull—is by diggin' in his pockets. "You musta banged ya damn head if you think that's 'posed to be makin' it worth my fuckin' while. Come betta, Cash, or it's a no-go. And I'm not fuckin' around."

"Aiight, aiight. I'll make it another fifty gees. Just handle the dude. His wife wants his ass stretched, ASAP."

My pussy pulled in my thong. The sound of that got me heated. "Then you need to get my seventy-five percent to me now. Otherwise, you'll have to send someone else on this one."

He sucked in his breath. "Damn, your little ass is really playin' hardball these days."

"I've learned from the best," I replied, tossin' the photo of this pasty-faced fool to the floor. "I want my money tonight."

"It'll be there."

"It better be," I said, snappin' the phone shut.

CHAPTER FOUR

At eleven a.m., my flight had safely landed at O'Hare International Airport. I loved Chicago, especially downtown, and had hoped to strut along Michigan Avenue to have lunch at one of the trendy restaurants that lined the strip, then do a little shopping, but I knew that wasn't my real purpose for being there so I decided to pick up my rental, then go check into my hotel suite. A bitch needed time to chill before it was time to do what I had come to do. The thought of this nigga with his white, clammy hands touchin' my body made my gut turn. *No wonder his bitch wants him dead. Probably gotta pencil dick, too,* I mused.

I made my way onto 90 East toward downtown Chicago, thinking about my life. At twenty-five, I had the life most bitches only dreamed about. I owned my own spot, was paid out the pussy, had e'erything I wanted, but somethin' still felt like it was missin'. I ain't sayin' I was on some lonely-type shit or some other crazy mess. It felt like...uh, fuck it. Shit ain't that serious. But in the back of my mind, somethin' was tellin' me I'd better get my ass outta this shit before all the shit I'd done caught up to me. A bitch in an orange or tan uniform wasn't a good look, and I wasn't tryna be the one. *Two more bodies,* I thought, makin' a right onto Michigan Avenue, *and I'm shuttin' shit down.*

Well, for a minute. Maybe travel the world, fuck a few foreign niggas, get my pussy ate and suck a few dicks on an airplane. But I had so much blood on my manicured hands that I wondered if I really had it in me to walk away from the thrill of it all. Holdin' a burner in my hand, pressin' it against a nigga's skull turned me the fuck on. Yeah, I was probably a sick, sadistic bitch, but I was paid and I'd be walkin' away with millions stacked.

I pulled up in front of the hotel and parked in the valet parkin' area, then stepped out of my busted-up rental—a fuckin' Aveo— and grabbed my satchel and carry-on bag, walkin' into the four-story lobby of this fly-ass hotel.

"Welcome to The InterContinental Chicago," an attractive young woman said, smilin' in my direction. "How may I help you?"

"I have a reservation."

"Your name, please?" I told her my name, then handed her one of my fake-ass identifications. "Oh, Miss Lewis, a package came for you this morning. I'll be right back." She went to the back to retrieve it, then returned. I already knew what it was: the supplies I needed to carry-out my job. While I got to fly all over the U.S. to handle these niggas, Cash's job was to make sure shit was in order. With the exception of his fat ass tryna shortchange me it was an operation that ran without any glitches. We all knew Cash was 'bout the business of killin', and a missed body was a missed bankroll. "Here you are," she said, returnin' with a medium-sized box.

I smiled. "Thanks."

"You're in Suite 6201," she said, handin' me my room key. "I hope you enjoy your stay with us."

"I'm sure I will," I stated, headin' toward the elevators.

Nine-thirty p.m., I was standin' out on my balcony admirin'

the view of the Chicago skyline, wishin' I was slumped over the railin' with a stiff dick diggin' my pussy out from the back. I needed some cock, and I was fuckin' disgusted that this job wouldn't be served up with a side order of thick dick. My private cell rang, breakin' my thoughts.

"Hello?"

"What's good, pretty lady?"

"Who's this?" I asked, smilin'. I knew it was the nigga from Studio 9. I'd written my number in the palm of his hand on our way outta the club. He and his mans 'n them had wanted to take us out to breakfast, but I asked for a rain check since I knew I had shit to do the followin' mornin'. Chanel had the nerve to try 'n be swoll 'bout it, but I didn't give a fuck. She'd get over it. He walked me to my car then I heard the chirp to that bangin'-ass Bentley parked beside my Benz. It was his. My pussy immediately got moist as thoughts of fuckin' him in the backseat of his whip and suckin' his dick while he was pushin' it down the turnpike came to mind. I kept my cool, but could see that my girls were gaggin'. Yeah, this nigga was paid, and I was gonna see what was really good with his fine ass as soon as I got back from handlin' my business.

"Grant," he said.

"Grant, who?" I asked, fuckin' with him.

"Oh, it's like that," he said, laughin'. "Let me find out you got a stable of niggas on your team."

I laughed. "Maybe, maybe not."

"Oh, word? Well, how can a nigga like me get on your squad?" he asked, dippin' his voice real low. I felt myself gettin' wet.

"That depends," I said, matchin' his low, sexy tone.

"On?"

"On how big ya dick is, and if ya know how to eat a pussy."

He laughed. "Well, shit, you ain't askin' for much. I got that covered."

"Is that so?"

"No doubt. You'se a sexy thing, and I'm tryna come through and spend some time with you. Show you how a real nigga treats a woman." Although the nigga had a street edge, he had this polished, sophisticated edge to him. That shit turned me on.

"And how's that?"

"Let me come scoop you up, and show you."

"I wish I could," I said, grinnin'. "But I'm outta town for few days. I'll be home Sunday afternoon."

"Oh word. Then hit me up when you touch."

"I will."

"Don't do nothing I wouldn't do," he said playfully.

"Well, that may be hard since I don't know what a nigga like you'd do."

He chuckled. "I feel ya, baby. Be safe."

"Thanks," I said, disconnectin' the call. I grabbed my purse and keys and headed for the door. I had someplace to be, someone to see, and a bullet to serve.

By the time I got to the Bucktown section of Chicago—an old warehouse district that had been rehabbed and turned into dance clubs and fly-ass lofts—it was almost ten forty-five. I pulled up in the parkin' area of this trendy spot Aqua, where my unsuspectin' victim would be. Not only was he a compulsive gambler, word had it he had a thing for pretty young girls, particularly black and Latin chicks. And since he couldn't keep his pecker in his pants, his wife probably wanted his ass ghost so she could collect on a million-dollar insurance policy he had. The bitch felt she deserved that and then some due to his years of cheatin' on her ass. *Whateva!* I wanted this shit to be over, and the sooner the better.

I stepped out of my rental rockin' a fly-ass hot pants jumpsuit and a pair of knee-high Gucci boots with stiletto heels. My hair was braided and tucked under a long black wig with short bangs. I made sure to rock something that flowed almost past my ass to give the illusion that I was one of them exotic bitches, which wasn't really hard to do since I already had the *look*.

When I walked into the club, I was surprised to see that this spot had a mixed crowd. I knew a bitch was gonna be all up in a lily-white shit hole with a bunch of snuff-chewin' hillbillies. Even the music was cute. I circled the club, scannin' the area in search of my mark. There were three bars and two dance floors, and the place was packed. *Shit*, I thought, *I could be here all fuckin' night lookin for this brown-toothed, limp dick nigga*. All eyes were on me as I made my way to the bar where I positioned myself so I had full view of the floor.

An hour goes by and I'm gettin' real sick of this postin' up at the bar and havin' all these duck-ass niggas tryna spit weak-ass game. The cat I'm lookin' for is nowhere to be found, and I was startin' to get vexed. But a bitch like me knows how to keep it cute. So I shook my ass a tease to get into the groove of shit. I almost wanted to hit the dance floor to pop my hips and toss a few drinks instead of sippin' on my flat-assed Coke. But I was there on business and drinkin' on the job was a no-no. I was so fuckin' ready to blow dust on the spot.

Well, as I'm 'bout to go into plan B, I turn to my left and there in all of his pasty-faced glory is my mark, dressed in all black, wearin' a slick-ass pair of Dolce & Gabbana shades with his stringy-ass hair pulled back in a shiny ponytail, makin' his way toward the bar and me. I turned around real slow and sexy-like, then leaned over the bar enough to allow my ass cheeks to peek from underneath the edges of my eighteen-hundred-dollar jumper. I shook my ass to the music, then gave the horny-ass niggas somethin' to go home and beat their dicks to. I could feel his eyes zoomin' in on my juicy ass. *Here kitty, kitty…that's right… come to momma, muhfucka…*

"What is a pretty young lady like you drinking tonight?"

I turned around, scanned this crab nigga real easy, then parted a phony-ass smile. "If I tell you, I might hafta kill you," I said, lettin' a sly grin spread across my face. He blinked, blinked again, then had the muthafuckin' audacity to show me his shit-stained teeth, cheesin' ear-to-ear. Ugh! *I'ma blast this nigga's grill out*, I thought.

"As pretty as you are," he said, eyein' me like he hit Lotto, "I'll take my chances."

"A risk taker," I said, matchin' his stare. "I like that."

"I only bet on sure things, baby. And I'd bet my life you're a winner."

"Your life?" I asked.

"Yeah, my life," he repeated.

Then your life it is, muhfucka. I smiled.

"Now, what can I get the beautiful lady?"

I went in for the kill. I licked my lips real slow and sexy-like and stared him down, before glancin' down at his crotch. I let the nigga see I was checkin' for his dick. "What I want, they're not servin' at the bar."

"In that case," he said, droolin' like a fuckin' hound dog, "I know someplace that is." He leaned in my ear and told me the room number to where he was stayin', then told me to meet him there in an hour, and to knock three times. I bounced from the club, switchin' my ass all the way out the door. When I got to my rental and was behind the wheel, I flipped open my cell and called Cash.

"What's good?"

"I'm restin' at the downtown Hyatt. Checkin' in 'bout an hour, then headin' out in forty."

"Bet. Enjoy your stay."

"I always do."

At one a.m., I dipped into the Hyatt Regency wearin' a black micro-mini dress and a pair of six-inch slingbacks, struttin' toward the elevators. When I got to the door, I knocked three times as instructed. He opened the door wearin' a white hotel robe, and his stringy hair was all over his head. His eyes were glazed. The pale-faced nigga looked coked the fuck out. But it was all good. I was gonna make this short and sweet. I gave myself ten minutes to stretch his ass, then bounce.

"Can I get you something?" he asked, shuttin' the door behind him. I walked over to the window and admired the view. His suite was overlookin' Lake Michigan, and the shit was sexy as hell. It was a perfect night to be fucked real rough out on the balcony, but definitely not with this trailer-park nigga. However, he did have me curious. I wanted to see if he had a little pink dick with a bunch of extra skin or not, before I blasted his ass. I glanced down at my watch. I had thirty-four minutes to spare. So, I changed plans.

"Yeah," I said, turnin' around to face him, "you can take off that corny-ass robe and let me see you jerk that dick while I play in my pussy, then I'ma let you fuck me deep in my fat, black ass." Lies!

He opened his beady eyes in shock, then smiled. Ugh!

"Don't play like you don't know what time it is," I said. "Why else you invite me up to your suite? To fuck this sweet, chocolate pussy with the creamy pink center, right?"

He licked his crusty-ass lips. The nigga looked like he was 'bout ready to nut on himself. He broke out into another one of his shitty smiles.

"You get right to the point. I like that."

"Life is too short to be wastin' time," I said, droppin' my bag into the green high-back chair, then pullin' my dress up over my hips, and slowly turnin' around. I bent over and slapped my ass, then pulled it open. "You ever see an ass this big before?" I asked him, lookin' at him over my shoulder.

He shook his head, runnin' his long tongue over his rusty lips. "No, can't say that I have."

"Then you ain't had no good ass until you had some black ass." I walked over to him and undid his robe. His dick was hard, and to my fuckin' surprise 'bout as thick as a cucumber. The nigga actually had a pretty dick for a white man, and if his face wasn't so busted, I probably woulda fucked him just for the hell of it. Not! I grabbed him by the base of his hard cock, glidin' my hand up to his mushroom head, pullin' him toward the bed. "Then, it looks like tonight's your lucky night. Now, lie back and beat that big white dick for me."

He sat on the edge of the bed, spread open his legs, then leaned back on one elbow, strokin' his dick. The more he stroked, the longer his dick got. "I want you to turn the light on over there on the table, then sit across from me and play in that sweet black pussy for me. Let me see you finger-fuck that pussy."

I smiled. "Oh, you wanna see how wet this pussy gets?" I asked, walkin' over toward my bag. I dropped it to the floor, then sat down, danglin' one leg over the arm of the chair. I glanced at the digital clock on the nightstand: 1:18. *Shit, I gotta hurry*, I thought, rubbin' my pussy. "Oooh, you gotta big dick," I moaned. "You wanna put that big white dick in this fat black pussy. You wanna fuck this tight pussy? You wanna eat this sweet pussy?"

"Yeah," he grunted, jackin' his dick fast and furious.

"Yeah, daddy, just like that...Mmmm. You wanna stick your tongue in my ass? Ooh, it feels sooo good," I said, pullin' open my pussy. "Look at this wet, pink pussy..."

The nigga was practically shakin' and droolin', pumpin' his dick in 'n out of his grungy hands, starin' at my pretty pussy.

His dick seemed to get thicker with each stroke. He was ugly as fuck, but his dick...humph, that thick, white dick and his fat, smooth balls had me wantin' to do some freaky thangs to his ass. The thought of handcuffin' and blindfoldin' him, then sittin' down on his dick and milkin' it with my pussy had me goin'. My hole was gettin' real hot. I dipped my finga in my slit. My shit was drippin'. "Close ya eyes, muhfucka, and make believe it's my lips wrapped around that big white dick, nigga."

He closed his eyes, and in that split second, I quickly reached down into my bag and pulled out my black silencer gun and stuck it behind my back.

"Oooh, you got my pussy so wet. Stroke that dick, daddy. You want me on my knees suckin' that dick?"

"Yeah, baby. I want them pretty dick-sucking lips all over this fat white cock. Turn off that light and bring your pretty black ass over here and suck all over this dick, you sexy black bitch." *Oh, yeah, you definitely 'bout to get ya fronts knocked for that, cracker bastard!*

"That's right, talk nasty, muhfucka," I said, reachin' over and turnin' off the light, then slowly walkin' over to him. The only light in the room was comin' from the bathroom. Just enough to make this scumbag nigga look like a damn glowworm. I eyed the digital clock: 1:32. I had eight minutes. "Lay back and close ya eyes, muhfucka. I got something real hot for ya ass."

Theesssrrpp! Before the back of his head made it to the bed, I had shot him in it. "That's for ya wife, nigga." I slammed the barrel in his mouth. *Theesssrrpp!* "And that's for ya dentist, muh-fucka." Blood gushed out from the back of his head, soaking up the bed. *Theessrrpp!* I shot him in his balls. "And that's for the black bitch, sucka." I was glad the only thing I touched besides his dick was the lamp, which I went back over and wiped before leavin' his ass splayed out on the edge of the bed with his brains oozin' outta his skull and less than a minute to spare.

CHAPTER FIVE

Gotta nigga on lock with this pussy heat…gotta sick head game that'll make the cock spit. Rockin' ya sheets…Got ya nigga clockin' me…tryna make a bitch nut lickin' the clit. Got ya nigga suckin' my tit…cum, nigga, cum…roll ya eyes up in ya head while I lap ya balls and wet ya dick…cum, nigga, cum…

Ten a.m. the followin' mornin', I was at Hartsfield-Jackson Atlanta International Airport, pickin' up my rental, then headin' toward the Buckhead section of Atlanta. I hated Atlanta. It was hot, muggy, and had more fuckin' traffic than a bitch could stand. I wanted to get to my hotel room, take another shower, and chill.

Two hours later, I was showered, changed, and struttin' through Lenox Square Mall loaded down with some bangin' shit outta Hermès, St. John Boutique, and Louis Vuitton. A few niggas tried to holla at a bitch, but I kept it movin'. I ain't gonna front, they were fine as hell, but they had the game fucked up if they thought I wasn't up on Hotlanta being the capital for dick-lovin', fudge-packin' niggas. Fuck what ya heard. I like my niggas strictly 'bout lickin' the clit and smashin' the pussy. I ain't got no time tryna play the guessin' game of who's on the creep suckin' dick and takin' it in the ass, that shit's for the birds. And I ain't the one! So, nigga, is you crazy?! Hell no, you can't get my muthafuckin' number. Ugh!

I glanced at my timepiece. It was almost two-thirty. I still had a few hours to kill before I made it do what it do. I hated when time dragged. I was so ready to get this shit over with. I began to tingle and get moist between my legs tingled, thinkin' 'bout that big-lipped nigga suckin' on my titties, and lappin' and slappin' my clit with his tongue. I couldn't wait to serve him a dish of this pussy.

When I finally finished shoppin', then gettin' over to UPS to have my shit shipped to Jersey, it was already five-thirty in the evening. A bitch was beat, and needed to take another long, hot shower, then catch a quick nap. I liked bein' well-rested and alert when doin' a job. As far as I was concerned, to be aware was to be alive. Bein' a tired bitch opened the door for mistakes, and a half-assed job. A sloppy bitch was a liability.

No sooner had I gotten out of my clothes and was makin' my way to the bathroom, when my private cell phone rang. I pulled it outta my red Hèrmes bag, then peeped the caller ID. It was Chanel.

"Hey tramp. What's good?" I asked, starin' at myself from the side in the hangin' wall mirror. Fuck a J-Lo, Beyoncé, or any of them wannabe-fab, stankin' video hoes shakin' and poppin' their asses. I knew I had a bangin'-ass body. If I were a clit and pussy licker, I'd bury my face all up in this fat ass. I ain't no nigga but I ain't gonna front, if I had a dick, I'd fuck myself silly.

"You trick. Where you at?"

"I'm outta town, why?"

She sucked her teeth. "Ho, you stay goin' somewhere."

"Don't hate, bitch. Instead of lyin' on ya back fuckin' them broke-ass niggas, step ya game up." Chanel and I were probably the tightest outta our crew. We lived and grew up in the same building across the hall from each other, and were both the only children of single moms who were Spanish, though her mother was full Puerto Rican. And they had both gotten knocked by a stiff black dick, so we shared a special connection and understanding of each other. It didn't hurt that she was also a fly chick with curly brown ringlets that bounced off her shoulders when she walked. And her body was almost as tight as mine. With her beautiful caramel-coated complexion, big brown doe-like eyes, and a beauty mole bitches dream of having over the right corner of her full lips, she looked fresh off the cover of a damn magazine. Chick was definitely a dime; but not quite as hot as me. I ain't hatin'. I'm just sayin'. That's my girl, fuck what ya heard. I'm keepin' shit real. Still at the end of the day, if I wasn't mad cool with her ass, or if I was one of them weak bitches worried 'bout the next bitch, chick could and would be a serious problem.

"I hate ya stank ass," she said, laughin'. "Ain't nobody fuckin' no broke niggas."

"Oh, I forgot. They ain't broke. Them niggas cheap as hell!"

"Least I'm fuckin'. Shit. You still ridin' them fingas."

"Yep, I sure am," I snapped, laughin'. "And them fingas know how to push the button and keep my pussy wet; and I ain't got to worry 'bout some nigga short-changin' me, either. Now, what's your excuse, ho? And what you want, anyway?"

"Yeah, yeah, yeah…whatever! Anyway, I was callin' ya ass to see if you wanna meet up for drinks tonight, but since you all ghost on a bitch, scratch it. Hit me up when you touch Jersey."

"Yeah, I'll do that."

"So, what's good with that nigga pushin' the Bentley? He get at you yet, or what?"

"Nah," I lied. Yeah, she my girl and all, but her pussy gets wet like mines. And chick likes to fuck like the next bitch. I had already peeped how she was tryna clock him in the club and out in the parkin' lot, so I already know what time it is. Until a nigga's ya man, it's open season. And a bitch in heat is always lookin' for prey. She don't care who else got their eye on it, get caught sleepin' and she's gonna swoop down on the dick and take ya spot. A hood bitch is always schemin'. It is what it is. "If he calls, he calls. If not, it's whatever," I said, sittin' at the foot of the king-sized bed. I leaned back on my forearm, then spread open my legs to let the cool air in the room hit my pussy. My nipples got hard as ice.

"I heard that. But the nigga was *fine*. And you can't tell me you ain't wonderin' how the dick's hangin'.'"

"Actually, I'm not," I said, lyin' outta my ass, 'cause on some real shit, I already knew I was gonna fuck him the first chance I got. But since e'erything ain't for e'erybody, there was no need for her to know that. I closed my eyes and leaned my head back tryna imagine him between my legs long strokin' this tight pussy. I ran my hand over my slit, then teased my clit with my two fingas.

"Girl, I don't know why not. That's the first thing I thought when I peeped him. The nigga looks like he got some bangin' dick. You need to stop frontin' and go 'head get you a taste."

See, I learned a long time ago that sometimes ya gotta know when to sit back, keep ya grill shut, and listen. Let a bitch flap her jaws 'cause if ya listen long and hard enough, she's gonna slip up. "Hmm…maybe," I said, pullin' my fingas outta my pussy and off my clit, then lickin' 'em. "But since you sound so ready to ride his dick down into the mattress, I'ma tell ya what. How 'bout you fuck him and let me know what's really good."

"If ya don't want 'em, I might," she said, gigglin'. I didn't even know the nigga, didn't even know if he was a good fuck or not, and for some reason I was startin' to get vexed that this bitch was seriously thinkin'—or fuckin' jokin—'bout tryna get at him. But I kept my shit in check, and let her ass keep talkin'.

"Well, the nigga ain't my man," I admitted. "It's open invitation, right? So do you."

"Nah, girl, you know I don't get down like that. I'd never do you like that. Another bitch, most def. But you my muthafuckin' peeps. You can try 'n front if ya want, but I know you was clockin' his ass. But, I ain't gonna front. A bitch could really use an upgrade on some dick 'cause Divine's shit ain't hittin' on nuthin'. The dick is thick as hell, but the nigga nuts in like six minutes. And he can't eat pussy to save his natural black ass. I swear if it wasn't for him payin' the note on this truck, I'd dismiss his ass."

I rolled my eyes up in my head. I hated when a chick dissed a nigga who was takin' care of her ass. Lousy fuck or not, a bitch needs to know when to keep her mouth shut. What might be a whack piece of dick to her, may be exactly what the next bitch needs to get off. I tell ya, some bitches 'bout as dumb as they come. They really think a wicked head game and a deep pussy is gonna put them on top. Yeah, maybe for a minute, but ya best believe once the verdict is out on the streets that ya ass is a trick, ya rep is a wrap. Believe that. Real niggas ain't tryna wife no hoes. Yeah, he gonna fuck her, might even splash up in her raw. He might even keep her laced in the hottest shit, but at the end of the day, she still gonna be a damn ho to him, real talk. And niggas run their mouths worse than bitches, especially when it comes to who's suckin' 'n fuckin' who.

Over the past two years, Chanel's been really gettin' it in with these niggas. Ever since she got played by this big-Willy nigga she was fuckin', she been straight wildin' out with the niggas. Divine is like the fourth nigga she's fucked in the last six months tryna keep her bills 'n shit paid. That shit is straight nasty to me. Get ya ass up and get a damn job! I mean, there's nothin' wrong with slayin' a nigga's pockets, but it's a dumb bitch who lets that shit be her only hustle. And these bitches kill me with no credit, no savin's, nothin' to fall back on. If they got credit, it's either maxed the fuck out or fucked up; and if they got a few dollars stashed, it's just that—a few damn measly dollars, nothin' major.

"Chanel, you do know you a certified trick, right? I mean, really. What the fuck! You sound like a real bird. What you need to do is find ya'self a hobby, take ya ass back to school, do somethin' constructive with ya'self instead of bobbin' ya neck up and down a nigga's dick, and chasin' niggas to support ya ass."

Oh, trust. I know if a nigga wanna trick his money on some pussy or brain, then oh fuckin' well. I think a real bitch holds shit down for herself, by herself. She knows how to make her paper, and get it poppin' without leanin' on a dick to do it. Hell, I know what I'm doin' is far worse than what she's doin'. But say what ya want. I'd rather slump niggas for a livin' than have them hump up in my guts for one. I might be many things, but a gold digger ain't ever gonna be one of 'em. I don't need a nigga lacin' me with ice 'n shit, payin' my mortgage, car note, or anything else, 'cause a bitch like me buys her own shit.

"Say what ya want," she said, soundin' offended. "Hustlin' these niggas *is* a job. And a bitch like me is gonna *always* hustle a nigga off his paper. Fuck what ya heard."

"Do you, sweetie," I said, gettin' heated listenin' to her stupid ass. "But tell me this. What's really good with a bitch who—after all the fuckin' and all the suckin' is done—has nothin' to show for givin' up her ass other than rug burns, a wet hole, and some shit that ya had to whore for? What's really good with a bitch with a pussy the size of a parkin' garage because she done let every muhfuckin' wanna-be balla run all up in her so she can get laced? Bitch, you bigga than that, that's all I'm sayin'. Get ya mind right."

"Yeah, whatever!"

On the real, the only reason I was comin' at her neck is 'cause she's my fuckin' peoples. Otherwise I wouldn't give a fuck. Do you. See, unlike Tamia and Iris, Chanel not only has street smarts, but the bitch is bright as hell. That makes her ass a serious threat. She graduated top in our class, and hustlin' niggas is all the bitch wants. She could be a lawyer, engineer, whatever! Humph. If her ass stopped trickin' for a minute she might see what I'm sayin'. But right now she's too wrapped up in a nigga's dick stroke and his pockets. Like my mother always said, "The smartest bitch can still be the dumbest bitch." And there ya have it!

"That nigga Divine is big on ya ass, Chanel. The nigga don't cheat on ya. And if he does, he keeps that shit tucked on the low. He don't bring drama to ya ass. He don't call ya out ya name, and keeps ya ass laced. And that still ain't good enough. You still got ya eyes and mind shiftin' to the next nigga. Keep up, and ya gonna find ya'self like the rest of them greedy bitches…with *nothing*."

"Bitch, I ain't call ya ass for no damn lecture."

"Whatever." I was done.

"And what is it you do again, huh, tramp? None of us seem to know since ya always top secret 'n shit."

I had to laugh to myself. A real bitch moved in silence. Thought she knew. Girls or not, the less they knew the better. The last thing I needed was one of them hoes sittin' around drinkin' and smokin' and blastin' off at the mouth. Then before ya know it I got feds 'n shit sniffin' 'round like fiends tryna be all up on mine. It's bad enough I have to watch how I make moves. Can't be flashin' and shinin' and tryna buy up too much shit without havin' some way to explain how I can afford it. Them feds got eyes and ears everywhere, listenin' and clockin' niggas. Lucky for me, my moms got major paper from her accident a few years back, so I can say she hit me off with gifts 'n shit. But still, a bitch gotta know how to move.

"And you never will," I said, lookin' over at the clock while getting up to go into the bathroom. *We been on the phone for almost forty-five minutes talkin' 'bout shit*, I thought. "Look, trick, love ya, but I got shit to do. I'll hit you when I get home."

"Fuck you, too," she said.

"I'll be sure to," I replied, laughin'. We hung up, then I jumped in the shower, rinsed my ass and pussy real good. When I was done, I dried myself off, took another one of the hotel's plush white towels and wrapped it around my body, then lay across the bed. I needed a power nap.

At ten p.m., I was in my target's room with my legs spread wide and bent at the knees, lyin' in the middle of his bed. I pressed the back of my head into the pillow and arched my back, palmin' the back of this nigga's smooth bald head as he ate my pussy inside out. The muhfucka's lips were heaven—soft, warm, and wet, and felt so damn good on my pussy. He dipped his tongue in, then flicked it across my clit a few times, then darted it back into my pussy.

"Yeah, nigga, just like that," I moaned. "Make me cum, daddy… yes, ooh…fuck me with your tongue, nigga." I pumped my pussy in his face, wrapped my legs around his neck, then begged him to fuck me deep. He flicked my clit with his thumb, then his tongue. He slathered my pussy lips with his wet mouth, then lapped up my kat juice the minute my slit started leakin'. The nigga was teasin' me, makin' my pussy churn. "Mmmm…oh, yes! Get all up in that pussy…make it nut, nigga…oh, yes!" I moaned again. "Feed my pussy, nigga."

He stuck two thick fingas in me, pressin' on my clit, flickin' his tongue while finger-fuckin' me. He moaned and slurped my pussy until I came in his mouth.

"Damn, baby, you taste good," he said, swallowin' my sweet cum, then lickin' his slick, sticky lips. *That's right, muhfucka, good to the last drop*, I thought, studyin' him as he got up from between my legs.

"It feels even better," I said, gettin' on my knees and spreadin' open my ass cheeks. I wanted him poundin' my pussy with his thick, long dick. "Come fuck my pussy," I said, lookin' over my shoulder as he rolled a Magnum down on his dick, which was smooth with big veins and curved to the right. The nigga slid his dick in, then fucked me from the back, deep and hard. "That's all you got, nigga? When you gonna fuck me, huh, muhfucka? Make my pussy nut, nigga. Make me feel the dick, punk."

"Yeah, you a nasty, shit-talkin' ho," he said, slappin' my ass. My pussy grabbed his dick. He slapped my ass again. My pussy grabbed his dick again. "Oh, you like a nigga slappin' ya ass, huh?" He pulled his dick out to the head, tip-drilled my hot hole, then plunged his dick back in me. I threw my ass up at him, backed my pussy onto his dick. "That's right," he said, slappin' my ass again, "fuck this big, black dick. Work that ass up on this dick."

"Stop teasin' me, nigga. I'm still waitin' for you to fuck me. Don't be scared. Beat this pussy up, muhfucka."

The more shit I talked, the harder he worked to rip my insides out. The nigga was fuckin' me so damn good, and grabbin' me by the back of the head. I had to keep pushin' his hands off my hair in fear he was gonna yank my wig off. I hated to have this fuck session end. I glanced at the digital clock. It read 9:50 p.m.

I straddled him and started ridin' his dick, bouncin' up and down on it. "Damn, fuck that dick, bitch," he said, reachin' around me and slappin' me on the ass. "Give me that wet pussy. Yeah, that's right, bitch, yeah…just like that. You like this big dick?"

"Yeah, nigga," I moaned, slammin' down on his dick. "This dick feels good."

It was ten o' clock. I had to hurry this along. "You like this tight pussy? You wanna nut up in my pussy, muhfucka?"

"Oh, shit. Yeah, that's what I'm talkin' 'bout. Ride that dick. You want me to bust this hot nut in your guts?" he asked, squeezin' my ass cheeks together to clamp around his cock. "Gotdamn," he groaned, "you got some good muhfuckin' pussy. That's right, make it grab my dick."

"Cum for me, daddy. Give me that nut, baby," I begged, squeezin' my pussy. "Oh, yeah."

"It's comin'. It's comin'. It's comin'."

I galloped harder.

"Give it to me, muhfucka. Yeah, baby, give me that hot nut."

"Mmmm, fuck. You ridin' the shit outta that dick."

The minute he closed his eyes and twisted his face, I leaned over, and pulled my Glock out from underneath the mattress where I hid it when he went into the bathroom. "Make that dick shoot for me, muhfucka. Uh, shit. Give me that nut, nigga."

"I'm cuummm—" *Theessrrpp!* I shot his ass between the eyes. A pool of blood seeped out from the back of his head. I climbed off him, pulled off the condom, then wiped him down. When I finished removin' the sheets and wipin' off any remainin' traces of my presence, I dipped outta his room and quietly took the elevator back up to my suite on the eighth floor. It was ten-thirty. I flipped open my cell and dialed.

"What's good?"

"I know why the caged bird sings."

"That's wassup. I'll get at ya."

"Bet," I said, shuttin' my phone, then headin' for the shower.

CHAPTER SIX

"*You have a collect call from…Naheem…at the Wyoming Correctional Facility. To accept this call, please do not use three-way or call waiting features or you will be disconnected. To accept this call…*" I waited for the computerized recording to finish, and pressed one. "Hello?"

"Aye, yo…'bout time ya ass is pickin' up. What, you ain't got no love for a nigga? I've been tryna get at you for a minute, but you ain't never home. What's good with you? I hear you out there doin' big things, shinin' and flossin' and got every nigga from here to Miami tryna get at your sexy ass."

I started laughin'. "You silly. Niggas ain't checkin' for me like that. It ain't even that serious. I'm chillin'. Yeah, it's been a while since we've talked. And nigga, you know I'ma always have love for you. I'm just doin' me."

"Yeah, aiight. I can't tell. I don't get no letters, no visits, nothin' from you. I thought we were bigger than that. I mean, damn! I know I'm not ya man 'n shit no more, but I'm sayin'…shoot a nigga a kite from time to time."

Humph. I wish the fuck I would. "You already know how I feel 'bout those visits. I'm not with 'em. And I ain't beat for writin' letters. I accept ya collects, so be thankful."

"Oh, word. It's like that now? When I was out on the bricks you wasn't talkin' all slick 'n shit. Now a nigga on freeze and you all brand-new. I see how you doin' it. It's all good, though. A nigga ain't gonna be down for long. The minute I touch, shit gon' change. And you better have that pussy nice and tight, too. I don't want you givin' up my pussy to none of them punk-ass niggas."

I sighed. "Whatever, nigga!" I said angrily. "Why must we go through this shit every time you call? I didn't get ya ass locked up, you did. Perhaps ya didn't get the memo. So, let me give it to ya now: I ain't no little-ass girl anymore. You can't spit that shit to me and think it's gonna be sweet. I'ma fuck who I wanna fuck."

"Yeah, aiight," he said, soundin' tight. I could tell by the tone in his voice that the idea of me ridin' another nigga's dick was a bit much for him. "So who you fuckin'?"

"None of ya muhfuckin' business, that's who," I said, rollin' my eyes.

He started laughin'. "Yeah, aiight. I'ma see what's really good with you in a minute, baby. Believe that. Fuck 'round and I'ma have another case."

Whatever! He's been sayin' that "in a minute" mess for almost five damn years, and his ass was still sittin' behind bars and barbed wire. I don't know what kinda time clock he was usin' but he needed a reality check, and quick. The nigga wasn't punchin' out anytime soon. I glanced at my 18kt timepiece dipped in ice. *This nigga is burnin' my jack with his bullshit*, I thought. *I really ain't beat for this shit tonight. He got two more minutes, then I'ma bang on his ass.* "Naheem, is there somethin' you want? 'Cause if not, it's been real. I got shit to do, so—"

"Aye, yo…what's good with ya peoples?" he asked, cuttin' me off. "I hear they out there real reckless with theirs."

"What you talkin' 'bout?" I asked, gettin' ready to flip into bitch mode. "Reckless how?"

"Well, from what I hear, ya girl Tamia out there bein' a real rabbit, poppin' E's 'n shit, and suckin' and fuckin' everything wit' a dick." I twisted my lips. *E pills?* This nigga musta banged his head on his bunk for real, talkin' that shit. Suckin' and fuckin', yeah, okay. And I know the bitch'll get lifted off some smoke. But pills, nah, that ain't even her flava. I kept my mouth shut, but inside I was ready to check his ass on the real. "And ya girl Iris out there fuckin' wit' this nigga from Long Island whose pushin' major weight, and he got her frontin' for him. And Tamia got that shit."

That shit? Of course a bitch's first thought was the Alphabets, 'cause that's the first thing you hear when someone's talkin' 'bout someone with the package. "What shit you talkin' 'bout?" I held my breath.

"She got herpes." Okay, on some real shit, I don't know if I was relieved that it wasn't HIV/AIDS or not. But a bitch was pissed that a nigga behind the wall was callin' me with this mess.

"Where'd you get that shit from 'bout Iris?" I asked.

"One of my mans I fuck wit' up in here is his peoples. And you know don't shit happen on the streets that we don't know 'bout."

"Hmm. And where'd you get that shit 'bout Tamia?"

"'Cause another one of my man's brothas was fuckin' wit' her for a minute on the low, and now he got that shit. He tellin' cats he got it from her nasty ass."

"Well, you got ya facts twisted. Ain't no way Iris frontin' shit for no nigga. She might be stuntin' his ass, but frontin' him? Nah, nigga, you got the wrong one. And I know damn well Tamia ain't on it like that."

"Nah, baby, real talk. My mans got flicks of ya girl Iris wit' his peoples, mad chillin'. I'm tellin' ya, dude got her straight rockin' his dick. The cat's stretchin' her neck, and got her pushin' them thangs for him. Matter of fact, he got like five or six bitches in his stable makin' that shit do what it do. And that shit wit' Tamia, I don't really know how true it is, but word to life this ain't the only nigga sayin' it. There's another cat she supposedly done did dirty, too. You know I'ma real nigga, and I ain't gonna say shit that ain't real."

"So, if you know all this, then why you askin' me? Both of 'em are grown-ass women. Iris can do whatever she wants. I'm not her keeper. And I ain't got shit to do with Tamia's pussy conditions."

"Yo, just tell 'em both to be easy. Shit is real hectic out there."

I knew what he meant. The streets were hot. ATF, TNT, FBI, DEA, SWAT, niggas were gettin' bagged and popped left and right. Iris knew this. It's on the news, in the papers, on the radio. The drug game, major paper or not, came with some serious risks. Some people gotta live it to learn it. And that mess 'bout Tamia, I refused to believe that shit. Yeah, when the bitch was in her teens she mighta got reckless with it, but she knew shit was too fuckin' serious now. A bitch could end up with some shit she can't get rid of. Fuck that, ain't no way this ho was bein' that damn stupid. But if it was true, then she'd get what her hand called for. A bitch can end up at the bottom of a river for some grimy shit like that.

"That's on them," I finally said.

"Yeah, but that's ya peoples. And one's fuckin' wit' a real live nigga, wit' a whole lotta enemies. I hope she knows what she's stepped into. And the other is playin' wit fire fuckin' these niggas' lives up. Some of these niggas she's fuckin' got families 'n shit."

I twisted my face up. "Okay, so you tryna say she's responsible for what the fuck these niggas bring home to their chicks. Fuck that! That's on their stupid asses for creepin', and for fuckin' a bitch raw. So, them niggas get what they get."

I hated that shit! Muhfuckas always wanna blame somebody else for their shit crumblin'. You play reckless, then you die reckless.

"Nah, I ain't sayin' that," he said. "'Cause them niggas should know how to move. But at the end of the day, she should be responsible enough to tell 'em."

"Oh, please," I snapped. "If the bitch wasn't bein' responsible fuckin' a nigga raw, what the fuck makes you think she'd be responsible enough to wanna tell the next muhfucka her pussy ain't right. Obviously, *she* had to get it from some nigga."

Okay, I ain't gonna front. Listenin' to Naheem's ass got a bitch sizzlin' mad. First I'm thinkin', why the fuck is he talkin' loose on the phone? I thought they listened in on all those lines. Then I'm thinkin', if what he was sayin' was true about Iris, I was gonna scream on that dumb bitch. Fuckin' a nigga pushin' weight was one thing, but bein' his gofer or *mule* was a whole other thing. We all knew a few chicks on lock for takin' the weight for some nigga. And while her ass is doin' *his* bid, doin' *his* time, he's makin' moves with the next bitch. We used to laugh at them silly-ass hoes.

And if that bitch Tamia was out here fuckin' niggas knowin' her pussy was rotten, and wasn't tryna tell them niggas, then that was some real foul shit. *What the fuck is these bitches thinkin'*, I thought. I needed to call them hoes.

"Who's the nigga Iris's fuckin' with?" I asked, already knowin' he wasn't gonna pass off that kinda info. I didn't even bother to ask him 'bout the nigga talkin' that shit 'bout Iris 'cause I wasn't tryna believe it.

"Ask ya girl."

I sucked my teeth, then took a deep breath. "Uh, why'd you call me again?" I asked.

He lowered his voice. "I was tryna bust this nut wit' you."

I rolled my eyes. "Nigga, please. Not today you won't. You betta take that shit somewhere else."

"Come on, ma, real quick. Let me hear some of that nasty shit you like."

I sighed. "Look, Naheem. I gotta go."

"Oh, so you just gonna leave a nigga's dick stiff."

"Well, if ya nasty ass kept ya hand outta ya pants and stopped strokin' while talkin' to me, the shit wouldn't be bricked the fuck up. So that's on you. Call me one day next week, aiight?"

"Yeah, baby. I can do that. When?"

I thought for a minute. "Hmm, like Wednesday or Thursday night." Those were days I knew I wouldn't be home. A bitch wasn't beat to listen to any more of his prison-yard gossip, and I damn sure wouldn't be phone-fuckin' him.

"Bet. You know I love you, right?"

"Like you love that bird you fuckin' with?"

"Oh, here you go. What, you jealous?"

I laughed. "Nigga, get a grip. That bum bitch ain't in my league."

"Maybe not. But she's holdin' a nigga down; more than what I can say 'bout you. You bounced on a nigga, so what was I supposed to do?"

I decided to ig that shit he was talkin' 'bout me bouncin' on his ass. As far as I was concerned he needed to get over it. "Do you," I said. "I ain't hatin'. I'm just sayin'…ya girl's a pigeon, that's all."

"But she's keepin' my dick wet, and my commissary up."

I knew all too well 'bout them hoes suckin' dick and a nigga finga-poppin' her pussy up in the visits whenever they could get it off. Yeah, them some real straight hood rat and rabbit bitches fuckin' a nigga in a damn visitin' hall.

"I bet she is. But she ain't wettin' it like I wet it. Ho can't even mind fuck ya right. And I *know* she ain't slayin' the dick like I slayed it, 'cause if she was you wouldn't be tryna phone-bone me. Bitch probably can't even stretch her neck. Yeah, you got ya'self a real door prize," I said, laughin'.

"Fuck so funny?" he snapped, gettin' agitated. He hated when I reminded him of how good this pussy and head game were. "I'm doin' what I gotta do to get through this shit, know what I'm sayin'? But a nigga tryna come home to you, real talk."

Wrong answer, I thought. For a second, I considered how he used to be dipped and paid, and how he used to have a bitch screamin' out his name and ready to climb walls every time he slammed that big, black dick in me. Oh, well. That shit was old news! His ass was locked the hell down, dead broke from spendin' hundreds of thousands of chips on lawyers 'n shit, and havin' a bunch of fiends and backward niggas on his team who either smoked up or hustled up his ends. He couldn't do shit for a bitch like me. Ain't no way in hell I'd give him any rhythm when he got out.

Keepin' shit real, I still had feelings for him, so I didn't have the heart to bust his bubble and remind him that shit was really over for us; that my love for him wasn't the kinda love a bitch had for a nigga she was tryna ride or die with. But a nigga behind the wall got enough shit to deal with; I figured ain't no use givin' him somethin' else to stress about. He'd find out soon enough.

"Yeah, okay," I said, gettin' off my bed to remove my jewelry. I stripped out of my clothes, then switched my naked, juicy ass into the bathroom to turn on the jets to my Jacuzzi. I decided to soak and unwind before I called Tamia and Iris. *Better yet*, I thought, *I'ma wait 'til I see them bitches, then I'ma see what's really good.*

"Aiight, baby. It's almost count. I'ma hit you next week."

"True," I said. We said our good-byes, then hung up. I went downstairs to my bar and poured myself some Hennessy, then rolled a blunt. For some reason, talkin' to Naheem had a bitch stressed the hell out. I came back upstairs with my things and went into the bathroom. I lit my candles, put in my Corinne Bailey Rae CD, then stepped into the tub. I slid my ass down into the bubbles, sipped my drink, lit my blunt and took two long pulls, leaned my head back, then closed my eyes, thinkin', rememberin'…

>>>

See, growin' up, all a bitch like me had to do was walk in a room and niggas would be tryna check for me the minute they spotted me. I didn't have to floss in front of no nigga tryna get his attention, poppin' my ass and titties. Hair, face, and wears, always on point! I stayed turnin' heads.

My moms not bein' able—or *maybe* not wantin'—to buy me the flavas didn't stop my flow. At eleven, I learned how to get the shit I needed and wanted, and by the time I was thirteen, I was a pro, makin' my own ends. There were a few boosters 'n shit who taught me how to lift shit—from jewelry to high-end pieces—so a bitch stayed laced in all the hot shit. And I kept my pockets lined. Anyway, the way my wears clung to my bangin' body, niggas knew what time it was. I was a real grade-A, top-shelf bitch. Like I told ya from gate, I was *that* bitch all the niggas wanted to fuck with. But I gave 'em no play.

Other than the young nigga I fucked for that burner to slump my mom's crab-ass nigga, there were only two cats back then who could ever say that they had fucked me. 'Cause unlike the rest of them young bitches, I wasn't hot in the ass. I wasn't lookin' for trouble and drama like a lot of them fast asses. I wasn't beat for chasin' bottom-of-the-barrel niggas hustlin' backward. You know. The niggas who hugged the block all day and all night, who stayed gettin' high but were always broke as hell, pullin' in enough peanuts to buy them a pair of constructs or a fresh pair of Jordans. I wasn't that kinda bitch. And I didn't stay runnin' the streets seven days a week like a lot of them hoes either. I took my ass to school every damn day instead of dippin' out, and did my shit right after school and on the weekends, feel me?

Goin' to school was one thing, but the minute that bell rang, I was tryna do me. And my moms didn't say shit. She let me do whatever I wanted and stay out as late as I wanted as long as my ass went to school. She didn't give a fuck if I got As or Ds, as long as I passed, and graduated, which I did.

Tamia's and Iris's dumb asses were too busy gettin' smoked out and fuckin' to be bothered with school. Not tryna dis them bitches and whatnot, but I understand why they fucked every nigga that came at 'em. A chick with low self-esteem will let a nigga do anything he wanna do to 'em 'cause he already knows she's all fucked up in the head. By the time they were fourteen, they had been through half the niggas from around the way, and had already been down to the clinic at least three times for some shit that some dirty nigga passed off. After a while, niggas knew to double-wrap 'cause they pussies stayed burnin'. Humph. Maybe that shit 'bout her havin' herpes was really true, who knows.

Anyway, Chanel was fuckin', too, but she had only one nigga she was lettin' smash. So she was straight. But them other two, forget it, they were straight hood rats with theirs; suckin' and fuckin' wherever and whenever they could get it in. But I'll keep it real—hoes or not, let some beef pop off and they were down for whatever. Like the time these bitches from Fort Greene tried to come through to get at Chanel and me over these two rusty niggas two of them bitches thought we was fuckin'. They came like six deep to fight us. Now, how the fuck you gonna try 'n come to someone else's hood and bring it? That's a no-no. I straight tic-tac-toed two of them hoes in the face with my razor. And Chanel stabbed two more with an ice pick. And when Tamia and Iris heard we were out there fightin' they ran 'round with hammers and put work in. We fucked them bitches up real good, then went back up to Tamia's buildin' and sparked up, laughin' all night at how we wrecked shop on they asses.

A lot of times, we'd rotate goin' to each other's spots, and sit up in each other's rooms gettin' blazed and gossipin' 'bout all the goings-on in the hood. Or we'd parlay with these niggas over in Bushwick. Other times, we'd get it poppin' over in Red Hook. Or we'd sneak uptown and chill with these older cats from Harlem and smoke and drink with them. But most of the time we'd squat over Tamia's 'cause her moms didn't give a fuck, and half the time she wasn't never there anyway.

Chanel and I would sit around and listen to Tamia and Iris swap stories about who they had fucked, how little or big the nigga's dick was, how they sucked dick, and what little trinket they had gotten for fuckin'. Although Iris was messy, fuckin' her mother's boyfriend and his son, Tamia was the real dirty type to fuck a nigga in the stairwell of his building if they couldn't get it in at his or her mother's spots. Or she'd sneak some young nigga up in her room and fuck him on her twin bed, then not change her cum-stained sheets for a week or two. I would sit 'n listen, like I do now. And a few times Tamia's nasty-assed sister, Tameka, would leave her bedroom door cracked and a light on so we could watch her fuck. They were straight nasty like that.

Chanel and I were always the hottest bitches out of the clique. And we still are. But, back then, a few times I would catch Tamia or Iris clockin' one of us outta the corner of her eye. Hate and envy seemed to always be wrapped up in their smiles. But I never checked 'em on it. Busted or not, they were still our girls, and they always had our backs. And we had theirs.

I'ma keep shit real and say Tamia and Iris really went from ugly-ass moths growin' up to some real live butterfly bitches. It's like them hoes transformed overnight. Too bad they could change everythin' else except their reps. A ho is always gonna be known as a ho. Real talk. That's one thing my moms made sure I knew. She'd beat me in the head nonstop 'bout keepin' my legs shut and not fuckin' none of them nasty no-count niggas, or not bringin' her no babies to take care of. Little did she know, fuckin' was the last thing on my mind. I was too busy lookin' for ways to make paper. Anyway, I don't really think me fuckin' was her issue—ending up like her was.

Shit. I didn't have my first boyfriend until I was sixteen. Yeah, that's right. Naheem. Oooh, my pussy used to get real wet thinkin' 'bout how good he used to dick me down. He stamped his name all up in this pussy, real talk. That fine black muhfucka was my heart. And I know I was his, which is why I didn't feel the need to let him know that I wasn't a virgin, that another nigga had already inched his dick up in me. See, in my head, since the young nigga had nutted in like ten minutes that shit didn't really count. So I didn't think it was necessary to bust Naheem's bubble. Besides, my pussy was still tighter than a muhfucka, and the fact that he had one of them long, thick, juicy dicks that stretched and pulled my pussy open made it that much easier to fake the funk with him. That nigga served me the dick Brooklyn-style, just how I liked it—rough, rugged, and real gully.

So as far as I was concerned, Naheem was my first. He was the first nigga who ate my pussy, the first nigga who fucked me in my ass, the first nigga who made me nut, the first nigga who splashed his dick milk down my throat, the first nigga I ever cried over, and the first—and *only*—nigga to ever get me pregnant. Yeah, a bitch got knocked when I was seventeen and a senior in high school. I had missed three periods so I already knew what time it was. I kept that shit on the low for real for real. My moms would have snapped. There was no way I was gonna be able to tell her without catchin' a real beat down. So Tamia got her cousin, Natalie, to take me to a clinic over in Queens where she and Tamia had gone and I got that shit sucked out with a quickness. And I never said anything 'bout it to Naheem. Please. The last thing I needed, or wanted, was a cryin'-ass baby holdin' me down, and I already know if I woulda told him that a bitch was pregnant, he woulda been tryna get me to keep it. And then my ass woulda been stuck raisin' it by my damn self, and luggin' it up and down the interstate to see a nigga in prison. Thanks, but no thanks. A bitch ain't beat for none of that shit.

Anyway, at nineteen Naheem was a grown-ass man to me. His swagger was so fuckin' official that every bitch on the scene wanted to fuck with him. The nigga's body was sick. His dick game was ridiculous. His knuckle game was tight. And he had the streets on lock. What I loved most about him was the respect he got. He wasn't some hand-to-hand nigga huggin' a block 'round the clock. He was the cat who made shit move. And when that nigga came through it was strictly to collect his paper; nothin' more, nothin' less. Muhfuckas knew what time it was when he rolled up. He either had niggas shook, or ridin' his nuts.

And I bagged him. That's right. The hottest bitch in the hood had his nose wide open. The nigga only had eyes for *me*. Yeah, muhfuckas, the chick with the fat ass, smooth, pretty brown thighs, and sexy-ass eyes. We'd chill, get blazed, pop a few bottles and fuck like two rabbits every damn day. I fucked with that nigga for almost two years until he got caught up in some dumb shit and got sent upstate. When that nigga caught a case for drug and weapons possession and got sentenced, I almost passed out. I ain't gonna front. E'erything in my fuckin' body went numb. It was like the air around me stopped movin'. I damn near suffocated.

On some real shit, I tried to hold the nigga down. But, hell… what was a fly bitch like me gonna do for ten years? Seal up my pussy, sit by the phone and wait for collect calls, chase the mailman down for letters, cry and have my stomach in knots after every visit 'cause it hurt leavin' him, spend my life bein' a prisoner's wife?

Well, I tried that. I really wanted to keep shit real and ride it out with him. What I felt for Naheem was probably the closest thing to love, 'cause everything in me ached without him. But the streets were callin' me. Time was testin' me. And almost two years into his bid, I told him I had to bounce. I was too young to have to put my life on hold for him. I didn't have it in me to hold my breath waitin' on appeals 'n shit. I couldn't hang on to empty promises that shit was gonna be right between us. I wanted to. I tried to. But shit was hectic.

So instead of goin' out like some crab-ass bitch, I told him face-to-face. The way his jaws tightened and his thick lips clenched, I thought he was gonna try 'n flex on my ass up in there. But he kept it cute and told me to do me. But the nigga was hurt. I heard

that shit in his voice, seen it in his eyes. Still, there wasn't nothin'
I could do 'bout it, I had to go. I told him I'd always have love
for him. And I knew I was gonna miss that pretty dick, but...fuck
that! With him on lock, I knew it'd be a long time before I got
to ride up on it any damn way. Niggas don't realize that when
they do time, the bitches holdin' them down is doin' time, too.
It takes a real special kinda bitch to stay true to a nigga on lock.
I wasn't the one. A bitch had a life. And sittin' up on a hot, funky
bus for two or more hours next to a bunch of stankin' ass hoes
bein' herded like cattle to see a man in prison wasn't a good look.
Not for a butter bitch like me.

CHAPTER SEVEN

*Pretty face...tiny waist...fat ass, got ya head fucked up...
dipped in the illest shit...fly from the top of her head...to the
bottom of her feet...the bitch got ya thinkin' shit's all
sweet...she's got ya toes curled tight and ya mind spinnin'
fast...got ya raw doggin' her deep in her ass...nigga wanted
a nut...fuckin' her was ya only desire...but turned out to be
ya worst mistake...dirty bitch got blisters and a nasty rash...
pussy full of pus...now ya dick on fire...dumb muhfucka, that's
what ya get for fuckin' a trick...*

I had just turned onto Chanel's street when my cell phone started ringin'. I picked up. "I'm a minute away," I said, then hung up. After speakin' to Naheem last night I wasn't really beat for bein' 'round Iris 'n them. But Chanel was beatin' me in my head 'bout chillin' so I gave in. Girls or not, I knew I was gonna have a hard time keepin' my mouth shut and not screamin' on them hoes. I had decided on my way over that I was gonna sit back 'n peep how they moved. However, I knew me, and a bitch like me ain't gonna keep her mouth shut too long. I'd like to think that a real bitch is gonna keep shit real, but I know every bitch ain't gonna be real so sometimes ya gotta watch how she plays her hand. Truth or not, if a nigga in prison is hearin' some shit 'bout ya ass, nine times out of ten, there's some fuckin' truth somewhere in the middle of all the bullshit. And truth be told, a bitch needed to know what type of hoes she was fuckin' with.

When I walked up to Chanel's apartment door, I could hear the music playin'. Lil' Kim's "The Jump Off" was bangin'. I rang the doorbell. A few seconds later, Tamia opened the door with a blunt hangin' outta her mouth and a drink in hand. I could tell by the glazed look in her eyes that her ass was already lifted. "What's good?" I asked, steppin' in and shuttin' the door behind me.

She took a pull from her blunt, then handed it to me. "Here, bitch," she said. "You already two blunts and three drinks behind the rest of us."

I looked at the blunt in her hand, shakin' my head. I wish the fuck I would put my lips on that shit after what I heard. Whether the shit is true or not, that bitch is nasty as far as I'm concerned. Uh, correction…the bitch has *always* been nasty. She's just nastier now.

"Nah, I'm good," I said.

"More for me, then," she said, puttin' it back up to her lips and takin' a deep pull.

"Where's everyone else?" I asked, removin' my jacket.

The smoke filled her nostrils as she blew it out of her mouth and through her nose. "In the kitchen," she answered. "Where else?"

I heard Chanel's loud-ass mouth comin' from down the hall-way. I hung my jacket up in the closet, then headed toward the kitchen. When I got to the doorway, a cloud of weed smoke hit me in the face. Chanel and Iris were sittin' at the table eatin' shrimp and gettin' their drink and smoke on. There was Rémy, Hennessy, Alizé, Absolut, Patrón, and weed for days all on the table.

"Bitch," Chanel started. "It's 'bout time you got here. I called ya ass three times."

"Well, I'm here now," I said, goin' to the sink to wash my hands. "What you bitches drinkin'?"

"Pick ya poison," Tamia said, handin' me a glass, "'cause we's 'bout to get lit the fuck up." She started dancin' in the middle of the floor when Cassidy's "I'm a Hustla" came on.

Iris handed Chanel the blunt. She took two pulls, then passed it to Tamia. I raised my eyebrow. When Tamia tried to hand it to me, I shook my head, wavin' it away. "Nah, I'm good."

"Oh, you ain't smokin' with ya bitches tonight?" Iris said.

Yeah, I'm smokin', I thought. *I just ain't smokin' that.* "I ain't fuckin' with you fiends like that right now."

"This bitch always on some extra shit," Chanel said, laughin'.

"So what's good with you, Iris?" I asked, pourin' myself some Rémy, then sittin' at the table next to her with my back toward the wall. I made sure I sat facin' everyone since I knew it was a matter of time before I started flippin' the script. Just in case shit popped off, I needed to be on point. These my girls 'n all, but after a few drinks and a couple of blunts, a bitch'll be ready to jump when shit gets heated. And since I'd changed my mind when I walked through the door and decided I was gonna bring it to these hoes, I knew it might get messy, especially since some bitches can't handle the truth.

"Shit," she said. "Just chillin'."

"Really?" I asked, reachin' for a plate and pickin' up four jumbo shrimp. "I hear ya pushin' shit for some nigga on Long Island, what's good with that?" I pulled a napkin outta my bag and discreetly spit my razor out. Yes, a bitch keeps a razor in her mouth at all times, and can spit it out and put it to a bitch's throat with a quickness. Fuck what ya heard. I never leave home without it.

"What?" she asked.

"Bitch, I ain't stutter," I said, dippin' my shrimp in some cocktail sauce, then poppin' it in my mouth. I shot her ass a look. "You heard what the fuck I said. So, is the shit true or not?"

Tamia and Chanel looked at each other, then at Iris, waitin' for her to answer.

"Yeah," she said, takin' a pull from the blunt. "I'm doin' a little sumthin'. Why?"

"Bitch, is you fuckin' crazy?!" I snapped. "What the fuck is you thinkin'?"

"I'm thinkin' a bitch got bills, and a bitch tryna make some paper. What, you gotta problem with that?"

"No, ho," I replied. "I gotta problem with how you makin' it. Outta all the muhfuckin' hustles out here you gotta be transportin' shit for some nigga. That shit is crazy to me."

"Well, that's you," she said. "I'ma do what I gotta do."

I shook my head, poppin' another shrimp in my mouth. "Does Justice know?" I asked, wipin' my mouth.

"Nah, that nigga don't know. And he ain't gonna know. Anyway, he ain't my muhfuckin' man. He's just somebody I'm fuckin'. I'm 'bout to give him his papers, anyway."

"You'se a real dumb bitch, for real," I said, rollin' my eyes. "I can't fuckin' believe you. We used to laugh at them bitches, and now you one of 'em."

"Whatever."

"So what's good with you and that other nigga you were fuckin'?" I asked.

"Please," she said as she reached for the Patrón, "he's just some side dick. Ain't nothin' poppin' with him and me." She filled her shot glass, then tossed it back. She set the glass back down on the table and continued. "As long as I can get into the clubs for free with my girls, then the nigga serves his purpose."

"Girl, you know I understand a bitch tryna do her," Chanel said, "but I'm with Kat. That shit's crazy. If shit gets hot, you know that nigga will hang ya ass to dry."

"It ain't even like that," she stated, gettin' all defensive 'n shit.

I sucked my teeth. "Why, because you fuckin' him?"

"Yeah, we fuckin' 'n all. But he ain't even on it like that. On some real shit, the nigga asked me to do him this solid. He's diggin' me, and I'm diggin' him. Real talk."

If that wasn't the dumbest shit I ever heard this bitch say. No nigga who is *really* feelin' you, or tryna wife ya, is gonna get ya ass caught up in some shit like pickin' up and movin' his packages. Fuck that. He's gonna try to keep ya ass outta that shit. Get his muhfuckin' niggas or some trick to handle that shit. I don't give a fuck what ya say. Now I might carry a nigga's gun into a club or some shit like that, like I used to do when I was fuckin' with Naheem, but that extra shit…you can kiss my beautiful round ass!

"Bitch, please," I said. "Like he's diggin' the other six bitches he got runnin' shit for his ass. Girl, the only thing that muhfucka is *diggin'* is ya back out. That nigga don't give a fuck 'bout you 'cause if he did, he wouldn't've asked ya ass to do no shit like that in the first place. So fuck what ya heard."

"You don't know what you talkin' 'bout."

"Yeah okay…if you say so. But I know all that nigga is doin' is usin' ya silly ass. And you too stuck on stupid to see it."

Tamia chimed in. "Kat, you always comin' outta the side of ya neck with shit. Iris is a grown-ass woman, so let her do her. If the nigga is tryna play her, she'll peep it, and in the end his ass'll get played 'cause that's how we do ours." She lifted her drink toward Iris. "Girl, I'm with you. Get that paper. Just know when to dip out."

"Exactly," Iris said, clickin' her glass with Tamia's.

"Bitch, fuck that. If we 'posed to be girls, then girls check each other when shit ain't right. And this shit don't sit right with me, so, I'm sayin' somethin'. But at the end of the day, I know the bitch is gonna do what she wants. But that still don't mean I ain't gonna call her on it."

"And you know I appreciate it, but I know what I'm doin'."

I stared at her ass like she had six heads and a dick hangin' outta each one of her mouths. "Humph. Yeah, okay. Who is this nigga, anyway?" I asked.

"Don't worry 'bout that," Iris replied, suckin' her teeth. "You don't need to know all that right now."

"Aww, shit," Chanel said. "So now we keepin' secrets from each other?"

"I'm not keepin' secrets. I need to keep this on the low for now. But, this bitch here," she said, flickin' her thumb in my direction, "tryna put me on blast 'n shit."

"Because I care 'bout what happens to ya dumb ass."

"Don't worry. I got this."

"Well, I tell ya what, Miss I Got This. When the nigga turns his back on ya ass, you make sure you got enough bail money to get ya dumb ass outta Rikers, and enough money for a lawyer to keep ya ass from bein' sent up the way, 'cause Tamia's broke ass ain't got it to help ya ass since she wanna be on ya team 'n shit."

"Whatever," Iris said. "I know you ain't talkin', bitch. You the biggest secret keeper up in this piece and ain't none of us ridin' ya clit tryna find out how you makin' ya paper."

"I ain't bein' no nigga's mule," I said, frownin'. "That's what the fuck I'm not doin'."

"Well, answer me this," Iris said, takin' another blunt from

Tamia. She took three pulls and passed it to Chanel. When Chanel tried to pull me into the rotation, I told her ass, *again*, I was good. "Is how you makin' ya ends legal?"

"Ho, what I do or don't do has nothin' to do with ya dumb ass runnin' drugs for some nigga. Don't try 'n flip this shit on me."

"Bitch, pass me the blunt," Iris ordered Chanel, who'd held on to it three tokes too long for Iris's likin'. "Your trick ass holdin' onto that shit like it's a dick or some shit."

Chanel took another toke, then exhaled. "Ho, bite me," she said, laughin', "with ya fiend ass."

I had had 'bout enough of this back 'n forth bullshit. Fuckin' with these hoes was startin' to give me a headache. A bitch needed a blunt! I reached into my Gucci bag and pulled out my stash. "Hand me a light," I said, lettin' out a deep disgusted sigh.

"Oh, bitch, what…you too good to smoke with us?" Tamia asked.

Chanel tossed me her lighter.

"Basically," I said, sparkin' up.

"Since when?" she asked with 'tude.

I eagerly took two pulls, then held the smoke in my lungs before lettin' it swirl up into my nose, and out of my mouth. Okay, this was startin' to remind me of that game Truth or Dare. See, a bitch who ain't ready to face the truth would rather be dared to do some off-the-wall shit, instead of facin' shit dead-on. But a real live bitch is gonna give ya ass the truth and even take the dare as a bonus. Tamia's raggedy-ass ain't gonna do either 'cause the ho ain't real with hers.

"Since I don't know where ya nasty-ass mouth's been, that's when," I answered, blowin' smoke up into the air.

"Bitch, and I don't know where yours been either," Tamia stated, cuttin' me the evil eye. "But that ain't never stop us from blazin' together before. And now you wanna be on some new shit. Fuck ya snotty ass, then."

"Ya right. You don't know where my mouth's been. But you ain't never heard no shit 'bout me either. You, on the other hand—"

"Wait a minute, bitch!" she cut me off. "What the fuck is you tryna say? You ain't heard shit 'bout me."

"Humph. We mighty defensive, aren't we?"

"I ain't defensive 'bout shit," she snapped.

"Ain't that special. Word on the streets is you got herpes," I said, takin' a long pull from my blunt. Everyone in the room almost chocked on their drinks and smoke.

"Get the fuck outta here," Chanel said, coughin' and wavin' the thick smoke outta her face. "Where'd you hear that bullshit?"

"Naheem called me last night and said some nigga up there got peoples on the bricks sayin' she gave it to 'em."

"Fuck that lyin'-ass nigga," Tamia said defensively. She poured herself another drink. "He don't know what the fuck I got."

I eyed her. "Well, what *do* you have?"

"The same shit you got, bitch. Fuck is you talkin' 'bout, tryna come at me on some bullshit. I'm real with mine, bitch."

"I seriously doubt it, ho!" I yelled at her. "You can say whatever the fuck ya want. But like I said before, you ain't never heard no shit 'bout me from no niggas or bitches. Believe that. But you, bitch, ya name has always been all up 'n down the streets. Ya name was floatin' all through the projects, ho. And you know it. So, please! You the one who had to start fuckin' with them Queens and uptown niggas 'cause most of Brooklyn had already ran up in you. Then when ya name started floatin' outta them niggas' circles, you crossed over the water and started fuckin' Jersey niggas. So, bitch, don't even clown. If the Centers for Disease Control ever got word on how much dick mileage ya pussy got on it, and the number of nuts dumped up in it, they'd have ya ass up on the Most Wanted Hoes list, so you can front if ya want."

"Fuck you, Kat!" She slammed her drink down onto the table. "You act like ya ass is so fuckin' on point. You got dirt under ya nails and rug burns on ya back, too, bitch."

I laughed. "Uh-huh, I sure do. But I don't have blisters on my pussy, bitch. See, the difference between you and a bitch like me is I know how to move. And, you, you real sloppy with your shit. Because you rockin' a few labels now don't mean shit ain't still poppin' off 'bout ya nasty ass. But I tell ya what. Since you so real with yours, ho, how many niggas used ya fuckin' throat to plant their nuts in, huh, you dirty bitch?"

"That's none of ya muhthafuckin' business."

"Oh, really?" I asked. "Since when? It never stopped ya ass in the past. Now all of a sudden who ya fuckin' ain't nobody's business." I started laughin'. "Trick, please. You always been a walkin' billboard for sex on the go. You been poppin' dicks in ya mouth like Tic Tacs since the sixth grade. And now you tryna be brandnew. And the funny shit is that after all the dicks ya ass done sucked and swallowed, you still on the bottom."

She started shiftin' her eyes and twistin' her ass in her seat. That's how I knew the bitch was lyin'. My moms always said, "Watch how a bitch acts when you confront her ass 'bout somethin'. If the ho ain't lookin' you straight in the eyes and if she starts actin' all fidgety 'n shit, then the bitch is lyin'. And if the bitch grabs her shit to leave, then she done told you what you already know." And that is somethin' I've always lived by.

"You know what, bitch!" she said suddenly, gettin' up. I slipped my hand down in my purse and grabbed my ice pick just in case this ho got froggish and tried to leap. Although I had my razor in my napkin, a know-it-all bitch like her needed to have some sense poked up in her a few times instead of bein' slashed up. "I'm sick of you always thinkin' you betta than somebody else. You ain't shit, bitch. Just because ya moms came into a little paper and moved ya conceited ass outta the hood don't make you no better, bitch! Just because you gotta little shine, that don't make you no better than me. Yeah, you might be bubblin', but you still a project bitch. But a bitch thinks she's too good for the hood now."

I looked at this bitch like she was half-crazy, tryna figure out what the fuck me movin' outta the hood had to do with her nasty ass. I bust out laughin'. "Yeah, tramp, I'm a project bitch, alright. Always was, always will be. But I ain't ever been no dirty one. Can you say that 'bout ya slutty ass?"

"Won't you bitches chill the fuck out," Iris jumped in. "Ya'll 'bout to fuck up my high for real for real with all this ying-yang, okey-doke bullshit."

"Nah, fuck that," Tamia said, snatchin' up her bag of weed and her Phillies and Dutches. "I'm out. This bitch done fucked up my mood."

I laughed. "Ho, run from the truth if ya want. But ya cruddy-ass just proved the shit is real. If ya pussy's flamin' and ya burnin' niggas, keep it real. That's all I'm sayin', ho. Be a real bitch 'bout it." The room got real quiet. Iris was shootin' me some serious rocks, like I really gave a fuck. I knew she didn't really want it 'cause if she did she woulda leaped. "What the fuck you ice-grillin' me for?"

She rolled her eyes. "Fuck you, bitch."

"Yeah, whatever," I said. I took another toke from my blunt, leaned back in my chair, and held that shit in my lungs.

I guess the tramp had a change of heart 'cause she tossed her shit back down on the table. "I'm goin' to the bathroom," she said, stompin' off. I knew the bitch was heated that I pulled her card. Oh well.

I slowly exhaled the smoke into the air, glancin' at Chanel. "Make sure when the bitch leaves, ya toss her glass in the trash and burn that toilet seat," I said. She rolled her eyes. Iris sucked her teeth. I picked up my glass and sipped the rest of my drink, smirkin'.

"You know you dead wrong, Kat, word," Iris said, regulatin' another blunt. "That's some real foul shit. You know we ain't never let no niggas or dick or who's fuckin' who come between us. We've always been down for each other. Why the fuck you come at her neck like that?"

"'Cause if the bitch got herpes then we need to know. She got us smokin' and drinkin' behind her nasty ass. That shit ain't fuckin' cool. And I'ma keep shit real. Muhfuckin' girls or not, if the bitch really does have that shit, and I catch it…I'ma shut her lights out. And I put that on e'erything I love."

I took another deep pull from my blunt, held it in my lungs, then let the smoke twirl around my tongue.

Iris and Chanel stared at me, shakin' their heads. But I bet them bitches put down that blunt they'd been passin' back 'n forth all night.

"Don't stop now," I said, laughin', stickin' both hands up and crossin' my fingas. "Ya'll bitches done got the cooties."

CHAPTER EIGHT

On some real shit, the other night had me lookin' at shit sideways. I mean, I got love for my girls 'n all. But, the more I was around them bitches the less I was feelin' 'em, especially Iris's and Tamia's triflin' asses. I guess my mental was much deeper than theirs. A bitch like me was lookin' at shit outside the fuckin' hood, while these broads were tryna stay chained to it. That ain't my flow. Don't get it twisted. I love the hood and all that it brings. But I ain't tryna live and breathe the shit every damn day, feel me? But I also knew that no matter where the fuck I went, I was takin' me with me. If I didn't change, then nothin' changed. But how can a bitch ever leave her past when the shit is constantly starin' me right in the fuckin' face? Even if I wanted to, which I don't, how can I ever forget where the fuck I come from when I gotta constantly keep comin' back to it? Fuck what ya heard. The hood is always gonna be in my blood. But what's wrong with a bitch wantin' some-thing better? Is it really so wrong? Hell fuckin' no!

I don't know why the fuck she still gotta live here, I thought as I pulled my truck up in front of my old buildin'. I flipped down my visor and checked my face, then watched as a group of kids came walkin' down the street—three chicks and four dudes, all 'bout thirteen, fourteen, passin' 'round what looked like a blunt as they walked and talked. They seemed to be havin' a live discussion, cursin' and laughin'. I glanced at the digital clock: 11:17 a.m. I smiled, rememberin' the days Chanel, Tamia, Iris, and I would be walkin' to catch the number 2 train to Flatbush Ave. to chill while gettin' lifted 'n talkin' shit. We'd be fresh to death in our matchin' wears, rockin' the crisp Nike Uptowns or Stan Smiths in our little bootie shorts and T-shirts knotted in the back. Our hair would be pulled back in tight ponytails with the bangs and we'd have our bamboo earrings or doorknockers swingin' and our gold name plates danglin' 'round our necks. And e'ery now and then we'd rock our matchin' gold fronts. Ugh! But you couldn't tell us bitches nothin'.

Nothin' had really changed since I moved outta the hood and outta Brooklyn two years ago. Gunshots were still poppin'; niggas were still droppin'; bitches were still stuntin'; muhfuckas were still gettin' high; the drug game was still live 'n kickin'. Same shit, different playas. The only difference, these little young niggas and bitches were more reckless with it than when I was out here. And now with this gang shit, the hood was real hectic.

As the group got closer to my truck, I sat a few minutes longer and watched an older woman who looked like she was in her fifties or so, carryin' two bags and her pocketbook, walkin' toward the group of kids. She was tryna get through the group, but no one moved outta her way so she could pass. Instead of gettin' in a confrontation, the woman tried to go 'round 'em. But one of the young girls—sportin' cornrow extensions and big danglin' earrings—just had to be a little bitch 'bout it and purposefully bumped into the woman, knockin' her bag outta her hand. Everyone in her posse thought the shit was funny and started laughin'. The woman gave them a glarin' look, pickin' up her things. I already knew if they tried to hurt her, I was gonna jump outta my truck and bring it to 'em. I cracked my windows to listen.

"Bitch, whut iz you lookin' at?" the young chick asked. The woman ignored her. "Dumb, old-ass bitch, ya lucky I'm in a good mood. Or me 'n my niggas would run ya shit."

I shook my head in disbelief, watchin' 'n waitin' to see if I was gonna have to jump outta my truck and set it off.

The woman stood, back straight, head high, and raised her hands. "I rebuke you...in the name of Jesus...in the name of Jesus...in the name of Jesus..."

"Be gone, old lady, or get ya shit split," one of the boys said.

"Though I walk through the valley," the woman said, "of the shadow of death...I fear no evil—"

"Fuck you!" they all yelled, laughin', then runnin' down the street.

I was so fuckin' disgusted. No fuckin' respect! These young niggas and bitches were on some real extra shit. Yeah, a bitch did her dirt growin' up: smoke, drank, fought and sliced bitches, boosted shit, got her party on and whatnot. But I was never disrespectful. Cussin' out and disrespectin' an old head was a no-no. I don't give a fuck how they came at ya. You kept ya grill shut and kept it movin'. I rolled up my windows and got out of my truck.

"You alright, ma'am?" I asked, walkin' 'round the front of my truck.

She smiled. "I'm fine, baby. Thanks. I don't know what's wrong with some of these kids today. They're just runnin' amok. No guidance. No respect. No regard," she said, straightenin' her rimmed glasses. "We are truly in the last days."

"You have a good day," I offered as I walked toward the project's entrance, ignorin' her comments. I really wasn't beat for a sermon. Not today. Not any day.

"You do the same," she said, speakin' to my back.

My cell started ringin' as I approached the entrance to my buildin'. I looked at the caller ID. It was Grant. I smiled, stoppin' to lean up against the railin'. I wanted some dick. And if he turned out to be a real nigga, I was gonna fuck him down into the mattress. *I hope the nigga can fuck*, I thought, answerin'. "Hello."

"Hey, beautiful," he said. "Did I catch you at a bad time?"

"Actually, I'm on my way up to see my moms. Can I call you back?"

"No doubt, but I'll hit you back instead. 'Cause I think you tryna front on a nigga. And I ain't havin' it."

I laughed. "Is that so? Well, that's what ya mouth says."

"That's what it is. I'll hit you back later on tonight."

"Aiight," I said, disconnectin' the call. My cell rang again. This time it was Chanel. "What's up, tramp?"

"Shit," she said. "What's good with you?"

"I'm here in Brooklyn, gettin' ready to go up to see my moms. Why, what's up?"

"Well, do you. Make sure you call me later. Some shit done popped off with Tamia and these bitches from Bed-Stuy over some nigga."

I rolled my eyes up in my head, suckin' my teeth. "Well, that shit's on her dumb ass," I said. "I'll holla back when I get back on the road."

"Make sure you do." *Yeah, whatever!* I hung up. A few months ago, a bitch woulda been amped the hell up, ready to strap up and wreck shop. But I ain't fuckin' with Tamia like that. This ho was on some extra shit, and I ain't the one. It'd be one thing if a bitch was straight dissin' her and tryna get at her for no reason, but some shit over a nigga who she probably had no business fuckin' any damn way...humph, I don't think so. The bitch is on her own, real talk. As a matter of fact, I really wasn't feelin' this visit with my moms, either. But I was already there.

When I entered my old buildin', I felt nothin'. Although the sidewalk was cleaner than I remembered, I thought back to when crack vials and needles littered the sidewalk and the playground in the back of buildin's four and six; when empty liquor bottles and shattered glass covered the ground. I could still hear the gunshots that rang like bells; the screams of mothers who lost another child to niggas shootin' and killin' each other over drugs and money and pussy and block takeovers. The shit was depressin'. I had spent so much time dreamin' 'bout gettin' the fuck away from here, 'bout bein' rescued from this hell hole, that my head and body were already long gone way before I ever bounced. My heart was still connected to the streets, it flowed through my blood. But it pumped at a different beat now. Don't get it twisted. I'ma be a Brooklyn bitch 'til the day I die. This life—four generations of livin' in the hood—is what I know, but I'd be damned if it was the only one I'd be livin'. Believe that.

I was glad the lobby was empty today. It was still dark and dirty and smelled like piss, but, usually, it'd be live and poppin'. I rolled my eyes when I got to the elevators and the shits were broken—*again*. I seriously thought about turnin' 'round and takin' my ass home, but decided goin' up eleven flights of stairs in heels was much better than hearin' my moms bitchin' 'bout me not comin' over. Not that I thought that she really cared one way or the other whether I came through or not, 'cause I know she didn't, but...she's still my moms and a bitch still liked to fantasize 'bout bein' wanted and missed. Shit, I thought, goin' toward the stairs, *e'erytime I come to this bitch these muhfuckas ain't workin'. What the fuck!*

As I climbed the stairs, I had to keep tryna not to step in someone's piss or spit. Nasty muhfuckas! I hurried up the stairs, and by the time I got to my floor, a bitch was wore out.

I knocked three times on the gray apartment door before the locks finally clicked and the door opened. "Well, looka here," my moms said, steppin' back to let me in. For some reason, she had that just-got-fucked look. Her thick, curly, shoulder-length hair was tossed all over her head and her face was flushed. She pulled the belt of her red silk robe tight 'round her waist. I could tell she was naked underneath. *Yep, she been fuckin'.* "The queen has finally decided to come grace me with her presence. Why didn't you call first?"

I rolled my eyes. "I didn't know I needed to make an appointment." I closed the door behind me. "Besides, you called me last week beatin' me in the head 'bout not comin' by or callin' you. I told ya I was gonna come through today."

"Well, I've heard that before, so I didn't hold my breath."

"Well, I'm here now. The least you could do is *act* like ya happy to see me. Damn."

"Humph," she grunted, switchin' her ass into the kitchen. At forty-one—I ain't gonna front—she looked much younger than her age, and still had a bangin' body. Then again, my grandmother was only sixty-one and she still had a body that would put some of these young bitches to shame.

I took a deep, disgusted breath. Just once I wished we were more like mother and daughter than two chicks who barely tolerated each other. Not that I expected a warm, mushy welcome, but damn! Some women should never have children. I'm convinced my moms was one of them chicks who shoulda kept her damn legs closed, or aborted 'cause she's never had the time, energy, or interest in raisin' me or nurturin' me. She'd rather be locked in a room with a nigga with her legs up over his shoulders than raisin' her own child. Sometimes I really wanna slap her. But no matter what, she's still my moms—fucked up or not.

"Lock my damn door." She yanked her neck 'round, glarin' at me. "You ain't been in that fancy place over in Jersey that long to forget where ya from. You know betta than to leave my doors unlocked." I shook my head, latchin' the five deadbolts. My thinkin' is, if ya so goddamn worried 'bout havin' ya doors kicked in, or bein' robbed, why the hell stay? Pack ya shit and get the fuck out.

From the outside, you'd never expect the inside of my mom's spot to be piped out with a crème-colored Italian leather sofa, plush brown carpet, marble tables, custom mirrored walls, a one-hundred-fifty-gallon tropical fish tank, and a fifty-two-inch plasma TV up on the wall.

When she came into her suit money, instead of movin' outta the projects and investin' in a house, she spent a grip redecoratin' 'n shit. Then she had the nerve to go out and buy a fuckin' 2006 Benz coupe that now looks like a damn hoopty 'cause muhfuckas stay scratchin' it up and breakin' into the shit. Humph.

Anyway, I asked her why she wouldn't move, and she flat out told me, "I ain't ever leavin' the projects. This is where I grew up and this is where I'ma die." Well, I looked at her ass like I would never relate. I mean, I mighta grew up in 'em, but I'd be damned if I ever wanted to stay and die in 'em. Keepin' shit real, I ain't nothin' like her. She is okay with her life. She is okay with never seein' or experiencin' anything outside of Brooklyn. Other than goin' to Harlem or the Bronx to visit her family, leavin'

New York—or Brooklyn, for that matter—would never happen. Oh, okay, if ya wanna count the bus trips she and my aunts make to Atlantic City to gamble. And even that's a big production. Fuck that. A bitch like me wanted to learn and see new shit. "That's the problem with ya ass," my moms had once said when I told her I was gonna travel the world when I grew up, "ya ass too busy daydreamin'."

Then when I told her I wanted to move to Jersey, she looked at me like I was outta my mind or somethin', as if movin' 'cross the water was a damn crime. "What the hell you gonna do way over there? Brooklyn is ya home. You might go, but ya ass'll be back. It's in ya blood."

I walked into the kitchen and pulled a chair out to sit at the table.

"So what you been up to?" she asked, openin' the refrigerator. She pulled out a carton of eggs and a pack of bacon. "You want somethin' to eat?"

I glanced around the small kitchen and rolled my eyes up in my head. There was dirty dishes piled in the sink, and the trash was overflowin'. *All this expensive shit up in this bitch*, I thought, *and the kitchen is still nasty. Ain't a muthafuckin' thing changed.* Outta the corner of my eye, I peeped a roach crawlin' alongside one of the cabinets, then another along the counter.

"Nah," I said, shiftin' in my seat, "I'm good. I ate already." Yeah, I lied. But there was no muthafuckin' way I'd eat shit outta that nasty-ass kitchen. She'd never have me eatin' roach eggs. The thought made me frown. I hadn't eaten outta that kitchen since I was twelve years old, and there was no way I'd start back now. "I've been chillin'. What about you?"

"Not a damn thing," she said, busyin' herself 'round the kitchen. I stared at her, takin' in the curve of her hips and the way her flimsy robe clung 'cross her titties, showin' her thick nipples. For some reason, her ass and titties looked much bigger than I remembered. "You know, Alberta over in buildin' four done got arrested for stabbin' her husband. She walked in and caught him fuckin' her best friend in their bed. She went off, stabbed his ass up real good, and she beat that bitch down real good, too."

"Hmm…" *Triflin' bitch*, I thought. *And I hope his slimy ass got his.* That was some shit. I couldn't even imagine what the fuck I'd do if I walked in and caught my man fuckin' one of my girls— well, uh, I do, but that's another story for another time. Bottom line, I woulda went the fuck off, too. But I don't know if I'da stabbed him. 'Cause unless she killed his ass, her goin' to jail is senseless. While the world is still rotatin' on its axis, and her ass is on lock, his muhfuckin' ass is still gonna be out fuckin' the next bitch. Fuck that shit, if you don't wanna kill his ass, then slice his muthafuckin' cock off. "Did she kill him?"

"No. But she gutted him real good. He's up in ICU."

"And where's she at?"

"I think she out on bail," she said.

"Humph," I grunted, shakin' my head.

Three more roaches came out to play. She saw them and started smashin' them with her hand, cussin'.

"Fuckin' roaches! I don't know why the ho next door don't fumigate her place. She's the only bitch in the buildin' that acts like she tryna keep 'em as pets." She caught my facial expression. "I don't know why you twistin' ya face up," she said, washin' her hands at the sink. "You act like you ain't ever seen a damn roach."

She reached under the sink and pulled out a can of Raid, then started sprayin' along the side of the cabinets, then 'round the back of the counter. The smell started to make me dizzy and sick to my stomach. I held my breath. She put the roach spray back, then started rinsin' pots and pans. I watched her as she pulled down a bowl, rinsed it, then started crackin' six eggs.

"Who you cookin' all them eggs for?" I asked. Before she could answer, a caramel-colored, hairy-chested, curly-haired nigga all tatted up, came into the kitchen, wearin' only a pair of flimsy gray sweats. He had that fresh-showered smell goin' on. The nigga's arms were chiseled and he had the nerve to have a damn six-pack. I peeped his long dick bouncin' and swingin' and knew the nigga didn't have any drawers on. Ugh.

The muhfucka coolly walked up on my moms and planted his thick lips on hers. The nigga didn't even speak, and I *knew* he saw me or at least *heard* us in here talkin'. I watched their tongues dart in and out of each other's mouths, like I wasn't even in the fuckin' room. He grabbed her ass. How fuckin' disrespectful was that shit? If I didn't clear my throat the two of 'em mighta started fuckin' right there. They stopped and he put his arm around her. My moms blushed, fixed her robe that had conveniently come untied, then said, "Baby, this is my daughter, Kat. Kat, this is Jawan, my fiancé."

Fiancé? I almost fell outta my fuckin' seat. I spoke to her last week and was there two months ago, and she not once said shit 'bout havin' no damn fiancé. She held up her hand to show off her ring finga. No wonder I didn't see it before. It was a tiny-ass, marquise-cut diamond ring 'bout the size of a pebble. What the fuck! I squinted my eyes and glared at her ass. She shrugged, then went back to fixin' her mystery man his breakfast.

He smiled, flashin' a chipped tooth. "So, this is my future step-daughter. I heard a lot 'bout you. Baby, you didn't tell me she was this fine," he said, walkin' over and extendin' his hand. I stared at him real hard, then at his hand. He had a tattoo of a panther with beautiful green eyes on his forearm. He was definitely younger than her, probably 'round late twenties or early thirties, I guessed. Humph. Oh, trust. I made a mental note to find out what was really good with his ass on the streets.

"It's Katrina," I said, with much 'tude. "And I haven't heard jack 'bout you." He dropped his hand. "How long you been fuckin' my mother?"

"Kat!" she yelled. "Don't start ya shit today or you can get ya ass up outta here. Baby," she cooed, like a damn silly-ass, dick-whipped schoolgirl. "Don't pay her ass no mind. She can be a real bitch sometimes."

He chuckled, lickin' his lips. "Nah, it's all good, baby. I can tell she's a real feisty one. Ya mom and I been *fuckin'*, as you put it, for a minute." He walked back over and planted another kiss on my mom's lips, then looked at me and winked. He slapped her on her ass. She giggled. I twisted my face. "So I guess we'll be seein' a lot of each other."

"I wouldn't hold ya breath," I said, rollin' my eyes. My moms shot me an evil look that said, '*Bitch, say one more slick thing and this muhfuckin' hot fryin' pan goes upside ya skull.*' She started cuttin' and dicin' up onions, tomatoes, and green peppers, then shreddin' cheddar cheese.

"Your breakfast'll be ready in 'bout ten minutes, baby. You want something to drink?"

He cut his eyes from me and turned to her. "That's cool. Yeah, bring me some orange juice. I'll be in the living room watchin' TV while you and ya daughter shoot the shit." He looked at me again, smirkin', then walked out.

"And why couldn't he get his own drink? He was standin' his ass right by the refrigerator." I spoke loud enough so the nigga could hear me. "Instead of plungin' his dick in and outta ya, he should make his ass useful and take out that trash."

She clenched her teeth. "Kat...don't...start. I mean it."

I ignored her. I tried to count the number of niggas she's had in my head, but lost count after number fourteen. Growin' up, e'ery six months to a year or so, she was in love with another nigga. Then when shit fell apart, she'd be somewhere balled up in a damn corner or locked up in her room cryin' over his ass. I swore I'd never be like her.

Like a puppet, she bounced around the kitchen fryin' up bacon 'n shit. She lowered the fire on the stove, then got a glass from outta the cabinet, rinsed it, went into the refrigerator and filled it with orange juice, then took it to him. I was too fuckin' through!

Okay, the nigga was fine, but I didn't give a fuck 'bout that. I didn't like him. Somethin' told me he was no fuckin' good. A bitch like me could peep a no-good muhfucka from a mile away. The only thing I wanted to know is where the fuck she met him and how long she'd been with him. As pretty as my moms is, for some reason she always liked niggas who had issues. Issues gettin' a job; issues keepin' a job; issues with drinkin'; issues with cheatin'; issues with gamblin'; issues with child support; issues with the law; issues with keepin' his hands off women; and the list went on. Issues, issues, issues...that's all she ever seemed to attract. Her pussy was a wet magnet for fucked-up men. And e'ery one of the niggas she picked up off the streets, she had to carry. Movin' his ass in, feedin' him, puttin' money in his pockets, cleanin' his ass up. She'd always put a nigga and his dick before me any day. Dumb women like her really made me fuckin' sick. Moms or not, as bad as I hated to admit it—no matter how hard I've tried not to—I had very little respect for her. And I was really startin' to like her less and less.

"So tell me. How old is he?" I asked when she came back into the kitchen. "He looks young enough to be ya son. Don't tell me you robbin' cradles now."

She sucked her teeth. "Shut your mouth. He's old enough. That's all you need to know."

"Humph. Well, what back alley did you find this stray in, and how long he been sniffin' around? Better yet, does the nigga work?"

"That's none of your gotdamn business. I don't question who you fuckin', so don't you dare go there with me. I'm the mother, not you. And don't forget it."

I took a deep breath, bit down on my bottom lip. Moms or not, I was ready to bring it to her ass. I tilted my head, raised my eyebrow. "Is that so," I said, smirkin'.

"What the fuck you mean 'is that so'? Bitch, don't get beside ya'self."

Bitch?!? I stared her down. "And don't you come out ya face callin' me out my name. I mean just how I said it. Take it how you wanna."

She stopped flutterin' her ass 'round, slammin' her hand on her waist. "Kat, I never put my hands on ya fresh ass, but I'm tellin' ya right now…keep it up and I'ma beat your ass for everything I didn't. You hear me?"

I rolled my eyes. "Yeah, whatever."

I knew sayin', "whatever" was gonna crank her up. She hated it. But she started the shit, so it was only a matter of time before it got hectic up in this piece.

"'Whatever' nothin'. I'm a split second off ya ass, Kat. I done warned you. For once, why can't you just be happy for me, instead of hatin'? You act like you jealous or something."

I laughed. "Jealous of what?"

"Of the fact that I got a man and you don't. That for once in my life I'm happy. This is why I didn't tell your ass about him, 'cause it's always the same bullshit with you."

"Are you serious? You sound real delusional. I ain't jealous of nothin' you got, especially a man you fuckin'. If havin' a man is what makes you happy, then good for you." I laughed at her, which I knew was gonna set shit off more. "You need help, sweetie. Real talk. 'Cause if havin' a man lay up on you is ya definition of happiness, then you can have it. And hatin' is the last thing I do, *trust*. I know ya track record when it comes to men, boo. And it ain't a good look."

"Bitch!" She yanked the knife off the counter and pointed it at me. Yep, this is how she comes at me. "I don't know where the fuck you get off thinkin' you can talk to me any way you want. Don't have me fuck you up in here."

Okay, so she never beat my ass growin' up, but verbally she'd get at me like I was a grown-ass woman, like I was a bitch on the streets. This is the kinda shit that kept me doin' me. But pullin' a muthfuckin' knife out on me was some new shit. And on some real shit, she was really pushin' my patience. I got up. It was time for me to get the fuck outta there. "I'm out," I said.

Her nigga was lampin' on the sofa with his big-ass feet plopped up on the table and his hands down in his sweats, watchin' some movie. He looked over at me and grinned. "Aiight, pretty. You be safe out there."

I igged him. "Bum-ass nigga," I mumbled. But obviously not low enough 'cause just as I unbolted the first two locks, she came runnin' outta the kitchen like a madwoman.

"And, Kat, don't bring ya ass back 'round here until you know how to talk to me."

"Get real," I snapped, facin' her. "You pull a fuckin' knife on me, and wanna…you know what? Fuck it. I'm out. You ain't gotta ever worry 'bout me comin' through this rathole again."

"Listen here, I'm 'bout sick of ya nasty-ass attitude, you ungrateful bitch. I mean what I said: Until you can respect me and my man, don't bring ya snotty, black ass back 'round here. I let ya ass get away with murder growin' up. I shoulda beat the shit outta ya smart ass a few times, then you wouldn't be up in here talkin' outta the side of ya neck at me, like I'm one of them bitches out on the street. That's what the fuck I shoulda done."

Ugh! Here she goes with this 'I shoulda beat ya ass' *shit again*. She sounded like a damn scratched record. And it was gettin' on my last muthafuckin' nerve. I finished unlockin' the rest of the bolts, then swung the door open, but before I walked out, I read her ass. Fuck what ya heard. She had it comin'.

"No, what ya shoulda been doin' was bein' a damn mother instead of chasin' behind sorry-ass muhfuckas who either used ya or beat ya damn ass. Like the nigga right there," I said, pointin' in his direction. "I don't give a hot flyin' fuck what you do, 'cause ya right. You a grown-ass woman, and you can fuck who the hell ya want. But you got ya facts twisted. Don't ever think you've been a damn mother, 'cause that's one thing you've never been."

"I kept a fuckin' roof over ya damn head!" she yelled. "And I made sure ya ass had food to eat. You never went hungry. You always had a place to lay your ungrateful-ass head. And when you wanted to take ya ass 'cross the river, I signed the papers and it was my muthafucking money that fronted ya shit, so don't fucking tell me what I've never done for ya selfish ass."

Oh, now we on this shit again, I thought. I slammed the door. Yes, we were gonna have it out for once and for goddamn all. I'd held a lotta shit in, and it was time she knew how I felt. Just how fucked up I thought she was. And I already knew if she raised up on me, this would be the one time I'd forget my manners and fight her like a chick from the hood. Keepin' it real, I wouldn't really straight-up duke her; she was still my moms. I'd remove my earrings and straight-up windmill her ass. And if her nigga wanted to be all up in the mix, then today was his lucky day. He was 'bout to get an earful. And if she even looked like she was gonna put her hands on me, he'd get to see firsthand how a live bitch rocks. That was my word.

I started clappin'. "So, what you want, a fuckin' medal? Yeah, you got my spot for me, but it was with *my* fuckin' money, so don't go there. And, yeah, you kept a roof over my head, but you kept bringin' crab-ass muhfuckas up in here, too. If they weren't layin' up on ya dumb ass, they were beatin' their dicks droolin' over *me*. And from what I can see, ain't much changed. You still stupid when it comes to a nigga. Like when I told ya ass that ya fuckin' man was comin' into my room, you acted like I was makin' the shit up. You believed that muhfucka over ya own daughter, talkin' 'bout I was probably shakin' my ass 'n titties up in his face; that I probably wanted him to fuck me. How the fuck you think that made me feel, huh?"

She stood there, lookin' at me like she didn't know what the fuck I was talkin' 'bout. "Kat, get the fuck out right now! I mean it. Get...out...before I forget you're my child and beat you the fuck down like a bitch in the streets."

"Bitch," I yelled. Yeah, I called my own mother a *bitch*. Oh, fuckin' well! What little respect I had for her as a mother was deaded the moment she pulled a knife on me. "It's obvious you *forgot* I was your child the moment you gave birth! So fuck what ya neglectful ass talkin'. You never gave a fuck 'bout me. The only thing you ever cared about was keepin' ya fat pussy wet, real talk."

Her nigga got up from off the sofa and grabbed her before she could run up on me. "Come on, baby, calm down. Don't."

She tried to break free. "No, Jawan. Let me go. This bitch done got too grown, callin' *me* a bitch. I don't know who the fuck she thinks she is. But it's time I brought her down a notch, and stretched her on her back."

"Chill, baby. She's probably upset 'bout not knowin' 'bout us gettin' married."

"Nigga," I snapped, "I don't give a fuck 'bout you and her gettin' married! I already know what time it is with ya bum ass. As soon as you run through her money, ya ass'll be ghost. And she's too fuckin' blind to see it."

His jaw tightened. "I'ma let that shit slide, outta respect for ya moms."

"Nigga, please! You don't really want it."

"Ho, I done told you to get ya ass outta here."

"C'mon, baby," the nigga said, pullin' her by the arm, tryna keep her from comin' up on me. "Let it go."

I stared at her long and hard. "That nigga must got some real good dick to have you pullin' fuckin' knives out on me and talkin' all reckless n' shit. But it's all good." I opened the door again, lookin' at her one more time. "As far as I'm concerned, ya ass is dead to me. So when he beats ya ass and fucks up all ya change, you got what the fuck ya ass deserves. And for the record, *bitch*, the only *ho* in this room is *you*. So do you, boo." She broke away from her nigga, and as she came chargin' toward me, I slammed the door in her face. As I ran toward the stairwell, all I heard was her yellin', screamin' and cursin' how she and my aunts were gonna fuck me up.

CHAPTER NINE

Young and restless…dumb and reckless…A nigga can't teach a girl to be a woman…can't teach her 'bout self-love… got ya wonderin' why she's runnin' away…why she's turned into a hateful bitch…look into my eyes…let me tell you why…while a bitch was lookin' for love in all the wrong places…a young girl was lookin' for direction…lookin' for love in her mother's eyes…searchin' for love in her embrace…but a bitch had no time…denied her…deprived her…chasin' dick was the only thing on her mind…now the young girl is a woman…and looks at her mother's ass with disdain…and no matter how hard she tries to explain…she has learned…she now realizes… a neglectful bitch will never understand her pain…

By the time I got back 'cross the water, I had already blazed two blunts and was feelin' right. But I ain't gonna front, I felt fucked up for callin' my moms a bitch 'cause no matter what, she's still my moms. But how she came at me was real fucked up. Moms or not, I'm not the fuckin' one. Still, a bitch broke down and called her to apologize.

"What?" she snapped when she answered her cell. Of course she knew it was me, thanks to caller ID.

"I'm only callin' to apologize for callin' you out ya name. But other than that—"

"Oh, hell no! Fuck ya apology, you disrespectful little bitch. I'ma bust that ass when I see you. You really fucked up, Kat. I don't give a fuck what you think I did or didn't do for you, I'm still ya gotdamn mother. I ain't never disrespect my mother, and she used to beat my ass with any-and-every-gotdamn-thing she got her hands on…"

That's because ya ass was fast 'n hot, I thought, rollin' my eyes.

"…But you, I just let your ass run wild. And now you done took it too muthafucking far. Since you think you so gotdamn gangster with yours; since you think you grown enough to talk slick and greasy to me, I promise you, ya ass is gonna see what it's like to really get it in with a Brooklyn bitch 'cause me and ya aunts—"

I couldn't believe this shit. My own mother was on some high school shit, talkin' like she was gonna have me jumped. For a woman who didn't drink or get high, the way she acted sometimes made me wonder. This was so over the top for me. The crazy thing was, she really had no idea *who* I was or *how* I got down. And I aleady knew in my heart, if they tried it, it would be messy. There was no way I was gonna ever let a bunch of bitches jump me, especially some old ones, family or not.

All the years she let her niggas disrespect her ass, and not once did she stand up to any of 'em. She'd fight a bitch in the streets before she went upside a muhfucka's head for puttin' his hands on her. She'd let him run her nerves down into the fuckin' ground, stressin' and wringin' her hands over a sorry nigga. And not once did she think 'bout, or consider, how that shit was gonna affect me—all that yellin' and screamin' and cursin' and cryin' and beggin' and breakin' shit. Not once did she fuckin' consider me! All the years she allowed me to do me without structure or restrictions or rules, she didn't raise me, and she damn sure didn't show me love. The streets did. Now all of a sudden she wanna be on some tough-girl shit, talkin' 'bout she's my mother and deserves to be respected. As far as I was concerned, she was a day late and a dollar too fuckin' short.

I lit another L. "Listen," I said, cuttin' her off, and takin' a pull off my blunt. "I ain't call you for all that. Do what you feel ya gotta do. I'm not pressed. I shouldn't've called you a bitch, but I said it, and I can't take it back. Nor do I wanna. 'Cause, keepin' it real, you *are* a bitch."

"I'm your mother!" she yelled.

"Then get over ya'self and start actin' like one."

"Kat, watch how the fuck you talk to me! I'm not one of them whore-ass bitches you run with."

"I can't tell," I said back.

"What?!?" she screamed.

"You heard me."

"Kat, what did I ever do to you for you to be so fucking hateful?"

Although I wanted to scream on her ass, I kept calm. I figured it didn't make sense to have both of us yellin' and screamin' like two wild bitches. "Okay, so either you really don't have a clue or this is your version of selective amnesia." I sighed, pausin'. I let the silence steady my voice and give me time to think before I spoke 'cause a bitch was ready to blast her ass. As I said, I've kept a lotta shit in with this woman. Out of respect. Out of some fucked hope that one day we'd have something that resembled a mother-daughter connection. But the older I get, the clearer this picture becomes. We will never, ever, be fuckin' close, and a bitch is tired of wishin' and hopin' for shit that ain't gonna happen. And

I'm fuckin' done with tryna hold on to somethin' that ain't worth holdin' on to. Yes, I know I'm 'posed to honor and respect my mother no matter what, but dammit…a bitch can only take but so fuckin' much. And right about now, this bitch had reached her limit.

"You want the truth, huh, *mother?* Well, how 'bout I give it straight. *You* opened up your fuckin' legs! *You* chose dick over me. *You* never had time for me. *You* treated me fucked up. No, you never beat me; you fuckin' ignored me. But as far as I'm concerned, that's worse than if you woulda beat my ass every damn day. Some kinda attention woulda been better than nothin' at all. No matter how hard I tried to love you, you never wanted to love me back."

"What kinda shit is that! Of course I loved you. I gave birth to you. I raised you. I made sacrifices. If that's not love, then I don't know what to tell you."

I was so fuckin' done with her. "You sacrificed what? What was it that you really gave up, huh?"

"My life!" she snapped. "I gave up my fucking dreams."

"And that's *my* fault? Oh, please. That's a bunch of shit. The only thing you spent ya life dreamin' 'bout was some nigga, and how big his dick was. The only thing you gave up was ya pussy. You couldn't be so bothered to be a fuckin' mother. But that's my fault, right? It's my fault ya ass tricked ya money and life up on dick, yeah, okay. Well, was it my fault ya ass got pregnant? Was it my fault ya ass had a bullshit job and we had to live paycheck to paycheck? Was it my fault my father fucked a slew of bitches and got locked up on ya ass? Was it my fault the niggas you ran behind tryna love didn't love you back? Yeah, it's all my fault that ya ass never wanted nothin' more than what ya already got. That's right, Juanita, blame me for your fucked-up, miserable life."

"Oh, now you done gone from callin' me bitch to Juanita. This is the disrespectful shit I'm talkin' 'bout. If you were in front of me, I'd knock your fucking teeth out."

"I seriously doubt I would sit there and let you get that off," I said, takin' two hard pulls on my blunt. I needed a drink. I got up from my seat and went downstairs to my bar to pour some Rémy in a glass. I tossed it back, then poured another. "If you didn't put ya hands on me when I was a kid, what the hell makes you *think* I'd let you put ya damn hands on me now? But tell me this. When you gonna start actin' ya age instead of tryna be on some 'round-the-way-chick shit? You can't compete with me, sweetie. If anyone has ever been jealous, it's been you," I said, walkin' back upstairs, then over to my balcony. I opened it and stepped outside.

"Kat, I'm tellin' ya ass right now. Keep disrespectin' me, okay, and see what happens the next time you bring ya ass to Brooklyn. I'm not gonna tell you no more. You had better start showin' me some muthafucking respect or you are gonna find ya ass beat the fuck down."

"Like I said, you need to act ya age, instead of runnin' 'round actin' like you still in ya twenties. You need to really let it go. If you want me to respect you like a mother, then, like I said, try actin' like one. Then again, you wouldn't know how to do that since you've never tried it. But you right. I don't respect ya ass. I never have 'cause you never gave me a reason to. Please don't come at me 'bout no damn respect 'cause at the end of the muthafuckin' day, if a bitch wants respect, then she gotta know how to give it, real talk.

"And, sweetie, please be clear. Just like you, I'm a grown-ass woman. And there's no fuckin' way I'ma let you, your sisters, or any other fuckin' bitch jump me or put their hands on me and shit's gonna be all sweet. I don't give a fuck if ya gave birth to me or not. It is what it is. Now, like I said, I apologize for callin' you a bitch. But I will never apologize for not likin' you or for not respectin' you. You brought that shit on ya'self. You've always been weak when it comes to a nigga. I'll be damned if I ever take responsibility for you bein' a fucked-up, neglectful mother. I'm done with you. Go get married, live a happy life, and leave me the fuck alone. You don't exist to me."

I snapped my phone shut on her ass before I said somethin' else that couldn't be taken back. When I finally walked back into the house and looked in my wall mirror, it was then that I noticed a bitch had been cryin'.

I don't need this shit right now, I thought as I tossed the cordless on the sofa, then climbed my ass up and around the spiral staircase. I was fuckin' drained and decided to take a long, hot shower, then take my ass a nap.

CHAPTER TEN

"Bitch, why you didn't call me back?"

"What?" I asked, wakin' up all groggy 'n shit. I'd slept so damn hard I wasn't sure if it was day or night. I had to look around to see where I was. After I took my shower, I remembered goin' back downstairs to get me another shot of Rémy and ended up takin' the bottle and a glass into my media room, smokin' another blunt, and listenin' to that crazy chick Amy Winehouse's *Back to Black* CD. The last song I remembered hearin' was "Tears Dry on Their Own" before dozin' off.

I yawned and stretched. "Girl, what time is it?"

"It's almost five-thirty."

"Damn," I said, sittin' up. "I musta been tired as hell."

"I thought I told ya ass to make sure you called me back."

"Unh-uh, don't do it. My mother got on her bullshit again. So you really don't want it, ho. Not today."

"Oh, shit. That bad?"

"Worse," I said. "She worked my fuckin' nerves down into the ground so bad I had to take three blunts and a bottle to the head to calm my ass down." I gave her the 4-1-1 on my visit with my moms and her nigga, then told her 'bout the phone conversation we had.

"Damn," Chanel said. "That's fucked up. And she really threat-ened to have your aunts jump you?"

"Yeah, ain't that some shit? But I tell you what. Let 'em try it."

"Kat, girl, you know I always got ya back. But fuckin' with ya crazy-ass aunts is like walkin' through Iraq bare-assed. They fuckin' crazy. You might wanna take that ass whoopin' and keep it movin' 'cause I ain't tryna rock with 'em."

I had to laugh 'cause she was right. Them bitches were noodles. First, there was Rosa, the oldest. She was forty-three with six kids and two grandchildren. Although she stopped usin' cocaine ten years ago, she still drank and carried a razor under her tongue and had no problem slicin' a bitch. Young, old, nigga, bitch, or in between—if ya came at her sideways on some greasy slick shit, she was gonna bring it to ya ass swift and clean. She wasn't one for a bunch of talkin', she'd just start slicin'. You wouldn't even know you'd been straight-edged until ya ass hit the concrete. She lived over in the Pink Houses, another one of Brooklyn's housin' projects.

Next was Elise. She was thirty-six and had spent almost eight years in prison for arson and aggravated assault and battery charges she got in '95 when she set her sons' father on fire while he was sleepin'. He had gotten some other bitch in her buildin' pregnant and Elise wasn't havin' it. She dropped her sons off over my grandmother's, then went back and torched his ass without blinkin' an eye. She's been home for close to four years and lives over in Red Hook with my two teenaged cousins.

Then there was my youngest aunt, Patrice, who was twenty-eight. She still lived with my grandmother over in Brownsville and only fucked niggas who were either drug dealers or gun run-ners. The bitch still boosted for a livin', drove a Range Rover, and always stepped outta her buildin' like she was that chick. But aside from the high-end wears and truck her nigga bought, the nutty bitch doesn't own a pot to piss in or a window to throw it out of. Just dumb, dumb, dumb!

However, on some real shit, she was the prettiest outta the four of 'em. With her jet-black hair flowin' down the center of her back and extra slick bangs, she had that Pocahontas look about her, with a body like a damn hourglass. Crazy thing, you would think that she and I would have been close since we were only three years apart and both fly bitches. *Not!* That bitch *hated* me, and make no mistake, there was no love lost between us where I was concerned either. But, keepin' it real, she was the only one of my aunts I used to look up to when I was growin' up. That's until the slimy bitch fucked my man, but that's another discussion for another time.

"Yeah, them bitches are crazy," I said, laughin'. "But they can get it, too. I'm not lettin' none of them hoes put their hands on me, and not rock with 'em. No, it's gonna be poppin'. And I already know Pat don't really want it."

"I hear you," she said. "But I'ma hafta sit this one out if shit pops off. I can't get caught up in no family–feud type shit. I saw how they get down when they jumped on that bitch, Tiny, at ya cousin's barbecue last year in Prospect Park. They wore that ho out. No, thank you, ma'am…I ain't fuckin' with ya aunts. The summer is comin' and a pretty bitch ain't tryna have her face dug out, and I definitely ain't tryna look like burnt toast. Please. I got no time tryna mend some damn fire burns."

I bust out laughin', thinkin' back on how the three of them had set it off on that bitch for talkin' slick to Patrice over some dumb nigga they both were fuckin', even though Patrice was really the one who provoked the shit.

It was an end-of-the-summer barbecue my cousin Manny and

his boys threw, and it was one of the very few times I wasn't beefin' with Patrice. The park was packed with niggas. The drinks were flowin', the music was rockin', and the grill was blazin'. Everbody was lit and feelin' real good. Then, as soon as Patrice saw Tiny—who was wearin' a burgundy weave and was stuffed in a cute Dolce & Gabbana denim mini-skirt, a sexy white midriff shirt, and a bangin' pair of Miu Miu strappy sandals—struttin' her big ass and double-D titties through the crowd toward the food table, Patrice started up.

"Somebody better get that fat bitch up outta here," Patrice had said to my aunt Elise, "before I end up goin' in her mouth. I'm sick of lookin' at her fat ass. Damn pork roll." Patrice and my aunt Elise were sittin' in their beach chairs passin' a flask of rum back 'n forth. They were definitely feelin' good.

Of course Tiny heard her since Patrice had said it loud enough that she could. But Tiny kept it cute and igged her, keepin' it movin'.

Elise stared at her, then grunted. "Humph. Let the bitch do her. She don't want it. Besides, I don't know why you mad at her ass any damn way. It's that nigga you should be pissed at. He's the one fuckin' the both of you. You don't know what the hell that nigga is tellin' her."

"Still, that bitch knows he's *my* man. And she still fucks with him."

I blinked, blinked again, then stared at this bitch, before steppin' the fuck away. I couldn't believe what I'd heard this ho say. I was so ready to remind her grimy ass of what she did to *me*, but decided to let it go otherwise it woulda been her and me thumpin' out that piece. Chanel had peeped it, too. Here she was, hatin' on the next bitch for fuckin' *her* man—who wasn't all that—when she had done the same fuckin' shit to me.

I laughed at how crazy the bitch sounded. "Mighty funny how what goes around, comes around," I said, rollin' my eyes. "Come on, Chanel, get ya shit and let's bounce before it starts gettin' hectic out here."

"Excuse you?" Patrice said to me.

"Don't," I warned, givin' her the evil eye. "Not today, boo-boo. Please don't."

"No, don't *you*, bitch," she said.

I laughed at her ass, but I knew if she got up I was gonna beat her face in. She kept it cute and kept her ass in her seat.

"What, you ain't got your aunt's back if shit kicks off?" Elise asked, lookin' at me all indignant 'n shit.

"Basically," I said. "You know me and Patrice don't get down like that. Besides, a bitch didn't come out here to be breakin' up my nails and gettin' all dirty 'n shit; especially for her ass."

"Whatever, bitch," Patrice said, rollin' her eyes. "You know you can get it, too."

"Is that so?"

"Both of you stop. No matter what the fuck is goin' on between the two of you, ya'll bitches still family, and when shit jumps off ya'll should be puttin' that bullshit to the side and have each other's back. Ya'll blood, and should never let no fuckin' nigga come between ya'll."

I laughed. "No disrespect, Aunt Elise. It's a bit too late for that. Any bitch who fucks my man ain't no damn family of mine. And a bitch like that gets what the fuck she gets." I looked over at Patrice and stared her down. "It's called karma, sweetie. Obviously, she didn't get the memo."

Aunt Elise's eyes widened. Patrice glared at me, but the only reason she didn't try to get at me was because she was too focused on Tiny. Chanel and I stepped off, leavin' them bitches lookin' like two fools. And just as we were makin' our way over toward the liquor, Tiny passed us, headin' toward where Patrice was sittin'. She offered a smile. Her beef with Patrice had nothin' to do with me, and she knew it. I smiled back, bouncin' my ass to Busta Rhymes's "Touch It" remix. The deejay had that shit pumpin'. When the nigga slipped "Make It Clap" on, bitches were poppin' them hips and niggas were tryna get they grinds on.

"Oh, shit," Chanel said suddenly. "Looks like it's 'bout to get messy out this bitch. Tiny and ya aunt over there beefin'.'" I turned around, cranin' my neck, and sure 'nough Tiny had her hands on her hips, and Patrice had stood up and they were goin' back 'n forth. Next thing I knew, Tiny slapped the shit outta Patrice. Patrice stumbled backward—and that's all it took. Tiny was yokin' Patrice's ass up, beatin' her down like a nigga. That's when my aunts Elise and Rosa set it off on Tiny, pullin' out razors and slashin' up her back, chest, and face. Blood was everywhere. Tiny hit the ground and all three of them started stompin' and kickin' her. Then Elise set Tiny's weave on fire. Bitches started screamin and scramblin', then guns started poppin' off. By the time my cousins were able to get my aunts off Tiny, the bitch's hair and scalp was in flames and she was all gashed up. Her blouse was shredded and one of her titties was hangin' out. Poor thing! It was terrible. They fucked her up somethin' terrible— all over some sorry-ass nigga and Patrice bein' the trouble-makin' bitch that she is.

"Well," I said, "hopefully they don't try 'n serve me. But since my moms on her bullshit, I don't know what might happen. She talkin' like the next time I'm in BK they gonna swoop down on me and bring it."

Am I really gonna have to watch my back with them bitches? I tried to imagine how they would come at me. I wondered if they'd wait until the next family gatherin' and set it off. Would one of 'em try 'n trick me into comin' over to their spot, while the rest of 'em hid in closets, then when my back was turned jump out and start swingin' off? Would they corner me, then pull out razors and start slashin' me up? I decided to keep my heat packed in my bag just in case.

"That's real fucked up," Chanel said.

"Oh well. It is what it is. I'm not pressed, *trust*. So, what shit Tamia done got herself in now?" I asked, changin' the subject. I really wasn't feelin' any of her drama, but I didn't wanna talk anymore 'bout my fucked-up mother or her crazy-assed sisters either.

"Some chick stepped to her about some nigga when she was downtown last week and threatened to whoop her ass the next time she called her man's cell…" Okay, this is where I started zonin' out. I was so sick of these bitches fightin' and arguin' over their half-assed niggas. I had no interest in entertainin' this shit. Been there, done that. And I had no desire to ever have to whoop another bitch's ass over a piece of dick. I swore after bangin' Patrice's face up that I'd never go there again. And I meant it.

➤➤➤

About a year after I bounced on Naheem, I started fuckin' with this nigga who everybody called B-Love 'cause he was from Bed-Stuy and got mad love from the streets for stayin' on his grind. The nigga was pushin' bricks and keys and had shops set up in different sections of his hood as well as in other sections of BK. He was the type of cat who knew how to get money and didn't give a fuck 'bout rollin' up his sleeves, puttin' in work and gettin' dirty. He didn't fuck with lightweight niggas. If you wanted him to build with ya ass, you had better come at him with some major paper and be talkin' 'bout makin' major moves, otherwise you'd either get laughed at or get ya wig pushed back for tryna waste his time. And he didn't slouch when it came to takin' what he wanted, includin' pussy.

He was six foot two, brown-skinned, well built, and had beautiful brown eyes that sparkled whenever he smiled or laughed. The nigga stayed rockin' a fresh, low fade cut with spinnin' waves, crisp sideburns, and a neatly trimmed mustache. Yeah, the nigga was finer than a muhfucka, with a big, long, thick, juicy dick that he *knew* how to use all night long. But the nigga was ruthless and didn't give a fuck who he pissed on. It was his arrogance and aggressive nature, along with his persistence, that made my pussy nut in my panties every time he looked at me.

With Naheem on lock and the money train runnin' low, a bitch had to get back on her grind, so I went back to boostin' to keep my shit right and keep a few dollars in my pockets at the same time. There was no way I was ever gonna pawn or sell all the jewels 'n shit Naheem had laced me with. I was still lampin' in his spot over in Crown Heights, but that shit was gonna fold in another two months. I didn't wanna go back to the projects and have to be up under my moms again. A bitch was feelin' real pressed 'bout her situation. So when Patrice and I walked up into this Jamaican spot on Atlantic Avenue, I spotted the nigga, B-Love, sitting in a corner booth with two other niggas, checkin' me out in my fly wears as we approached the counter to place our orders. I knew then I had hit the jackpot. But Patrice was already tryna get her digs in. The bitch was salivatin', tryna get her shine on. So I played it cute, stepped aside and let her bounce her ass around, click-clackin' and poppin' her gum like a real hoodrat.

"You see that nigga right there," she had whispered. I glanced his way. "That nigga is getting paid out the ass. And word is he got a dick like a horse."

I shrugged like I wasn't fazed. But I already knew who he was and had heard how he was movin'. Naheem would mention his name and talk about how he wanted to cut into his pockets by takin' over some of his spots. Besides, I had bumped into him several times at a few VIP parties, and once down in AC. He'd always have some cute chick on his arm, but the bitch wasn't no real winner like me. And I was always on Naheem's arm, and he loved showin' his hood beauty off. So when B-Love kept starin' at me instead of Patrice, I knew he knew I was *that* bitch, so I gave him somethin' to look at. I slowly twisted my body a taste so he could get a clear view of how my jeans wrapped around my apple-bottom ass like a glove.

"Okay," I said, frownin', "And?"

"And I'm tryna ride that shit and run his pockets."

I rolled my eyes. *I doubt it, ho*, I thought, cuttin' my eye over at him, *but if you say so.* The nigga winked at me, then blew a kiss. I rolled my eyes again, this time at him. He said somethin' to his boys, then I heard him start laughin'. His boys looked over at us, grinnin'.

Patrice peeped them lookin' over at us and got all agitated 'n shit. "What the fuck they laughin' at?" she asked, gettin' ready to turn it up.

I shrugged. "Girl, ignore them niggas. It ain't that serious. They want some attention. Somethin' a bitch like me don't give."

She sucked her teeth. "Yeah, right."

I rolled my eyes, but let the bitch's remark slide.

When our orders came, we paid for our food, then found a table three tables away from them. Patrice's dick-thirsty ass made sure she posted her ass in the seat directly across from him so that everytime he looked up, he'd see her face. But he was too busy tryna clock me on the sly and Patrice knew it, but she kept on tryna shine. Patrice mighta been older than me, but the bitch didn't really know shit 'bout a nigga like B-Love. A nigga like him wasn't gonna openly fuck with no busybody bitch who needed and wanted attention. A real nigga recognized a gold-diggin' bitch a mile away. Yeah, he'd fuck her, but a bitch like that would bore him to death. She'd be another one of his jump-offs who he laced with shit, but he wasn't gonna put no cash in her hands. Uh-uh. What a nigga like him wanted was a top-of-the-line, classy bitch who knew how to be a lady in public and a freak behind closed doors. A bitch who didn't have to open her mouth to get noticed. When she walked into a room, her beauty spoke for itself, and her presence commanded attention. She didn't have to go lookin' for it. Yeah, Patrice rocked the fly wears and was a beauty, but she wasn't that bitch. She was fuckable, but she wasn't gonna be wifey to a nigga like B-Love. I knew it and B-Love knew it…it's just too bad Patrice's ass didn't know it.

After he and his boys finished eatin', they got up from their table and walked past us. I could feel the nigga burnin' a hole in my face, but I igged him. "How you beautiful ladies doin'?" he asked. "Ya'll sisters or something?" Although he was talkin' to both of us, he had his eyes on me. I looked up and stared at him, givin' him a fake half-smile. He was dipped in ice and chunky jewels, but I wasn't pressed. Well, I was…but he didn't know it. Patrice spoke.

"No, baby, I'm her aunt. And I can't speak for her, but I'm doin' lovely. Thought you knew. What's good with you, big daddy?

How can a chick like me chill with a fine nigga like you?" Oh, this bitch was really reachin'. I picked at my food, unimpressed, while she tried to get her ho on.

He smiled. "Oh, word. I heard that."

"You got a girl?"

"Nah, baby. I'm just fuckin'. Why, you tryna get it in?"

"That depends," she said, soundin' like a real pigeon. I grinned on the sly. He was baitin' her ass and she was playin' right into it.

"Oh, on what?"

"On how you treat a bitch like me."

"Is that so?"

"Absolutely."

I faked a yawn.

"What's good with ya peoples?" he asked her, eyein' me. Patrice cut her eyes at me, then rolled 'em, like I gave a fuck. She shrugged her shoulders. He spoke directly to me. "What's up with you, baby girl? Cat got ya tongue?"

I looked up at him, real slow 'n sexy-like. "I'm eatin'," I said, slowly slidin' my fork in my mouth, then pullin' it out, "and I ain't beat for no convo."

He grinned. "Yeah, I like that. A pretty chick who knows how to keep her mouth shut." I tilted my head and was gettin' ready to blast his ass but he spoke up before I could get started. "No disrespect, feel me? I'm just sayin'—"

"No, nigga, I don't feel you, and I don't know what you sayin'. I speak when I wanna speak, and to whoever I wanna speak to. Don't get it twisted. I ain't no nigga's puppet."

He burst out laughin'. "You feisty and fine. Yeah, I like that."

I got up to go to the bathroom, suckin' my teeth. "Whatever, nigga."

When I got back from the bathroom, he was gone. And Patrice

was hot. I ain't gonna front, I was hopin' he was gonna still be there, but I knew enough to know that a nigga like him wasn't gonna be waitin' too long; not yet anyway. I sat down to finish my food, grinnin'.

"Bitch, why you have to act all stank 'n shit? You knew I was tryna get at him. That nigga is paid."

"What the hell my attitude got to do with you gettin' ya ass wet?" She sucked her teeth.

"Well, did you get his number?" I asked, suckin' the meat off a chicken bone. Juice dripped from my lips. I licked them and my fingas.

"No, bitch."

"Well, then, I guess he wasn't interested."

"How you figure?" she asked with her face all twisted up 'n shit.

"'Cause ya ass is a gold digger and he peeped ya shit a mile away."

"So the fuck what? That nigga couldn't keep his eyes off me. And I'm gonna have him, watch."

"Okay, if you say so."

"Bitch, I *know* so."

"I said, okay, ho. Back up off me. It really ain't that serious. He might fuck ya dumb ass, but a nigga like him ain't beat for tryna wife no damn groupie chick."

She stared me down, but I ignored her ass and kept on eatin'. When we were done, we stepped outside and who the fuck was curbside, leanin' up against a piped-out, brand-spankin'-new 2001 metallic silver Benz, but the one and only B-Love—live and direct. I ain't gonna front, the nigga looked good as hell in his powder-blue Sean John sweatsuit with an oversized white tee and a pair of crispy white Uptowns with the powder-blue Nike swoosh and sole. The nigga's neck was glistenin' with ice. Patrice immediately got all hyped 'n shit the minute she saw him.

"See. I told you, bitch. The nigga's out here waitin' to get at me."

He grinned. "Hey, baby girl, let me holla at you for a minute." She started walkin' over to him, throwin' an extra shake in her thick hips. "No, not you, ma. Ya peoples." She stopped in her tracks. I smirked, watchin' her face crack. But I didn't move. Instead, I folded my arms across my chest, and stared him *down*. "Yo, I ain't gonna bite you, baby. I just wanna talk to you."

"You wanna talk, you come to me," I finally said. And that he did. The nigga walked up on me, almost pressin' his body up against mine, and looked down at me. I looked the nigga dead in his eyes. Didn't budge or blink. "Can I help you?" I asked.

"Yeah," he said, smilin'. "You can tell me ya name." His cinnamon-fresh breath smelled like Dentyne chewin' gum.

"Unless that info's gonna add value to ya life, it ain't important."

"I'ma call you Baby Girl, then."

"Knock ya'self out," I replied, tryna keep from smilin' while watchin' Patrice standin' at the corner with her arms folded tight. The bitch was sick. She had no time for the cat who was tryna rap to her. She wanted the real prize, and it was standin' right in front of *me*.

"You still fuckin' with that nigga Naheem?"

"Excuse you?" I asked with major 'tude. I was surprised he'd ask me about a nigga I knew he knew was locked the hell up.

"I asked you—"

"I know what you asked me," I said, cuttin' him off. "Why you wanna know?"

"'Cause a pretty thang like you," he said, lickin' his lips and sizin' me up, "needs to be fuckin' with a real nigga doin' real things instead of fuckin' with some nigga behind the wall. That nigga can't do shit for you."

"And who said I needed someone to do somethin' for me?"

He smiled. "Do you?"

"Nope," I lied. "I make shit happen on my own." Well, that was partially true. But a nigga like him would help me stay on my feet. I looked down at my watch. It was gettin' late.

"You got somewhere to be?"

"Maybe," I said. He stepped in closer. I stepped back. "Umm, is there a reason why you all up on me?"

"Yeah, 'cause I dig you."

I laughed. "Nigga…"

"Kat," Patrice called out. "I'm goin' to the truck. Don't be out here all fuckin' day either."

"Yeah, whatever," I said, wavin' her on. *And pick ya face up on your way, trick.* I looked back up at him. "You don't even know me."

"Maybe not," he said, lickin' his lips again—thick, beautiful, kissable lips made for eatin' my pussy and suckin' all over my titties and toes. This nigga was so fuckin' sexy. But I wasn't gonna gas his head. I played him to the left and kept shit light. "But I've seen you several times. And I *know* you've seen me, *Kat*." He smiled. "Interesting name; just like you. And so far, I like what I see. So stop tryna front like you ain't beat."

I rolled my eyes all dramatic 'n shit. Knowin' damn well I really was frontin', I simply ignored that last remark. "Do you always stand outside of restaurants tryna pick up chicks?"

He laughed. "Baby Girl, let me school you on somethin'. I run these streets. I don't hafta try 'n do shit. Pussy and money come to me."

"Well, then, let it keep comin' to ya. 'Cause I ain't the one."

"Maybe not," he said, grinnin'. "But *you* the one I'm gonna wife. Now let me get ya digits so I can get to know you better."

I stepped away from him. "Well, since you run these streets, and shit comes to ya so easily, I guess you can figure out a way to get at me."

He laughed. "So you just gonna walk off?"

"Yep," I said. "Enjoy ya night." I walked off, leavin' him with a grin on his face. And if I knew nothin' else, that nigga was gonna track me down. And I was right.

Two weeks later my cell phone rang and when I peeped the caller ID, I wasn't familiar with the number, but I picked up anyway. "Hello?"

"So, now that I got ya number, Baby Girl, you gonna let a nigga take you out or do I hafta beg?"

I smiled. "I'm impressed," I said. And I meant it. "But I don't know you to go out with you. And beggin' ain't ya style, especially a nigga who got pussy comin' to him real easy." I already knew the nigga was not used to puttin' in work with bitches 'cause they threw themselves at him. Dumb bitches! And I could tell by his attitude that he was the type of nigga used to gettin' what he wanted. But I wasn't gonna make shit easy for him.

He laughed. "Yeah, but I want you."

"Well, I'm not available."

"So do I need to come ring ya bell?"

"You don't know where I live."

"Try me," he said, laughin'.

"You fuckin' crazy," I said, laughin' with him.

"I'm crazy for you, Baby Girl. And I'm tryna get at you. I'll be at ya spot in a couple of hours."

"Nigga, you not invited. So don't even try it. You come here and you gonna find ya ass standin' out on the stoop."

"Oh, word. You'll really do a nigga like that?"

"Yep, try me."

And sure enough, the nigga showed up at my door two hours later, ringin' the buzzer. I hit the intercom to see who it was. When he announced himself, I reminded him that he wasn't invited, and refused to let him in. I ain't gonna front, I was gassed. He was gonna be my damn meal ticket. But I wasn't gonna act all hungry 'n shit.

I couldn't believe this nigga. He stood outside all fuckin' night. It was after three in the morning when I finally gave in and went downstairs and walked up to him. He grinned. "Yeah, that's what I'm talkin' 'bout, Baby."

"Are you crazy?" I had asked, pullin' my robe tighter and tryna keep a straight-face. "Why are you standin' out here like you have nowhere else to go?"

"'Yeah," he said, flashin' his sexy smile, "as a matter of fact I am. And a crazy nigga like me got nothing but time on his hands. So unless you brought ya fine ass out here to invite me up or go for a ride, then this is where I'm gonna stay. So what's it gonna be, pretty baby?" His hungry eyes roamed all over my body.

"I'm sorry, but you can't come up," I said, turnin' to leave. "And I'm not ridin' nowhere with you. Good night."

As I turned to walk away, he grabbed me by the arm, pullin' me toward him. "Hold up, ma. Let me give you something to think about tonight." He backed me up against the wall of my buildin', then pressed his body into mine, kissin' me and pressin' his already hard dick into me. Yeah, the nigga was aggressive, not some soft, weak cat scared to take what he wanted—just how I liked it. His free hand snaked its way inside my robe, rubbin' the inside of my thighs until he found my wet pussy covered by red silk panties. His index finga pressed on my clit and he rubbed it fiercely until I moaned. I reached for his dick and almost fainted when I felt how long and thick it was. I let out another soft moan, then came to my senses and pushed him away before he got a chance to stick his fingas inside of me. "I ain't that kinda bitch," I finally said, breakin' outta his grip. "You want this pussy, then you gonna have to earn it." He leaned in to kiss me again, but this time I turned my head. "Good night."

"Yeah, I'ma wife you," he said, lettin' me go, then backin' away. "You mine. Believe that. I'll be back tomorrow and I ain't takin' no for an answer."

"Whatever," I replied, headin' toward the door. Every day for a week straight, he came through ringin' my doorbell, and each time I refused him. Then he started sendin' me two dozen yellow roses for a week. When that didn't work, he started sendin' teddy bears rockin' diamond necklaces around their necks, tennis bracelets, or diamond earrings, until I finally gave in.

For almost a year we were goin' strong. The nigga started lacin' me with bangin' furs and jewels, takin' me on expensive trips, and kept the cash flowin'—no matter the amount, no matter for what, I got it. I was the Bonnie to his Clyde. Wherever he went, I went. Everyone knew I was his; and whatever bitches he had suckin' his dick, they knew to play their positions and not bring drama to me. I fucked him any-and-every which way he wanted, nonstop. He moved me outta Crown Heights into a cute co-op off Eastern Parkway across from the Brooklyn Musuem. A bitch was catchin' feelins for the nigga hard, and was really thinkin' he was the one.

But I quickly learned that shit ain't always what it seems. That everything that glitters ain't always gold. That lovin' a nigga some-times comes with a price. A bitch was slapped into reality when I decided to come back early from a two-week trip to Hawaii, the one he paid for as a gift for my twentieth birthday, but couldn't go because he swore he couldn't get away. He also laced me with two-carat diamond studs, a diamond necklace, and ten thousand dollars. He even paid for Chanel to go in his place. So instead of stayin' the full time, I flew home four days early to surprise him 'cause a bitch was missin' her man and wanted to be fucked into a coma for her birthday instead of layin' on a beautiful beach with another bitch. But the surprise was on me.

I walked up on him fuckin' Patrice doggie-style in the same bed he had been fuckin' me in many times before. She was moanin' and groanin' and beggin' him, callin' him big daddy this, and big daddy that. I stood in the doorway and watched him slap her on the ass, and tell her how good and wet and fat her pussy was. I listened to her tell him how much she wanted him, how much she loved his big dick. Listened to her ask him to leave "that bitch"; heard him tell her he would never leave me, that I was always gonna be his wifey, but she could always get the dick on the low. I stood stone still and watched my own blood fuck my man, and the nigga I practically gave my heart to play me like a fuckin' fool. A bitch was boilin' mad. I wanted to kill 'em both, but I kept it cute. Just as he was 'bout to cum, I took a deep breath, then walked in.

"So, this is what a nigga who says he loves a bitch does when she's gone—he fucks my muthafuckin' aunt."

He looked up. "Oh, shit," he gasped, pullin' his dick outta Patrice. Shock was all over their faces as they both tried to scramble off the bed. His dick was slick from her pussy. Her hair was tossed every which way. I was too through. Not only was he fuckin' her, but the nigga was fuckin' her *raw!*

I walked closer to the bed. "Oh, nigga, don't stop. Keep on

ridin' that ass. The bitch got some good pussy, huh? Is the shit better than mine, muhfucka?"

"Wait a minute, Baby Girl, let me explain. It's not what you think."

I put my hand up. "'Baby Girl' my ass, nigga...it's exactly what I think. So save it. You can't explain shit to me." Patrice looked at me wide-eyed and sweaty as she tried to hurry up and cover her naked body. "Bitch, I done already seen ya titties floppin' up and down and ya ass spread open like the Harlem River, so there ain't no need to rush on my account, ho." I stared her down. "Yeah, bitch, you finally got what you wanted. I hope the nigga's dick was worth it. How'd you like that big dick up in ya guts, bitch?" She igged me; just kept puttin' her clothes on. "You hear me, bitch, how long you been fuckin' my muthafuckin' man?"

"Six months," she replied. B-Love's mouth dropped open.

"Yo, she's buggin'. We ain't—"

"Shut ya lyin' ass up, nigga! This is between me and this bitch here."

"Yeah, I'm fuckin' ya man, and what?!" she yelled on some real tough-girl shit. "You knew I was diggin' him, and instead of steppin' off you, jumped up on his dick, so it's fair exchange. Now you—"

And before the bitch could finish tryna talk greasy, I charged at her, clawin' at her and punchin' up her face. This was no longer 'bout him; I already knew I was gonna handle him later. At that moment, it was 'bout that bitch disrespectin' me; it was 'bout her crossin' the line; and it was 'bout me fuckin' her up to let her know she had crossed the wrong one.

"You triflin' dirty bitch!" I screamed as I knocked her down, then jumped on her and continued beatin' her face in. "I'ma fuckin' kill you, bitch." She tried to scratch at my face to get me off her, but I was hittin' her so hard and so fast that she couldn't get her nails in. "You wanna fuck my man, ho. Fuckin' trick! You want him, bitch, you can have him!"

B-Love tried to pull me off of her. But I was a wild woman, swingin' and punchin' and screamin' with all my might. "Kat, stop it! Get off her. Come on, baby." He finally got his arms up under mine and yanked me off of her. My legs were swingin' wildly, kickin' her in her head, face, and chest.

"You'se a dead bitch!" Patrice yelled as she scrambled to her feet and tried to come at me. Blood was pourin' outta her mouth and nose. Her neck and chest became a battleground filled with bruises and long, deep scratches, exposin' white meat. "I'ma fuck you up for jumpin' on me, bitch." I raised both of my legs up and kicked her in her chest, sendin' her flyin' backward. She stumbled into the wall.

"Yo, bitch," B-Love yelled at Patrice while tryna restrain me, "get ya shit and get the fuck out! Let me handle this."

"Get the fuck off me!" I screamed, tryna kick, bite, and break outta his grip. "Get your muthafuckin' grimy-ass hands off me, nigga! You fucked my aunt, you fuckin' snake-ass bastard. And you tryna save her from gettin' her ass beat. Fuck you, nigga!"

Patrice grabbed the rest of her shit and ran out the door. "This ain't over, bitch!" I screamed at her. "Trust me. I'ma see you, you dirty ho. And e'erytime I do—be ready to rock, *bitch!*"

B-Love tried to calm me down, but I wasn't hearin' shit he had to say. He held me tight, refusin' to let me go while I screamed, cried, and called him every name in the fuckin' book. He kept apologizin' over and over, kept beggin' me to forgive him. The damage was done. Slob and spit and snot was e'erywhere. I cried all fuckin' night. And the nigga thought all my tears were over him. Little did he know, he had awakened a beast that I thought I had buried, a beast that craved blood, a beast that longed for revenge, a beast that would not rest until it was served; and I sobbed all night tryna fight it back. But it was too late. This thing inside of me was alive and hungry and needed to be fed. And I was the bitch to feed it! Fuck love, fuck forgiveness—my mind was made up. The only thing that would soothe its hunger was death.

≻≻≻

"...I don't know why the fuck her dumb ass gotta fuck with someone else's man. That shit is just fuckin' crazy to me," Chanel continued, bringin' me back to the coversation. "Then she got the nerve to have me out 'n about with her ass last night at Mars 2112 and not say shit to me about havin' beef with these bitches until after shit popped off outside. Four o'clock in the goddamn morning, and these bitches tryna set it off right there in the middle of Times Square. I'm so over that ho right now. What the fuck I look like, tryna fight them big booga bear bitches in my wears. Had the bitch told me shit was hectic I woulda rocked a pair of jeans and some constructs instead of bein' out in my two-thousand-dollar Chanel dress and diamond-crusted heels, feel me?"

I sighed, rollin' my eyes. I *hated* bitches who knowingly slept with another chick's man. It's one thing if a nigga lies to you and gets you all caught up in his shit, and it's a whole 'nother thing when a ho just don't give a fuck. Fuck what ya heard. That's grounds for a serious ghetto-style beat down!

"Humph. Better you than me. I ain't fuckin' with Tamia like that anymore. The bitch is too damn reckless, and I ain't diggin' it. So, since she wanna be fuckin' these niggas, knowin' they got girls 'n shit, then she gets what she gets. Somebody is gonna stretch her ass if she doesn't slow her roll. I really don't know what the fuck is wrong with these bitches. Did I tell you her ass is poppin' E's?"

"Say what?" she asked, surprised. "Get the fuck outta here, no way!"

"That's what I hear."

"Who told you that bullshit?"

"A source that I'm slowly startin' to believe," I said. "I almost didn't wanna believe it, but the way them bitches been movin' I don't put shit past either one of 'em now. I meant to confront her ass 'bout it the other night, but I got sidetracked with Iris's nasty ass."

"Humph. Girl, I'm done."

The Kat line started ringin'. I got up and pulled it out of my D & G bag, then checked the number. It was Cash. Don't ask why I always checked the number, knowin' damn well he was the only nigga callin' on that line. I just did outta habit, I guess. I let it go into voicemail.

"...I've heard it all," Chanel continued. "But poppin' pills, Kat, c'mon...that's a bit much."

"Listen, don't shoot the messenger. I'm just sayin'. The next time you talk to her ass, ask her."

"Oh, trust. I will," she said, pausin'. "Well, let me go. Divine is on his way over. I swear he gets on my last nerve, but—"

"The nigga takes good care of you."

"Exactly," she said, laughin'. "But that's not what I was gonna say."

"Well, it's all you should be sayin'. 'Cause if ya ass keep followin' behind Tamia and Iris, ya gonna end up losin' a good thing. So be thankful for what ya got."

"I know, I know."

"Uh-huh, bitch. Don't say I didn't try 'n warn ya," I said, lookin' at the clock. It was almost seven p.m. I yawned, coverin' my mouth. "Oh, shit. Excuse me. I'm fuckin' beat. Hit me up tomorrow."

"Later," she said. I closed the phone shut, then retrieved my other cell and checked the message Cash had left me. I rolled my eyes, listenin'. He had another job for me; this one in San Diego. *I ain't beat for him right now. I'll call that nigga in the mornin'.* I stripped off my clothes and headed upstairs in my white-laced panties. Until my next mark, it was gonna be another vibrator night.

CHAPTER ELEVEN

Yeah, muhfucka...caught ya ass with ya pants down...deep strokin' it from the back...dick slick from the next bitch... all caught up in bustin' ya nut...as a matter of fact, ya never suspected I'd be watchin' ya...never realized there'd be a price to pay...thought you knew...I ain't one to play...ya best believe... fuckin' over a bitch like me...tsk, tsk...ya worst mistake... look me in the eyes...ain't no need to lie... you been busted muh-fucka...Surprise, surprise, nigga... welcome to ya demise!

You know, on some real shit, sometimes I wonder if a bitch is a borderline psychopath, or if I'm just straight sadistic 'n shit. I mean, I really get off on fuckin' these niggas, knowin' that in a matter of minutes, I'm gonna take their lives. It does somethin' to me. It really gets my pussy hot and poppin' ridin' a muhfucka's dick, then splatterin' his brains. It's like I'm goin' through an out-of-body experience or some shit, watchin' the shit in slow motion while floatin'.

I read somewhere once—uh...yes, a bitch can read—that there were different degrees and types of psychopath. You know, a crazy bitch or nigga who is just straight noodles; someone who doesn't feel shit for or 'bout nobody else; a bitch who goes bananas over the littlest shit. Well, that's not me. I do care 'bout others. I just don't care for a bitch who tries to play me. And I care even less for a nigga who tries to be on some slick shit. Hold up. Yes, I can be manipulative and calculatin'. *No*, I'm not dishonest. I keep shit real. I give it raw, whether you like it or not. *Yes*, I always try to be two steps ahead of the next muhfucka. *Yes*, I can be dangerous. And? That still don't make me a psychopath, or a bitch on some serial killer-type shit. *No*, there's no sympathy or remorse for what I do. *Noooo*, there's no fuckin' guilt. Guilt for what? Please. I provide a service, one I like to refer to as mercy killin'. Yeah, that's right. I put muhfuckas outta they misery. Even when a nigga don't know he's miserable, or that he's worn out his welcome in the world, I'm the bitch that's gonna bring his ass peace of mind.

Anyway, I also read somewhere that obsession, greed, and revenge were three reasons why someone ended up bodied. So take ya pick. But I can't offer ya ass no convo on bein' a bitch obsessed 'bout nothin', and I damn sure can't tell you shit 'bout bein' a greedy bitch. Oh, but revenge…now you talkin'. And as the sayin' goes, payback is a muthafucka!

It's said that *most* vengeful murders aren't thought out, or premeditated. It's done outta anger. Humph. Not with me, trust. 'Cause if you cross me, I'm the type of chick who's gonna plot on ya ass, fuck all that actin' on impulse. Like I always say, an impulsive bitch is a reckless bitch. So, fuck what ya heard. If I'ma slump ya ass on some revenge-type shit, you best believe I'ma slow walk ya ass. I don't give a fuck if it takes days, weeks, months, or years. I'ma smile in ya face, mind-fuck ya, then lay ya ass to rest.

By the time I was twenty, I had already had another nigga's blood on my hands. Yeah, I bodied B-Love, and? Like most niggas, he was so wrapped up in gettin' his dick wet that he didn't think twice 'bout the consequences if his ass ever got busted. I didn't give a fuck how many times he apologized, or swore he'd never do it again, his ass couldn't be trusted. As far as I was concerned, he was no different from the crab-ass nigga who snuck into my room every other night and played in my pussy. And he confirmed what I already thought, what I already knew at fifteen—that the only way to stop a no-good nigga in his tracks was by dumpin' a clip in his ass. Fuck what ya heard. I had no time to be stressin' over no cheatin'-ass nigga. I was gonna get over him, move on with my life, and chalk this shit up as another reason why a nigga couldn't be trusted. So now…instead of one body on my hands, I had two.

For three weeks after I busted B-Love's little fuck party with Patrice—before I shut his lights, splatterin' his brains—the nigga dipped deep in his pockets, lacin' me with dough, jewelry, flowers, cards, shoppin' sprees, and every other fuckin' thing else niggas do to make up when they know they done fucked up a good thing. And while he was spendin' his loot, beggin' and apologizin' and professin' his love for me, thinkin' shit was gonna be peace, I was plottin' on how I was gonna take him out.

He wanted pussy; he craved its warmth so much that he couldn't control himself from runnin' his dick up in my fuckin' aunt—I didn't give a fuck if she was tryna get at him or not. What the fuck I care 'bout her brushin' her titties all up on him and braggin' 'bout how sick her brain game was; 'bout how deep and wet her pussy was. Why should I give a fuck 'bout how he never meant for it to happen; that he just got caught up. The nigga still crossed the line. He allowed his dick to think for him. Allowed it to fuck her raw, fuck her in our bed. And now he had to pay the price.

And, *yes*, the cost of fuckin' with another bitch's pussy was death!

As far as I was concerned, pussy and money were a weak nigga's downfall. The more they had, the more powerful they thought they were. It gave them a false sense of security. B-Love's delusions of bein' invincible made it that much easier for me to set this nigga up lovely. Like I said, he didn't give a fuck 'bout me, so I didn't give a fuck 'bout takin' his life. There's one thing I can't stand: a weak nigga or bitch!

See, the funny thing 'bout death is you never know when it's gonna come snatch ya. Yeah, it's a fact of life, it's guaranteed to us. But when it comes in the still of the night to silence you, to yank ya last breath outta ya chest, there is no time for plannin', no time for thinkin'. When ya least expect it, when ya least prepared, it swoops down on ya and pulls ya under. And it's the element of surprise that excites a bitch like me.

"You still want that bitch's pussy?" I had asked, bouncin' up and down on his dick. I was fuckin' him down into the mattress, givin' him this pussy nice and wet and tight, grippin' and milkin' his dick for the last time.

"No," he said in between grunts. "Oh, shit. Damn…Oh, shit. Damn, baby, this pussy good."

Yeah, okay, I heard this before, I thought, glarin' in his face. His eyes were half-closed, the lazy slits of a nigga bein' sexed *down*. "Better than that bitch's?" I asked, slowly liftin' my hips up 'til my pussy wrapped just the head of his dick. I twirled my hips a tease, slid halfway down his thick shaft again, then back up to the head. I did that eight or nine times, then slammed all the way down on it, hard, buryin' all of his dick deep inside me. I thought I would be nervous 'bout what I was plannin' to do, but a bitch was gettin' turned the fuck on, knowin' that I was in control. I was *that* bitch, capable of bringin' pleasure or—in his case—

death. I wanted this nigga to feel just how deep and wet I could get; wanted him to feel the heat of my boilin' rage. I reached behind me and started jugglin' and rollin' his balls in my hand.

"Yes…oh, fuck!"

"Whose dick is this, nigga?"

"Yours, baby…damn. Uh…oh, shit! It's all yours…"

Liar!

"How many more bitches you fuckin'?"

"None," he said in between deep breaths. He was drenched in sweat, pantin' and moanin'. "Fuck, baby…Aaah, shit." He thrust his hips up into me, matched my rhythm. "I dismissed 'em all, baby. It's you and me, baby." *It shoulda always been you and me.* I slammed down on his dick again, and moaned.

Liar!

"You sure 'bout that?" I lifted my hips up again, and didn't move while he threw his hips up, stabbin' and jabbin' up my pussy.

"Yesss, baby."

Liar!

I slammed my pussy back down on his dick.

"Aaah, shiiiiiit…you fuckin' 'n wettin' the hell outta this dick, baby girl…Damn…Uh…oh, shit…your pussy's tighter than a fuckin' cat trap."

Hmmm, cat trap, I thought, smilin'. *How fittin'. I like that.* I galloped up and down, fast and hard, on his dick, rubbed my pierced clit, then came all over his dick. My warm, sticky juices dripped outta me and down his thick shaft. "Cum for me, nigga," I said, grindin' and buckin' my hips. "Bust ya dick in my guts, nigga." He pumped deep and hard and fast in me, placed his hands on my hips and went for his. "Yeah, muhfucka, you love this pussy?"

"Fuck yeah!" he grunted.

"Would you die for this pussy?" I was smearin' my wet pussy all up and down and around on his dick, grippin' it.

"Damn, baby…What you tryna do to a nigga? Oh shit…"

Inside I was laughin' my ass off. This nigga had no clue.

"Answer the question," I said, moanin'. I lifted my hips, then slowly repeated it. "Would"—slammed down on his dick. Lifted my hips, again—"you"—slammed down on it again—"Die"—lifted my hips again—"for"—slammed down on his dick again—"This pussy?"

I could tell the nigga was losin' his mind. He was gruntin' and moanin' and twistin' his face up. "Oh, shit…Yesssss, you my world, pretty baby."

I leaned forward, stuck my right titty in his mouth. He sucked and licked all over it, like the greedy muhfucka he was, then moved over to my other titty. We both were in a zone. He was tryna bust off, and I was tryna nut one last time before it was over. I kissed him on his lips. Slid my tongue in his mouth, then started suckin' on his tongue like it was his big, juicy dick. The same black, veiny dick he used to fuck my aunt with.

My pussy was hot 'n poppin'. I lifted up and started pinchin' my hard nipples, ridin' down on his cock and grindin' my clit. *Damn, this nigga got some good dick. Cheatin'-ass bastard!* "I'm cuuuummmin', daddy…oh shit…uh…ooooh…"

"Yeah, baby," he repeated, lookin' me in my eyes, "I'd die for you…wet this dick up…yeah, that's it…oh, fuck…you ready for this nut, baby?"

I leaned forward, pressed my body close against his, then reached under the side of the mattress and felt for my .380 with the silencer. I gripped it and kept my hand hangin' over the side of the bed, waitin'. I whispered, "Yeah, daddy, I'm ready for your nut. Oh, yes…uh, uh…you got my pussy real wet with ya big, black dick, nigga!" My pussy was so overheated from the thought of this cheatin'-ass muhfucka's blood and brains and chunks of his skull bein' splattered all over the place, a bitch almost had the shakes from just knowin' what was 'bout to pop off.

The minute he closed his eyes, I lifted up and hid my right hand behind my back, then placed my left hand on his chest and bounced up and down on his dick and waited…

"Here it comes, baby…Aaaah, aaah, aaah…I'm cuuu—"

Thessrrpp! I shot him right between the eyes.

"Welcome to the *Kat* Trap, nigga!"

I got up off his dick and stared at his lifeless body, then glanced at the clock. It was two in the mornin'. I rushed into the bathroom, sink-washed my pussy, then splashed water on my face. Reality set in, and now a bitch had to put the rest of her plan in motion.

I spotted the jeans he had worn earlier over in the corner on the floor. I raced over to check inside his pockets for the keys to his three lockboxes he kept hidden in a secret compartment up in the ceilin' of his walk-in closet. There were three sets of keys with at least fifteen different keys on each ring. I grabbed them and went into his closet, knockin' boxes of sneakers and hard-bottoms off the shelves. I ran back into the kitchen to get one of the barstools, then climbed up on it and lifted up the corner panel. I pulled it down, tossin' it to the floor, then reached for the metal boxes. I pulled each one down, then tried every key until I found the ones that opened each box. *Bingo!*

There were forty thick rolls of hundreds wrapped with double rubberbands in the first box; another forty rolls in the second box; and the third box had thirty-two rolls. Each roll had one hundred crisp hundred-dollar bills. *You* do the math.

Next, I went into his other closet to try the keys on the custom-designed floor safe hidden underneath the carpet. I dragged the dresser outta the way, pulled back the rug. I almost screamed when I saw that it was a combination- *and* key-lock safe. Here I was on my knees, with a body in the next room, and a bitch wanted to snatch up as much of the nigga's cheddar as I could. Fuck what ya heard. The nigga owed me for my pain 'n sufferin' and for me havin' to use a bullet on his ass. And I was gonna take e'ery muthafuckin' dollar up in that piece.

I leaned back on my knees and thought. *Okay, think, bitch. What would that muhfucka use as his combination?* I tried a first set of numbers—nothin'. I tried again—still nothin'. I took a deep breath, rubbed my sweaty hands across my ass, then tried the numbers in his birthday: 9-26-8-0. When the shit clicked, I almost passed out. I opened the door and smiled. There were stacks and stacks of benjamins.

I knew this wasn't even half of what he was holdin'. He had a safety deposit box at Citibank, probably loaded with cheddar. And he had guns and drugs tucked away at his stash houses. But who gave a fuck! This paper was gonna set a bitch up lovely and keep my ass from sinkin' until I figured out my next move.

I jumped up, snatched my Louis Vuitton duffle bag, and started fillin' it with the money. Once I cleaned e'erything out, I tossed some clothes and other personal items in another bag, then I put e'erything back in its place. Made sure I wiped the bathroom down, and his body. Just before I was ready to bounce, I glanced over at B-Love one last time, wishin' things coulda turned out different. *Oh, well.* "Be careful what you ask for, muhfucka," I said, walkin' over to the bed and tossin' the covers up over his body and head, "'cause you just might get it."

I tossed all of his keys into my satchel, and smiled when I remembered his secret spot over in Prospect Park. I'd only been to it twice, but I knew it was where he kept major paper. *Nigga, thanks to you and your cheatin'-ass dick, you just helped a bitch bubble up.* I quietly snuck out of the buildin', then drove the two hours back down to AC where I already had a suite at the Borgata. I was smart enough to drive down earlier that afternoon to check in. I dropped off my bags in the room, then turned right back around and drove back to Brooklyn. If anyone asked, I was gamblin' and partyin' all night—alone.

The next afternoon I walked back up in that piece like e'erything was e'erything, then ran outta the apartment, screamin' hysterically through the hallway, bangin' on doors. By the time Brooklyn's finest arrived on the scene I was a mess. They were at the crime spot, tryna piece together clues to who took down one of the street's biggest, most dangerous known drug dealers. They questioned e'erybody in the buildin'. And of course, no one heard, seen, or knew shit. They even had the fuckin' nerve to interrogate me. But a bitch kept it cute. I rocked and screamed and cried through the whole questionin'. Finally, the muthafuckas left me alone. I guess they felt I was too damn distraught to offer up any info. I took one of the detective's cards and promised to call him if I remembered anything. I never did.

A week later, B-Love was bein' buried. The church was packed. Bitches and niggas were e'erywhere. His poor mother cried and passed out. His sister fell into his coffin and had to be dragged up outta there. Oh, it was a mess. Some of his niggas swore on their seed's head that they would bring it to whoever murked him. Chicks he fucked and was still fuckin' before I smashed his lights out were all hysterical 'n shit. And that fuckin' ho, Patrice, even had the nerve to show her face. I guess the bitch thought I wouldn't turn it up at a funeral. Please. The minute I saw her ass up at the coffin, I jumped up and charged her. And me and this ho *rocked*.

"Bitch!" I screamed, "I told you be ready to fight whenever I saw your slutty ass." We were gettin' it in right there in front of his casket. Funny thing, neither one of us spit out our razors to use on the other. Humph…go figure! "You still want him, bitch?" I yelled, slappin' and punchin' the shit outta her. We turned the church out. B-Love's nephews and a few of his boys had to pull us apart. "Get that bitch outta here 'fore I kill her!" I screamed, before fallin' down to my knees. I broke down cryin'. If that wasn't an Academy Award–winning performance, then dammit, I don't know what was.

His body wasn't even in the ground good, and I was already back at our spot packin' my shit. Besides the money, jewels, and furs, I walked outta there with e'erything that wasn't glued or nailed down, never lookin' back.

Although a lotta niggas in the hood was sayin' B-Love was set up, the cats in blue had already figured it was an inside job. But they didn't invest much time or energy into tryna track down his killer—the bitch who had sat right in front of 'em with snot and spit flyin' e'erywhere. Although I wasn't a suspect, they called me in for questionin' again, but nothin' came of it, so they had to let it go. As far as they were concerned, B-Love was just one less dealer on the streets, destroyin' lives and bringin' down the community. They would eventually close the case as another murder unsolved. And a bitch like me would get away with slumpin' a nigga—*again*.

CHAPTER TWELVE

Okay, since you know how I get down, you can see slumpin' muhfuckas comes easy to me. My first two bodies were strictly personal 'cause a bitch felt wronged. As far as I was concerned, they deserved what they got. Not only for me, but for anyone else they fucked over. But a bitch ain't on that revenge shit anymore.

I ain't gonna front. A bitch was mad nervous the first time I had to actually body a nigga that hadn't disrespected me, or tried to play me close. I mean, blastin' a nigga who fueled my anger was one thing, but killin' a muhfucka who I had no beef with, was a whole 'nother situation, feel me? But trust. I promised myself that I would never murk anyone else for personal reasons. Well, okay, not at the moment. 'Cause on some real shit, if a muhfucka tried to play me again—I just might have to take his head off. I really can't say I wouldn't slump his ass, feel me?

Anyway, no matter what type of beef I might have with another bitch, I will never, ever, push a slug in her ass. I'd either fight the ho with my hands, or slash her ass up with a blade. But killin' another chick was and will *always* be a no-no. Well, that is, unless the bitch is tryna body me, then it's open season for an all-out slaughter. And I'm definitely not fuckin' with political figures. That comes with too many risks—well, at least for me.

Anyway, I had made this very clear to Cash when I agreed to work with him. No chicks, no children, no niggas caught up in politics. And I meant it. Anythin' else was fair game.

Call me what ya want, contract killer, hit man—or in my case, the hit bitch. The only difference between me and the others in the murder game is that I added my own twist to the shit. As you already know, I fuck the niggas first. Twisted or not, I don't give a fuck. As far as a bitch like me is concerned, ain't no sense in takin' a nigga's life without givin' him a taste of pussy for the last time. Call it mercy fuckin'. I mean, on some real shit, the nigga's already 'bout to catch it, so why not fuck 'im, feel me? Hell, it's the least a bitch who loves to fuck could do. In the end, I get to get my fuck on without niggas tryna put my shit on blast, and get *paid* in the process. A bitch can't beat that.

On some real shit, though, this fuckin' world is so gotdamn goddamn crazy. And there are some really sick muhfuckas out here who have no problem puttin' a hit out on someone for their own personal, political, or professional gains. From silencin' witnesses to eliminatin' rival drug leaders, gang leaders, or politicians who refuse to take bribes; from bitches and niggas lookin' to collect on insurance policies or estates to someone who just wants out of a fucked-up relationship but is bein' forced to stay—someone is always ready to pay out the ass for a hit, and it ain't 'bout race. These white muhfuckas and bitches are real gangsta with theirs. And the shit that really cracks me the fuck up is the fact that most of these fools really think just because they've hired someone else to do their dirty work that their dumb asses still can't be linked to the murder; that they can't go down for the shit too if one of us gets knocked. Uh, hello...ya ass ordered a body to go, duh!

It doesn't matter whether ya ass got an airtight alibi 'bout bein' outta the country or in some spot where many people see ya ass and can verify ya whereabouts. You still can catch the heat, trust. Yeah, I mighta pulled the trigger, but at the end of the day, it was the *customer* who paid for the shit, so his or her ass can be found guilty, too. Don't get it twisted. Yes, a bitch did her homework before gettin' all caught up in this. And I'm aware of the legal shit that comes with what I do. Still, there's somethin' 'bout bein' on top of a nigga, ridin' his dick, anticipatin' puttin' a slug in his head that turns a bitch on.

Anyway, dependin' on the needs of the person puttin' out the hit, some of our hits are obvious murders, while some are staged as either suicides or accidents. Others, the only ones I take, are the hits where, after the muhfucka's been slumped, the bodies are destroyed so that it looks like a disappearance instead of an actual murder, feel me?

Although a bitch like me is considered a professional killer, I typically only like the hits where there is not much danger involved. Fuck what ya heard. A bitch ain't tryna get caught up in no shit way over my head. I like my hits simple. My motto: fuck 'em and slump 'em. No hassles, no drama, no damn confusion.

CHAPTER THIRTEEN

*A bitch is in heat…come stoke this fire…got a nigga lustin'
with desire…got a bitch's pussy poppin'…spark a blunt, got
that chronic liftin' ya… as I sit 'n spin on ya dick…fat ass
clappin' ya, deepthroatin' ya…neck snappin' ya…got ya knees
shakin'…bust ya nut, nigga…sexy bitch with the slanted
eyes…deep, wet pussy makin' ya weak…got ya eye on the
prize…fuck what ya heard…I'm a hustler baby, a bitch from
the streets…*

Seven a.m., the Kat line started ringin'. I let out a disgusted sigh. I was too fuckin' beat to be bothered, so I
let it roll into voice mail. A few seconds later, the
beepin' started to let me know the caller had left a message. I
turned over in my bed, yankin' the covers up over my head. A
few minutes later, the shit started ringin' again. Again, I let it go
into voice mail. This time the caller didn't leave a message. It
rang again. "What the fuck!" I screamed, jumpin' outta bed,
then snatchin' it off the dresser. *Next time I'll put this bitch on
vibrate,* I thought as I opened it. "Yeah."

"You get my messages?"

"Messages? I got the one from last night," I said, yawnin' and stretchin'. "I haven't checked my phone for any others. I was gonna call you when I woke up. So why is you callin' me so fuckin' early in the mornin'?"

"'Cause I wanted to hear ya sexy voice," he said, laughin'. I let out a disgusted sigh. He got the hint. "Nah, on some real shit. I need to know ASAP if you in on this next gig before I send someone else."

I really wasn't feelin' up to it, but since I'd never been to San Diego before, I decided to go, do a little sightseein', and see what was really good there. *Mmm, I could really use some dick.* "When?" I asked, slippin' on my silk robe, then slidin' my feet into my slippers. I opened up the glass door to the balcony, then stood in the middle of the doorway and let the cool mornin' air rush in. My nipples hardened under my robe.

"Like yesterday."

"Send me the paperwork. And if I accept, I want my money—"

"I know, I know. I got you."

"Humph," I grunted. "Make sure you do, Cash. I'm really not beat for cussin' ya black ass out again."

He laughed. "Yeah, keep talkin' nasty. You know that shit gets my dick hard."

I rolled my eyes and igged his ass. But I had heard his ugly ass had a long, thick, juicy, black dick, though. Ugh. The thought of that fat, nasty nigga smashin' me down into a mattress, smotherin' me and sweatin' and gruntin' on top of me, made my stomach turn. But the freak-nasty bitch in me wanted to see the nigga's dick. I shook away the thought.

"Expect ya package sometime this afternoon," he said. "Then hit me back when you look the shit over."

"Aiight," I said.

"Right back," he snapped.

"I heard you, damn!"

"Oh, aiight...One!"

"Later." I said, disconnectin' the call.

I went downstairs and fixed myself two scrambled eggs with cheddar cheese, four slices of turkey bacon, then sliced some cantaloupe and strawberries. When e'erything was ready, I pulled out a stool and sat at my counter, then dug in while flippin' through my latest edition of *Sister 2 Sister*. I thought 'bout sparkin' a blunt, but decided it was too early in the day to get lifted. Besides, I needed to cut down on smokin'. That shit was startin' to fuck my memory up. And a bitch can't have that.

Three hours later, my package arrived and just as I was gettin' ready to go through it, my private line rang. I looked at the number and smiled. It was Grant. "Hello," I answered, tossin' the envelope on the counter. *I'll get to this shit later.*

"Yo, what's good, pretty baby? Can a nigga get some love today? I'm tryna come through and scoop you."

"Oh yeah, and do what?" I asked.

"Come on, ma. Don't play. You already know."

"What, you tryna get ya dick wet or somethin'? 'Cause if ya are, I ain't the one."

He laughed. "Nah, baby, I ain't on it like that. I'ma grown-ass man; if a nigga wanna get up in some pussy, I'll tell ya straight up."

"Hmm. Yeah, okay. So, where ya tryna take me, 'cause ya ass ain't sittin' up in my spot."

"Let's start with dinner. Let me get ya address and I'll be through around six."

"Where you comin' from?" I asked, tryna decide if I wanted him all up in my face tonight. It was bad enough I never called him when I got back from Chicago, and I didn't pick up when he called back last night. I can be real funny-style when it comes to niggas. Besides, once ya ass is always accessible to a muhfucka, he starts expectin' the shit. I ain't the one. I learned never let a muhfucka know he got ya ass on lock, otherwise he starts takin' ya ass for granted. Then I gotta dump a clip in his ass. Besides, he seemed like the type who liked for chicks to be all up on his nuts. Well, that's cute 'n all. But a bitch like me ain't beat for sweatin' no nigga's balls.

"Newark," he said. I pursed my lips. *Hmm*, I thought. *What the hell.* I gave him my address and directions to my spot. "Bet. I'll see ya at six, *sharp*."

"I'll be ready. But if ya a minute late, it's a wrap. A bitch like me don't wait on a nigga for nothin'."

"I hear ya, baby. But be clear. A nigga like me ain't tryna have ya wait."

"Yeah, that's what ya mouth says."

"And that's what it is. Oh, and wear something sexy."

I laughed. "Oh, what…you ain't know? Nigga, I was born sexy."

"Oh, my bad," he said, laughin'. "I forgot who I was fuckin' with."

"Exactly," I responded. We said our good-byes, then I ran my ass upstairs to figure out what the hell I was gonna wear. It was a little after eleven, so I had seven hours to show this nigga how a sexy bitch rocks it. I made a quick phone call to my girl Gabby's salon in SoHo to get my hair done, along with a mani and pedi. Thank God she was able to fit me in. There was nothin' worse than a chick tryna be fierce with chipped fingernails and man hands and a pair of gorilla feet. I grabbed my keys and bounced out the door.

At exactly six p.m., my doorbell rang. I checked myself in the wall mirror and winked. My cinnamon skin was flawless. No need for makeup; just a splash of lip gloss to accentuate my already pillowy-soft lips. And my silky, naturally long hair hung past my shoulders. I opened the door, smilin'. I ain't gonna front. The nigga was finer than I remembered. He was dipped in a bangin' black Versace button-up and black slacks that hung just right and clung in all the right spots. I peeped the bulge behind his zipper and grinned. I was glad I decided to wear a black Yves Saint Laurent jersey halter set—fortunately for me, my titties didn't sag or flop all over the place so I could go braless—with a pair of black Louis Vuitton six-inch stilettos. I started to rock one of my diamond necklaces, but decided against it. I didn't wanna overdo it. So I kept it cute, and stuck in my diamond hoop earrings. The nigga stood in my doorway, droolin'. "Is this sexy enough?" I asked, slowly turnin' around, givin' him a nice front and back view of my bangin' body. Yeah, I was teasin' the nigga, oh well. "Can you put this on for me?" I asked, handin' him my tennis bracelet.

"Hell yeah," he said, takin' the bling and claspin' it around my wrist. "You killin' it, baby."

"Good," I said, throwin' my hips and bouncin' my ass—just enough to let him know what was poppin' underneath my wears as I walked toward my dinin' room table. "I just need to get my bag, then I'll be ready to bounce." I felt his eyes on me as they followed the outline of my hips, trailed along the humps of my juicy ass. I grabbed my black and white Dooney & Bourke, set my alarm, then followed him out the door.

"So, where you takin' me?" I asked, slidin' into the passenger seat of his Bentley Arnage RL. The smell of fresh money filled the car's cabin and made my nipples harden. I immediately pressed my legs together to keep my pussy from suckin' in my thong. A nigga caked up always got me wet. Still, although I was impressed with the nigga's whip, I kept it cute and acted like I'd been ridin' in one all my life. I learned a long time ago to never let a nigga think he's schoolin' you on shit. Just sit back 'n act as if ya was born to live it. Yeah, this nigga was paid. But the beauty of it all was that a bitch like me didn't need his paper. I smiled. I had come a long way from the days of needin' a nigga.

"Sit back, relax, and enjoy the ride, baby," he said, flashin' his sexy smile. He started the engine, then backed out of my drive-way. "No need for a bunch of questions. Let a real nigga show you how it's done."

I did what I was told, sat back, and got comfy in my seat. I smiled when Teedra Moses' "Take Me" came on. "What you know 'bout Teedra?" I asked, shiftin' my body toward him. I was impressed. "A lot of peeps are sleepin' on her."

"Yeah, she's kinda dope," he said, glancin' over at me.

I smiled. "I'm surprised."

"'bout what?" he asked.

"That a rugged nigga like you digs her," I answered. "You don't seem like the type that would know anything 'bout her."

"Wow," he said, laughin'. "Well, stick with me, baby, there's a lot more surprises in store. 'Cause I ain't ya average cat. Don't get me wrong. I can rock it hardcore with the best of 'em, but every now and then I wanna hear that soft, sexy shit, feel me?"

I laughed. "I feel ya, daddy. I ain't mad. I guess it doesn't hurt that she's also pretty."

"Yeah, she is. But she can't hold a candle to you, baby."

"Good answer," I said, smilin'.

I leaned back in my seat, then sang along quietly to "You Better

Tell Her" when it came through the stereo. I felt him stealin' glances at me while he drove, but I kept my eyes straight ahead, starin' at the road and swayin' to the music. E'ery now and then I gave him sideways glances on the low, tryna figure out what was really good with this nigga's flow.

"So what kinda niggas you into?" he asked, lookin' at me as we stopped at a red light.

I stared back at him. "Why, you puttin' in an application?"

He chuckled. "If I want the position, I'll just take it. So answer the question."

I grinned. "To answer ya question, I'm into niggas who ain't scared of pussy; a nigga who knows how to eat it up and beat it up." He laughed. "Real talk," I continued. "I hate a nigga who can't fuck, and don't eat pussy."

"I can dig it. On some real shit, though, you talkin' like you know how to take a dick and suck a dick."

"I ain't scared to put the work in, if that's what ya askin'."

"Okay, so what else you look for in a cat?"

"He gotta know how to keep shit real," I stated. "I can't stand a lyin'-ass muhfucka, or a nigga who thinks I'm some weak chick he can mind-fuck. That's when the bitch comes out, and I gotta bring it to him. Anyway, I'm into a nigga who knows how to keep his dick in his pants and who ain't easily impressed by a bitch tryna offer him some pussy. A nigga who ain't beat for creepin' with the next bitch. I'm into a nigga who knows how to hold it down *in* and *out* of the bedroom; a get-money type nigga who handles his business without bringin' that street drama up in my space."

He nodded, takin' it all in. "I hear ya, baby. So why you don't have a man?"

I thought for a minute before I spoke. Flashes of all the bitches I knew who lived and breathed a man came to mind. Bitches who couldn't live without a man, who thought not havin' one was the end of the world, that somehow they were nothin' without one. Bitches who would sell their souls for a stiff dick rammed up their ass. I shook the images outta my head. The thought of ever becomin' one of them weak bitches made me sick to my fuckin' stomach. Ugh, how I hate weak bitches!

"'Cause a man don't define me," I finally said, lookin' directly at him, "and havin' a man isn't something I need."

"Sure you do," he said, grinnin'.

I frowned. "How you figure?"

"'Cause a woman has needs, and no matter how many times she says she doesn't *need* or want a man, at the end of the day, she still wants to feel loved and needed and wanted. She still wants a man to make her feel special."

"Then she's a damn fool," I snapped. "A chick shouldn't haveta have a man to make her feel special. She *should* already feel special. She shouldn't have to rely on a man to be loved. She *should* already love herself."

He smiled. "It's more about companionship. Having someone she can feel connected to; someone to spend her life with."

Humph, fuck all the extras. Just give me the dick. I shrugged my shoulders. "I guess," I said.

"So, you don't wanna spend ya life with someone special; have someone you can share your hurts and fears with, someone you can grow old with?"

I took a deep breath. A bitch wasn't ready for this discussion. "I don't think about it," I said honestly. Hell, most niggas were too muhfuckin' shady for my likin'. And some of 'em acted worse than bitches.

"Oh, okay. Let's switch gears. Since you don't seem to need anyone to handle ya emotional needs, how about having a man to handle ya sexual needs?"

I held up both hands and wiggled my fingas. "This is what these are for," I said. "They never let me down."

He smiled. "Okay, but what about those nights when you wanna feel something thick up in ya guts?"

"Oh, not to worry," I said, smilin'. "That's what my collection of dildos is for. And if I just need a quick touch-up, I have a thick mini-vibrator to take the edge off. Two double-As and it's good to go all night long. No stress; no mess. I can just nut and go."

He laughed as he drove toward the Lincoln Tunnel. "Oh, shit," he said, grippin' the steerin' wheel and tryna keep his eyes on the road while lookin' over at me. "You funny as hell, word up. I see you got a answer for everything."

"Yep," I agreed. "I'm *that* bitch; I thought you knew."

"So I see," he said, pullin' up to the toll booth. He handed the busted chick in the booth a twenty. "Well, I guess since you don't seem to need or want a man, there's no sense in me tryna push up on ya."

"That's on you. I just know I'm not gonna expect much. Expectations open the door for disappointments, and I'm not the one."

"I feel you," he said, holdin' his hand out for his change. The ho was so busy tryna check for him she had to recount the money. I rolled my eyes. The old me woulda been on some real extra shit and woulda blasted her ass.

When he pulled off and made his way through the tunnel, I looked over at him and said, "I guess you got a lotta bitches checkin' for you."

"Nah, not really. I mean, there's a few. But it ain't that serious."

"Uh-huh," I said, half-believin' him. It wasn't like I was tryna make him my man. Hell, he could fuck whoever he wanted. I just wanted to test ride the dick for myself. But, still, a bitch wanted to know how he did him. "So, how many baby mamas you got?"

"None."

"How many bitches you fuckin'?"

"Two."

"Oh, and what...you tryna add me to the list?"

"Maybe," he said, glancin' over at me. I smiled. I was really diggin' him. "Why you smilin'?"

I slowly shook my head. "I don't share."

He grinned. "Oh, so what you sayin', you tryna have me all to yourself?"

"Maybe," I said, lickin' my lips and starin' at him real sexy-like, "maybe not."

"Yeah, aiight." He laughed, weavin' in and outta traffic through midtown. "You got a lotta shit with you, but it's all good."

I smiled, but said nothin'. The rest of the ride we were both silent, listenin' to the music 'til he turned down Lexington. I peeped Bloomingdale's on Fifty-Ninth, and automatically knew where we were headed: Mr. Chow's, my all time fav Eastside spot where fashionistas, money-makers, and celebs frequented, and the food was bangin'. Yeah, it was pricey, and definitely not a spot for a penny-pincher, but it was well worth it. I smiled, thinkin' 'bout the last time I was there, sittin' two tables away from Beyoncé and Jay-Z. And four tables over was the one and only Donald Trump, politickin' with a group of associates. Oh, yes, it was definitely a spot for a bitch like me—rich and beautiful. "Hmmm...how'd you know I like Chinese?"

"I don't know, educated guess. You seemed like a Peking duck kinda chick."

I laughed. "Yeah, okay. I got ya duck, alright."

He laughed with me. "As long as I can have it with sauce, I'll take it however you got it."

"Uh-huh," I said, grinnin'. "I bet you will."

After he parked across the street, he opened the door to let me out, then grabbed my hand and held it as we walked up to the restaurant. Once we were seated and our food finally came to our table, a bitch was so fuckin' hungry I coulda ate a horse. I had the chicken satay appetizers and shrimp toast with the bangin' sweet brown sauce, then the spicy green shrimp. Grant had the shrimp with glazed walnuts and crunchy seaweed and chicken skewers. We ate, drank, and laughed like we had known each other for years. By the time we finished our third drink, I learned he was born in Hollis, Queens, but was raised in Newark. Played football in high school, and went to college on a football scholarship, but dropped out after his second year when he got hurt and couldn't play ball anymore. He had three brothers and two sisters and was the middle child. He was twenty-eight and was ready to settle down.

I ain't gonna front, the nigga made me feel real comfortable. He was smooth and sexy and so damn fuckable. And let me tell you. After three glasses of Pinot Grigio, a bitch wanted somethin' more than that light, fruity shit. A blunt and some Rémy XO woulda really set it off and had me lifted and right. But I kept it cute, and sipped on the rest of my wine, grinnin' and flirtin' and buildin' with this fine-ass nigga in front of me. He grinned back and we both already knew what it was. *Yeah, muhfucka, I'ma have my pussy all over ya face in no time.*

After we finished dessert and another round of drinks, Grant paid the bill, then took my hand and led me out the door. His big, warm hand made my pussy tingle. And as soon as we got back into his whip, he reached over and started kissin' all over my neck and rubbin' my titties and circlin' my nipple with his thumb. My nipples hardened and I let out a moan. It felt like a bitch's whole body was bein' electrocuted. Sparks shot through me. His hands were big, strong, and soft...and his touch was sendin' a bitch over the edge. I had to stop him before I ended up fuckin' him in the front seat of his whip. My mind was tellin' me to push him off me, but my body was in need of a thug-nigga's touch. It had been so fuckin' long since a bitch had a real nigga slay this pussy. I couldn't think straight.

Since the only niggas I've fucked and sucked for the last four years have been the ones I've slumped, fuckin' them allowed me to get my nut off and not have to worry 'bout a nigga puttin' me on front street. Murkin' their asses made fuckin' them that much easier. They'd take my slutty deeds to their graves.

I know I'm a ho like the next bitch, but...fuck! Not on the first date. Not in the front seat of a car. Not in a parking lot. No. No. No. No. I heard the words in my head, but can't remember sayin' them. A bitch became a fuckin' mute. My tongue was stuck in the back of my throat, right where I wanted his dick to be. *Oh...my...God!*

He nibbled on my chin, lightly brushed his thick, soft lips against mine, then pulled away, flickin' the tip of his tongue against my upper lip. "I better get you home," he finally said in his deep, sexy voice. Just like that! He had a bitch's thong drenched. Had her pussy cracklin', and..."I better get you home" is what he hits me with. What the fuck?!

Oh, no this nigga didn't, I thought, pressin' the heat from my pussy shut between my legs. *This nigga is teasin' me.* He went to start the ignition, and before I knew what was happenin', a bitch had climbed up on him and straddled his lap, and was tonguin' him *down*, and grindin' my pussy into him. I sucked on his long tongue like it was a dick, twirlin' my tongue around his. I hadn't kissed a real nigga in *years* and…his lips, my lips, his tongue, my tongue…made my body shiver. He started thrustin' his hips up into my pussy, grabbed hold of my ass with both of his hands and started squeezin'.

"I wanna fuck," I whispered in his ear. "You got a bitch on fire." I sucked on his earlobe, traced his ear with my tongue.

"Yeah, baby," he moaned. His head was pressed back on his headrest, and his eyes were half-closed as his fingas found the center of my wet pussy. He slid his hand under my dress and pulled at the string of my thong. He slid one finga, then two, inside my slit.

I moaned. "Mmm…you got some thick fingas."

"That's not the only thing thick," he said in between soft, warm kisses on my lips.

"That's what ya mouth says."

"And that's what my dick says."

His fingas stirred my hole. "Deeper," I said. Twinge of desire shot from my asshole all the way to my clit, like sparks. The steam from my pussy could have fogged up the tinted windows. I arched my back, pressin' up against the leather steerin' wheel. I reached underneath me and felt the thickness of his dick pressin' against his slacks. He was stirrin' my pussy up just right, and I was on my way to bustin' a thick nut. My body started buckin'. "Mmmmm…you wanna feed me that dick, daddy?"

"Yeah, baby." He brushed his lips against mine, losin' his fingas in my wetness. I moaned again. "That's right, baby. Bust that nut for daddy; wet daddy's fingers." I clenched his fingas with my pussy, started grindin' deep and hard on his hand, bit him on his bottom lip, and nutted all over his fingas. Sweat dripped from my face.

"Damn, you got a a nice, hot pussy." He smiled, pullin' his cummy fingas from outta my hole. Then he fucked a bitch up when he stuck them in his mouth and sucked the cream off 'em. "Mmmm…and it tastes like honey, too." He kissed me on the lips, then stuck his fingas in my mouth. He watched me, grinnin' as I sucked them down to the knuckles. I ran my tongue in between each one, then climbed off him and sat back in my seat. My nut ran down between my legs as I shifted in my seat, tryna fix my short dress so my wet ass wouldn't stick to his leather seats.

I flipped down the visor to check my face. I smiled. Sweaty and all, a bitch's face was still in place. "Shit," I said. "This was a real bird move."

"What?" he asked, startin' the ignition and pullin' outta the space.

"Lettin' you run ya fingas all up in me."

"Nah, baby," he said real easy-like, lookin' over at me. "It's all good. You ain't rustlin' no feathers. This was just the beginning of what's to come. You'se a real dime. And I'm tryna be the man you need. Real talk."

I smiled. "Oh yeah. And what makes ya think I need a man?"

He grinned. "'Cause ya body told me all I needed to know."

I sucked my teeth. "Whatever, nigga!" I snapped, playfully hittin' him on the arm.

He bust out laughin', makin' his way back to my spot.

CHAPTER FOURTEEN

At ten a.m. the followin' mornin', I was sittin' in my office lookin' at the flick of my next target. He was a nice-lookin' older cat with a full beard, a thick nose, and full lips. I read his stats: *48, 5'10", 198 pounds, divorced. Hmm*, I thought, tossin' his photo on my desk. *I wonder if I should fuck him or just suck his old-ass dick*. I already knew if his ass had a bunch of extra skin flappin' 'round his cock, I wouldn't be suckin' on shit.

I got up and walked to my master bathroom and turned on the shower, then went into one of my bedroom walk-ins and pulled down my yellow Tumi bag. I tossed some wears and cosmetics in the bag before goin' back into the bathroom to shower. My flight to San Diego was at one-thirty, and I needed to get ready to make my way to the airport.

At four-forty their time, I landed at San Diego International Airport. After I got my bag, I headed toward the shuttle bus to pick up my rental—a burgundy Toyota Corolla. My destination was the Humphries Half Moon Inn & Suites on Shelter Island. My mark was conveniently stayin' there for some type of week-long business conference and typically stayed in his rooms alone, so unless he was totally committed in a relationship, or was strictly suckin' dick, enticin' him with a dish of this deep pussy would be easy, just the way I liked it. On some crazy shit, I often wondered what I'd do if one of my targets proved to be a bit more challengin' than I hoped for and refused a bitch some dick. Unfortunately, I'd have to go into plan B: straight sharp-shoot his ass on the spot, then peel rubber. Ugh, that'd be some real borin' shit!

Ten minutes later, I was turnin' onto Shelter Island Drive and slowly makin' my way to the hotel. When I saw the entrance, I pulled into the packed parkin' lot and strutted my way to the front desk. Keepin' shit real, I was really diggin' the hotel's layout. All these big tropical trees and exotic flowers 'n shit had me thinkin' I was in some kinda paradise or somethin'. The receptionist smiled as I walked through the slidin' glass doors.

"Hello, welcome to Humphries Half Moon Inn and Suites."

"Hi, I'd like to check in."

"Sure, your name, please?" I smiled and gave her one of my aliases. For this trip, I was Natasha Simmons. I handed her my fake ID. The room, as with all the others, was already paid for through Cash. Don't ask how, 'cause on some real shit, I've never asked, and I honestly didn't give a shit how or what he did to make it happen; or where and how he got his connects. I was only 'bout the business of killin', feel me? All that extra shit was of no concern to me.

"Oh, yes, Ms. Simmons," she stated, clickin' the keyboard with her thin fingas. "Here you are. We have you in one of our marina-view suites. I think you'll find it to be lovely as it overlooks the marina and the tropical garden. And at night, you'll be able to see downtown San Diego. Will you need more than one key?"

Bitch, save all the goddamn extras and just give me my fuckin' room key. I forced a smile. "Sounds wonderful. Umm, no. One key will be fine." I signed the printout.

"Here you go," she said, handin' me the key. "You're in Marina Suite 105." She pointed in the direction I should go. "It's out this door to the left, then around the side on your left. You can go all the way around the building, or you can cut through the garden pathway. Oh, I almost forgot. We have a package here for you. Hold on. I'll go get it." She went into a back office, and reappeared a few seconds later with a medium-sized box.

"Thanks," I said. It was already close to seven-thirty, and a bitch was starvin', not to mention tired. I wasn't plannin' to slump my mark until tomorrow so I had some time to chill. In the meantime, I was gonna jump in the shower, then head to the mall and grab a bite to eat. "Oh, and can you tell me where your nearest mall is? Something with high-end fashion."

Chick's eyes lit up. "Oh, you want to go to the Fashion Valley Mall. It's in Mission Valley off Friars Road. Here, let me write down the directions. It'll take you about fifteen minutes to get there, but they have some fabulous stores."

"Perfect," I said, takin' the directions from her.

Once I got to my suite, I tossed my bags onto the extra bed, then looked out on the triangular-shaped patio to enjoy the view. Since I was already pressed for time, I decided to head to the mall, shop a bit, then find somethin' to eat. If the opportunity to meet my mark presented itself, I'd fuck him tonight, then again tomorrow before I shut his lights. I stepped back into the room, closin' and lockin' the patio door, then headed out the door.

By eight-fifteen, I was walkin' through Bloomingdale's on my way to the Louis Vuitton store in search of somethin' hot. I wanted to slay them bitches back home with a cute bag or a slammin' pair of heels. My cell started ringin'.

I reached into my chocolate Bottega Veneta and pulled it out.

It was Chanel. "What's good, tramp?" I said, forgettin' my destination and goin' toward Saks Fifth Avenue instead.

"Shit. Where you?"

"At the mall," I said.

"Ooh, bitch," she replied. "Which one, Paramus or Short Hills?"

"Neither," I said.

She sucked her teeth. "Well, which one then? Shit. You coulda hit me up to roll with ya ass. You know I can always use a new pair of heels. You stay tryna dip on a bitch."

"Whatever, ho," I said, laughin'. "I'm at Fashion Valley Mall, and the shit is *fiiiyah*. They got some—"

"Fashion what? Is that some new shit in Jersey?"

I rolled my eyes. "No, bitch," I said. "San Diego."

She sucked her teeth, laughin'. "*San Diego?* What the hell?! I swear ya ass down with the secret society or some shit, as much shit you keep on the low. When you gonna be home?"

"In a few days," I said, runnin' my hands over this bangin'-ass black Donna Karan wrap-and-tie jersey dress. I looked at the tag: $2,495.00. Now the old me woulda boosted the shit quick, fast, and in a muthafuckin' hurry; I'da had that dress plucked from its hanger. "Listen, ho. I'm tryna get my shop on. I'll hit you back when I touch."

"Whatever. Oh, shit"—she snapped her fingas—"I almost forgot why I called ya ass. You know that dude ya moms is fuckin'?"

For some reason my stomach knotted up. "Yeah," I said slowly. "What about him?"

"Well, word has it that the nigga got outta prison sometime last year. I think for robbery or some shit. The nigga's from Brownsville."

"Okay and?" I said, eyein' another Donna Karan creation, this slick-ass slip dress. *Hmmm, I'd wear the fuck outta this.*

"I just thought you might wanna know."

I rolled my eyes, shiftin' my cell from one ear to the other. "On some real shit, Chanel, I don't give a fuck. That's my mother's shit. Not mine. When I said I was done with her ass, that's what the fuck it is."

"I hear you, girl." She paused. "Anyway, I don't know if I should say anything, but since you my girl 'n shit…"

I frowned my face up. "You shouldn't say shit to me 'bout what?" I asked, runnin' my hands along the rack of designer wears.

"Well, you might wanna know that the word is ya moms is knocked up."

I almost dropped the fuckin' phone. "Say what?!?"

"Yeah, girl. Ya moms was down at the doctor's office yesterday with that nigga."

Pregnant? I ain't gonna front. Hearing that shit had a bitch's head spinnin'. She couldn't even raise me right. *Unh-uh, ain't no way in muthafuckin' hell her neglectful ass would be that damn dizzy to let another child slip outta her snatch*, I thought.

"Where'd you hear that shit?" I asked.

"Well, you didn't hear this from me, but Tameka works at some doctor's office over on…damn, I think it's Atlantic Ave. Anyway, she told Tamia ya moms was up in that piece."

Okay, now I'm pissed. This bitch, Tameka, is not only disclosin' confidential shit, but she's flappin' her jaws to her gossipin'-ass sista. That shit was fucked up. And I was gonna check that bitch when I saw her.

"Well, that's on her dumb ass." Although I said that shit, I'm not sure if that's what I really meant. "Besides, goin' to a doctor doesn't mean her ass is pregnant. She coulda been there for a check-up or somethin'."

"Hmmm, I guess."

"Hmm...nothin'," I snapped. "What the fuck is that retarded bitch runnin' her fuckin' mouth for any damn way? Yeah, you right. You shoulda never told me this shit. 'Cause now, I'ma see Tameka's trick ass. And it ain't gonna be cute. How the fuck is she gonna be workin' in a doctor's office, tellin' bitches who's comin' and goin' outta that muhfucka. Let me go," I said, stormin' outta Saks. This ho had fucked up my mood. I peeped the time. It was already a little past nine p.m. The mall was gonna be closin' soon any damn way. I needed to get back to my hotel and take off this fuckin' hot-ass wig and take out these contacts. And, if I had it my way, fuck my frustrations away.

"If you gonna call ya moms, don't tell her you got that shit from me. Just ask her."

"Whatever. I'm out." I disconnected the call, walkin' toward the exit. I was too fuckin' through. I really wasn't sure if I wanted to call my moms or not. Even though in my mind I was sayin' I really didn't give a fuck, my heart was sayin' some other shit. Either way, whether she was knocked the fuck up or not, I was gonna push Tameka's muthafuckin' biscuit in for puttin' my mom's business on front street. So the fuck what if I ain't fuckin' with her. That shit was still low budget. Fuckin' bum-ass bitch! Ugh, I needed a damn blunt.

On my way out to the car, my cell rang again. It was Grant. "Hello."

"What's good, beautiful?"

"You," I said. I don't know why, but a bitch was cheesin' all hard 'n shit and I didn't even know what the nigga's dick stroke was like. Though a chick like me ain't needy 'n shit, it would be kinda nice to have some steady dick to ride. *It's been a long fuckin' time*, I thought, placin' the earpiece over my ear, *since I've fucked a nigga I didn't have to kill.*

"You miss me?"

"Nigga, please," I said, laughin'. "You got the wrong number. That's that other bitch you got suckin' ya dick."

He laughed. "Nah, baby. I got the right number. You the chick with that sweet, hot pussy I'm tryna get up in."

I pushed the button to the alarm, opened the door, then slid into my rental. Before puttin' on my seatbelt, I dug through my bag and pulled out a half-lit blunt I had smoked earlier that mornin', then lit it. "Take a number and get at the back of the line, then. 'Cause the wait's gonna be a while." I puffed the blunt, takin' in long, deep pulls as I started the engine, then backed outta my parkin' space. I exhaled, and the smoke filled the car.

"Oh, word. Then I guess you don't know me. I'm bum-rushin' niggas to the front spot, then I'm snatchin' ya sexy ass up and puttin' this dick to you." I laughed, almost chokin'. "You aiight?"

"Yeah, I'm good." I coughed again. "Oh, shit. You got me chokin' 'n shit. You silly as hell."

"Nah, it's all good, ma. I'm just fuckin' with you."

"Oh, so what you sayin' is, you don't want none of this pussy?" I joked. "You don't wanna see how deep ya dick can go, and just how wet it can get?"

"Hell yeah!" he said excitedly. "Just say the word, and I'm there; strokin' all up in it."

"Oh, now you soundin' all eager 'n shit."

He laughed again. "I am, baby. I am. You got a nigga's shit bricked, real talk. But I can wait. Trust me. I'm a real patient-type cat."

"And good things come to niggas who wait," I said, gettin' back on Interstate 15, hittin' sixty. Ugh, if I'da been in my own whip, I'da been pushin' a hundred by now. I ain't gonna front, talkin' to him and smokin' that blunt had me feelin' real relaxed and fuckin' horny. A bitch was ready to fuck. *I'ma do this mark tonight.* "Listen, I'm outta town for a few days and I'm on my way back to the hotel. Can I hit you up later?"

"Most def," he said. "Be safe, baby."

"Thanks. I will," I said before disconnectin' the call.

By the time I got to back to the hotel it was almost 9:45, and I still hadn't eaten. So I ordered some Chinese food from this spot up the street from the hotel and had it delivered. Since it was only Monday night, and my mark still had another four days left at his conference, I had hoped to quietly knock on his door to try 'n get a feel of this nigga. If things went well, maybe get a dose of dick tonight, and again two more nights before I slumped his ass. But of course I got sidetracked and ended up chillin' in the room.

Besides, Cash had called just before I got outta my rental to see what was good. He wanted me to murk his ass tonight, but I told him no. I assured him I'd have a bullet in the nigga's head before midnight Wednesday. I wanted to watch him for a minute— see how he moved, then make my move. In the meantime, I wanted to do a little sightseein', and see what was poppin' with the nightlife. I had heard the Gaslamp Quarter was live Thursday thru Sunday, and a bitch wanted to stretch this trip out as long as I could to see all of what beautiful San Diego had to offer.

After my shower, I blazed another blunt and paced the floor in my purple lace panties with my titties bouncin' free and my hair wrapped in a white towel. I glanced at the digital clock on the nightstand: 11:19 p.m. I slid open the patio door, then stepped outside. I smoked my blunt, starin' out at the marina. It was absolutely gorgeous and peaceful out. Definitely a night for deep, slow fuckin'.

I finished the rest of my blunt, then slid my hands down in my panties. I pressed on my clit, brushed my finga 'cross it, teasin' it while lightly pinchin' my nipple. A bitch was horny! *Unh-uh, I need more than this.* I stopped what I was doin' and raced back into the suite. I dumped open my bag, grabbed what I needed, took a towel from outta the bathroom, then went back outside.

I laid the towel across the patio chair, sat down, then draped my legs over the arms of the chair and slid the head of my dildo into my pussy, teasin' my slit with the tip. I rested my head on the back of the chair and pushed my make-believe dick in halfway, then quickly pulled it out. I did it again and again until I couldn't take it anymore, then plunged it deep into my pussy. I moaned. I wanted some *real* dick bad, needed to be fucked rough. I slammed my dildo in and out of my pussy with one hand and jerked my clit off until I shot my nut all over the dildo. I pulled it outta my wet, sticky pussy, then sucked the juices off it. A bitch was spent. I got up and took my ass to bed.

Seven a.m., I was up, showered, dressed, and on my way out the door for breakfast in the waterfront restaurant. If my hunch was right, I'd catch my mark there. I walked through the tropical garden, and couldn't believe how beautiful it was. The parrots and pond set it off just right. I peeped the pool and all the swayin' palms and decided I'd have to do a few laps before I bounced.

When I stepped through the door of the restaurant, I quickly scanned the area. *Voila!* Just like I suspected, my mark was sittin' at a corner table, readin' a newspaper and drinkin' a cup of coffee. I had to give it to him, for an older cat, the nigga was fine and definitely fuckable. I switched my ass toward an empty table two tables away from him. I made sure I sat where he could see a fly bitch in all her goodness. Even in my brown bob-cut wig and brown contacts, I was sexy and sensual. I stood up and removed my brown crochet poncho. Underneath, I was rockin' a brown one-piece Lycra cat suit. The shit clung to every curve, wrappin' 'round my ass and titties like a perfect glove, while showin' off the imprint of my fat pussy. I had it zipped down low 'n sexy, lettin' a muhfucka know what time it was with my titty game.

After the waiter took my order, I got up and headed toward the bathroom, passin' my mark's table. I caught his eye, and smiled. His eyes lit the fuck up as he returned the smile. "Good morning," he said.

"Good mornin'," I replied, keepin' it movin'. I took my time in the bathroom, standin' in front of the mirror. I pressed on another coat of lipstick, then twirled a strand of hair, makin' sure it was on point. The last thing I needed was tryna be fierce with a lopsided wig piece. As I was comin' outta the bathroom, I hoped my mark was still at his table. He was. And I purposefully threw an extra shake in my ass as I walked by, takin' my seat. I swept my eyes 'round the room to see what was what. There were a few square-type niggas at another table with two nondescript bitches, and a slew of white muhfuckas, definitely nothin' to write home about. *Humph*. Then came this blonde-haired, blue-eyed, bombshell-type chick outta the bathroom. She walked by with her head up. *She musta been in the stall*, I thought as she waltzed by.

This ho was dipped in ice. I peeped her Jimmy Choo slingbacks and Louie Louis bag. *Alright, you betta work, bitch!* I glanced over my shoulder to see who she was with. She took her seat at a table on the other side of the room with a cluster of white chicks with they faces beat to death with a bunch of pressed powder and whatnot. But you could tell them bitches were paid out the ass.

When my order came, I peeped my mark glancin' over at me several times. I smiled at him and slid my fork in and outta my mouth nice 'n slow and very sexy-like, lickin' my lips. He smiled back. *Yeah, nigga, I know you want some of this good pussy. I see it in ya eyes. Don't worry, muhfucka, I'ma let ya dip ya tongue up in it.*

I even peeped a few white cats eyein' me on the sly. They knew a classy bitch when they saw one. And I was servin' it lovely. E'ery so often, my target would look up from his paper, and I'd flirt with him with my eyes just to fuck with him. There's somethin' 'bout the way a man looks at me that lets me know just what's on his mind. I took a few more bites of my fruit salad, sipped my glass of water with lemon, then slowly got up to leave. I watched him eye me as I slipped my poncho over my head. I flirted with him with my eyes, then smiled. He smiled. I winked and blew him a kiss, then turned on my heels and sashayed toward the exit, lookin' back to catch him with his eyes glued to my ass. I smiled again, then strutted out the door.

Then the next two mornins I did the same shit, eyein' him real sexy, lickin' my lips and whatnot, baitin' his ass, then gettin' up and leavin' abruptly. I was fuckin' with the muhfucka, lettin' him know what was really good without words. And he obviously heard me, 'cause on the fourth day, he got up from his seat, walked over to my table, and spoke. *That's right, big daddy, come on over to lil' momma.*

"Mind if I join you?"

I let my eyes linger over his body, focused on the center of his crotch, then slowly looked up into his eyes. "Not at all," I said, smilin'.

He went back to get his things, then returned to my table and sat across from me. "So, tell me," he said, leanin' forward in his seat and restin' his elbows on the table. "What's a beautiful woman like you doing here all by herself?"

I stared into his eyes. Although I knew they were brown, they almost looked black. And they sparkled. I noticed specks of gray in his mustache and beard. Damn, this old nigga was fine.

"Waitin' for a man like you," I said as I licked my lips.

He smiled, blushin' 'n shit. "Is that so?"

"Absolutely."

"Stanley," he said, stickin' his hand out to me. I allowed my hand to get lost in his grip. *Hmm...I can't wait to feel them big hands squeezin' this ass, I thought.*

And I'm horny. I smiled. "Natasha," I offered. Then we spent the next thirty minutes talkin'. He was an architect from Upper Marlboro, Maryland, and had been in San Diego for over a week. Although I was actin' like I was really listenin' to him while he rattled on 'bout his corny-ass architecture conference, I wasn't beat. I nodded and smiled, and gave him what looked like my undivided attention. But the only thing on my mind was tryna figure out how I was gonna get into his room, get at his dick, then shut his lights. I ain't gonna front, his deep Barry White-soundin' voice had my pussy lips flappin' open. But the nigga—fine and all—was a fuckin' bore. And that's capital, B-O-R-E. Humph... I could see why his wife divorced his tired ass. I tried so fuckin' hard to look interested in him goin' on and on 'bout his buildin' designs and his love for classical and jazz music. Oh my God, I wanted to splatter his fuckin' brains right there on the spot.

About another ten minutes into the conversation, I got up and excused myself to go to the bathroom. I had to put this muhfucka outta his misery quick. I looked under the two stalls to make sure no one else was around, then flipped open the Kat line and called Cash.

"Yo, what's good? You take care of that, yet?"

"Tonight," I said.

"Cool. Make it happen," he replied. "You the only one takin' three and four days to handle ya business, tryna make vacations out the shit. I want this square handled tonight, Kat; you holdin' my peoples up with ya bullshit."

I sucked my teeth, rollin' my eyes. "I said tonight, nigga. Damn. Look, I gotta go. I'll call you later."

"Don't—" *Click.* I disconnected the call, walkin' outta the bathroom back to the table.

"Sorry 'bout that," I said, sittin' back down. I glanced around the room and noticed there were hardly any people there. *Good. The fewer people who see us talkin' the better,* I thought.

He was sippin' on his second cup of coffee. He set his cup down and smiled. "No problem. So…you never said what brings you to beautiful San Diego."

You, muhfucka, I thought. "Change of scenery," I told his ass, lickin' my neatly painted lips.

"Is that right?"

I nodded, keepin' my gaze on him.

"So, is this change for business or pleasure?"

I eyed him real sexy-like, then slowly licked my lips again. "Both," I answered, claspin' my hands together on the table. I leaned in. "Listen. Let me ask you this to get it outta the way before I go any further with this. You married? 'Cause I ain't lookin' for no drama from the Mrs." Even though I usually know the answer to this question, I always like askin' just to see what a nigga's gonna say. Nine times outta ten, the muhfucka's gonna lie outta his ass.

"Divorced," he stated. "And you?"

"Besides bein' very horny, I'm single."

He laughed. "Interesting combination," he said, starin' at my titties. I stuck my chest out more, givin' him a better view.

"They feel even better," I told him.

He let out a nervous chuckle, then cleared his throat. "I guess you can say I'm weak for…uh, a beautiful woman." *Like most muh-fuckas*, I thought. He glanced at his watch. "Oh, shoot. I gotta get going. I wish I could stay longer and talk, but I gotta swing past my room before my conference starts. How 'bout we get together tonight; say, like, eight? And we can finish where we left off."

I decided I had better go for the kill, and let his ass know what it was. "If we get together tonight, talkin' is not what I'm lookin' for." I leaned in, lowerin' my voice. "A thick dick is. Can you help me with that?"

He grinned, but I could tell I had caught his ass off guard. "I think I might be able to figure out something without much talk."

"Then I promise to make it a night you'll never forget."

"Is that right?"

"Yes, it is. I just hope you can handle a young bit—chick like me."

He stood up, smilin'. "Oh, I'm sure I can handle it. Eight o'clock good?"

Yeah, muhfucka, it's good. You just make sure that dick is good. I licked my lips. "I can hardly wait."

He leaned into me, then whispered into my ear, "Room 110. See you tonight."

I smiled, slowly noddin' my head. "Yes, you will, daddy. Yes, indeed you will."

For the rest of the day, I lounged 'round the pool, took a nap, then went downtown to take in the sights. I even tried one of them fish tacos e'ryone said I had to try. Yeah, okay? I'm still tryna figure out what the hype was all about. Chunks of cod fish, shredded cabbage, and a bunch of white cream stuffed in a tortilla didn't do it for a bitch like me.

Eight p.m., I was knockin' on my target's door wearin' a black car coat, a matchin' cap, and black spiked, knee-high boots. I scanned the area to make sure the coast was clear. I was glad no one was around to see me at his door. Besides, I couldn't have a picked a better night to get at him. The hotel was havin' some kinda blues concert on the grounds, so the music was loud and most of the guests were there. He opened the door, and I quickly stepped in.

"Hello, beautiful," he said, closin' the door behind him. "I'm glad you came. I was hoping you weren't gonna stand me up."

I set my bag on the wooden desk. "I'm a woman of my word," I said, unsnappin' my coat, then lettin' it hit the floor. Underneath, I had on a sheer black teddy. "And I never turn down the opportunity to suck on a big chocolate dick. You do have a big dick, don't you, daddy?"

He smiled, openin' his white terrycloth robe. "I sure do," he said, pullin' it outta his striped boxers.

Mmmm, it was thick; even soft. And the dick was cut! My mouth watered. "Then come on over to Momma and let me wrap my soft lips 'round it, while I play in my hot pussy. I hope you can nut more than once, baby, 'cause tonight I'ma show you how a young chick does it."

"I'm sure I can manage. It's been a long time since I've had some young, tight pussy."

"Then tonight is ya lucky night." *Muhfucka*, I thought to myself. "Now come give me that big dick."

"Damn, baby, I see you don't waste any time."

"Why should I?" I asked, walkin' over to his patio and lookin' out. He had a beautiful view of the hotel's tropical garden. Humph. I woulda loved fuckin' his ass under one of them palm trees. Oh, well. I turned back around to face him. "We're all on borrowed time. And I don't have any of it to waste. So I wanna get it all in while I can. Now stop with all the extras and bring that fat, black dick over here so I can wet it up for ya."

"And you're demanding," he commented, grinnin'. "I like that." He turned off the hall light, leavin' the bathroom light on, slowly makin' his way toward me.

As he walked over to me, I noticed the nigga was slightly bow-legged. And his thighs were muscular. For an old dude, the muhfucka had a nice, strong body. I pinched my nipples, then ran my hand across my pussy. The minute he walked up on me, I dropped down to my knees and snatched his boxers down, where they stayed wrapped around his ankles as I took his soft dick into my mouth, slowly suckin' and kissin' and lickin' all over it, twirlin' my tongue 'round the head until it started to get thicker and longer.

"Aaaah, shit. Damn, you know how to suck some dick," he said, dippin' at the knees. I lifted up his balls and started suckin' and lickin' on 'em while usin' my soft hands to jack off his dick. "Damn, girl! Oh, shit…you tryna make me bust this nut, huh?"

I nodded and moaned, lookin' up at him. "Give me that sweet milk, daddy."

"Yeah, pretty baby," he said, grabbin' me by the back of my head. *Oh, no you don't, nigga!* I quickly removed his hand before he accidentally tangled his big-ass hands up in my wig. "Wet daddy's dick up, baby girl…"

A bitch started gettin' real nasty with it, spittin' and slobberin' all over his cock, makin' a lotta smackin' and poppin' sounds with my lips and mouth, then lickin' up the spit from around his balls.

"Oh, shit…oh, shit…oh, shit…" His left leg started shakin'. I reached up and started squeezin' his muscular, hairy ass with my hands, swallowin' his dick balls deep, like only a true dick sucka can. The nigga's dick was nice 'n hot and tasted so fuckin' good. My pussy was drippin'. My clit was throbbin' for this muhfucka's tongue on it. I got up, then pushed him backward on the bed.

"I want you to eat my pussy, daddy," I whispered, crawlin' up on top of him, like a panther in heat. I sucked on his nipples, allowed my tongue to circle around 'em, kissed down his stomach, then brushed my lips over the head of his dick, then turned around and straddled his face. "Fuck me with ya tongue," I purred, lowerin' my pussy down on his lips. I took his dick back in my mouth and sucked him like a hungry, cum-guzzlin' trick while he licked and lapped and ate my pussy. I moaned. "Uh…hmmm… oh, yes…"

After I nutted on his tongue, a bitch was ready for some dick. Besides, I didn't want this muhfucka thinkin' it was okay for him to nut in my mouth. So I shifted my body 'round and started lappin' at his fat balls, jerkin' his dick.

"You ready to fuck me, daddy?" I asked, sittin' up and lickin' and suckin' my nipples. "You ready to put that dick in my tight pussy?"

He nodded. "Yeah, daddy's ready to fuck that young, sweet pussy." The nigga lay there like he was ready to dick me raw. Oh, hell no! I looked at his ass like he was fuckin' crazy.

"Well, get ya ass up and get a condom," I snapped. When the muhfucka told me he didn't have any, I was fuckin' through. Do you hear me? Done! "What?!" I yelled. "You jokin', right?"

He sat up on the bed, leanin' back on his forearms. "Sorry, babe, when I travel I don't usually carry condoms with me. I don't usu-ally get offered pussy from beautiful young women. Besides, I thought you were gonna bring some."

What the fuck! I took a deep breath, gettin' up off the bed. A bitch was in heat, and this muhfucka wasn't even prepared to stoke my fire. I walked over to the other side of the room and yanked up my bag. I dug inside it while walkin' back over to the bed. Though his balcony door was closed, you could still hear the band blarin' outside. I wrapped my hand 'round what I needed.

"Well," I said. "I guess that means there'll be no pussy for you. And since you gypped a bitch from gettin' her fuck on, I'ma hafta shut ya lights out early," I said, pullin' out my Glock and spittin' a bullet in his forehead. His head jerked backward before he had a chance to open his mouth. "Night-night, muhfucka!"

I wiped his ass down and e'erything I touched, then removed his sheets. I stared at his big dick and rolled my eyes. *Damn you!* I leaned over and licked it one last time, then threw the comforter over his body and snuck outta his room.

Back in my suite, I opened up my cell and called Cash. "I know why the caged bird sings," I said, pullin' off my wig and takin' off the rest of my costume.

"That's what it is," he replied. "It's 'bout damn time. I'll get at you."

I said nothin', just hung up. I glanced over at the clock on my nightstand. It was nine-thirty. "I'm takin' my ass down to the Gaslamp Quarter tonight to get my dance on before I jet tomorrow," I said aloud, layin' 'cross the bed and spreadin' open my legs, then reachin' for my dildo. "But first I'ma finish gettin' my nut off." *How that dumb muhfucka not gonna have a goddamn condom,* I thought as I plunged the head of my dildo inside my hungry, soppin'-wet pussy. *I shoulda shot his bitch ass in his fuckin' nuts.*

CHAPTER FIFTEEN

Got ya tremblin' while I'm wettin' ya dick…eyes rolled back…face twisted up…moanin' my name…hands grippin' my ass…got that pussy heat on ya balls…got ya buckin' ya hips…titty on ya lips…yeah, nigga…give me ya nut…run ya dick up in my guts…yeah, muhfucka…spit ya shit…

Three weeks later, and after many nightly phone conversations, and several more dinner and lunch dates, a bitch was finally on her knees bein' fucked down lovely by Grant. We'd been fuckin' for almost an hour, and he had rocked my pussy in six different positions before wantin' it doggie-style. I got up on all fours, spread open my ass cheeks with my legs spread wide, pressed my head down into the mattress, and arched my back while he ate my pussy from the back, tongue-fuckin' me before slidin' his dick up in me.

He started hittin' my walls and stretchin' the back of my pussy so good, I started to shake. And the nigga had me on fuckin' fire. I was so worried 'bout whether or not he could fuck, and the muhfucka slayed my pussy a new rhythm. His dick game was tight, his slurp game was serious, his money was right, and he was *fine*. It was after my fifth nut that a bitch realized he was that nigga I had dreamed 'bout growin' up. He *was* the nigga I'd been waitin' for to scoop a bitch up and love.

"Damn, baby, you wet," he said, pumpin' his dick deep, fast, and furious inside of me. "Damn, this pussy good." My pussy was hot, tight, and creamy from the big horse dick he was servin' me. He was diggin' my guts out.

"Yeah, nigga, fuck my pussy," I grunted, pullin' my ass cheeks open wider so he could make the dick do what it do. He slammed it in me. I kept my head down, arched my back, and pumped my hips. "Uh...mmmph. Yeah, just like that. Mmmph... harder, muhfucka." His balls slapped against my pussy while it swished and splashed juices all over his dick. "Beat this pussy up, nigga."

He slapped my ass with his big-ass hands. The shit stung, but it felt good as hell. "You like talkin' shit, hunh?" he asked, smackin' my ass again, and again, and again—alternatin' from one cheek to the other while slammin' his dick in and out of me. He had my ass bouncin' and shakin' all over the place. I groaned and moaned. "I don't hear you talkin' shit now...what was all that slick shit you was poppin', hunh?" I shifted forward. "Nah, baby, don't start runnin' from this dick, now." He slapped me on the ass. "This pussy's mine."

"Nigga, ain't nobody runnin' from ya dick," I gasped, backin' my ass up on him, pumpin' my hips. I started grabbin' his dick with my pussy. "Nigga, this pussy was made for takin' dick."

He slapped me on the ass again, then pressed down on the small of my back with one hand on top of the other, pumpin' in and out, movin' like a runaway slave. "Yeah, baby...that's right, give me that pussy..."

"Fuck my pussy, nigga. Oh, yes, just like that...fuck me!"

I was throwin' this ass back at him, grippin' his dick.

"Aaah, fuck, yeah...that's right; keep talkin' shit," he said, rapidly slammin' his dick in and out of me. My hot juices sloshed all over his dick as his balls slapped the back of my pussy.

I held back a scream. Oh, my fuckin' God, the nigga's dick game was fire! But I wasn't gonna let 'im know it. I threw my ass back at him. "When you gonna start fuckin' me instead of runnin' ya mouth, muhfucka. When you gonna put ya dick in me?"

The nigga was slayin' my pussy a mile a minute. I had the muhfucka workin' for that nut. Had him goin' deep, fast, hard, long, and strong. Sweat dripped off his face down on my back. "Oh, you can't feel this dick?"

"Uh...Mmmph, no, nigga," I grunted, throwin' my ass up on his dick. "You teasin' me with that little-ass finga." He grabbed me by the hips, liftin' me up off the bed like I was a wheelbarrow, then slayed my insides a new rhythm. It felt like he was tryna knock my uterus off the hinges. "Mmmm...oh, shit...oh, shit..."

He was grindin' and snappin' his hips into me, makin' his balls slap up against the back of my pussy. "What you moanin' for? I thought you said you couldn't feel this dick. I thought you said I was fuckin' you with a little-ass finger." I reached between my legs and started rubbin' my clit. The nigga was fuckin' a bitch silly. I started comin' and comin' and comin', squeezin' my pussy around his dick. "Damn, baby...oh, shit. Damn, you 'bout to make me bust this nut up in ya..."

"That's right," I whispered. "Cum for me, big daddy...give me that hot nut, muhfucka."

"Where you want it?" he asked, gruntin' and groanin' and sweatin'.

Even though he had his dick wrapped, the thought of suckin'

my pussy juice off his dick had me shakin'. A bitch loved tastin' her creamy nut on a nigga's big dick. And if he ended up bein' my man, that's how I'd take it—raw. "Down my throat," I said, clampin' my pussy around his dick. "Let me suck the nut outta ya."

He chuckled. "Yeah, that's wassup." He pulled out, removed the rubber while I quickly turned around and took his dick into my mouth, then swallowed that shit inch by inch until I had the head of his dick down in my throat. I played with his heavy balls. "Oh, shit. You suckin' that shit. Yeah, baby. Suck daddy's dick."

"You like that shit?" I asked, twirlin' my tongue 'round the head of his dick.

"Yeah, baby...aaah, shit yeah. Suck that dick."

I hummed and licked and swallowed his cock until he shot his thick nut. By the time I pulled his dick outta my throat and started suckin' the head, he had bust another load. I licked my lips, and slurped up the cream from around his balls, then pulled him toward me by the back of his neck and slid my tongue into his mouth, givin' him a taste of his own juices. My thing is, if a nigga can't kiss me after I let him bust his nut in my mouth, then that ain't the muhfucka for me. And, on some real shit, the muhfucka would never get piped out again.

Anyway, after we finished kissin' and whatnot, he held me in his arms. And I felt somethin' I had never felt before. Safe.

"Damn, girl," he said, runnin' his fingas through my hair. I wasn't one of those bitches who got heated when a nigga dug his hands in her hair, 'cause a bitch didn't have to worry 'bout no tracks 'n shit gettin' yanked or his hand gettin' stuck. "You keep suckin' and wettin' this dick the way you do, and you gonna have a nigga fall for your sexy ass."

I lifted my head from his chest, and looked at him. I'm a bitch who knows how to suck a nigga's dick, and fuck him until his head is spinnin' and his knees are shakin'. And I knew, once a bitch got inside a nigga's mind, she'd eventually get into his heart too.

"Maybe that's what I want."

"It's all good," he said, rubbin' the side of my face. "I dig your style. You the type of chick a nigga like me needs in his life."

I smiled. *'Cause I'm that bitch*, I thought.

Silence.

"So what does a beautiful woman like you do? You in school, workin'…what's really good with you?" he asked, runnin' his hands up and down the curves of my body, then cuppin' my left titty with his big hand.

I looked up at him again, stared him dead in the eyes. "I'm a villainess," I said.

He busted out laughin'. "Yo, you funny as hell," he said, still laughin'. "Nah, seriously, how you making ya paper?"

For some reason, I wanted to spill my guts and tell his ass my whole life story. There was somethin' 'bout him that made me wanna keep shit real with him. But I didn't wanna spook the nigga. So I kept it cute. I shifted my body and took his dick back into my mouth until it bricked up again, slobbered all over it, lapped his hairy balls with my tongue, then climbed back up on top of him. I slid down on his dick and did what I do best… welcomed him into the Kat Trap.

CHAPTER SIXTEEN

Almost a month had passed since I saw my moms or even spoke to her ass, but the shit Chanel had told me 'bout her bein' knocked the fuck up was still floatin' around in a bitch's head. And it was fuckin' with me. I wanted, needed, to know what was really good with her ass. But I also wasn't beat to call her. Call it pride. Call it stubbornness. Call it whatever the fuck you want. Bottom line, I wasn't callin' her. But I called Tamia's ho ass instead.

"Hello?"

"Bitch," I snapped, "don't front like you don't know who the fuck it is. I know ya ass saw my number come up."

"Humph," she grunted, suckin' her teeth. "Whatever."

I could tell the bitch was still salty, like I gave a fuck. I kept on pressin'. "What's good with ya trick ass?" I asked.

"Not a damn thing, bitch. Now what you want 'cause I know this ain't no fuckin' social call."

I laughed. "Ho, I know ya ass ain't still heated."

She sucked her teeth. "The fuck I ain't. Bitch, that was some real foul shit you pulled at Chanel's, tryna come at my neck all sideways 'n shit. On some real shit, I ain't really feelin' ya ass right now, Kat."

"Bitch, get over ya'self," I snapped. "Ain't shit changed, ho. You still my bitch. I just wanted to know what was really good with ya ass."

"Well, you didn't have to try 'n play me out 'n shit. You coulda came at me differently."

I sighed. "Tamia, please…shoulda, coulda, woulda. Since when ya ass get all sensitive 'n shit? I heard some shit, and I asked ya silly-ass about it. You said the shit wasn't true, so why the fuck is you still stressin' over it? But on some real shit, I don't give a fuck 'bout ya fuckin' attitude. Like I said, you still my bitch. But, you actin' like you wanna get it in or some shit. And you already know what it is. So, don't do it."

"No, bitch," she snapped. "*You* know what it is. It's whatever."

I took a deep, slow breath. "Oh, so you really tryna get it in over some dumb shit. Bitch, I will push ya muthafuckin' wig back, and you know this. On some real shit, don't go there. I can't believe you really tryna bring it when you know I will straight rock ya ass." I bust out laughin'. "Bitch, you done really let all that nut up in ya guts go to ya fuckin' knotty-ass head, for real."

"You know what, Kat, I am so fuckin' sick of you, bitch. Real talk. Chanel 'n them might let ya ass come at them any kinda way, but—"

"Bitch, what the fuck Chanel 'n them got to do with this?"

"—I ain't the one. Fuck what ya heard," she continued. "I'ma grown-ass woman and how you tried to get at me was on some real shady shit." Oh my God, I was so ready to blast this ho's ass. I bit down on my bottom lip and let her continue. "Ever since you left Brooklyn you really been on some extra shit, and I ain't feelin' it. Instead of clockin' what the fuck I do, you need to worry 'bout ya own shit. You act like you better than somebody;

like you can't be touched. Bitch, you bleed like I bleed. You shit like I shit. You ain't the baddest bitch around, be clear. 'Cause you can get it, too."

"Wow, I musta really hit a nerve."

"Nah, bitch, you ain't hit shit. I just don't 'preciate how you tried to shine on me. That shit was jacked the fuck up."

"Okay, you already said that."

"And I'ma say it a thousand more times if I want, and *what*, bitch?"

Deep breath.

Silence.

"Are you done?" I finally asked, really tryna hold my tongue. "'Cause you do know, bitch, I really don't give a fuck. You do know this. But if you need to get ya shit off, then do you." Yeah, she was heated, but no matter how much shit she popped, I knew this ho didn't really want it.

"Fuck you, Kat. I hate ya ugly ass."

I laughed. "Bitch, is there anything else you gotta say, that you wanna say, that you think you need to say? 'Cause I ain't call ya ass for this."

"Well, what the fuck you call for, then?"

"What's the name of that doctor's office Tameka works at?"

"I don't know," she said. But I could tell the bitch was lyin'.

"Well, let me get her number so I can ask her myself."

"You know I don't give out nobody's numbers 'n shit."

"Humph. Well, call her and give her mine 'cause I need to speak to her."

"Why, you pregnant or something?"

"No, bitch, I ain't pregnant. But, I heard my moms was up in that piece. So, I need to see what's good."

And when I catch her ass, I'ma dig in her fuckin' face.

"Well, then, why the fuck you don't call ya moms and ask her?"

I rolled my eyes. "Obviously, bitch, I'm not speakin' to her. Duh, now follow the yellow brick road and call ya damn sista, and tell her to call me."

"Yeah, whatever."

Since we were addressin' shit and the bitch was already vexed with me, I figured I might as well keep shit goin'. "By the way, what's good with them E's?"

"What?" she asked, soundin' shocked. "E's? What you talkin' 'bout?"

I sighed, suckin' my teeth. "I'm talkin' 'bout *you* poppin' E's, that's what."

"Who told you that?"

"Is it true?" I asked, iggin' her ass. I hated when bitches asked who told someone somethin' 'bout them. I'm like, who the fuck cares who said it; either the shit's true or it isn't.

"I do my thing from time to time," she said. "Why?"

I shook my head. A part of me had hoped the shit wasn't true; that hatin-ass bitches and niggas were just talkin'. But from the looks of things, e'erything Naheem said was true. "'Cause the streets is talkin'," I stated, soundin' real disgusted. "But on some real shit, I wasn't tryna believe it."

"Why is muhfuckas all up on my clit? Damn, can't a bitch do her without niggas clockin' my moves? What the fuck!"

Okay, now the bitch was tryna shine like she was a rock star or some shit. "Well, maybe it's the company you keep. Obviously them niggas you gettin' it in with don't give a fuck 'bout you. They got you soundin' real loose 'n shit. Maybe you should chill out for a minute."

"Bitch," she snapped, "don't judge me. I'm doin' me. And whoever don't like it can eat my big, black ass."

"Trick, ain't nobody judgin' ya dumb ass. If anything, I'm tryna come at ya ass on some real shit. I don't like what the fuck I'm hearin' 'bout you. And if we girls 'n shit, then I should be able to confront you about it. You should know I'm a real bitch. I ain't gonna grin all up in ya grill, then kick ya back in. I'ma come at you on some woman-to-woman-type shit. Now, do you have the herpes or not?" The bitch got quiet. For a hot minute, I thought the ho hung up on me. "Hello, you still there?"

"Yeah, bitch."

"Well?"

"I'm not answerin' that," she said. "That's none of ya muhfuckin' business."

"Sweetie," I said, gettin' up from the sofa and walkin' into the kitchen. I opened the refrigerator and took out the cranberry juice, then poured some into a glass. "You just did." I gulped it down, tryna ease the dryness in my throat from talkin' to this chick. For some reason, I almost felt bad for her ass. Why, I don't know. 'Cause at the end of the day, the bitch deserved whateva the fuck her hand called for. "You betta be careful 'cause niggas is really sayin' you burnin' 'em."

"Oh, well," she said.

I screamed on her ass. "Oh, well?!? Bitch, is you fuckin' crazy? What kinda shit is that? If your ass got that shit, you need to be gettin' ya ass treated, then chalk it up as a lesson learned, instead of tryna spread that shit, fuckin' up people's lives 'n shit."

"Kat," she said, sighin'. "You do you, and let me do me. I'm not puttin' a gun to a nigga's head. If he wanna fuck raw, then we fuckin' raw; if he wanna wrap up, cool. If not, then the shit's on him. Fuck at ya own risk. If he doesn't give a fuck, why should I?"

Needless to say, a bitch was through. "You know what," I said, rollin' a blunt, "that's some real grimy shit you doin', real talk."

"Well, right now, that's how I'm livin'. I'm like whateva. Muh-fuckas didn't give a fuck 'bout me—"

"So you turn around and do the same shit. Bitch, if you don't give a fuck 'bout you, then what the fuck makes you think a nigga should? You gotta look out for you first. And that means protectin' ya'self and makin' a muhfucka strap up. Fuck all the extras. You playin' Russian roulette. Next time you might end up with somethin' worse."

"Obviously, I didn't get that memo. And it's a bit late. So yeah, if the mood hits me, I'm suckin' and fuckin' and poppin' E's. We all gotta die someday."

Let me tell you. I knew right then and there that this chick was turnin' into a real live cum-guzzlin', junkie bitch. Okay, okay, maybe she wasn't a junkie yet, but with the way her reckless ass was movin', it was only a matter of time.

"Well, are you at least on some kinda medication or somethin'?"

"Kat, listen. I don't wanna talk 'bout this. It is what it is. So don't be askin' me a bunch of questions. I don't need ya tryna air my business out."

Oh, my fuckin' God, this hoodrat bitch was actin' like she was a damn victim; she's the one makin' choices to be loose in the ass, fuckin' e'erything movin', and she wanna act like somebody raped her ass or somethin' and gave her the shit.

"Me, air ya business out? Bitch, is you suckin' on paint chips or somethin'? I don't gotta air shit out. Niggas got ya stank ass all over the front page of the street news. You a walkin' billboard, ho. So, get real." I grunted. "Uh. You know what… forget it. Like you said, you a grown woman, so do you. But I think ya ass is playin' with fire."

"That's ya opinion."

"You right, it is."

"Well, when I ask for it, then it'll matter. Until then, I don't give a fuck 'bout ya opinions 'n shit. So do me a favor and keep 'em to ya'self."

"Oh, trust. You ain't gotta worry," I said, takin' two pulls on my blunt. "I'm done. From this moment on, I'ma keep my mouth shut. Just have your sister call me. I need to speak to her."

"Whenever I talk to her, I'll let her know."

"Do that," I stated. "Oh, and one more thing."

"What?"

"Grown-ass women don't still live in the projects with they mammies, sneakin' niggas into they bedrooms."

"Fuck—"

I ended the call on her ass. Silly bitch!

Two days later, Tameka's monkey ass finally hit me up. And the bitch came at me with major 'tude. But instead of blastin' her ass like I wanted to, I kept it cute. "Hey, girl," I said. "What's good?"

"What's up?" she questioned, soundin' all paranoid 'n shit. "T said you were tryna get at me. What you need?"

"Well, I wanted to know the name of that doctor's office you work at."

I could see the bitch twistin' her lips up, lookin' at the phone. "Why you wanna know that?" she asked, soundin' all tight 'n whatnot.

I sighed, then paused. "Because I need to get tested, ASAP," I lied.

"Well, that's not what T said. She said you was tryna get at me 'bout your moms 'n shit."

Well, if you knew that already, bitch, why the fuck you askin'. I shook my head, rollin' my eyes. I thought for a quick minute how I was gonna come at her. Although I wanted to really dig in her ass over the phone, I knew if I did she'd hang up, then I wouldn't get what I wanted. And right now, my only focus was gettin' at her. Keepin' shit real, I didn't know if my issue was really with her flappin' her fuckin' gums or if it was 'bout the idea of my moms bein' pregnant again. I was feelin' some kinda way that the bitch barely wanted me growin' up and now…humph. I ain't even goin' there, not now, anyway.

"I…well, on some real shit, I had heard my moms was up in ya spot. I woulda asked her where the spot was, but we beefin' again. And I ain't beat to call her ass 'bout shit."

"Humph. Ya'll at it again. That's a damn shame."

And so is ya damn grill, I thought. "Anyway," I said, pausin'. "I think a bitch is knocked."

"Get the fuck outta here?!" She laughed. "Not Miss I Got My Shit Together. Humph. Now, that shit's priceless."

I don't know what the fuck she thought was so goddamn funny, but I humored her dusty ass, anyway. "I know, right," I said, givin' this bitch one of my phony laughs. "A bitch got caught up in the dick. Hey, shit happens—even to the best of us."

"So why you ain't tell Tamia? She didn't say shit 'bout you bein' knocked up. What's good with that?"

This stupid bitch, I thought. "'Cause I didn't tell her," I said. "That's why."

"So, what you tryna do?"

"Well, right now, I need to be seen. I haven't given much thought to what I'ma do after that. A bitch ain't tryna have no baby." I threw that in for good measure.

"Well, I can schedule you to see one of our doctors next—"

"Girl, can I get somethin' sooner? I'm already two months late. A bitch is stressed."

She sighed. "Let me see." I heard papers shufflin' in the background. "Hold on," she said. I smiled. *Yeah, I'll hold on alright, ho.* Well, the bitch had me on hold for almost five minutes. "Okay, I can get you in to see one of the doctors tomorrow at three forty-five."

"That's perfect. Umm, can you do me a favor?"

"Sure, if I can."

"Well, can you keep this on the low until after I find out what's really good with me?"

"Girl, you know how I do. We from the same 'hood. I got you. Just let me know how you make out."

I laughed to myself, rollin' my eyes. *Yeah, bitch, you right. I know exactly how you do.* I already knew the minute I hung up her he-mannish ass was gonna be on the phone with Tamia's infested ass. And then she got the fuckin' nerve to ask me to let her know how the fuck I make out. This nosey bitch knew I knew that if I really was goin' there for an appointment, she'd have her pudgy-ass nose all up in my file.

I sighed for effect, actin' like I was relieved. "Thanks, I owe you."

"Oh, trust. I'ma hold you to it."

Oh, please. When I finish with ya ass, the only thing ya gonna be holdin' is ya face.

She gave me the address. I twisted my face up when I saw that it was on Pacific Avenue. *Hmm,* I thought, *I thought Chanel's ass said the spot was over on Atlantic. That bitch can't get shit straight.*

After I took down all the information, I asked her crusty ass if she was gonna be there when I got there. I already had it planned out in my head how I was gonna walk up in that piece and go dead in her mouth, and if she wanted to rock after that, then we could get it in. And once Tamia got wind of it, I already knew we'd be at it, too, 'cause that's how they do. But it was all good. It wasn't like her ass added any value to my life any damn way. My mind was already made up that I was cuttin' her off so if she wanted it, she could get it, too. There was definitely more than enough ass-whoop to go around.

"No, I'm outta here at two-thirty on Wednesdays."

Fuck! "Oh, that's too bad. It's been a minute since I saw you. What time you get off on other days?"

"I'm usually outta this box 'round seven-thirty, why?"

"'Cause we need to plan to hook up for drinks 'n shit. My treat." I was really gassin' her ass. Ain't no way I'd ever be caught dead anywhere with this hoodrat, with her tired and late wears. Now I had to consider how I wanted to get at her. Either bum-rush her ass at the front desk, then drag her through the fuckin' office, or wait for her slutty ass to come out the door, then straight-rock her grill in. Bottom line, I wasn't gonna go up in the projects to fight chick; even if it was where we were both from. The difference was she still lived there. I didn't. No, a bitch needed to get at this ho off grounds, on neutral territory.

"Now you talkin'," she said, soundin' all excited 'n shit. I could see the drool runnin' outta the sides of her raggedy mouth. The bitch was a straight-lush. "That's wassup."

"Most def. Oh, one more thing..."

"What's that?" she asked.

I smiled, flippin' the script. "Watch ya face."

"Excuse you?"

I repeated myself. "I *said*, watch ya face."

"Bitch, you tellin' me to watch my face for what?"

Now, on some real shit, I coulda just caught the ho on the low, but that's not how I get down. I'm the type of bitch who's gonna let you know from gate what it is. I want you to be ready to rock. I want ya ass to be constantly lookin' over ya shoulder. I wanna keep a bitch on her toes 'cause ya never gonna know when I'm gonna come at ya.

"'Cause I'ma bust you in ya muthafuckin' mouthpiece when I catch you for flappin' ya jaws 'bout my moms comin' through."

"Oh, fuck that. You got the wrong one, bitch. My name ain't Tamia. Don't get it fucked up. This hood bitch will beat ya little ass the fuck down if you even think about tryna bring it. Now try it if you want."

I laughed at her low-budget ass. "Like I said, watch ya face, bitch. And that's what it is."

I pressed the end button on her ass, savin' her number in my phone, then flippin' it shut. *Sooner than you think*, I thought, walkin' into the kitchen. I glanced up at the clock. It was 11:30 a.m. I decided to fix myself breakfast, then lay 'round the house for the rest of the day. I wasn't gonna get at the bitch today 'cause she'd be expectin' it. So I was gonna let the ho do her for a minute, then rock her snotbox open the minute I caught her ass slippin'. But knowin' Tameka's ass, she was already on the phone with Tamia poppin' shit, and would be tryna figure out a way to bring it before I did. Funny thing, a bitch like me would be ready—whenever, wherever, however. Believe that!

CHAPTER SEVENTEEN

Dangerous and unpredictable...swift on her feet...silent in her tasks...got no time for hustlin' backward...that's a bitch like me...have ya doin' shit you'd never do to ya chick...have ya beggin' to slay me with ya dick...you ain't ready for a bitch like me...cool, calm, collected...I gave ya a run...but now ya finished... it's lights out, muhfucka...ya lifelines been disconnected...

Summertime in New York is always what's poppin'. Harlem, Brooklyn, the Village, SoHo, you name it. There was somethin' for e'eryone to get into. The streets were live. And a bitch could get caught up in its heat. There were niggas dipped e'erywhere, straight flossin'. Stereos blastin' the hot beats from the sickest whips; dick-thirsty hoes on the stroll; packs of bitches stuntin'; homeless pushin' carts; young cats wildin' out; street vendors tryna get their hustle on. Anything ya want...whatever ya lookin' for, find a block, and find ya pleasure. New York was alive!

The energy and excitement was enough to make a bitch forget 'bout bullshit niggas and stress. Today was no different as me and Chanel made our way through mad traffic up the West Side Highway to One Hundred fifty-fifth to see what was poppin' off at the courts. We were two fly bitches posted up in a slick-ass whip, rockin' some of the illest wears. Oh, yes, today Ruckers Park was the hot spot. And we were 'bout to see what was what.

At first I wasn't really beat for takin' the ride, but Chanel twisted my arm by tellin' me she wanted to go to show her support for the Sean Bell All-Star team, which was formed in memory of the young cat Sean from Jamaica, Queens, who was gunned down for no damn reason by the muthafuckin' cops. Fifty fuckin' shots fired, ugh! E'ery time I thought 'bout that shit it made a bitch wanna squat up on a rooftop and start pluckin' muhfuckas off.

Anyway, before I knew it I was scoopin' her ass up and we were on our way, blazin' trees and talkin' mad shit and laughin'. My God, the park was overflowin' with frontin'-ass and hood-rich niggas! Ballers, brawlers, and shot-callers were all over the place, and the streets were jammed with cars. Music was blarin' e'ery-where. And niggas and bitches were gettin' their party and dance on. Even I felt like poppin' it a bit, but I kept it cute and just bopped my head a few times, and threw a few extra shakes in my ass.

We was lookin' all fly 'n whatnot in our wears. I had on a pair of denim short-shorts and a cute white sheer pullover blouse with a plungin' neckline over a white lace bra, and a pair of black fuck-me pumps that made my smooth, pretty-ass legs look more shapely. I snickered at the bitches whose faces cracked as I walked by with my black Hèrmes Lindy bag hangin' in the crook of my arm. I had them bitches gaggin' and droolin'. And Chanel kept it cute 'n sexy in a short white halter dress that showed off her thick thighs. She had on a bangin' pair of tangerine-colored Dolce & Gabbana strappy sandals and rocked a fly-ass tangerine hand-bag. We both had our hair pulled up off our faces so the sun could hit the ice in our ears just right as we sauntered through the crowd, killin' 'em.

A bitch's pussy got real moist when I peeped Nas's sexy ass, standin' on the sidelines. Fat Joe—well, he ain't so fat anymore—was out on the scene as well. And I spotted a few other hip-hop shakers 'n movers mixin' and minglin'. Hunc Records was givin' away prizes for makin' free throws and different jump shots around the court. Of course, Sean Bell's name was announced over the loudspeaker several times and folks cheered as his team slayed muhfuckas on the court. There was so much goin' on 'round the court that a bitch had a hard time stayin' focused. There was dick and body out for days! And there was also a slew of vultures waitin' to swoop down on some hard cock. I had to pull out my binoculars so I could scan the sights without missin' a damn thing.

Ugh! I let out a disgusted grunt when I spotted Cash's ugly ass standin' over by the fence talkin' to a group of flossed-out niggas. I can't even front, ugly or not, the nigga was dipped in a bunch of ice and had a bangin'-ass pair of black shades on his busted face. Crazy thing, I kept my eye on him longer than I shoulda, watchin' him grab at his dick while he talked. I swear I thought I seen a big-ass lump danglin' up in them designer sweats. For a split second, I wondered what the nigga's dick game was really like since I had heard the muhfucka could fuck like a stallion. Oh, my God, the heat and the blunt I had smoked on the way up had a bitch buggin' for real. I shook away the thought.

"What's wrong?" Chanel asked, lookin' 'round to see what I was lookin' at.

"Nothin'," I said, glancin' at my watch. "What time is this shit over?"

"Why?" she asked, rollin' her eyes. "You got a date with some dick or somethin'?"

I sucked my teeth. "No," I shot back, "you my date, you sexy-ass ho."

She chuckled. "So, then answer me this, smart-ass: why is two fly bitches sittin' down instead of tryna see what's good?"

"Because we ain't thirsty like the rest of these hoes out here."

"Says who?"

"Says me, bitch."

"Humph," she grunted, standin' up. "Speak for ya'self. A bitch lookin' for some new dick for the summer."

I rolled my eyes. "Well, go on and get ya ho-stroll on, then. I'm keepin' my ass right here. I ain't beat."

"Then I'll get at ya in a few. I wanna see what's really poppin' out here."

"Whateva," I said, tryna keep my eye on the niggas runnin' up and down the court. On some real shit, I couldn't tell you shit 'bout who was doin' what 'cause a bitch was really only cock watchin', tryna see whose dick was doin' the most bouncin' 'round in they shorts.

A nigga tryna get at Chanel disrupted my peep show. "Yo, ma," he yelled from a few seats away, "what's good wit' ya fine self? Let me holla at ya."

I looked over my shades to see what his grill looked like. He was a light-skinned cutie—a bit too bright for me, though—with short, wavy light-brown hair. His wears were aiight, but nothin' to get a bitch's pussy moist over.

"Ugh, not," Chanel said, puttin' the palm of her hand out to stop him. "I'm checkin' for heavyweights, so go run along, little one."

A few peeps laughed, but that didn't stop the nigga from tryna come back at her. "Yeah, okay. This little boy got ya heavyweight, aiight. I'll split that ass right down the middle."

"Nigga, puhleeze. I wouldn't even let ya busted, crab ass lick the shit outta my ass." She flicked her fingas at him. "So, poof... be gone!"

Before dude could open his mouth to say somethin' else, she turned to me and said, "See ya. I'm out. Hit me on the cell when you ready to meet up."

"Whateva, bitch," I said. "But when ya ass ends up with nothin', fuckin' with these niggas, don't say I didn't warn ya." She threw her hand up, wavin' me off, switchin' and bouncin' her way off into the crowd. I looked around and peeped a few niggas with they eyes locked on her big ass.

My cell phone rang. I glanced at the number, then flipped it open. I stuck my finga in my right ear, tryna block out some of the noise. "Hello?"

"I got my eye on you, baby."

"Say, what?" I asked, lookin' around. "Where are you?"

"What you lookin' around for?"

"Oh, what, you spyin' on me, now?" I said, laughin'.

"Yeah, I got eyes everywhere; thought you knew."

"Nah, I didn't. So, did these little eyes of yours see me suckin' ya dick and ridin' ya ass down into the mattress last week?"

He laughed. "Nah, but right now they see a bunch of niggas sittin' around a real dime-piece tryna get what's mine."

I rolled my eyes, suckin' my teeth. "Oh, please. I ain't thinkin' 'bout these niggas."

"Yeah, aiight. What you thinkin' 'bout then?"

"How 'bout I'll tell ya when I see ya?"

"Yeah, you can do that," he said. Some nigga sittin' next to me tapped me on the shoulder to ask me somethin'. I looked at his ass, then igged him, rollin' my eyes.

"Aye, yo, don't have me hurt nobody out here."

"Grant," I said, laughin', "where the hell you at, nigga?"

"Look in back of you." I craned my neck all the way around, and there his fine ass was, sittin' five rows in back of me with a bunch of niggas dipped in jewels. I didn't remember seein' his ass sittin' there. Then again, I wasn't lookin' for him. He smiled at me, gettin' up from his seat and makin' his way down to me. I was glad I had my shit in the space where Chanel had been sittin'. He sat down beside me. "Hey, beautiful," he said, kissin' me on the neck.

I smiled. "Oh, you tryna mark your territory, huh?"

"And you know it," he stated, wrappin' his arm 'round me. He kissed me again. "You look good as hell. I peeped your sexy ass when you first came in. Niggas was breakin' they muhfuckin' necks tryna see who you and ya peeps were. They were like, 'Oh, shit, check out shortie in them jean shorts. That sexy bitch is bangin', word is bond, son...'"

I laughed. "You so damn silly."

"Real talk, baby. I had to check a few of them cats. But I was diggin' it on the low, though. I was like, 'Damn, my baby is fiiiyah.'"

I laughed. "Oh, so I'm ya baby now?"

"Don't play. You know what it is."

"Humph," I stated, twistin' my lips. "As long as you know I ain't playin' the second or third spot to no other bitch, then it's all good."

"No doubt," he said, leanin' in and tryna kiss me on the lips.

I turned my head, playfully mushin' him.

"Oh no, nigga, I don't think so. Until ya ass is my man, I'm still on the market."

He laughed. "Baby, I'm shuttin' shit down. So, fuck all that shit you talkin' 'cause your fine ass is with me."

Needless to say, we half-watched the game, and talked. This nigga kept his hands on me the whole time, lettin' the rest of them muhfuckas know who had the real door prize. I really didn't mind, though. It was nice to have a strong arm wrapped 'round me. He wasn't my man, and he may never be, but in the meantime he definitely was gonna be some steady dick.

"So, you ready for me to tell you what I was thinkin' 'bout?" I asked, grinnin'.

"No doubt, baby, no doubt."

I leaned in and whispered in his ear, "I was thinkin' 'bout how good that big, juicy dick of yours felt in this tight pussy"—I slipped my hand on the inside of his thigh and lightly rubbed it— "and I'm thinkin' 'bout how I wanna nut on ya tongue tonight."

He smiled, fannin' his legs. The nigga's dick was brick. I squeezed it on the low, and smiled back at him. "See what you do to me?" he said.

"And I'm gonna do even more when I get up on this long dick," I whispered, flickin' my tongue in his ear.

"That's wassup, baby...no doubt." And for rest of the game, I kept my hand on his dick and watched the Sean Bell team house muhfuckas on the court.

CHAPTER EIGHTEEN

"Aiight, baby, I'ma hit you up later tonight," Grant said, givin' me a big bear hug and kissin' me on the cheek. I had to laugh to myself at the nigga tryna shine in front of his niggas like he had already bagged a bitch. But I let 'im live 'cause it was kinda, hmm...cute. And the nigga was too fuckin' fine to let any of the thirsty bitches who stood around droolin' think anything different. He looked over at Chanel, who had returned after she finished collectin' her numbers for the night. Some hoes gotta be greedy. I rolled my eyes, shakin' my head. "It was nice meeting you," Grant said to Chanel.

"You too," she said, smilin' at him, then glancin' over and raisin' her eyebrow at me. Like, *you betta fuck him or I will, bitch!* "I hope I'm gonna see more of you. Kat needs a real nigga to keep her ass in line."

"Oh, word? Then I guess it's her lucky night."

She smiled. "Alright now...let's get it poppin'."

I laughed. "Don't listen to her crazy ass. She's delusional. And, you"—I turned to Chanel—"stop puttin' ideas in his head. Makin' it sound like I'm pressed for a nigga and some dick."

"Oh, you not?" they both asked, bustin' out laughin'.

I gave 'em both the middle finga. "Fuck ya'll hatin' asses."

He grabbed me again and whispered in my ear. "I'ma come through and beat that pussy up tonight, baby. So make sure you answer ya phone."

I smiled. "Maybe I will, maybe I won't."

"Yeah, aiight, don't play." He looked over at Chanel. "Yo, ma, make sure ya girl don't have a bunch of niggas all up in her grill when I bounce."

"I got you," she said, grinnin'. "Trust me. Kat needs a nigga like you."

Grant winked at me. "I'm out."

He walked over to his boys. They were like ten deep and posted up in the cut, waitin' for him and watchin' Chanel and me at the same time while tryna holla at some of the chicks that were flouncin' and bouncin' all 'round the niggas, lookin' and actin' real thirsty. As Grant made his way over to his niggas, I spotted Patrice with two of the several gold-diggin' bitches she rolled with. I ain't gonna front, the bitch kept it cute in a pair of blue Baby Phat pencil jeans that were cuffed up to her ankles, and a white wife beater with the word "bitch" stretched across her titties in gold and crystals. She had a gold coin belt draped around her waist and a bangin'-ass pair of stilettos on her feet.

I rolled my eyes.

"This bitch," I said to Chanel, gesturin' my head over in her direction. Chanel peeped her. "All these heads out here and I gotta see her fuckin' face. Let's bounce."

Chanel shook her head, lookin' over my shoulder. But since she didn't say nothin', I didn't bother to turn around. I just figured she saw someone she knew. She twisted her face up.

"Who the fuck is this ugly nigga tryna creep up behind you, puttin' his finga up to his big-ass lips tellin' me to 'ssh'?" I turned around, suckin' my teeth. It was Cash.

"What's good?" he asked, walkin' up on me, grinnin'. The jewels around his neck and in his lobes lit up like mini lamps, all bright and whatnot. I can't front, the nigga's swagger was serious—ugly or not. But on some real shit, I was surprised he was even comin' over to me. I can count on one hand the number of times he's actually acknowledged me when we were out in public. And if he did, he'd either do it with a nod or a wink of the eye. Other than that, he usually kept his interaction strictly over the phone, with the exception of those rare times when he called a "family meetin'"—as he called 'em—to discuss "business." And even then, the family meetin' would only be him, me and one of his henchmen. The nigga typically met with his hit team on some one-on-one type shit. He never met with all of us together. He liked keepin' who he had on his squad on the low, which was fine by me.

"I see you got these niggas out here buzzin' all around ya sweet ass," he said, leanin' into my ear.

I rolled my eyes. "Whatever." He stepped back and eyed me up and down, then looked over at Chanel, who turned her back on him. I bet if her ass knew how deep the nigga's pockets were she woulda been all up on his dick tryna suck the skin off it. He licked his lips. "What's good with ya peoples?"

"She's off limits and she ain't beat," I stated, twistin' my lips up.

"I can dig it. What about you, what's good with you?"

I wasn't sure if his question was on some gettin'-his-dick-wet type-shit or not, but I decided to check his ass just in case. "Nigga, I know you not tryna come at me on some extra shit. Don't have me curse ya ass out in this bitch."

"Yo, ma, chill with that shit. I ain't on it like that. I'm talkin' 'bout what the fuck you tryna get into tonight, that's it. You always thinkin' somebody tryna get in ya damn drawers or some shit. Geesh."

"Yeah, whateva, nigga," I said, smirkin'. "I know how you do."

"Yeah, well, not tonight. I got my sights on somethin' else." I peeped him starin' at Chanel's big, juicy ass.

I rolled my eyes, suckin' my teeth. "Anyway," I continued, "I'm not sure what' I'm doin' tonight. Why?"

"Come through the Forty-Forty. Me and a few cats got somethin' poppin' off tonight." He had one of those Forty-Forty purple memberships so he was always throwin' parties 'n shit, but I had never officially been invited to any until tonight. Hmm…it made a bitch wonder why now all of a sudden. I'm sure it had somethin' to do with his nasty ass tryna get up on Chanel's clit. I can't front, the bitch was flawless and her body was

bangin' in her wears. The nigga peeped her style, so he knew what time it was.

Of course Chanel's ears perked up the minute she heard Forty-Forty club. The bitch loved to party. Anywhere there was gonna be drinks, dicks, and dollars her ass was gonna be 'bout it. She turned around, droolin'. I grinned at her. "You down to go to the Forty-Forty tonight?" I asked her.

She glanced over at Cash, then me. "What time?"

"Oh, you couldn't speak to a nigga, but now you wanna know what time you can come shake ya pretty ass."

She rolled her eyes. "Whatever."

He eyed her. "Does 'whatever' got a name?"

"Cash," I said, pointin' to her, "this is my girl Chanel. Chanel, Cash."

She rolled her eyes.

"That's better," he said, grinnin'. Then the nigga started lookin' at her like he was ready to fuck her on the spot. "Have the cats at the door come get me." He looked at me, then winked at Chanel. "And you, beautiful, I'ma get at you later."

"Don't hold ya breath," she replied. "You can't afford me." Cash just laughed at her dumb ass, walkin' off.

"What the fuck so funny?" she asked, vexed.

This ho is so busy chasin' ballers 'n shit, but had no fuckin' clue. Hell, I was glad she wasn't feelin' him. I didn't want her tryna get at the nigga any damn way. That's the last thing I needed.

I sucked my teeth. "Bitch, let's go," I snapped, brushin' past her. "Fuckin' with you, I need a damn blunt."

By the time we finally got to the club it was a little after midnight and hot 'n poppin'. Dripped heavy in ice, with niggas clockin' us in our wears, me and Chanel made our way up to the Rémy Lounge. I had on a canary-yellow chiffon Chanel pullover blouse that hung real low 'n sexy in the front and back, showin' off my perky tits and smooth back, with a pair of white Gucci pencil jeans—and, yes, with no panties—that melted over e'ery delicious curve of my body, and a bangin' pair of six-inch Balenciaga slingbacks. Chanel kept it cute in a sexy white Christian Louboutin wrap dress with a pair of white Christian Louboutin crystal "Vamp" stilettos.

There was a group of thug niggas dipped in jewels playin' PlayStation 2, and I peeped 'bout seven or eight model-type chicks among a group of pigeons sittin' on the oversized leather bed, cacklin' and cawin' like real birds. A few of 'em got up and started finger-poppin' and shakin' they hips—clearly for attention—when Rihanna's "Umbrella" came through the speakers.

I spotted Cash at the pool table with a bunch of his niggas; they were talkin' shit back 'n forth. I could tell they had a team game goin' on. I glanced at Chanel and smiled.

"You thinkin' what I'm thinkin'?" I asked her outta the side of my mouth.

"And you know it," she said, followin' behind me. We heard a few "damns" and "oh, shits" as we walked over to them, disruptin' their flow. Even a few bitches kept they eyes on us. It was all good. *All eyes on me, bitches.* Chanel and I kept it cute, and posed for the audience.

"I see you made it," Cash said to me, but he was eyein' Chanel. "And you brought Miss Whatever with you." He smiled. Chanel gave him one of them phony smiles. He introduced us to the niggas, then leaned into my ear. "Yo, hook a nigga up with ya girl."

"You silly as hell, nigga," I said, laughin'. "She's off limits."

He didn't get the hint. "I ain't tryna marry her gold-diggin' ass; I just wanna get in them drawers."

I rolled my eyes. "Drop dead, nigga," I said, catchin' Chanel givin' me the eye. She ice-grilled Cash.

"Yo, that's fucked up. But it's all good."

"Whatever," I said, lookin' over at the niggas 'round the table. "Me and my girl got next." Chanel looked at me, then smirked. She knew what it was. We was 'bout to run 'em.

"Bitch," Chanel snapped, puttin' her hand on her hip, "what the hell you doin'? You know I can't play no fuckin' pool."

"So what," I said, "I ain't that good either, but we can still get it in."

I peeped all the niggas 'round the pool table had stopped talkin' and the niggas who were shootin' pool were now standin' with they sticks in they hands, lookin' all bug-eyed 'n shit at me.

I laughed. "What, ya'll niggas scared to play with two dime bitches?"

"Dig, beautiful," this cross-eyed nigga rockin' a navy-blue Yankee fitted cocked to the side said, "I don't mean no harm, but maybe you and ya girl might wanna come back when ya got ya game up."

A few niggas laughed.

"No harm taken," I said, eyein' him with my hand on my hip. "Like I said, me and my girl got next."

Cash and a few other niggas laughed.

"Rack 'em up, then, baby," this short, cock-diesel-type nigga with shoulder-length dreads said. "I'm 'bout to house ya fine ass."

I eyed him real easy-like. He was a brown-skinned cutie with a thick neck; definitely fuckable, but my clit didn't jump so I knew his paper wasn't long enough to handle a bitch like me. "Oh, is that right, little man?"

"Little man? Yeah, okay. But I got a big stick," he drawled.

"With little-ass balls," I said back. "And a big-ass mouth. And you'se 'bout to get the snot whipped outta ya."

His boys laughed.

"Oh, looks like we got a shit-talker in the room."

"And I can back it up," I said, shiftin' my bag from one arm to the other.

Cash jumped in. "Yo, I love you, my nigga, but I'ma haveta ride with Kat and her peoples on this one."

"Yo, fuck you, nigga," one of his boys said, laughin'. "Ya black ass just tryna get some ass."

"Yeah, that, too," Cash replied, laughin' and eyein' Chanel at the same time. "But, I'm tellin' you niggas, don't sleep. I bet these beauties are real beasts."

I rolled my eyes. I was gettin' restless and was ready to bring it to them niggas. "Listen, muhfuckas, are we gonna play or are ya'll niggas gonna stand here bullshittin'?"

"Oh, okay, I see you one a them gangsta chicks."

I smiled. "I'm from Brooklyn, nigga...thought you knew."

"Let's do this, then, pretty baby," the stocky nigga said. "By the way, I'm Leo, and"—he pointed to this golden-brown nigga with light-brown eyes and light-brown curly hair—"this here is my nigga Bronze."

I introduced myself and Chanel to 'em, then walked over and started rackin' the balls. By now there was so much hype in the air 'round us that niggas and bitches had stopped what they were doin' and were all comin' over and standin' 'round tryna see what all the excitement was 'bout. Once again, all eyes on me, bitches!

Then outta nowhere this fine brown-skinned nigga with spinnin' waves said, "I got a twenty on them two fine shorties."

The cornball nigga was tryna clown us.

"I'll double that," said this other nigga, laughin', with a bunch of razor bumps under his chin and neck, lookin' like a damn burn victim. The niggas were really tryna play us close. I shook my head. Then another one spoke up.

"Yo, fuck that. I got five beans on my mans 'n them. Word up."

Okay, five hundred dollars wasn't enough to get a bitch's pussy wet, but it was a start. Me and Chanel glanced at each other, thinkin' if we played it right, we was 'bout to house these muh-fuckas for some major paper. Before you knew it, 'bout thirty muhfuckas was diggin' in they pockets ready to get it poppin'. Most of 'em had they bets on the niggas, which was all good. Even a few bitches wanted in, but they rode with the dick. But them soft hoes and niggas were all pullin' out peanuts. And I ain't the one.

"What, that's all you cheap niggas got?" I asked, openin' up my Balenciaga bag and pullin' out a roll of hundreds. "If ya pockets light, then say they light." I smirked. "But don't try 'n play a dime-piece like me." I tossed the roll on the table. "Two rounds, double or nothin'."

Some nigga named Skratch took the knot and tossed it over to Cash, who started countin' it. When he finished, he started smilin'. "Well, my niggas...looks like ya'll gonna need to come hard or go home. I got five G's in my hand. Let's make it do what it do."

"Ah, shit...this gonna be like snatchin' candy from a baby," Leo said, laughin' and lookin' over at his partner. "Ya'll sure you wanna lose ya paper?"

"That's chump change, nigga," I said, walkin' over to the rack wall, gettin' my stick. "Besides, even if me and my girl can't really play, I'ma always be a winner, baby." I winked at the nigga. Chanel walked over and stood in wait while some nigga tried to get at her. She igged his ass. The niggas were tryin' hard to keep they eyes off our asses, but we was killin' 'em. I threw an extra shake in my hips, just to fuck with 'em.

Chanel sucked her teeth. "You always draggin' me into some shit. Hand me a stick, bitch." I held in my laugh.

Leo broke strong, and that's all she wrote. Four balls clanked in. The niggas were stripes. We were solids. A few niggas were talkin' and laughin' but most of 'em had they eyes pressed up on the game. Niggas had cheddar ridin' on the table and didn't wanna miss shit. The rules were simple: call ya pockets, two rounds, winner takes all.

Tie-breaker if each team lost one round.

He sank two more balls, then missed. I handed Chanel my bag. Took my stick and leaned in, spread my legs and bent over, givin' muhfuckas a ringside view of my fatty. Yeah, I was fuckin' with 'em. I pointed to the corner right pocket with my stick, then licked my lips real sexy-like. I took my eye off the table for a hot minute and caught the stares of a few niggas eye-ballin' me. I made one shot; *missed* the other.

"Bitch," Chanel snapped. "You know ya ass can't play this damn shit, and we 'bout to lose."

Bronze laughed. "It's cool, baby," he said, chalkin' his stick, "we don't mind takin' ya money. I'll even buy ya drinks the rest of the night." He gave his boy some dap, then slayed the rest of the game. Niggas was gettin' real amped. "Rack 'em up, baby."

I bit my lip. Chanel sucked her teeth. The nigga Leo broke again, strong. This time only three balls went in. Again, the niggas were stripes. He sank one ball; missed the next.

Chanel took her stick, picked up the chalk, then asked, "What's this for?" Niggas and bitches started laughin'. She shrugged. "What?"

"Bitch," I snapped, "just try 'n hit a damn ball in. And we're solids."

"I know, I know. Damn." She leaned in, let her titties smile at all the happy niggas, then sank a ball in. She jumped up, actin' all excited 'n shit. The bitch had the niggas goin'. They was really lookin' at us like we were two dumb hoes. She re-chalked her stick between her shots, rockin' the table. Niggas started shiftin' 'round, bitches started grinnin'. "Eight ball, corner pocket. Oh, I'm so nervous." I wanted to bust out laughin' at her theatrical ass. She stood straight, shook out her hands, took a deep breath, then leaned back over.

My eyes swept across the room, checkin' the niggas. I peeped the way Cash was lookin' at Chanel like he was ready to throw her ass 'cross the pool table and deep dick her down. The nigga even grabbed at his dick a few times.

"C'mon, girl," I said, "you can do it." My lips broke into a wide smile the minute the shiny black ball sank. We jumped up and down, screamin', actin' all hyped 'n shit. "Rack 'em up, muhfuckas," I said. Chanel unpinned her 'do, shakin' out her thick, curly hair, then ran her fingas through it. The way she did it was sexy as fuck. I looked around the room again and noticed a few niggas' jaws were tight. I smiled again.

"Good game," Leo said. "Let's see how lucky ya'll get now."

I laughed, shakin' my ass over to the table. A few niggas was tryna get my attention with they eyes, but I igged 'em. "Yeah, yeah, yeah," I said, chalkin' my stick. I shook out my hands, closed my eyes real tight, then stared at the table.

"Oh, yeah," I heard someone say, "ya'll niggas got this. Chick's game is whack." A few niggas snickered.

"Yeah, yeah, yeah," I said, cuttin' my eyes over at him. "And so is ya dick game, muhfucka." Niggas started clownin' him. That shut his dumb ass up. I took a deep breath, then made a strong-ass break. Four balls scattered in.

"Stripes," I called out, smilin'. I heard a few niggas chucklin' and talkin' 'bout gettin' lucky or some shit like that. But a bitch kept her eye on the table, tryna map out my next move. I was ready to get my drink and smoke on and was gettin' bored with clownin' these muhfuckas. I glanced over my shoulder at Chanel and grinned. She smiled. Then I straight-housed them niggas, leavin' them gaggin'. "Eight ball, side pocket," I said, watchin' it sink. "Run me my money, niggas." I high-fived Chanel. Niggas who had paper on us was cheerin' and two-steppin' 'round, talkin' mad shit. The rest of the niggas was mad tight.

"Good game," Leo and his boy, Bronze, said. We shook hands. "Yo, let me get ya number. I like how you move," Leo stated.

"I bet you do. But we gonna keep it on the table. So run me my money, little man."

"Yeah, aiight. I'll show you little, alright."

"No, lil' daddy, the only thing you gonna show me is my paper. 'Cause you and ya nigga just got got. Bye-bye," I said, wavin' him on. Chanel started laughin'. The nigga was swoll.

Cash walked over to us, grinnin'. "Yo, why you game my mans 'n them?" he asked, handin' me a stack of paper.

"'Cause I'ma hustler, nigga. That's what we do. Thought you knew." I tossed the money in my bag.

He laughed, eyein' Chanel. She rolled her eyes, then twisted her face up. "Ugh! Why you all up in my damn face?"

"'Cause you fine, baby—"

"What you ladies drinkin'?" a nigga with a deep sexy voice asked us, cuttin' Cash's ass off. The muhfucka was the color of tar, but had beautiful smooth skin with shiny black brows, long eyelashes, beautiful big, dark eyes, and a head full of thick curly hair. He was rockin' all white and the ice around his wrist and ears told me he was paid. Fine! Fine! Fine! That's all a bitch can say. He was 'bout six feet two and I could tell the nigga got it in at the gym the way his white muscle shirt hugged his chest and stretched 'round his huge arms. Chanel peeped him, too, and her whole 'tude changed. She answered before I could open my mouth.

"Surprise us," she said, eyein' him all sexy-like and grinnin'. He smiled. And a bitch almost passed the fuck out when I saw those straight, white teeth and deep dimples. Cash peeped how we was checkin' for his sexy ass.

"Oh, I see how ya'll do. This pretty muhfucka come 'round and ya'll ready to toss the pussy at him, but a nigga like me can barely get love. What, I ain't black enough for ya asses?" he asked, throwin' his arms open. Everyone laughed. He introduced the sexy dude as Coal. I smiled. The name fit him perfectly 'cause that's exactly how black he was. But ugly he was not. This muhfucka Coal was a beautiful, black diamond. I could feel my pussy churnin' as I imagined havin' my legs up over his shoulders with him shovin' his tar-black dick in and outta me. I would bet my 960-dollar heels that the nigga had some good dick. But if he didn't, he still could get it. Hell, the muhfucka coulda had a little dick and one nut, and…um, well, maybe not. I snapped to my senses and almost hit the fuckin' floor when Cash said that fine, black, sexy nigga was his nephew.

Chanel let out a disgusted grunt.

Coal eyed me, then Chanel, and grinned. "One surprise for two beautiful ladies coming right up," he said, walkin' off. We— uh, correction—*I* excused us from Cash since Chanel was in bitch mode. I igged it, but as soon as we found a seat on the wrap-around sofa, I confronted her ass.

"Bitch, what's up with the stankness?" She reached into her orange Hèrmes bag, pullin' out a pack of Doublemint. She took a stick, then offered me a piece. I shook my head. "No, bitch," I snapped. "I wanna know why you actin' all shady 'n shit." She looked at me like I was buggin' or somethin'. "Don't look at me like that. You know what I'm talkin' 'bout. You did that shit at the park, too, but I didn't say shit. Now you here servin' it. So what's good?"

She rolled the gum up in her mouth. "How you know that nigga?"

"Who?" I asked, playin' stupid.

"That nigga Cash."

"I met him a while back when we were playin' the Brooklyn Café," I said, hopin' she wouldn't ask nothin' else. "Dude was tryna get at me at first, but once I made it clear he wasn't my flava he fell back. I run into him e'ery now and then. Why?"

She looked over at him, shakin' her head. "I don't like him."

"Girl, you don't even know him," I said, laughin'.

"I don't have to know him to know a snake when I see one." She looked me dead in the eyes. "And that nigga over there"—she nodded toward Cash—"is a Mojave rattlesnake."

I had to laugh, rememberin' Chanel's crazy fascination with reptiles. She knew e'ery type of snake listed, and the Mojave rattlesnake was one of the deadliest snakes in the world. And Cash was definitely a dangerous-type nigga.

"So I guess the nigga can't get no pussy from ya?" I asked, still laughin'.

"Bitch, is you serious? Not hardly. That nigga will never splash his venom up in me. Hell, I wouldn't even fuck his grimy ass with Tamia's pussy. And we both know how much mileage that has on it." We cracked up laughin'. Nothin' else needed to be said.

We sat takin' in the sights, pointin' out which niggas were hot and which were not; which chicks were bangin' and which were busted.

We peeped a few niggas walkin' 'round the room carryin' six-hundred-dollar bottles of Dom P and eight-hundred-dollar bottles of Krug, drinkin' outta them shits like it was water. Neither of us were really impressed. But the nigga who did impress us was Coal when he came back with a twenty-five hundred-dollar bottle of Rémy Martin Louis XIII. I think Chanel and I were both ready to drop down low and suck the nigga's dick.

He walked over to us, smilin' that Crest-white smile. "I figured top-of-the-line beauties deserved a top-of-the-line drink," he said, handin' us the bottle with two snifters. "Enjoy."

"What, you not gonna drink with us?" Chanel asked, eyein' him up and down. Now the bitch was all flirty 'n shit.

He made a slight gesture with his head to the left of us. Chanel and I peeped a brown-skinned chick draped in some ill shit over in the corner with two other high-post bitches. She stopped talkin' and looked over in our direction for a hot second, then started talkin' and laughin' again. Without words, we already knew— the bitch was gettin' the dick.

"Not tonight," he said, smilin' and lickin' his lips. "Maybe some other time."

"I like the sound of that," Chanel said. This time the bitch *and* her girls looked over at us. Chanel kept on flirtin'. "Maybe we can set somethin' up for later." I elbowed her ass. I was not beat to be havin' no shit pop off with some bitch over some dick; especially some dick I had no intentions of fuckin' *or* suckin'.

He grinned at both of us. "Are we talkin' a two-for-one special?"

Me and Chanel looked at each other, then back at him like he had been sippin' on bleach or some shit. This muhfucka was tryna get it in with the both of us. "Nigga, please," I said, rollin' my eyes. "Nice try, but no cigar. This is between you and my girl."

He smiled, shruggin' his shoulders. "Can't blame a brotha for tryin'."

Chanel slid the tip of her pierced tongue across her tangerine-painted lips. "So…like I was sayin', maybe we can make it happen."

"Maybe," he replied, cuttin' his eyes back over to his chick, then eyein' Chanel like he was ready to slam his dick in her mouth. "Figure out a way to get me your number without lettin' my girl catch you and we can make it happen. But be clear. I'll give ya the dick, but there's only one chick who'll ever have the top spot." He gestured his head back over toward Miss Thing.

Chanel smiled. "Oh, trust. That's all I'm ever gonna want."

"Then so be it," he stated, pourin' us our first drink. "Get at me with ya number without gettin' caught and it's all yours." And with that said, the nigga spun on his Ferragamos, leavin' Chanel and me gaggin' as he walked over to his chick and planted a kiss on her lips. She wrapped her arms around him, lettin' e'eryone know he was hers. I wasn't mad at her 'cause I woulda probably did the same damn thing to let them bitches know what time it was. Too bad she thought she was the only one.

"That bitch can't handle a nigga like him," Chanel said as we sipped our drinks. The shit was so fuckin' smooth goin' down. My nipples got real hard as the heat went through my body. "And I know that gold-plated bitch ain't wettin' his dick right. A nigga like that needs a bitch with that platinum pussy in his life." She lifted her drink up in Coal's and his chick's direction, smiled, then took another sip. "Enjoy him while you can, honey, 'cause I'ma be fuckin' ya man and runnin' his pockets before the end of summer."

I rolled my eyes, laughin'. Crazy thing, I knew the bitch was serious. "I need another damn blunt," I said, gettin' up to go to the bathroom.

CHAPTER NINETEEN

Close ya eyes...count to ten...ready or not here I cum...nuttin'
all over ya tongue...the shit done got good to ya... got ya
moanin' 'n groanin'...beggin' a bitch to wet ya dick... yeah,
just like that...make it pop, nigga...yeah, don't stop... get it
hot, nigga...beat it up 'til you make it drop...

I didn't stumble back up in the house until almost seven a.m.
We shut the damn 40/40 down, then hung outside blazin'
and talkin' shit to niggas who were tryna get at us. And a
bitch was lit the hell up. Do you hear me? I'm talkin' extra fucked
up. At first we kept it cute, sippin' from our glasses 'n shit, but
after the fourth round, we tossed our glasses and started neckin'
that Réemy straight to the head. Niggas were buggin' when they
came by to congratulate us on our game and saw that we had
dried the bottle out. Muhfuckas couldn't believe how long and
deep our necks were.

Ugh! Between all the trees and the liquor a bitch was spent. I
don't even remember drivin', or how the hell I got the fuck home.
All I know is, when I woke up I was layin' in a pool of vomit and
e'erything 'round me was spinnin'. Fast. My stomach felt heavy
and rumbled up in knots. I sat up in bed, glanced at the digital

clock. It was 12:15. I still had on my Chanel blouse, and still had one leg in my jeans with one shoe on. Oh my God, I was gonna throw up. I jumped outta bed and bolted toward the bathroom, barely makin' it to the toilet. I fell down on my knees and tossed my guts up all over the rim of the toilet, then started huggin' the bowl. I was sweatin' like a horse and heavin', and as I was throwin' up, somethin' warm started runnin' down the back of my legs and onto the floor. Ugh! A bitch had shitted on herself. I was too fuckin' through!

I don't know why the fuck I got all liquored up like that, but I was payin' for it out the ass and I was a hot shitty mess—literally and figuratively. I wrapped a few sheets of toilet paper around my hand and attempted to wipe my ass, but started throwin' up again. I was wiped the fuck out, and didn't even have the strength to finish wipin' my ass. I left the tissue up in the crack of my ass and tried to crawl back to my bed. But I never made it. I fell out facedown on my white-marbled floor.

I don't know how many times I heard the dull chirpin' in my ears, but when I finally lifted my head up from the bathroom floor, it took me a minute to come to my senses and realize that the noise was comin' from outta my bag that was right in the middle of the bathroom. I had no fuckin' idea how it got there. The noise stopped, then started up again. Somebody was really tryna get at me. I stretched my arm out and grabbed my bag, draggin' it across the floor, then diggin' through it.

I looked at the screen, slowly pullin' myself up off the floor. "Hello," I said, rubbin' my head. I stood up and stared at myself in the mirror. My hair was matted, and streaks of crusty vomit were 'round the sides of my mouth. I pulled off my wrinkled shirt and threw it in the corner, pulled the dried-up toilet tissue from outta my ass, tossin' it in the toilet, then flushin'. I felt like throwin' up again when I noticed dried-up shit on my floor.

"Damn, baby, you left a nigga hangin' with his dick in his hand last night. Word up."

I groaned, reachin' under the sink cabinet and pullin' out the liquid Lysol and a sponge to wipe up my mess. "I wasn't on it like that. I ended up goin' to the 40/40 club with Chanel."

"I musta hit your sexy ass up mad times; you straight-dipped on a nigga."

"My phone was in my bag," I said, throwin' the sponge in the trash, then puttin' the bottle of disinfectant back. "I didn't even hear it ringin'."

"Oh, word? Well, while you were shakin' ya ass all up in them niggas' faces, I had to take it down with a stiff dick."

"Aww," I said as I washed my hands, then ran water into the bathtub. I poured in some Pooka Pure & Simple lavender bath crystals. "Poor baby. I apologize. Is there anything I can do to make it up to you?"

"Yeah, you can let me come through and get up in that good pussy again."

"Well, I guess we can arrange for that to happen." Although I said it, I really wasn't beat for a nigga to be crawlin' all up over me, groanin' up in my ear, or breathin' up in my damn face. Not today, and definitely not the way I was feelin'. "What you gonna be doin' tomorrow?"

"Tomorrow? Nah, baby, you got it fucked up. I'm comin' through now."

"Now?!" I said shocked. "You jokin', right?"

"Hell, nah, I ain't jokin'. I wanna see you today, right this minute."

"Unh-uh. You can't come through now."

"What you mean, I can't come through now?" he asked, soundin' like he had an attitude. "You got some other nigga up in there?"

Now, had a bitch been in her right frame of mind, I woulda slayed him a new asshole for tryna question me like I was his girl 'n shit. 'Cause on some real shit, that questionin' mess and havin' a nigga check for me did not work with me. I guess that's why a bitch was single. But since I was all off centered 'n shit, I let it go and actually answered him.

"Not hardly. I'm hung the fuck over, that's all. And I'm just wakin' up."

"Okay, and?"

"I look a hot, sloppy mess."

He laughed. "And even in all of ya hot sloppiness, I bet ya still fine as fuck."

"Yeah, okay," I said, laughin'. "But, I still wanna chill and lay down. That's it."

"That works for me," he said. "You can lay in my arms and we can chill together. I had you on the brain all muhfuckin' night, word up. You had a nigga on brick. I'm comin' through. So go do what you gotta do, and I'ma see you in 'bout a half-hour or so."

"I'm not openin' the door," I said, slidin' down into the water. It felt so damn good. I moaned.

"Say what? Aye, yo, don't play with me."

I was too weak to argue with his ass. "I'm not playin'. I'm dead-ass."

"So what you sayin'? You ain't beat to lay up in a nigga's arms? You gonna deprive me from seein' ya fine ass 'cause you went out and got twisted last night? Yo, that's real cold, baby." He lowered his voice. "Come on, baby, I got just what the doctor ordered to make ya feel better."

"Oh, yeah…and what's that?"

He laughed. "I'll show you when I get there." He hung up before I could speak. Instead of callin' his ass back, I flipped the phone shut and placed it on the tub ledge, then laid my head back, slid my hand between my legs, and closed my eyes, smilin'.

"Mmmm…uh…uh…mmm," I moaned as Grant rammed his dick in me for the third time since he had gotten to my spot over two hours ago. The nigga musta been on Viagra or some shit 'cause he just kept goin' and goin' and bustin' off back to back, changin' the condom, then slidin' his dick back up in me. I swear I had no intentions of givin' this fine muhfucka some pussy when he walked up in here lookin' and smellin' all fuckin' good with his fresh cut, fly-ass Gucci runnin' suit, and crispy Air Force Ones. But when the nigga stripped down to his silk boxers and all that dick started swingin' and bouncin' around, a bitch forgot to say no when he started kissin' and rubbin' and lickin' all over me. And the minute he wrapped his soft lips around my titties that was it. Shit started feelin' good and the next thing I know his dick started callin' me loud 'n muthafuckin' crystal clear: "Kat…Kat…Kat…suck me, bitch…drop down on ya knees and wet this big-ass dick." And that's just what I did.

"Uh…" I groaned as Grant pulled his dick outta me again, slowly slid it back in, then tip-drilled me, before slammin' it back in. He banged my pussy deep with 'bout twenty fast strokes, slayin' my pussy to pieces, then grindin' up in me nice 'n slow another twenty strokes, before pickin' up his pace. "Oh, fuck… damn, nigga…Oh, shit…I'm cummin'…"

"That's right, baby, wet daddy's dick up," he grunted, slappin' my ass, then reachin' up under me and playin' with my swollen clit. "Put that sweet cream all over this long, fat dick." I can't even front. As hung over as I was, the nigga had a bitch goin'.

I started throwin' this pussy up on his dick, suckin' and lickin' all over my titties. The deeper his dick went, the wetter my pussy got; the hornier I got, the freakier I wanted it.

"Open up my ass," I said in between a string of moans and groans, "Uh...Mmm...stop teasin' me, nigga...fuck me..." He grabbed me by the hips and started speed fuckin' me, poundin' in and outta me.

"Aaah, shit...damn, girl...this pussy hot...Oh shit, I'm 'bout to bust...where you want it?"

"That's right, nigga," I said, grindin' and windin' my hips. "Give me that nut in the crack of my ass. I wanna feel it run down into my asshole." He pumped a few more times, jabbin' his dick in and outta me with deep rapid strokes before pullin' out. He snatched the rubber off, then started jerkin' his shit.

"Open them pretty ass cheeks up for me," he said, gruntin'. I dug my fingas into my ass and pulled open my soft cheeks as wide as they would go, givin' him a full view of my tight asshole and soppin' wet pussy. "Yeah, baby," he said, slappin' the center of my crack with the weight of his brick-hard dick, "you got a pretty brown hole. You gonna let me get some of that?"

I was so fuckin' heated that this muhfucka coulda fucked me in any and e'ery hole all night if he wanted. Thought he knew. "Yes...oh, yesssssssss!" I screamed, pumpin' my hips like only a ho in heat can. "Wet it with ya nut, muhfucka, then shove ya dick in it." He rubbed and slapped his thick, heavy cock on my ass, then laid it in the center of my crack, rubbin' the shaft against my asshole, then splattered his nut all up in it.

"Oooooh...aaaah...yes..." I started cummin' as his warm, sticky cream slid down into my asshole, drippin' along the back of my pussy. As he smeared his nut in with his thumb, I heard him tearin' another condom wrapper with his teeth, then placin' the rubber over his still-brick dick. I looked back at him, smilin'. "That's right, nigga...run ya dick up in my ass," I said, archin' my back.

I felt the pressure of his dick as he slowly tried to push the tip of his mushroom head into my hole. "Come on, baby...open that ass up for me." He pushed in further. "That's right, baby..."

"Uh...mmm," I moaned, jerkin' forward.

"Don't run, baby...take this dick."

He pushed farther.

"Ooooh...uh...mmmm...oh, yes..."

"That's right...Mmm...yeah, baby...that ass's openin' up."

He pushed further.

"Oh, yes...uh...damn, nigga."

"Come on, baby, take daddy's big dick."

He pushed farther.

"Uh..."

"It's almost there, baby..." He pushed further. "Yeah, just like that...come on...open that sweet ass up for me."

A bitch was startin' to shake. He only had half his dick in. And it was hurtin' and startin' to burn, but feelin' oh so fuckin' good at the same time. It was delicious pain. The kinda pain that shot through my back, crashed up into my stomach, then exploded onto my clit. And by the time he finally got e'ery inch of his nine in me, I had already nutted twice. I arched my back, then buried my face down into the mattress and bit down on the sheets as he grabbed my titties and pulled at my nipples until he had me floatin'. The pressure and heat from this nigga's dick up in my ass had my pussy drippin'. A bitch was on fire!

"Yeah, that's it...it's all in now," he moaned, gettin' into a nice, deep groove. Once I loosened up and got comfortable with his dick inside me, I started pumpin' and windin' and slammin' my hips back. "Yeah, you like that dick, don't you? That's right, baby, fuck daddy's dick…" The muhfucka pumped the hell outta my ass, stretchin' my hole beyond capacity. And I was backin' it up on him, bouncin' and shakin' my ass. "Oh shit, girl…that's it… throw that ass up on this dick…yeah, baby… uh, shit…"

"Aaah…uh…mmm…damn, nigga…uh, I'm cummin'…" I moaned. The nigga had my insides rumblin'. It felt like my uterus was shakin'. "Uh…oooooh…" I was gettin' ready to explode from my asshole to my pussy.

"Damn, baby…ya ass is so tight," he said, grindin' deep inside my ass, then grabbin' me by the hips and long strokin' it. "Aaah, shit! Oh, fuck! This ass is so damn hot and wet. Aaah, fuck! This big dick got you nuttin' out ya ass? That's right, baby…cum all over daddy's dick…"

And together, we moaned, groaned, screamed, and nutted 'til we both passed out sticky, sweaty, and exhausted.

I'm not sure how long we slept, but when I finally opened my eyes, Grant was spoonin' behind me, slidin' his dick back up in my still wet and well-fucked pussy. I swear the nigga was tryna fuck me to death. And this went on from the time the sun went down 'til the sun came up the followin' mornin'.

Eight a.m. the next mornin', the smell of all-night fuckin' was still in the air, and a bitch was still floatin'—and sore—from the dick Grant served me. I can't front, the nigga felt good inside of me, and when he asked if he could hit this pussy raw, I almost caved in and let him. Real talk, I wanted to feel how good the dick woulda been skin to skin. But I ain't no weak bitch so I told his ass no. Ain't no way I was gonna play myself, knowin' the nigga ain't mine. When his cell kept goin' off, it was what a bitch needed to remind her ass that the nigga's fuckin' two other bitches on the regular. Yeah, the dick was right. And, yeah, a bitch wanted to feel his nut up in her. But ain't that much good dick in the world to have me playin' Russian roulette with my fuckin' life, feel me?

As much as I enjoyed havin' a stiff dick up in me, and a nigga layin' next to me in bed, the reality of him not bein' my man was as bright as the fuckin' sun that was startin' to shine through my blinds. Though there was somethin' 'bout the nigga's style I was really diggin', I wasn't beat to be sharin' a nigga and his dick with another bitch. And I definitely wasn't down with no Casanova-type nigga who was givin' the dick to a slew of bitches.

Grant was still sleep, snorin'. Well…actually, it sounded more like purrin', and rightfully so after the balls-deep dick suckin' I put on his ass last night, then again early this mornin'. Had the nigga's whole body shakin' as he twisted up his face and moaned and begged, tryna get me up offa his shit 'cause he wasn't ready to spit.

The nigga's phone started goin' off again. He was either in a deep coma or was layin' there iggin' it. I shook his ass. "You need to answer ya shit, or turn it off," I said.

He grunted, stretchin' and rollin' over. "What time is it?" he asked, pickin' his phone up off the nightstand, glancin' at the time, then checkin' the caller ID. "I ain't beat," he said, turnin' it off.

I smirked. "Somebody is really tryna get at ya ass. Don't you think you should listen to ya messages?"

"Nah, they can wait," he responded, gettin' outta bed. He stretched again. His dick was thick and heavy, stickin' out like a bat. A bitch's mouth started droolin'. He walked into the bathroom, leavin' the door open. I heard the stream of heavy piss hittin' the water, then the water from the faucet. He walked back into the room. I frowned my face. "What?" he asked, lookin' all stupid 'n shit.

"Nigga, flush my toilet. That's what."

He sucked his teeth. "Oh, here you go." But he took his ass back up in there and flushed it.

"And I hope you put my lid down," I said. He came back into the room, then slid back into bed, pullin' me into him.

"I want some more of that good pussy," he said, runnin' his hand over my titties, squeezin' my nipples, then runnin' his hands up and down my leg. He started searchin' for my pussy, but I clamped my legs shut and pumped his brakes.

"Let's be clear on some things," I said, facin' him eye-to-eye. "This pussy is not at ya disposal—whenever, however, or wherever you want it. We fucked all through the night and through the wee hours of the mornin', and it was all good—"

"But," he said, pressin' his body up against me. He kissed me on the lips, then sucked on my lips.

"I'm tryna talk to you," I said, turnin' my face.

"I'm listenin'," he said, squeezin' my ass and kissin' me on my neck. The heat from his breath made my skin tingle. He started grindin' his hard dick into me.

"I'm serious, nigga."

His hand slid between my legs. His fingas played with my clit. "I'm serious, too. Go 'head, tell me what you want, baby."

This nigga was fuckin' with my head. All my thoughts, e'erything a bitch wanted to say, got stuck in my brain. I let out a moan. "I want…uh, I mean…"

"That's right, baby," he whispered, slippin' and dippin' his two fingas in and outta my pussy. "Let daddy give you what you want."

I moaned again.

The phone rang. It was my house line.

"Let it ring," he said. "Whoever it is...let 'em call back. Right now, you all mine."

After the eighth ring, it stopped. My heart started racin'. "I told you this pussy ain't at ya disposal," I said, clampin' my legs 'round his hand. He dug his fingas deeper, like he was searchin' for somethin'. He pressed harder, deeper, brushed my clit with his thumb. Found what he was lookin' for. I let out a loud moan, humped his hand, yanked my head back and started buckin'.

"That's right, baby...yeah, just like that. Bust that nut for daddy." I grabbed his dick, stroked it. Nice 'n slow. Squeezed it; rubbed my finga over the slit, felt the precum seepin' outta the head of his dick. "Yeah, baby. See what you do to me? You got my dick on brick."

"We need to talk." I pushed out in between another moan. The nigga had another nut swellin' up inside of me.

"I'm listenin'," he said, kissin' all over my face, my lips, then my neck. He took his free hand and grabbed my titty, then leaned over and stuck my nipple in his mouth and started suckin' all over it like he was thirstin' for milk. I thought he was gonna stuff my whole titty in his mouth. He gently rolled my nipple between his teeth, then pressed down, lightly tuggin' it.

I let out a loud moan.

He pulled his fingas outta me, stuck 'em in my mouth, then rolled up on top of me while I sucked my sweet sticky juice off of 'em. I opened my legs as wide as they could go so he could lay his dick on my pussy, teasin' my clit.

"Fuck...oh, God..."

"You gonna let me put this dick up in this good pussy?" he asked, breathin' all heavy in my ear. His dick was feelin' so good pressed up between my swollen lips. My clit throbbed. "C'mon, baby...let daddy get up in this wet pussy."

Now, I know a bitch said no—well, at least I thought I did—but, somehow the shit didn't sound like me. The nigga had his hands roamin' all over my body, and was kissin' all over me—my face, my neck, my shoulders, my titties, my stomach, my pussy, my knees, all the way down to my toes. Then he turned me over and started kissin' the bottom of my feet, my calves, the back of my thighs, my ass cheeks, my asshole, then all over my back. And before I knew it, he had pulled open my ass and slid his long dick deep into the back of my pussy. E'erything I thought I wanted to say to his ass 'bout thinkin' he was gonna fuck me whenever he wanted, 'bout him thinkin' he was gonna have me and them two other bitches on his cock, 'bout not tryna put claims on me, 'bout me not bein' built to compete with no bitch for a nigga's attention, went right outta my head.

"Uh...mmmph...oh, yes," I moaned. "Mmmph...mmmph... uh..."

"Yeah, baby...this good, tight pussy's all mine...is this hot pussy mine, baby?"

Hell no! I screamed in my head. But the words got jumbled up in the back of my throat and came out soundin' like a string of deep moans. He locked his arms up under mine, then slow fucked me, askin' the question again. The nigga had my pussy poppin' like a firecracker; sparks were shootin' all through me. I pumped and twirled my hips, clutchin' his dick with my pussy muscles, but a bitch never said one way or the other if this pussy was his or not. Sometimes it's just best to let a muhfucka think what it is he wanna think, so that's exactly what I did. I moaned and groaned and nutted all over his dick, never sayin' a word.

CHAPTER TWENTY

"Bitch, you got a lotta fuckin' nerve, talkin' reckless to Tameka," Tamia spat into the phone.

I rolled my eyes. I knew it was only a matter of time before this ho was gonna call tryna get at me. But on some real shit, I wasn't in the fuckin' mood.

"Bitch, get over it," I snapped. "That shit you talkin' happened almost two weeks ago. I ain't even thinkin' 'bout ya trick-ass sister. If I wanted to get at that bitch I woulda been served her, trust."

"Yeah, whatever," she huffed, blowin' air into the phone. "You always tryna talk slick 'n greasy, bitch. You need ya ass beat down for real, for real."

"Well, it won't be that ho who does it," I said, shiftin' the phone from one ear to the other. "And it definitely won't be you."

"Whatever. You don't really want it."

"No, ho, *you* don't want it."

"Kat, on some real shit, I ain't beat for ya ass, okay." She blew into the phone again. "I swear, bitch, if this wasn't an emergency, I wouldn't even be fuckin' with ya stank ass."

"Bitch, what are you talkin' 'bout…emergency? What the fuck happened?"

"I know you and ya moms beefin' 'n shit, but I thought you

might wanna know she left up outta here on a stretcher. I think her and that dude she's fuckin' with got into it."

I blinked, blinked again, pullin' the phone from my ear and lookin' at it before puttin' it back up to my ear. "Excuse me?" I asked in disbelief. "What did you say?"

"Ya moms left in an ambulance. I heard she was unconscious..."

Tamia's voice started driftin' as I thought about all the muh-fuckas my mother let run in and outta her life; all the times I watched her balled-up, cryin' over a nigga; saw her face all beat the fuck up, heard her beggin' a muhfucka not to leave her. Countless times she got caught up in bullshit off-again, on-again relationships. Niggas knew she was weak, and they knew what to say to get her right where they wanted her—lost and all fucked up in the head over 'em. Muhfuckas smelled her weakness a mile away. And I hated them for usin' her, and I hated her even more for bein' weak and stupid enough to let 'em.

I felt like my life was flashin' before my eyes as I half-listened to Tamia and thought 'bout all the times I ran in tryna pull a muhfucka up offa my moms, or jumped in the middle to keep the nigga from hittin' her, or how I'd fight him, and she'd somehow always find a way to flip the script and blame me, like it was my fault the nigga was beatin' on her ass. Like it was my fault the nigga bounced. And she'd spend days, sometimes weeks, not fuckin' speakin' to me, ignorin' me, treatin' me like I was fuckin' invisible, takin' her fucked-up life out on me. This is the woman I'm 'posed to feel sorry for; the woman I'm 'posed to trust and love when she always puts a muthafuckin' nigga before me. I'm 'posed to embrace her with open arms like she really ever gave a fuck 'bout me. Yeah, well...I tried that shit. And it got me no-fuckin'-where. I'll be damned if I get sucked back into tryna save her ass from herself.

"...We all outside, and they takin' her to Kings County," she continued. "The police got the nigga all cuffed up 'n shit."

I sighed. "T, thanks for callin', but she's on her own. I ain't breakin' my neck for her ass, not this time. Not ever again, real talk. I'm done tryna save a ho who ain't tryna be saved."

"Kat, that's real fucked up. That's ya moms, regardless."

"Oh, well. Life is fucked up, and so is she. So she gets what she gets. And that's what it is."

"Bitch, is you fuckin' nuts? You mean to tell me you can't get over yourself for one minute to check for ya moms?"

I sucked my teeth. "Exactly," I said. "Let's be clear: I don't give a fuck. So pump ya brakes. I don't get up in ya relationship with ya moms, so don't try 'n serve it up in mine. That chick, moms or not, is a grown-ass woman, and she's responsible for her own choices, not me. So, I ain't tryna get caught up in 'em. She's made her choices, and I'm makin' mine. And a bitch chooses to keep my distance from her ass."

I didn't give a fuck 'bout what Tamia, or anybody else, thought for that matter. I was done. At some point a bitch gotta stop lettin' muhfuckas fuck with her head. I mean, damn...how many times a muhfucka gotta smear shit on a bitch before her ass realizes it ain't chocolate? Give me a fuckin' break. I don't care how many times I try, I will never, ever, be able to wrap my mind around a chick lovin' a nigga more than she loves herself. On some real shit, what kinda fool is she? I mean, if that's what it takes to be loved, then I'ma be one old, lonely ass, dick-deprived bitch 'cause I'll be damned if I ever let a nigga beat my ass, disrespect, or try 'n play me.

"That's real fuckin' heartless."

"And on some real shit, Tamia, so is fuckin' niggas raw when you know you got blisters on ya pussy, so don't come at me, bitch."

"Bitch," she yelled, "Fuck you!"

"No, sweetie, fuck you," I snapped back. "You need to check ya'self before you try 'n check me on shit, for real. I 'preciate you hittin' me up 'n shit, but do me a favor, don't call me again. I don't wanna hear shit else 'bout Juanita Perez."

I hung up on her ass. Then found myself thinkin' 'bout my father. I hadn't given his nonexistent ass a thought in years. And all of a sudden he popped up in my head. I wondered if he ever beat my mom's ass, or was he too busy dissin' her with other bitches. On some real shit, I closed my eyes and tried to see his face, tried to remember what the nigga looked like in my head, but the shit was a big blur. He was a fuckin' invisible man to me, a faceless stranger. At this point in my life, he wasn't much more than a figment of my imagination.

I took a deep breath, then slowly blew it out. Tamia's ass had stressed a bitch out. I tore through the house lookin' for a damn blunt. When I found my stash, I opened a box of Phillies, took one out, split the shit down the middle with my razor, then packed it with trees. I rolled the shit up nice 'n tight, then sparked up. The shit was good as hell. I rolled two more 'cause I knew I was gonna need 'em before the day ended.

Ten minutes later, my cell started ringin'. This time it was Chanel. "Hello."

"Kat, girl, I just got off the phone with T. Sorry to hear 'bout ya moms. She told me how you started spazzin' out 'n shit."

"Don't be sorry for her ass," I said, walkin' downstairs to my media room. I knew Tamia's gossipin' ass couldn't wait to get off the phone so she could call Chanel. I plopped down on my butter-soft, cranberry leather sofa. "She got what she deserved. I wasn't spazzin' 'bout nothin', trust. I kept shit real with the bitch, and she wasn't tryna hear it."

"Kat, I don't think anyone deserves to be beat on."

"Well, maybe not. But when you keep allowin' fucked-up niggas in ya life, then you gonna keep gettin' fucked over and fucked up. It is what it is. As far as I'm concerned, if a bitch can't learn her lesson after the second or third time, then her dumb ass deserves to get her biscuit pushed in. I have no respect for a bitch who lets a man define her happiness—or worse, who she is as a woman."

"Whether she learns or not, niggas shouldn't be puttin' they hands on no woman, Kat. And you know it. I don't care how many times she chooses the wrong muhfucka."

"Well, guess what? We can agree to disagree. But at the end of the day, a woman needs to take responsibility for her choices in men. Period. If her ass keeps choosin' the same type of nigga, then maybe she needs to take a long, hard look in the mirror, and stop makin' excuses. A bitch's choices are 'bout her, not 'bout what the fuck some nigga does to her silly ass. If she doesn't love herself, then how the fuck she gonna expect a nigga to love her? And if she doesn't know how to love herself, then guess what? You can't expect a muhfucka to know how to either. I don't care what you or anyone else says, muhfuckas only gonna do what you allow 'em to do to ya."

"Yeah, you right," she said, sighin'. "It's still fucked up."

"Well, when bitches stand up and stop makin' fucked-up choices, then maybe it won't be that way, but it is. And it's always gonna be that way 'cause you and I both know that there's always gonna be a woman out here who can't live, think, breathe, or move without a man, or a dick stuffed in her ass. We both know there are a bunch of hard-pressed bitches out there who will put up with almost anything a muhfucka dishes out to her ass."

"True," she said, pausin'. "So, I guess you dead serious 'bout not goin' to the hospital, or at least callin' to make sure ya moms is aiight?"

"I'm serious as a fuckin' heart attack," I said.

"Don't you wanna know what happened to her?"

"She got her ass beat, *again*," I answered, takin' a deep toke on my blunt. I blew the smoke up into the air. "So what else is there to know?" I paused, waitin' for her to respond. When she didn't, I continued. "Not a damn thing. It was only a matter of time before it happened. When she gets sick and tired of bein' sick and tired of openin' her legs up to fucked-up niggas, then maybe she'll wake the fuck up and make some changes in her life. But until then, I ain't beat. 'Cause I know like you know, the first chance she gets, she'll be right back on her knees suckin' that nigga's dick. And if it's not his, it'll be some other muhfucka's. So, no thank you. I'll have no part in what the fuck she does."

It got real silent for a minute and I knew Chanel was thinkin' 'bout what to say next, but she knew she'd catch it so she let it go. "I feel you," she finally said, sighin'. "Anyway, listen…I was gettin' ready to dial ya number before Tamia hit me up. Have you heard from Iris?"

"No, why?" I asked, pickin' up this book, *Get Money Chicks*, I had bought at Borders a few days ago, off the glass table, then flippin' through it. "Her dumb ass is probably somewhere mulin' for that nigga." I shook my head, glancing at a chapter where one of the dumb-ass chicks in the book was doin' the same shit. Humph. These stupid bitches are e'ery where! "Bitches nowadays too busy tryna do them to give a fuck 'bout pickin' up a phone to let a bitch know they aiight, so I wouldn't even stress ya'self."

"Well, I wouldn't be if her moms hadn't called me lookin' for her, and Tamia hasn't heard from her either. That's not like her.

Her moms sounded real worried. She said she hadn't heard from her in three days, and she's not answerin' her cell."

"Humph. The bitch's probably laid up somewhere with a dick shoved down her throat," I stated, tossin' the book back on the table. There was no need to read shit 'bout a bunch of dumb bitches when I already knew two dumb ones up close 'n personal. I sparked another blunt, then pulled it deep into my lungs until the shit burned. I coughed.

"What, you blazin'?" she asked.

"Yep," I said. "Straight to the muthafuckin' head. I'ma get lifted all fuckin' day."

She laughed. "With ya fiend ass. Save me some."

The call waitin' beeped. I glanced at the number. It was my aunt Rosa. I let the shit roll into voicemail. "Why, you comin' through?"

"Hell yeah," she replied, soundin' all excited 'n shit. I could almost see the bitch droolin'. "I'm throwin' on some clothes right now. I'll be there in half an hour."

"Who's soundin' like the fiend, now?" I asked, laughin'.

"Whatever, ho," she said, joinin' in my laughter. "You need me to pick up anything while I'm out?"

"Nope."

"Bet. I see ya in a minute."

"Lata, trick." As soon as I hung up with Chanel, the Kat line rang. I answered, "Yeah?"

"What's good, pretty baby?"

I rolled my eyes. "Life," I said. "Now tell me what I gotta do to get you outta mine?"

He laughed. "Oh, shit. That's cold. But, if ya really wanna know, then I'ma keep shit real. Let me take ya fine ass away for the weekend so I can slide this big, black dick up in ya guts."

Cash was one funny muhfucka. I couldn't even get mad at the nigga 'cause I knew he was talkin' shit. But I still had to check his ass. "Muhfucka," I said. "I'd take two to the head before I ever let you run ya dick up in me. I don't give a fuck how big it is. Believe that."

"Then you need to let me eat that pussy."

I shook my head, laughin'. As ugly as his muhfuckin' ass was, his dick and tongue game were probably wicked. On some real shit, the nigga looked like he could tear some pussy up. The imprint of his thick dick flashed in my head. *What the fuck is wrong with me*, I thought, shakin' the image outta my head. My private cell started ringin', then my house phone. I let them shits go into voicemail.

"Wrong answer, nigga. You can't even sniff my pantyliner."

"Damn, you sure know how ta crush a nigga's spirits. Let me stop fuckin' with you. I mean, don't get it twisted; I'd dick and tongue you down in a heartbeat, stretch that fat ass right out the box, but I know you ain't havin' it. I like talkin' shit to ya nasty ass, ma."

"Yeah, whatever," I said. "Now, how can I help you?"

"I got some outta town work for ya."

My phones rang again.

"Oh, yeah," I said, goin' upstairs to put somethin' on before Chanel got here. I had been chillin' in my lace panties. "Where and when?"

"Vegas. In three days."

Even though I'd been to Vegas in February for All-Star weekend, I hadn't really gotten a chance to take in much of the happenin's. Besides, it was so fuckin' packed I couldn't really move like I wanted. So goin' back was all good. I figured I could hit the Fashion Show Mall on the strip to hopefully buy some bangin' shit, check out that show Zumanity at New York-New York, and maybe even gamble it up a bit.

"Cool. I'll fly out a day or two early and chill."

He laughed. "Why the fuck I know you was gonna say that shit?"

"'Cause that's how I do mine. You already know."

"Do you, ma. Just make sure you handle ya business on time. I don't want none of that bullshit you pulled in San Diego. Matter of fact, I shoulda docked ya ass for holdin' shit up."

Against my better judgment, I decided to fuck with the nigga. "Cash, if you ever fuck with my money, you'll never get any of this pussy, feel me? But if ya keep my paper flowin' like ya 'posed to, then one day I might invite ya to slide ya tongue up in it. So if you ever wanna taste of this sweet pussy, don't fuck with my paper."

"Yeah, aiight," he said, lowerin' his voice. "Keep fuckin' with me, Kat, and I'ma end up takin' it, ya heard?"

"And ya'll end up with a bullet in ya skull, muhfucka."

"Damn, baby, you get my dick hard e'erytime you talk like that. Word up."

"Ugh. Send me the paperwork, along with my paper, Cash."

"You'll have e'erything you need tomorrow afternoon."

"Good."

"Be easy," he said, hangin' up. I swear he makes me fuckin' sick sometimes. I glanced at the clock and noticed Chanel's ass was late as usual. It was 3:15. I figured the ho would be another hour or so, so I decided to take a quick shower.

By the time Chanel rang my doorbell two hours later, I was already on my third blunt, and a bitch was lifted lovely.

"Ho," I snapped, swingin' the door open, "I thought you said you was gonna be here in a half hour. You betta be glad I like ya yellow ass or you'd be standin' outside."

"Whatever, tramp." She laughed, walkin' in carryin' a bangin'-ass, white pebbled leather Prada weekend bag. She was lookin' all fly 'n whatnot in a slick-ass white linen jumper and a pair of strappy heels.

"I know you don't think ya ugly ass is stayin' the night. I ain't runnin' no damn ho house."

"I can't tell," she said, closin' the door behind her and followin' me into the kitchen. "They have ya ass listed in the Yellow Pages under 'Hoes for Rent.'" She dropped her bag by the door, then walked over to the refrigerator and opened it.

"Whatever, bitch," I said, throwin' my hand up in her face. I pressed the Bose remote and Me'Shell NdegéOcello's "Dead Nigga Blvd., Pt. I" blared through the speakers.

"I'm hungry as hell. What you got to eat up in this piece?"

"Not a damn thing. You know ain't shit domesticated 'bout me."

She sucked her teeth. "And that's why ya ass can't get ya'self a man."

"Whatever, ho," I said, dismissin' her with the flick of my hand. "I'm good. You worry 'bout keepin' ya ass a man."

"Speaking of which," she said, closin' the fridge door, then leanin' on the aisle counter. I pulled out some menus from outta the counter drawer, then tossed them to her. I puffed the blunt, watchin' her flip through each one. "Divine told me to tell ya ass 'wassup.' That nigga funny as hell. He started buggin' when he saw me packin' my overnight bag. He was like, 'Where the fuck ya ass goin?' Then as soon as I told him I was chillin' with you tonight, he was like, 'Oh, aiight.'" She started laughin'. "But let it be me tryna chill with T or Iris, and the nigga starts straight blackin' for real. That nigga's crazy. He really can't stand them two."

We each pulled out a stool and sat at the counter.

"Humph, I wonder why," I said sarcastically. "What you wanna eat?"

"Let's do Chinese. I want the garlic shrimp with brown rice. And two spring rolls. You treatin', right?" I rolled my eyes, pickin' up the cordless to call our order in. "Thanks, babe," she said, smilin'. "And why the fuck you hoggin' that damn blunt, bitch. Puff, puff, pass...I'm tryna get my smoke on too, greedy heifer."

"Kiss my ass, trick," I said, takin' another pull, then handin' it to her, laughin'. I started rollin' two more.

When Me'Shell's "Priorities 1-6" came on, Chanel closed her eyes and started swayin'. "I love this chick. She's the fuckin' truth." She took another toke from the blunt, then handed it to me. I took two pulls and swayed with her.

"Yeah, she ain't to be fucked with," I agreed. "These weak-ass chicks in the game don't really want it with her."

We sliced open six more cigars, removed the tobacco, then packed 'em with weed. I watched Chanel as she expertly slid her tongue across the cigar paper like she was lickin' the edges of a dick to moisten it, before fillin' it with trees. She rolled the last blunt between her thumbs and index fingas, then placed it on the table with the rest of 'em.

"On some real shit, I think she's too deep for a lotta these bitches out here. Her musical style is so damn fly to me."

I nodded, takin' a pull from the blunt while Chanel lit another one. I closed my eyes when "Andromeda & the Milky Way" came on. We sat in silence, smoked, and grooved to Me'Shell. The funky soul beats were so fuckin' tight that I wanted to light candles, lay my head back, and drift into a zone.

"Would you let her eat your pussy?" Chanel asked outta the blue, fuckin' up the mood. I almost choked.

"What?" I asked, shocked.

She repeated the question. "Would you let her go down on you?"

"That's it, bitch," I said, reachin' for the blunt, "no more smoke for ya ass. You talkin' real sideways now."

She started laughin' 'n shit. "I'm just sayin'."

I raised my eyebrow, placin' my hand on my hip. "Bitch, is there somethin' you tryna tell me?"

"No, I'm just sayin'. I mean, she really does her thing, musically. And some of her joints got a freaky-sexy groove that be makin' me wanna get it in."

"Well, ho, you make sure you ain't tryna get it in here. I don't wanna split ya shit up for tryna get at my pussy."

"Bitch, please," she said, laughin'. "I ain't on it like that. I was just askin'. Besides, you ain't my type."

"Mmm-hmm. Yeah, aiight. Try that freaky shit if you want."

"Whatever…aaah, shit," she said, jumpin' up when the song "I'm Diggin' You" came on. "Bitch, you need to burn this shit for me. Who made this mix for you? The shit is tight."

"I did," I said, watchin' her shake her big, round ass and swing her hips. On some real shit though, if I was into chicks, I'd probably strap on a dildo and rock her ass. But I wouldn't tongue-fuck her. That was out. This ho done had too many dicks up in her. I frowned at the thought of havin' my face between her legs. Ugh!

My phone rang. I picked it up off the counter and glanced at the number. It was my aunt Rosa again. I sat the phone back down. Two minutes later, my cell rang, then my home line again. I turned my cell off.

Chanel looked at me, then the phones. She took a pull from

the half-blunt, then exhaled the smoke up into the air. "Don't you think you should at least check ya messages? It could be 'bout ya moms."

I shrugged. "I ain't beat."

She opened her mouth to say somethin', but I raised my brow and gave her a warnin' look to keep her muthafuckin' mouth shut. And she did.

Thirty minutes later we were sittin' at the table eatin' our food, drinkin' and smokin' mad trees. My phone kept ringin' off the hook, and I kept iggin' the shit.

Chanel set her fork down and eyed me. "Kat, you—"

"Don't," I warned, liftin' my index finga to stop her.

She raised her hands up. "Okay, you got that." She picked up her fork and started eatin' again. In between her forkfuls of shrimp, she asked, changin' the subject, "What's good with you and that fine nigga Grant?"

I eyed this bitch, but kept it cute. "We been talkin'," I offered, slowly slidin' a forkful of vegetable lo mein into my mouth. I chewed, then swallowed. "We actually went out a few times."

"When?" she asked, surprised. "And why am I just now hearin' 'bout it?"

"A few weeks now," I told her, tryna front like it was no biggie. "I didn't say shit 'cause there ain't shit to say. We kicked it a few times, and we'll see what happens."

"Please tell me you gave the nigga some pussy."

"And why would I do that?"

She popped her eyes open, and bobbed her neck back 'n forth, makin' suckin' sounds with her lips. "Uh, duh, 'cause ya ass ain't tasted dick since dick tasted you."

I laughed. "You're a fuckin' nut."

"Uh-huh," she said, laughin'. "Somethin' ya ass needs." She looked at me, tiltin' her head, then raisin' her eyebrow. "So you went out a few times with dude, and you didn't even grind up on the nigga."

"Nope," I lied. "Not yet."

"So you don't even know if the nigga's packin'?"

I shook my head, shiftin' my eyes 'round the room, then started rollin' another blunt. On some real shit, I don't know why I felt like I had to lie to her, but I didn't feel like discussin' his dick game with her, which is what the bitch would be askin' next if I told her the truth. We always had a rule that if we were diggin' a nigga we'd never ask the other 'bout his dick skills, but the way her hot ass was checkin' for him at the club, I would have to watch her real close if I did decided to fuck with him. Girls or not, a bitch's pussy tended to think for itself when it came to fuckin' someone else's man. Fuck what ya heard. A bitch in heat has no conscience. I sparked another blunt, took two pulls, then handed it to her.

"I ain't on his dick like that," I answered.

"Hmm...well, speakin' of dick," she said, takin' a pull of the blunt. "Oh, fuck..." *Psssph. Psssph.* "This is some good shit." She took another pull, then held it in her lungs before blowin' it out.

"Bitch, will you shut ya fiend-ass up, and tell me what the fuck you was gettin' ready to tell me."

She took another toke from the blunt, then passed it back to me. "I fucked that fine nigga Coal."

"Get. The. Fuck. Out. Bitch, you lyin'. When?"

She started gettin' all amped 'n shit, tellin' me how he called her a few days after she had slipped him her number at the 40/40 Club. She told him she wanted to fuck and he was down, but couldn't get at her until his chick went outta town on business or some shit. And as soon as she did, he'd be ready to dig her guts out. I tilted my head and stared at her ass in disbelief.

"What? Why you lookin' at me like that?"

"Un-fuckin'-believable," I said, stickin' a forkful of sesame chicken in my mouth. "I can't believe you fucked him."

"When have you ever known me to lie on some dick?"

"Never," I admitted, grinnin'. I twirled my fork. "Go on… when and where did this illicit affair take place?"

"Two nights ago," she said, dippin' her spring roll in a plate of duck sauce, then takin' a bite. "The nigga hit me up and told me to meet him at the Brooklyn Marriott, and that's all she wrote. The nigga had the room for two days, and we fucked day and night. Girl, that muhfucka got an extra-thick, black dick, and can go the distance. Oh, my God, Kat, that nigga can fuck. It ain't all that long, but when I tell you he knows how to use that shit, oh, my God. Humph. I can see how a bitch falls in love with a nigga's dick. He fucked me so good, I started to shake."

I laughed at her silly ass as she rapidly shook in her seat like she was havin' a seizure or some shit.

She stopped. "Kat, that muthafucka almost had a bitch in tears."

I shook my head, chucklin' at the thought of Chanel's ass boo-hooin' while gettin' dicked down. Now I've had my share of some good dick, but not any good enough to make a bitch break down cryin'.

"And where was Divine while you were out gettin' ya pussy stretched?"

"In Miami doin' him. You know if his ass is around ain't no way I'ma be able to ride another nigga's dick. Hell, that nigga would be tryna get some pussy as soon as I stepped back up in the house.

And you know a bitch gotta give her pussy at least three days' rest to snap back, feel me?"

I laughed. "You'se a damn fool."

"Fuck that," she said, handin' me the blunt, "I might be a ho, but I ain't a messy one. There's three things I won't do, and that's let a nigga who ain't my man go raw in me, let a nigga nut in my mouth, and fuck my man right after fuckin' another nigga. That's straight nasty and an absolute no-no, which is why I live by the three-day rule. So the only way I'm fuckin' another muhfucka is when I know Divine's ass is outta town and I got at least three days to regroup."

I shook my head in disbelief. "And did the nigga hit you with some paper?"

"Nope," she said. "That's not what I wanted from his ass."

I blinked, then blinked again. Now, I knew if the nigga was Cash's nephew, then he was a get-money nigga. Ain't no way Cash would have that nigga bummin'. Then again, if he fucked as good as she said he did, maybe his chick was lacin' his ass. Nah, fuck that, that fine, black muhfucka had to be sittin' on some ends. "Well, did you at least get a handbag or some heels outta his ass?"

"Nope," she said, twistin' her lips and frownin' up her face. "That's what I got Divine for."

"So what happened to all that 'I'ma be fuckin' ya man and runnin' his pockets before the end of summer' shit?'"

"Oh, please," she said, wavin' me on with her hand, "he can keep whatever's in his pockets. I ain't beat."

I stared at her ass. Now, either this bitch had changed her gold-diggin' ways or that nigga Coal had literally fucked her brains inside out, 'cause the ho looked at me like I had snot and boogas hangin' from outta my nose or some shit.

"Okay, so you're sayin' you wanted nothin' from the nigga?"

"Not a damn thing. Just a ride on that sweet, black dick; that's it."

"Wait a minute, so you fucked this nigga, knowin' he got a chick, just for the hell of it when you got a nigga who laces ya ass lovely?

"Yep," she said, grinnin'. "And the nigga fucked me like the world was endin'."

"Bitch, is you serious?"

"I sure am. Now, don't get me wrong. Divine holds it down, and I dig him for it. But like I told you a while back, his dick game is real whack. Granted, the nigga can fuck nonstop if you let 'im. However, no matter how many times I try to teach him, he still insists on fuckin' me like a damn bunny rabbit, and bustin' off all quick. I'm sorry, but all that quick humpin' and nuttin' ain't doin' it for me. I don't care how many times he can get it up. At the end of the day, I need a nigga who knows how to rock this pussy inside out."

I rolled my eyes. I tell you, bitches ain't ever fuckin' satisfied. If they got a nigga who's lacin' they asses and treatin' 'em right, it ain't good enough. The bitch'll still find somethin' to complain 'bout. He can't fuck, his dick ain't big enough, he's too fuckin' borin', he ain't hood enough, he ain't rough enough, blah, blah, blah. Give me a fuckin' break!

"So you mean to tell me you'd risk losin' a nigga who treats you right for some dick from a muhfucka who ain't comin' to the table with nothin' but a hot nut and who ain't ever gonna leave his chick for ya ass."

She stared at me, then blinked. "Hell yeah," she said, snatchin' the blunt outta my hand, then puffin'. "I ain't tryna marry the nigga. I fucked him for a tune-up. He stretched this pussy out, knocked the sides around, and now I'm good. If we hook up again, cool. If not, no biggie. I wanted to fuck 'im and I did. But a muhfucka who got a wifey ain't someone I'm tryna check for."

"So you sayin' you don't want 'im for ya'self?"

"Not hardly," she said, twistin' her lips up. "Why the fuck would I want that? That nigga ain't shit for creepin' on his chick."

"And neither are you, ho," I said, laughin' while lightin' another blunt. "For fuckin' on a nigga who thinks he done wifed ya hot ass."

She laughed. "Well, as far as I'm concerned, a ho who ain't ready to be wifed is a ho playin' house. And that's exactly what the fuck I'm doin'."

"Humph," I grunted, stickin' another forkful of lo mein in my mouth. "And it's shit like that that causes a nigga to push a bitch's biscuit in. You hoes need to stop playin' niggas. Just keep the shit funky, and let the muhfucka know what time it is."

"Yeah, whatever. Niggas stay playin' us. It is what it is. You play or get played; you already know."

"What I know is, you gonna end up with ya grill wrecked if you don't get ya mind right. It's only a matter of time before the shit catches up to you, trust."

We passed the blunt back 'n forth for a while, sayin' nothin'. I left Chanel in her thoughts and she left me in mine. Me'Shell NdegéOcello's song "Faithful" came on, and I smiled, shakin' my head. *How fittin'*, I thought, hummin' along. I guess she was right when she said no one is faithful.

My house phone rang again, breakin' the silence. I ignored it. Chanel glared at me. I rolled my eyes, suckin' my teeth. "Aiight, aiight," I said, pickin' it up and answerin' it. It was Rosa again. "Hello."

"Kat?"

"Yeah?"

"This is ya Aunt Rosa," she said, soundin' outta breath. I exhaled, pushin' my plate to the side. "You need to get down to Kings County Hospital ASAP. That nigga ya moms is fuckin' with done beat her ass. I told her not to fuck with that punk ass, but…"

I placed the phone up against my chest, coverin' the receiver. "Bitch," I hissed at Chanel, mean-muggin' her ass. "Go downstairs to the bar and fix me a hit of Rémy." She laughed, gettin' up from her seat. "On second thought, make that shit two hits."

I put the phone back up to my ear.

"…he done broke her jaw and beat her face in."

I closed my eyes tight. Bit down on my bottom lip.

"We've been tryna reach ya ass all damn day," another voice jumped in. I frowned. It sounded like Patrice, but I wasn't sure.

"Who is this?" I asked, lightin' another blunt. I already knew this conversation was gonna turn real messy in a few minutes.

"It's Patrice," she said, suckin' her teeth.

"We're on three-way," Aunt Rosa stated.

"Why?" I asked. Chanel came back into the kitchen with two drinks in her hand. I snatched the one she handed to me, gulped the shit down in one quick motion, then reached over and took hers from her and gulped that one down. The shit burned goin' down.

"'Cause ya moms is in the fuckin' hospital," Patrice snapped. "And we've been blowin' ya fuckin' phone up, leavin' messages 'n shit, and you don't even have the decency to call a muthafucka back. Duh, now follow the yellow brick road, bitch."

"Fuck you, you cum-guzzlin' bitch!" I yelled back.

"Will ya'll two bitches shut the fuck up," Aunt Rosa said, "with all this back 'n forth bullshit for one goddamn minute. Kat, you need to get to the hospital."

I rolled my eyes. "For what?"

"For what?!?" they both yelled.

"Bitch, is you serious?!" Patrice screamed.

"Didn't you hear a word I fuckin' said, Kat?" Aunt Rosa jumped in, soundin' real tight. Please, like I gave a fuck. "I just told ya ass that ya moms is in the goddamn hospital and you need to get ya ass over to Brooklyn *now!*"

I started buckin' my eyes and twistin' up my lips, mockin' her ass. Then the bitch started goin' off on one of her tangents 'bout how she wished one of her kids would come outta they faces talkin' shit the way I did, disrespectin' my moms; 'bout how she can't believe I'd come out my neck talkin' all sideways 'n shit after e'erything my moms had done for me.

What the fuck? I thought, shakin' my head.

"I can't fuckin' believe you," she said. "I woulda banged ya damn grill out."

"Oh, my God." I laughed. "Aunt Rosa, please don't tell me you back on that shit again."

"*Whaaat?!?* Kat, don't have me slap the shit outta you. My name ain't Juanita. I'm ya aunt and all, and I love ya ass to death, but ho, I'd cut ya muthafuckin' throat if you ever come at me like that again."

"Rosa," Patrice jumped in. "I told ya ass how fuckin' disrespect-ful Kat is. She don't give a fuck 'bout nobody but herself. She stay talkin' slick 'n greasy."

I laughed at both they asses.

"Bitch, this shit ain't funny," Aunt Rosa said.

"You right, it ain't. But ya'll tryna come at me on some tag-team shit is."

"Rosa, I don't even know why you bother. I already told you

what it was with this bitch. Kat be on some other shit. Now you see why I don't fuck with her like that."

That did it. Between the drinks and all the trees, a bitch was ready to bring it to 'em. I read both of them hoes. "No, *bitch*," I snapped, "I don't fuck with *you*. Don't get it twisted."

"Kat, watch ya fuckin' mouth," Rosa said.

"No, you watch yours," I said back. "You called me. I didn't call you. And then you got the nerve to have me on fuckin' three-way with Pat's whore ass. So now let me tell both of you one goddamn thing. Patrice, you already know I don't give a hot fuck 'bout you, bitch. So you can suck shit and die. And on some real shit, I'ma be the bitch to spit on ya fuckin' grave. And Aunt Rosa, I love you too, boo. But don't get the shit twisted. The only thing Juanita ever did was spread open her muthafuckin' legs, and let niggas run over her. So fuck all that extra shit you talkin'. How the fuck you know what the fuck she's done for me when ya ass stayed coked the fuck up when I was growin' up?

"You don't know what the fuck she's done for me—I'm sick of bitches tellin' me 'bout what the fuck she did for me. Poor Juanita this, poor Juanita that. Well, newsflash, bitches: Poor Juanita is a grown-ass woman who keeps makin' the same fuckin' mistakes. Ya'll can go run ya happy asses down to the hospital and do whatever the fuck you gonna do. But don't call my fuckin' house 'bout shit 'cause I don't wanna hear it. As far as I'm concerned, the woman who gave birth to me is dead."

Aunt Rosa gasped. "Kat, I swear on e'erything I love, I'ma beat ya ass when I see you."

"Well, stand in line," I said, cuttin' my eyes over at Chanel who was starin' me down.

"I bet your fucked-up ass don't even care that that nigga stomped ya mother all up in her stomach, and she done lost her baby, do you?"

"Why should I? Good for her silly ass," I snapped, "and good for him. The nigga saved her dumb ass from fuckin' up another child's life."

"You know what?" Aunt Rosa stated. "Juanita was right 'bout ya ass. You'se a fuckin' crazy bitch."

"Thank you very much," I said sarcastically. "I'm glad you finally figured it out. Now, like I said, don't call my muthafuckin' house again."

I hung up. Chanel was lookin' at me in shock. She opened her mouth to say somethin', but I shut her ass down. "Don't open ya trap to say shit," I warned, givin' her ass a threatenin' look. "If you don't wanna get tossed up outta here, go on downstairs and bring up that bottle of Rèmy and let's make it do what it do. 'Cause right about now, a bitch is through."

Three a.m., I was tossin' 'n turnin'. I sat up in bed, tryna adjust my eyes to the dark. I was sweatin' and had a splittin'-ass headache. At first I thought it mighta been from all the drinkin' and smokin' with Chanel from the night before, but the more I thought 'bout it, the more I realized it wasn't the same kinda feelin' I usually got after a night of gettin' lifted. It was different; one I couldn't put my finga on. It was like I had some kinda nightmare or somethin', but a bitch couldn't remember dreamin' 'bout shit.

I took a deep breath, and looked 'round the room. My blankets and pillows were all on the floor. I stretched my arms up over my head, then leaned over and turned on the lamp on my nightstand. I picked up the telephone and retrieved my messages from my home phone. I inhaled, exhaled, then listened.

"Kat, this ya Aunt Rosa. Ya mother's in the hospital. That nigga of hers done beat her up real bad. She's at Kings County."

"Kat, where the hell are you? This is Rosa again. I'm tryin' to get in touch with you. You need to answer ya damn phones. This shit's important. Call me the minute you get this."

"Kat, this is Patrice. You need to call us immediately. Some shit went down with ya moms, and we 'bout to bring it to that nigga. He done fucked up, puttin' his hands on her."

"Kat, answer ya damn phones. Shit! I know you fuckin' see my goddamn numbers comin' up. This is ya Aunt Rosa. Call me the fuck back, *asap!*"

I deleted them, along with the six other messages I didn't bother listenin' to. I flopped back 'cross my bed and stared up at the ceilin'. *She's still ya moms, Kat…That's real fucked up…I bet you don't even care that the nigga stomped ya mother all up in her stomach…He beat her face in…*

I closed my eyes and fought back tears, tryna understand why she kept gettin' her ass caught up in bullshit with muhfuckas, wonderin' when she was gonna get sick and tired of lettin' niggas beat her ass and disrespect her. Watchin' my moms jump from one man to the other over the years had made me realize that women like her have a lotta emotional issues. They gotta be sick. 'Cause ain't no muthafuckin' way in hell a healthy bitch gonna put up with half the shit these chicks put up with from a muhfucka.

So what you gonna do, Kat? I questioned in my head.

"Not a muthafuckin' thing," I answered out loud. "I didn't put her ass in that situation. So why the fuck do I have to feel some kinda way 'bout it?"

Because she's still ya moms, I thought.

I took another deep breath, then picked up the phone and dialed 4-1-1 for the number to Kings County. "Hello, I'm callin' 'bout Juanita Rivera," I said when a woman answered the hospital switchboard. "She's a patient there."

"Okay, hold on...let me see." She placed me on hold, then returned. "Let me connect you to her floor." The hospital music came back on for a moment, then someone else picked up. "ICU, how can I help you?"

"Um, yes. I'm callin' about Juanita Rivera. I was told she was in the hospital."

"I'm sorry, information 'bout patients is strictly—"

"Ma'am," I said, takin' a deep breath before I cursed her ass out. "No disrespect to you, but I'm Ms. Rivera's daughter and I wanna know how the fuck she's doin', *please.*"

I heard her gasp. "Your name?"

"Katrina Rivera."

"Ms. Rivera," she said, soundin' all professional and whatnot. "Your mother is in stable condition. She has two broken ribs, her mouth is wired from her jaw being broken, and she has a fractured eye socket."

I bit down on my lip, clenched my fists. "Thank you."

"She's been asking for you."

"That's nice," I said sarcastically. "You can tell her I send my regards." I hung up, wipin' tears from my face.

CHAPTER TWENTY-ONE

Ready or not, it's 'bout to go down...wet 'n horny...ready to fuck...got a fat clit for ya tongue...a hot pussy for ya dick... lick, lick...click, click...and chrome for ya dome...lights out, muhfucka...ya time's up...

The following mornin', after Chanel's ass finally left up outta here, I was sprawled out on my sofa lookin' over the photo of my next mark. I glanced at his stats: 36, five foot eleven, 211 pounds, brown hair, brown eyes. Humph. He was a smooth, dark chocolate with thick eyebrows and dreamy bedroom eyes. He had a short, fade-type haircut with a neatly trimmed mustache and goatee. He kinda reminded me of a darker version of that fine-ass model Keston Karter. Humph. And that's who I was gonna pretend I was fuckin' until it was time to splatter the nigga's skull; then he'd become another missin' link in someone's life.

The ringin' house phone distrupted my thoughts. I picked up on the third ring without payin' attention to the number that flashed 'cross the caller ID. "Hello?"

"Kat, this is ya Aunt Elise."

I scrunched up my face, wonderin' why the hell she was callin', although I really knew why. Elise never, ever picked up a phone to get at me, so I knew the only reason she'd be callin' now was 'cause it had somethin' to do with my moms. "Hey, Aunt Elise," I said, forcin' myself to sound happy to hear from her. "How you been?"

"Good," she said. "But this ain't a social call. I'm callin' 'cause ya moms up in that hospital and e'rybody else been up there to see her but you. Now, I know the two of you don't always see eye-to-eye, but that's ya mother, Kat. No matter what she's said or done to you, that is still ya mother. And right now you gotta be big enough to put aside your feelings and be by her side. That's what families do."

I kept my mouth shut and listened. On the inside I was so ready to shut her ass down. I wasn't beat to hear her shit. However, outta my three aunts, she was the one who always treated me like a daughter so I gave her respect on the strength of that. But, I already knew if she came at me sideways, I'd bring it to her, too.

It's too early for this shit, I thought, glancin' up at the wall clock. It was 11:08.

"My sister is laid up in a hospital bed, and she needs her family by her side. That includes you, her daughter. And I expect you to make it your business to get your ass there. Do you hear me, Kat?"

"Yeah, I hear you," I said, pacin' the kitchen floor.

"Good. So, what time should I tell your mother you're coming?"

I sighed, closin' my eyes. "You can tell her…" I paused, takin' a deep breath. "You can tell her, I'm *not* comin'."

"What?" she asked, actin' like she didn't hear me. "What did you say?"

I repeated myself, pullin' a chair out from the kitchen table and sittin' down. "I said, I'm not goin'."

"And why not?"

"Because…" Humph. I wished I had a damn recorder to push play e'erytime I had to make my "fucked-up mother" speech. I sighed. "Look, Aunt Elise, no disrespect to you. That's ya sister, not mine. That woman, mother or not, has put one man too many before me, and I'm done tryna be a daughter to someone who has never wanted to be a mother. So you can tell her I send my regards. But that's all she'll ever get from me. I got my own life, and I don't ask her for shit. Whatever decisions I make, I make them knowin' that if the shit gets me caught up, I gotta get myself outta it without her. And she needs to do the same 'cause I'm over her."

"I don't believe I'm hearin' this shit come outta ya fuckin' mouth." I almost wanted to laugh. I knew it was only a matter of time before she dropped all that proper grammar 'n shit. "Rosa and Patrice told me you were gonna say this bullshit. I've never got at ya ass, Kat, but I will if you don't make it ya business to get ya ass down to that hospital to see about ya mother."

"Aunt Elise, listen, sweetie. I would love to go back 'n forth with you 'bout this. But my mind's made up, and there's nothin' you or anyone else can say or do to change it. So, all ya threats mean nothin' to me—"

"Now, wait one goddamn minute, Kat—"

"No," I snapped, cuttin' her off, "you wait. I'm not gonna argue with you 'bout this shit. I said I'm not goin' and that's what it is. I love you, Aunt Elise, but do me a fuckin' favor and stay outta my relationship with my moms."

"Kat, who the fuck you think you talkin' to, hunh? You must don't know who the hell I am."

"No, I know exactly who I'm talkin' to and who you are. Like I said, I'm not tryna disrespect you, but you callin' my house tryna get at me. And I'm not the one,; aunt or no aunt, it makes me no never mind. I know that's ya sister 'n all, but she brought this shit on herself. And you know it. So she gets what she gets. Like I told Aunt Rosa and Patrice, ya'll can run up to that hospital all ya want, but I ain't the one."

"So let me get this right," she said. I could tell she was clenchin' her teeth. "You mean to tell me that you are turnin' ya fuckin' back on your own mother. Is that what the fuck you're tellin' me, huh, Kat?"

"Basically, that's *exactly* what I'm tellin' you."

"How the fuck you gonna turn ya back on her? That's your mother; she's ya blood."

"The same way she turned hers on me," I responded. "Now, I'd love to continue this conversation, but I have more important things to do. So you take care of ya'self, Aunt Elise."

"Kat—"

"Love you, but I gotta go," I said, cuttin' her off, then hangin' up on her ass. Now, trust, if I still lived in Brooklyn them crazy bitches would already be camped outside tryna get it in with me. I shook my head. "I swear I hope they don't try it on my time," I said out loud.

When the phone rang again, I rolled my eyes. I knew it was her callin' back to bring it, but when I looked at the caller ID this time, it was Naheem callin' from prison. *Oh, no, not today, nigga,* I thought. *You betta call that bird you got suckin' ya dick 'cause I ain't the one.* This nigga had been blowin' my shit up for the last three weeks tryna get at me. I started to pick up to curse his ass the hell out for constantly callin' like he was my man or some shit. I done told the nigga it ain't that type of party, and to stop tryna burn my damn phone lines up. Yet the muhfucka still thinks 'cause we was fuckin' that I should accept his collects anytime he calls. Humph. Muthafuckas kill me.

Anyway, for the rest of the day I layied around, got lifted, listened to some beats, watched a few flicks, ate, and played in my pussy. Before I knew it, I was knocked the fuck out.

At like four in the afternoon, all my phones started ringin' at the same time. First it was both cell phones, then the house line. I jumped up, all groggy 'n shit, rubbin' my eyes. I had to look around to see where the hell I was. I reached over and grabbed the cordless off the coffee table, then looked at the caller ID. It was Naheem callin' again. I *tsked*, answerin', "Yeah?"

I got up off the sofa to get my cell phones from the bar while the automated voice went through its bullshit recordin'. Cash had left a message on the Kat line. Grant and Chanel had called on my other line.

"What's good, ma?" Naheem finally said over the noise in the background. "Where you been? I've been tryna get at you for a minute."

Who the fuck this nigga think he checkin' for? "Nigga, you got the wrong number. I don't answer to you. Now why the fuck you callin' here?"

"Oh word, it's like that?"

"Yeah, nigga, it's like that. What the fuck! You called here earlier today, and now here you are callin' again. What the fuck ya ass got to say to me that's so important that you gotta call here back to back like we still fuckin'?"

"Yo, chill ma," he said, keepin' his voice calm. "Why you snappin' on a nigga?"

"'Cause ya black ass keep callin' here like you hooked on retarded or some shit, that's why."

"Damn, baby, I ain't tryna beef with you. We ain't talked in a minute—"

"Nigga, what the hell you mean 'we ain't talked in a minute'? I spoke to ya ass a month or so ago. And ain't shit changed since then."

"Listen," he said, sighin'. "I wanted to hit you up to see what was good with you. It ain't that serious. If you didn't wanna talk, you shouldn't had picked up."

Ohmyfuckin'God, I was ready to bring it to this nigga. But, I let 'im live 'cause I already knew, first thing in the mornin', I was havin' my fuckin' number changed. Between his nutty ass and my crazy-ass family, I was done. "Naheem, you know what? You right. I shoulda let the shit go into voicemail. But I didn't. Now, what the fuck you want?"

"Yo, is ya peeps still pushin' them thangs?"

I frowned. "Nigga, is you fuckin' serious?! You actually callin' here to ask me some dumb shit like that?"

He blew into the phone. "Yo, hold the fuck up, Kat, real talk. I've been lettin' you come out ya neck all greasy 'n shit, but on some real shit. Don't get it twisted. Just 'cause a nigga's on lock don't mean I can't still get at that ass if I want. Now, I'm only askin' 'cause if the bitch is still ridin' the train, you need to tell her to get the fuck off and lay low. Shit's hot; for real, for real."

Why the fuck is this nigga callin' me with this shit? And why the fuck is he so concerned about what the fuck Iris is doin'? Why the fuck he keepin' tabs on her ass? This nigga actin' like he's been fuckin' this bitch. This is the shit I started thinkin' in my head. Then all of a sudden I started thinkin' back to when he was out on the bricks and how Iris was always grinnin' in his face or comin' over to our spot prancin' her ass 'n titties all up in Naheem's face. Back then, I didn't really pay the shit no mind 'cause he never gave me a reason to doubt his ass. But now…hmmm, a bitch gotta wonder what was really good with the two of them. Okay, now a bitch's temper is 'bout to kick in. If that bitch fucked him while I was with him, I was gonna run straight in her mouth. Fuck the fact that I deaded the shit between him and me years ago. The fact that the bitch was all up in my face, knowin' she had fucked him was just cause to take her face off, real talk. As far as I'm concerned, if a bitch in ya circle fucks ya man, then the ho done broke a cardinal rule. And her ass gotta be handled.

"Naheem, why the fuck you care?"

"I don't," he shot back. "I know that's ya girl 'n shit."

"Nah, muhfucka…wrong answer," I said. "Come again, nigga. Ain't no fuckin' way you callin' me with this shit 'cause she's my damn girl. Who the hell you think you talkin' to? You ain't checkin' for no-muthafuckin'-body unless you gonna benefit. So either somethin's in it for you, or you done fucked the bitch. So which is it?"

He got quiet.

"Naheem?" I shouted.

"What?"

"I asked you a question, nigga. That's what."

"I didn't hear you."

"Nigga, don't fuckin' play me. You heard what the fuck I said. Now, did you fuck Iris or not? And be real with it."

He sucked his teeth. "Here you go with this shit."

"Here I go with what shit, Naheem? If you a real nigga like you say you are, then keep shit funky and be real with yours. Did you fuck the bitch or not?"

"Uh, listen," he said, lowerin' his voice.

"'Uh, listen,' what, nigga?" I said, clenchin' my teeth. "Speak up. I can't hear you."

"C'mon, Kat, let's not do this."

"Nah, nigga, don't give me that 'let's not do this' shit. You callin' here, burnin' my fuckin' jack, askin' me 'bout some other bitch all concerned 'n shit like you got it in with her. You need to tell me what's really good, muhfucka, and you need to do it right now. So I'ma ask you again—was you fuckin' her?"

"Yeah," he said.

I felt blood rush to my head. I sat down.

"But—"

"'But' hell," I snapped. "So, you fucked her while we were fuckin'?" I asked, but I said it like I already figured the shit out.

"Only a few times," he said. "But it was when you and me first started dealin' with each other, and then I deaded it."

"How many months before you ended the shit?"

"Like four or five. But she was only suckin' my dick 'n shit. Hell, she was dustin' the whole block off."

"And that's supposed to make the shit better? Nigga, do you know I'ma fuck her up when I see her? You do know this, right?"

"Kat, c'mon, don't go there."

"Don't go there, hell. I'm already there. I'ma take that bitch's face off."

"I already told you I was fuckin' her way before I caught feelin's for you. Once I fell for you, I cut her ass off."

"Yeah, but the bitch was still prancin' her ass all up in ya face, and smilin' the fuck up in mine. And the bitch was probably laughin' behind my back, too. And you didn't say shit. Now I see why she was always tryna come through and chill 'n shit. The bitch had ya dick on her breath, and ya nut on her tongue. Yeah, that ho-ass bitch got a beatdown comin'. I don't give a fuck how long ago it was. And that's on e'rything I love. And you know what, I ain't tellin' that bitch shit. I hope they run up on her ass, and the nigga shits all over her, real talk."

The nigga started repeatin' himself, tryna explain how he had been fuckin' with Iris off and on before I stepped on the scene, but it was on some DL-type shit. He claimed he was just fuckin' her and lacin' her with a few dollars e'ery now and then, but wasn't tryna wife her ass 'cause he already knew she was hot in the ass, and was fuckin' 'n suckin' e'erything movin'. He was just lettin' her wet his dick whenever he felt like trickin'. I listened to his ass go on and on until I couldn't take it anymore.

"You black, muthafuckin', retarded-ass piece of shit, you already said all this." I called this nigga e'ery fucked-up name in the book, just straight disrespected his ass. And the nigga didn't say shit. He just kept his mouth shut and let me go off. Then, when I finally stopped blackin', he had the muthafuckin' nerve to ask me if I was all right. *Am I all right?*

"Yeah, nigga, I'm all right. I'ma always be all right. Believe that. That fact that you was playin' me with this bitch is one thing, and the fact that this ho was all up in my face frontin' like we was girls 'n shit is another. But on some real shit, I'm more pissed that you never once said shit to me 'bout you fuckin' this bitch *before* you got with me when you knew I was cool with her ass."

"I wanted to tell you, but she wanted to keep the shit on the low. It wasn't really nothin' major anyway," he said, tryna make light of the shit.

"Oh, fuckin' really? Then answer me this: why is it you made sure I knew 'bout all the other bitches you were smashin' 'cept her ass, hunh, nigga? Why was that? She tells you not to say anything and you ride with that shit. Why? Was you fuckin' that bitch raw?"

He was silent.

"You know what, nigga, forget it. Don't even bother answerin' that 'cause it's not like you still my man, so really, the shit's not that serious to me. However, I'ma still rock that bitch when I see her for tryna clown me all these years."

"See, here you go," he said, suckin' his teeth. "Kat, that shit is dead. Besides, ain't like you and me still fuckin'. You dumped a muhfucka, remember?"

"Yeah, nigga, I remember. *And?* That ain't got shit to do with the fact that you was fuckin' her while fuckin' *me*; that's all I need to know. Ain't shit dead until I beat her ass the fuck down, then you can talk to me 'bout shit bein' dead. And you lucky ya ass is behind the wall 'cause I'd get at ya ass, too, nigga. If I woulda known this shit from gate, I woulda never fucked with ya monkey ass."

He laughed. "Oh, shit. Why I gotta be a 'monkey ass'?"

"'Cause that's what the fuck you are. Now, do me a favor and don't call my fuckin' house no goddamn more."

"Yo, I know you hot right now, but you don't mean that shit. I know you still got love for me."

"Nigga, you don't really know me then." I hung up, then called Iris's ass. Her phone went straight into voicemail, but I couldn't leave a message 'cause her box was full. I called Chanel.

"Hey, Kat," she said, soundin' all cheery 'n shit.

"You talk to that bitch Iris yet?"

"Nah, no one has still seen or heard from her ass. Why, what's wrong?"

"Ain't shit wrong; let that bitch know I'm straight rockin' her fuckin' grill in when I see her, so her best bet is to stay far the fuck away from me."

"Bitch, what is you talkin' 'bout? What the fuck done happened?"

"Chanel, I'ma ask you somethin' and I want it raw."

"Aiight, you got that. You know I'ma always be real with mine."

"I hope so, 'cause if you not…" I paused, sighin'. Chanel was my fuckin' girl, but I knew if the bitch knew 'bout this shit all along, I was gonna have to cut her ass off for real. And I might end up goin' in her mouth for keepin' the shit from me. I took a deep breath. "Did you know Iris was fuckin' Naheem while we were dealin' with each other?" I asked, holdin' my breath.

"What? When?" she asked, soundin' surprised. But I still wasn't convinced. "Kat, ain't no way Iris would go there. I mean, I know she could be messy, but she knows how we roll. And if she woulda told me some shit like that you know I woulda checked her ass, then put you on. Fuck that. You my muhfuckin' people, and that shit ain't cool, Kat."

Okay, maybe she didn't know, but I bet that bitch Tamia did. Those trick bitches were two peas in a pod. They always knew who was fuckin' and suckin' who. Hell, them bitches done tag-teamed plenty of niggas together, so yeah, Tamia's ass knew.

"Yes, the bitch would. And she did." I told her about the phone call from Naheem and how it had me lookin' at shit sideways.

"Damn. That's some real foul shit. Kat, on e'ery thing I love, I had no idea. She never told me shit 'bout fuckin' him."

"Chanel, I promise you, I'ma wear that bitch out when I see her."

"Oh, well," she said, sighin'. "That's my girl 'n all, but she brought that shit on herself. So she's gonna have to wear that ass whippin'."

"You know what, do me a favor. Forget we even had this conversation."

"Hunh?"

"Don't tell that ho shit when you talk to her ass. Let the bitch think e'erything's e'erything, like shit's all sweet."

Like I told ya'll before, I like to always let a bitch know what it is, so she can be ready to rock when she sees me comin'. But since that bitch wanted to be on some slick shit, fuckin' my man right up under my nose, then I was gonna catch her ass off guard and drop her ass. As far as I'm concerned, if the bitch grinned up in my face after ridin' my man's dick, then I had to wonder what else her messy ass did while smilin' up in my face. Then again, what the fuck did I expect? This is the same bitch who fucked her own stepfather and her sister's man when we were in high school. So, no...this dirty bitch fuckin' Naheem ain't really no damn surprise.

"You got that," Chanel said.

"Aiight," I said, glancin' over at the digital clock on the microwave. It was almost five o'clock and I hadn't done shit all day. I needed to do laundry and still hadn't packed for my trip to Vegas. "Listen, I'm out. I got shit to do. I'ma get at ya later."

"Well, fuck you too, ho," she said, laughin'. "Holla back."

"Love you, too, slut," I said before hangin' up.

I went down into the laundry room, tossed a load of clothes in the washer, then took my ass upstairs to pack. When I was finished, I turned on my stereo and pressed the remote button for CD. DMX's "X Gone Give It to Ya" came on. I lit a blunt, flopped back onto my bed, then slid my right hand inside my pink lace panties and played in my curly, triangled patch of hair, slowly brushin' my hand over my clit, then along the openin' of my pussy. I needed a good fuck to take the edge off, 'cause a bitch's nerves were truly rattled. And fuckin' myself was not gonna do it—not tonight. Ugh! I removed my hand and played with my right nipple until it hardened. I continued to puff on my blunt, pinchin' and tweakin' my nipple until my blunt was almost down to a roach, then jumped up off the bed. "Fuck!" I said out loud as I headed toward the bathroom. "I need some fuckin' dick in my life." Although I coulda called Grant's ass to come through and dig this hole out, I really wasn't beat for him, not at that moment. Besides, I didn't wanna give the nigga too much pussy too soon 'cause then a muhfucka starts buggin'.

I went back downstairs to the laundry room, put the load of clothes into the dryer, then went back upstairs to take my shower. Twenty minutes later, I climbed in bed with thoughts of ridin' a long, black dick before I drifted off to sleep.

At two-fifteen the next day, I had arrived in Vegas, checked into Bally's, received my travel package, and was now standin' in the elevator on my way up to the seventh floor to my hotel room. My cell phone started ringin'. It was Grant.

"Hello?"

"Yo, what's good, baby?"

"You," I said, smilin'.

"Oh word? You been thinkin' 'bout me?"

"Yep," I said.

"Oh, word. What you been thinkin' 'bout?"

I giggled, slidin' the hotel key card into the door. I walked in, droppin' my bags on the spare bed. "I've been thinkin' 'bout suckin' that big, thick, black dick of yours, and you feedin' it to me real slow, then fuckin' my throat, stretchin' my neck."

"Damn, baby. So what you sayin'? You tryna let a nigga come through or what?"

I sighed, removin' my shoes, then slippin' outta my clothes. "I wish. I'm outta town."

"Damn, again? Where you at now?"

"Vegas," I told him.

"Oh word? What you doin' out there?"

"I have a business meetin'."

"So why you talkin' all slick, gettin' a nigga's dick brick 'n shit when ya ass ain't even around for me to bang that shit up?"

"'Cause I'm horny," I said, slippin' my hands in my panties, then rubbin' the front of my pussy, imaginin' his face between my legs. I lay 'cross the bed and spread open my legs, bendin' at the knees. "I want you to fill my horny, wet pussy up with your gushin' hot nut, nigga."

"Fuck! You really know how to get a nigga goin', word up. You ain't gonna be out there givin' none of that pussy up, are you?"

I laughed. "Nigga, please. It ain't that type of party," I lied, knowin' damn well in a matter of hours I was gonna have my pussy juice smeared all over another muhfucka's face, then I was gonna be ridin' down 'n dirty on that dick. I tried not to think 'bout it, so to keep myself from feelin' any kinda way 'bout fuckin', I kept remindin' myself that it wasn't personal; that it was strictly business. Then why the fuck was I feelin' bad 'bout lyin' to his ass?

"I'm horny as fuck," he said. "Damn, I was hopin' to get up in you today."

"Oh, I'm sure you got someone else lined up to take my spot," I said, half-jokin'. I got up and opened up the box containin' my gun for the night, then lay back on the bed.

"I ain't beat for them." He sounded serious. But when it comes to a muhfucka and his dick, you can never be too sure. "The only pussy I'm checkin' for is yours."

"Oh, it's like that?"

"Real talk," he said, lowerin' his voice. "When you comin' home?"

"Thursday," I said. "Why?"

"Stop playin'. You know what it is."

"Oh, what…you tryna bag me?"

"I already did," he said, laughin'. "Thought you knew."

"Ooops, I don't think I got that memo."

"Yeah, aiight. Well, you got it now. You mine, baby."

I smiled, closin' my eyes and picturin' him holdin' his big dick in his hands, jerkin' that shit off nice 'n slow while I rolled my tongue under and 'round his balls, then pulled 'em into my mouth one at a time, gently suckin' 'em. Hearin' his voice and rememberin' how good he fucked me the last time we were together had my pussy tinglin'.

I slipped outta my red panties, spread open my pussy lips, then rubbed my unloaded .357 back and forth, up and down, against my slit until my pussy got real wet 'n creamy.

"Whatchu doin'?" I asked in a whisper that almost got caught in my throat, pushin' up against the butt of my gun and the risin' nut that was buildin' up on the tip of my clit.

"Gettin' ready to jump in the shower," he said. "Why?"

"You naked?"

"I'm in my boxers. Why?"

"I want you to slide your dick up in me," I said into the phone low 'n sexy.

"Oh, word? You tryna get shit poppin' and you not here so I can get off?"

I pushed the barrel of the gun into my pussy, then moaned. "I want some dick," I told him, grindin' and moanin'. "I'm so horny. Squeeze ya dick for me."

"C'mon, baby," he whispered. "Don't start this shit, you got my shit throbbin'."

"Stick ya hands in ya boxers and play with it for me."

"Girl," he said in a deep whisper, "why you fuckin' with me? You know I'ma wanna fuck."

"Take ya dick out and stroke a nut out for me, daddy. Make

believe you rammin' that long, black dick deep up in this tight, sweet pussy. You wanna feel this hot pussy wrapped 'round ya cock, big daddy?"

"Aaah, shit, girl. You got my shit all swollen 'n shit."

"Mmm-hmm," I moaned. "Just how I like it."

"Oh, word? What you wanna do to this big dick?"

I closed my eyes and pictured his shiny dick in my head. I could see the thick veins runnin' along the shaft of his cock.

I could see the tip of his dick leakin' with clear, sticky precum. I could feel the heaviness of his hairy balls in my hands as I gently tugged on 'em before slippin' 'em into my mouth. I pinched my clit and let out a moan. "I wanna ride that shit deep, wet it up with my sweet cream, then suck the nut outta it."

"Word? What else you wanna do to daddy's big dick?"

I flicked the barrel of the gun against my clit, rollin' my left nipple between my fingers, then slippin' the gun in and outta my pussy. My slippery slit grabbed and pulled at it. I let out another soft moan. "I wanna…Mmm…deep throat that shit…let you bust ya nut down in my throat…uh…then…Mmmph… I wanna ease that long, black dick in my tight, hot ass…Mmmm… ooooh…then I want you to bury that shit deep inside of me and slow fuck my asshole…"

"Oh, shit…you think you can handle all this dick?"

"I know I can. But first, I want you to take this pussy, nigga. Fuck it like you own it." I started poppin' 'n slappin' the mouth of my pussy with my hand, causin' my clit to stiffen and my juices to drip. I slipped the tip of the barrel back inside of me, slowly moved it in and out, then pushed it deeper into me. "Fuck me, nigga…Uh, aaaah…slam ya dick in me…oh, daddy…fuck me…"

"Damn. You got me hornier than a muhfucka. Fuck! Stick ya

fingers up in that pussy for me. Make daddy's pussy pop for me. Can you do that for me, baby?"

"Mmm-hmm," I moaned, pullin' the barrel outta my pussy, then pressin' on my clit with the butt of it, before slowly slidin' the barrel back into my slippery hole. The steel tip felt good up against and in my pussy. I pushed the gun deeper inside, lettin' out a loud moan. "Fuck me…oooh, aaah…oh, yes…fuck me…"

"Yeah, that's right, baby. Come all over them fingers for me. Give daddy that sweet pussy juice. Yeah, baby…you feel this dick up in you." The nigga's voice dipped into a husky whisper. I could tell he was strokin' that dick deep and hard.

"Yeah, nigga, stroke that dick for me…splash that hot nut deep up in this tight pussy…"

"Mmmph…oh, shit…fuck…"

"Jerk that big dick, nigga."

"Aah, shit…you want daddy to plant this nut up in ya guts?"

"Yeah," I panted, "bust ya dick up in this wet, hungry pussy."

"Yeah, baby…daddy's gettin' ready to spit his nut up in ya."

"Oooh, give it to me. Give it to me. Give it to me. Mmm… bang ya dick in me…fuck meeee."

He moaned. I moaned. Then we both came in loud, earth-shattering grunts. On some real shit, we sounded like two howlin' wolves. But it was all good. We held on to the phones, pantin', tryna catch our breaths 'n shit.

"Damn, baby, that shit was good," he said, lettin' out a loud grunt. It sounded like his breath was stuck in his throat. "Fuck! I can't wait to get up in you."

"Me either," I said, suckin' my cream off the tip of the gun's barrel, then slidin' my hands between my legs. My pussy was so fuckin' wet and achin' for a stiff dick. That shit we did was nothin' but a tease for a bitch like me. I was ready for some sweaty, deep-strokin'-all-night suckin 'n fuckin'. I hoped that was exactly what was in store for me later on.

"Damn, my shit is still hard. I'ma tear that ass up when you get home."

"Yeah, yeah, yeah," I said, laughin', "promises, promises."

"Yeah, aiight. You won't be sayin' that when I got ya ass pinned down into the mattress."

"Whatever, nigga," I said, yawnin'. "Oh, excuse me. You done wore me out."

He laughed. "You can't hang."

"Nigga, please. Don't get gassed."

"Yeah, aiight. Listen, baby...I'ma get ready to jump in this shower. Make sure you hit me up the minute you touch."

"I will."

"Be safe."

"And you keep them bitches off ya cock."

He laughed. "You got that," he said. "I'll see ya when you get home."

After we hung up, I decided to take a cat nap. I closed my eyes and fell into a deep sleep. When I finally opened my eyes and glanced at the digital clock on the nightstand, it was 8:18 p.m. I had slept for almost four hours. *Fuck!* I said in my head as I jumped outta the bed and raced to the bathroom to turn on the shower. I needed to get down to the casino and hopefully find my mark at one of the poker or blackjack tables. If all else failed, I'd make my way to his room up on the eighth floor and invite myself in. One way or the other, tonight I was fuckin', then shuttin' this nigga's lights out.

Once I finished my shower, I stepped back into the room with a plush white towel wrapped around my body and another wrapped around my head. I moisturized my body, then dried my hair and braided it nice 'n tight in two French braids, then pinned the ends under and placed my auburn Beverly Johnson mid-length wig with spiral curls on my head. I stood in the mirror, adjusted the wig, then tossed the curls with my fingas. I applied a coat of bing-cherry lipstick to my luscious lips and some mascara to enhance my already thick lashes and sexy bedroom eyes, then dabbed Chanel No. 5 behind both ears, on my wrists, and along my cleavage.

Once I was satisfied with my look, I retrieved my gun, screwed on my silencer, then tossed it into my black lambskin shoulder bag. Next, I slipped into my black spandex catsuit, then stood in the hotel mirror, peepin' myself from all angles, admirin' the way my wears wrapped around my body and hugged my fat ass, titties, and pussy lips. I puckered my lips real sexy-like, smiled at myself and winked, then headed out the door to the casino.

The casino was so fuckin' packed that it took me almost forty minutes to finally spot my mark. He was sittin' at a twenty-five-dollar blackjack table with two other heads, a chick and another nigga who favored a shorter, stocky version of Morris Chestnut. As luck would have it, the seat next to my target was open. I took my seat, then opened up my purse and put five hundred dollars down onto the table. We made eye contact. I smiled and he smiled back at me.

I placed my bet, and of course, lost the first three rounds. But shit picked up after that and I started slayin' shit. I purposely touched my mark a few times in excitement and made small talk with him in between hands. After 'bout an hour or so, I was so ready to get my drink on, but knew I had to stay focused so I kept it cute and drank watered-down cranberry juice. Ugh! I spent another two hours at this table, thankfully winnin'. A few times I slyly licked my lips at him. He grinned, but the nigga knew what time it was. The more drinks he ordered from the cute little barmaid, the more receptive he became. But a bitch was really gettin' bored with this table shit. I was a slot machine ho and wanted to shift gears for a minute, but 'cause I needed to play this nigga close, I kept my ass glued to my seat, constantly glancin' over at my mark, and smilin'. Besides, I was ready to fuck. So I was more than happy when the nigga started collectin' his chips. That was my cue to start packin' up my shit as well.

"Oh, you had enough, too, huh?" he asked, strainin' to keep his eyes from wanderin' all over my body. I could tell the muh-fucka was feelin' good from all those shots of scotch he drank, which was fine with me.

"Yeah, I'm done," I said, eyein' him seductively. "That was cute, but I'm ready to get into somethin' else now." I stared at him, tiltin' my head. I hoped the nigga got the hint, or at least took the bait. When he did, I smiled inside. *That's right, nigga, you hear this pussy callin' you, don't you?*

"Oh, yeah, what you have in mind?"

"Well," I said, not wantin' to sound too eager 'n shit. "You feel like goin' somewhere for a few drinks..." I paused, gaugin' his body language. The nigga was practically droolin'. "...then see where the night takes us?"

"Hopefully, someplace we both wanna be," he said, smilin'.

"Well, let's start with drinks. Are you here with anyone?"

"I'm out here with a few of my boys. And you?"

"I'm solo, baby. But hopefully, that will change," I said as we slowly walked through the crowd. I was glad I had caught him by himself, but now I needed to make sure the nigga wasn't sharin' a room with one of his boys. That woulda posed a major problem 'cause there was no way I could body the nigga in my room. I was relieved when the nigga said he was restin' solo.

"Well, tonight's ya lucky night," he said, lickin' his top lip, then slowly pullin' in his bottom lip. "And I have just the place in mind where we can go get those drinks, before we move on to *bigger* and wetter things."

"Well, lead the way," I replied, grinnin'. "I love big, and I'm *always* wet."

"Then we should get along just fine."

I followed behind him, takin' in his broad shoulders, his nice ass. I imagined my nails clawin' up his back, then sinkin' into his ass cheeks as he thrust his dick into me. I had to shake the thoughts of him fuckin' me outta my head before I jumped up on his back and fucked him on the spot. He slowed his pace and we walked side by side, makin' our way over to the Indigo Lounge. It was cute, and very laid-back. We found a seat at an empty table where we ordered drinks and got better acquainted. After 'bout the third round of drinks, he started really feelin' himself, talkin' like he was ready to put some work in.

"Damn, baby," he said, lickin' his thick lips again. "You fine as fuck. I didn't even get ya name, beautiful."

"It's Maleka," I lied.

"Oh, that's wassup. Mark," he stated, fannin' his long legs open and closed. Usually when a nigga started that shit 'round me it meant he was tryna keep his dick in check.

I smiled. "Am I makin' you nervous or somethin'?" I asked, pullin' in my bottom lip.

"Nah, baby," he said, finishin' his drink, then settin' the glass down on the table. "I'm just ready to go somewhere a little more private, if you know what I'm sayin'."

Yeah, I already knew what time it was, but I decided to fuck with him anyway. "And then what?" I asked, slowly sippin' on my drink, then eyein' him over the rim of my glass.

"And then whatever happens happens."

"Well, if I'm goin' somewhere private with you, you need to know I'm tryna wet ya dick, then get that nut. Bottom line, I'm tryna fuck. Can you handle that?"

"Oh, no doubt," he said, givin' me a wide-ass smile like he hit the lottery. I could tell I had the nigga's dick swoll by the way he was fannin' his legs a mile a minute. And when he finally stood up, the lump in the front of his pants told me all I needed to know. "Let's make it happen."

I smiled, gettin' up, allowin' him to lead the way.

By one a.m., I was up in my mark's standard hotel room, spread out on the bed, on my stomach, bobbin' my neck, gulpin' down the nigga's dick like it was a smoked beef sausage.

"Slap my ass while I'm suckin' ya dick," I told him. He did, and I moaned. "Slap it again. Make that shit jiggle, nigga." He did, and I moaned again. I circled the openin' of his short, thick dick with the tip of my tongue, lappin' at the tiny droplets of precum that leaked from its fat mushroom head. Mmmm, it was sweet tastin'. Okay, on some real shit, even though the nigga dished up a short order of dick, he made up for it in thickness, and in balls. His muthafuckin' balls were the size of juicy, ripe plums. And his dick was almost as thick as my damn arm. Humph. My pussy lips started quiverin' as I stroked his dick with one hand and slowly sucked on his balls, rollin' them around with my tongue.

He gasped, then moaned. "Oh, shit, baby. Damn, you workin'

the hell outta my balls." He thrust his hips and let out another moan as I took both of his balls deep into my warm, wet mouth. "Oh, shit," he whispered. "I want you to suck this dick, baby. Stop teasin'. me, and put this fat dick down in ya throat."

I smiled. Little did the muhfucka know suckin' on his fat balls already had me wantin' to suck his dick down and deep throat that shit, so I was more than happy to oblige. My mouth watered and my pussy was wet and slippery for what would come after I finished servin' him brain. I looked up, grinnin' at his ass lookin' down at me all lusty and whatnot. I opened my mouth and swallowed that shit whole, pressin' my nose up into his pubic hairs, gulpin' him down, gently pullin' and squeezin' and milkin' his balls. I hummed and bobbed my neck until the nigga's knees shook.

"Oh, fuck…oh, shit…uh," he moaned as I ran my hands along the back of his muscular thighs, then grabbed onto his ass and dug my nails in, slurpin' the shit outta his dick. "Aaah, uh… damn, girl, you got that shit on lock."

I moaned and groaned and wet his dick up real good until a bitch couldn't take it no more. The heat from my pussy had my juices boilin'. I pulled his dick from outta my throat, then started spittin' all over it and makin' poppin' noises over the head of his dick with my lips and mouth. And just when I knew he was 'bout to spit his milk, I pulled up off the head of his dick, bringin' him to the edge, then lettin' the nut roll back into his balls. Yeah, a bitch was fuckin' with him. I was ready to have this nigga's tongue in my creamy, pink snatch.

"Why you stop?" he asked, tryna catch his breath. "Why you teasin' me?"

"I wanna nut on ya tongue," I said, pushin' him back onto the bed, then straddlin' over his face. I lowered my pussy onto his mouth, and my fat lips immediately opened up to receive his long, wet tongue. "Oh, shit," I whispered as I leaned forward and took his dick back in my mouth. We both moaned. He thrust upward into my mouth, and I ground my hips downward onto his. "Mmmm…uh…mmmm…oh, yes…"

The tip of his dick leaked gobs of clear, sticky juice, and I greedily lapped it up, feelin' a thick nut buildin' up inside of me. I pumped my hips and pussy down onto his face, and fucked his mouth and tongue until I bust my nut.

He licked up all my juices, sucked on my clit, darted his tongue in and out of my hot cunt, then slid his fat fingas into my slippery, steamy hole. "Oh, shit…let me put my dick in this pussy," he said, slidin' two more fingas in, then twistin' and pumpin' them knuckles deep. I slid his dick in between my titties and gave him a nice slow titty fuck, while flickin' my tongue across the head of his dick. "Aaah, shit…oh, fuck…damn, you gon' make me cum," he moaned. "Where the fuck you been all my life?"

Waitin' to put a bullet in ya skull, muhfucka, I answered in my head. "Cum for me, nigga," I urged, bouncin' my titties up and down on his dick. "Then I'ma let you fuck me deep in this hot pussy. You wanna fuck this pussy, daddy? Wanna let me wet ya dick with this good pussy?"

"Yes," he groaned. "Oh, shit." He pulled his fingas outta my sweet, creamy pussy and sucked 'em. "Damn, baby, your pussy tastes good." I took his dick back into my mouth, then sucked him until he exploded, shootin' ropes of hot dick cream all over my titties and neck. "Aaaaah…oh fuck!"

He fell back on the bed, spent, sweatin' and breathin' heavy. I glanced at him over my shoulder and saw his eyes were rolled up in his head. I smiled, then got up off him and straddled him, leanin' in and kissin' him on his pussy-stained lips. Mmmm. I loved tastin' my pussy on a nigga's lips and tongue. And I loved suckin' a muhfucka's dick that's been smothered in my pussy juice. Too bad I couldn't marinate this muhfucka's dick in my pussy, then suck him off. Oh, well. I glanced at the digital clock on the nightstand. It read: 2:17 a.m.

I rolled over and grabbed the white hand towel on the night-stand, then wiped his cum off my body. I tossed it on the floor, then lay next to him with my naked body pressed against his, watchin' him fall into a deep sleep. I soaked in his beautiful dark features, wonderin' why his wife wanted him earthed. Did he cheat on her? Did he beat her? Was he sittin' on loads of cheddar that she wanted to get her greedy hands on? Was it for the insurance money?

When his breathin' became light snores, I knew he was out for the count. *Just like a nigga*, I thought, slowly easin' outta bed. *Bust a nut and fall right out.* I quietly opened my bag and pulled out my gun, hidin' it behind my back while walkin' back over to the bed on my tippy-toes like the nigga was gonna hear me comin' 'cross the thick-ass carpet in my bare feet. I started to blast his brains out right then and there, but a bitch's pussy needed to be stroked. And I damn sure wasn't gonna deprive myself of an opportunity to test ride his thick cock before shuttin' his lights. But, on some real shit, I already knew if he woke up before I got back over to the bed and was able to slide my piece under the mattress, I was gonna blast his ass on the spot. Luckily for him—and me, he didn't 'cause a bitch wanted to ride that thick, choco-late dick. My eyes swept 'cross the nigga's body, takin' in e'ery muscular inch of him. I pinched my nipples, starin' at his dick, restin' up on his big balls. Oh my God, this nigga's chiseled-up body had a bitch leakin'. Fuck all this sleepin'. It was time to wake this muhfucka up and finish gettin' my fuck on so I could dispose of his ass quick, fast, and in a hurry.

"Wake up, big daddy," I whispered into his ear, stickin' my tongue in, then slowly suckin' on his earlobe. "I'm ready to fuck."

He groaned and stretched, slowly openin' his eyes, smilin'.

I inched down toward his dick and took him back into my mouth until his dick thickened and got hard as steel.

"Yeah, baby, you like that dick, don't you?" I nodded and moaned, slurpin' and lickin' all over his cock while playin' with my clit. "Oh, shit...."—he grabbed my arms and pulled me, tryin' to get me up on top of him—"C'mon, let me stuff this dick up in you before you make me nut."

I stopped suckin' his dick and looked up at him. "Where's ya condoms? I don't fuck without a wrapper on."

He smiled, gettin' up. "Hold on, let me go get one." He hurried to the bathroom and came back. He rolled the condom down on his dick, then climbed up over me as I spread open my legs to invite him into my hot pussy. He slowly pushed the head of his dick in, worked his way into my hole until he had all of it inside of me. He gasped from the tightness and warmth. I gasped from him stretchin' my walls with his thickness.

"Oh, yes," I moaned. "Work that fat cock in me," I said, pullin' my legs up to my chest as he braced his hands on my shins, pushin' my legs wider apart, 'causin' my pussy to spread open. His dick slipped all the way in, then slipped out a few times. "Stop teasin' me, nigga. Keep ya dick in me." He finally got his groove right, then started poundin' the inside of my pussy. "Yeah, nigga... just like that. Oh, yes...fuck me...fuck me...fuck me, big daddy."

He grunted and deep stroked me; fucked me long and hard as

my pussy clutched his dick, pullin' him deeper inside. "Oh, shit, you got some good pussy," he moaned in my ear. He sucked his bottom lip in, then bit down on it. His face twisted. "Damn, this shit is so fuckin' good…" I glanced over at the clock: 2:47 a.m. I hated for this shit to end, but I needed to hurry this along.

"Fuck this pussy from the back, daddy," I said as he pumped a mile a minute. I grabbed him by his hairy ass, dug my nails in. Sweat dripped from his face down onto my chest. "Uh…oh, yes."

A few more strokes and we changed positions. I arched my back, leaned my face down into the mattress, and let the muhfucka dig my pussy out from the back. He rocked me slow, then fast, then deep before slowly pullin' his dick out to the head, then plungin' it back in. He did that 'bout six or seven times before a bitch lost count and felt a nut swirlin' up inside of me.

"Stop teasin' me, nigga. Feed my pussy that fat dick," I breathed, glancin' at him over my shoulder. "Slap my ass, daddy. Act like you wanna own this pussy."

"Oh, you wanna talk shit," he said, slappin' my ass; rapidly alternating from one cheek to the other while slammin' in and outta me.

"Yeah, nigga, just like that. You want me to nut all over ya dick? You wanna see my sweet, pussy milk coat ya dick?"

"Oh, shit…" He grabbed me by the hips and started pumpin, grindin' and snappin' his hips into me. "Yeah, baby…oh shit…"

"Fuck me…oh, yes…fuck me!"

I guess the pussy started gettin' real good to the nigga 'cause all of a sudden he started buckin' and gruntin' and moanin' and talkin' real freaky-like. The nigga almost sounded possessed or some shit. But it was turnin' me the fuck on. The muhfucka had a bitch all sweaty and whatnot.

"Yeah, bitch, I'ma bust this nut way up in ya pretty-ass guts. This's my pussy now, bitch. I'ma fuck the shit out you all night. Damn, you got some muthafuckin' good, wet pussy. Yeah, this shit's nice and tight. It's mine, right, baby? This good pussy all mine?"

These niggas kill me with that shit, askin' a bitch if her pussy's his. Sometimes I wanna scream, "Yeah, muhfucka, for the moment! I got it out on loan to ya dumb ass." But I always keep it cute and let the nigga think what he wants. Anyway, the more shit he talked, the wetter my pussy got. The harder he fucked me, the hotter my pussy got. The muhfucka had my insides on fire. My juices gushed out, 'causin' his dick to splash in and out of my wetness.

"Yeah, nigga," I moaned. "Fuck ya pussy, muhfucka. Mmmph. That's right, get all up in ya pussy."

I almost lost it when the nigga wrapped his hands up in my wigpiece and started yankin' me by the back of my hair. I threw my hands up over my head and held on for dear life. Oh my God, I thought the nigga was gonna rip the shit right offa my head. I had to reach in back of me and pry his damn hands outta my wig. I was glad I had that shit packed on tight with a bunch of bobby pins. But, I still couldn't take any chances with him snatchin' my shit off.

"Let me get on top, and ride ya fat cock," I said, hopin' to get in control of the situation before he had my wig in his mutha-fuckin' big-ass hands. Thankfully, he was ready for me to ride him down into the mattress. He slowly pulled his dick outta me.

We changed positions, and this time I straddled on top of him, then reached up underneath me and stuffed his dick up in me. That was better. I made a note to myself to never, ever, let another nigga I had to body hit this pussy from the back. From now on, I'd be on top at all times. I slammed down on his dick. Gave him the ride of his life, then leaned over and reached under the mattress for my gun. I held it in my hand, grindin' down on his dick, pressin' and brushin' my clit against the shaft of his cock.

I let out another loud moan, glancin' over at the clock: 3:15 a.m.

"Aaah, shit," he groaned. "I'm gettin' ready to nut, baby. Oh, shit…this pussy. Is. So. Fuckin'. Good."

"Give me that nut, daddy," I said, tightenin' my grip on my piece. "Bust all up in ya pussy, baby."

"Oh, shit…"—he thrust deep up into me, grabbin' me by the hips—"I'm. Cum—"

Theessrrpp!

I shot him between the eyes, then continued ridin' him until I came all over his dick again. When I was finished, I rolled up off of him, wiped his ass down, removed the sheets, then tossed the spread up over him. I quickly slipped into my clothes, gathered my shit, then quietly walked outta his hotel room.

I pulled my phone outta my bag, turned it on, dialed Cash's number, then pressed send. "What's good?"

"I know why the caged bird sings," I said, walkin' off the elevator toward my hotel room. I slid the key into the door.

"That's what it is. I'll get at you."

"Yeah, make sure you do," I replied before hangin' up.

CHAPTER TWENTY-TWO

Three weeks later, word on the street was that that nigga who beat my mom's ass was out on bail, and she was released from the hospital. *Good for her,* I thought when I heard the news. I still wasn't fuckin' with her ass. They were probably holed up in her room fuckin' like two banshees. Interestingly enough, she had tried callin' me a few times. I guess to let me know she was outta the hospital. Then again, knowin' her ass she was gonna try to come at me on some other shit—even with a wired-ass jaw she was probably gonna try 'n pop shit. I guess she knew not to leave me any damn messages 'cause I wouldn't listen to 'em if she did.

I hadn't really been playin' Brooklyn too heavy either. Most of my time was spent in SohHo, midtown, or the upper east and west sides. Other than that, I kept my ass in Jersey. Chanel was already talkin' 'bout movin' back to Brooklyn. And on some real shit, I was really startin' to miss Brooklyn as well. There was somethin' 'bout its vibe and a Brooklyn nigga's swagger that made a bitch's pussy moist. And I was seriously thinkin' 'bout sellin' my spot and buyin' a cute brownstone somewhere over in Prospect Park or the Grand Army Plaza area. But I also liked the luxury of bein' 'cross the water away from all the hustle. Besides, my spot was laced lovely.

Anyway, I still wasn't fuckin' with Tamia's crusty-pus-pocket ass either. And Iris's dumb ass finally popped up on the scene after bein' ghost for almost a week and some change, talkin' some bullshit 'bout travelin' with that nigga she was mulin' for. Humph, whatever! The bitch stayed away from me, and didn't return my phone calls. I knew it had nothin' to do with her knowin' that I knew she had sucked Naheem's dick, 'cause when I called her ass I kept it real cute, actin' like I wanted to get caught up. The bitch didn't wanna hear my mouth 'bout how she was makin' her ends. Not that I had any room to come at her neck 'bout it, but...humph, fuck her! Either way you looked at it, the bitch had it comin'. It was only a matter of time before the ho slipped or got caught up.

Chanel tried to convince her to stop fuckin' with that nigga and runnin' drugs for his ass. But the bitch said she knew what she was doin'. I told Chanel not to even stress that shit. If the bitch wanted to be a mule, then let her. Sometimes you gotta know when to let a know-it-all bitch do her 'cause that's the only way they gonna learn. Bitches like Iris gotta fall real hard, bang they heads, then get up and start runnin' in circles before they realize they done got they asses stuck in the middle of a fire. So when Chanel called me all frantic and whatnot last night, I knew Iris's day had come. I was pissed that I didn't get a chance to smash her fuckin' lights in first.

"Kat, girl, you not gonna believe this shit," Chanel said, talkin' all fast 'n shit. "Hurry up and turn on ya TV. Iris done got her dumb-ass grill splattered all over the news."

"What?!" I shrieked, jumpin' up off the sofa and racin' over to get the remote off the entertainment center. I turned the power on, then started flippin' through the channels. "What channel?"

"Two, four, seven, take ya damn pick," she said. "Hurry up and turn the shit on."

I pressed the buttons for channel two, and almost passed the hell out when I saw Iris's face plastered on the screen, along with eight niggas and two other bitches, behind the white reporter chick with the pressed-powder makeup. "Breaking news," she said, talkin' into the camera. "Federal authorities have dismantled a global drug ring in New York, New Jersey and Connecticut allegedly headed by a Long Island man authorities have identified as Marcellus Bryant…"

"Can you believe this shit?" Chanel asked, interruptin' my concentration. "They gonna slay her dumb ass. Didn't we get at her 'bout this shit a few months ago?"

We? Humph. I shook my head, iggin' her ass. "Chanel," I shot back, "will you shut the fuck up and let me finish listenin' to what the bitch is sayin'! Geesh."

"…Undercover DEA agents bought large quantitities of cocaine about a year ago and that purchase has led to the arrests of twenty-eight people, seizure of more than three million dollars' worth of cocaine, a hundred-and-fifty pounds of marijuana, and close to five-and-a-half million dollars' worth of Ecstasy tablets. Along with the drugs, authorities confiscated a cache of assault weapons, pistols, swords, bulletproof vests, and approximately two-hundred-and-eighty thousand dollars in cash in making arrests over the past four months. Marcellus Bryant, thirty-two, who commanded and controlled the New York nexus of the drug ring, was arrested this morning along with…"

I couldn't believe what I was hearin' and seein'. The shit was unreal. Like I said, I knew this shit was gonna happen. I didn't know it was gonna pop off so soon, and to that fuckin' degree.

This bitch was in way over her head. And I bet her ass didn't have no paper stacked for bail, or lawyers. Retarded bitch!

"Her mother is gonna flip her noodle when she hears this shit," Chanel said. "Hold on, T's callin' on the other line." I rolled my eyes, listenin' to the reporter list the rest of the fools arrested while she had me on hold talkin' to Tamia's smutty ass.

"...and Iris Pines"—the news camera zoomed in on her grill then showed her bein' escorted in handcuffs by five agents— "twenty-four, of Brooklyn, New York, who was in possession of a black gym bag containing fifty pounds of cocaine, more than five-and-a-half pounds of heroin, and approximately a hundred thousand dollars in cash. The defendants are being held on bails ranging from forty-five thousand to five million dollars..."

Humph, I thought, *they 'bout to fry that ass up real good. This bitch is goin' to the furnace!*

"Kat, girl, you still there?" Chanel asked, flickin' back to me.

"Yeah, ho. I shoulda hung up on ya freak-nasty ass."

"Whatever," she said, laughin'. "Ain't this some shit?"

"Not really," I said, turnin' the TV off. I had enough. "She knew the shit came with risks. She knows enough chicks who done got caught up in that shit to know shit ain't sweet. But she still got down with it. So, I can't feel no kinda way 'bout it. She gets what she gets. And they 'bout to bring it to that bitch's head."

"Damn, that's fucked up, Kat. She's 'posed to be ya girl 'n shit."

"The fuck she is," I snapped. "Not after findin' out that bitch was fuckin' Naheem."

"Oh, damn, my bad. That shit slipped my mind."

"Well, it didn't slip mine," I said. "That bitch got just what the fuck she deserved. I wish I coulda dropped her ass first. But it's all good. I'ma be front and center when that bitch gets sentenced, trust. And then I'ma go pay her ass a visit when they ship her ass up the river—and knock her dead in her grill."

"Oooh, Kat, you wouldn't," Chanel said, shocked.

"Then I guess you don't really know me. That slut crossed the line. It woulda been different if I didn't know the bitch, but she was frontin' like we were all fly 'n whatnot. Oh, no, that bitch got a ass whippin' comin' to her special delivery."

"I wonder if she's gonna be able to post bail."

"Probably not," I said. "That ho was too busy splurgin' on bullshit to be thinkin' 'bout stackin' her ends. All I know is the bitch had better not call me askin' for no change to help her with shit—especially not after findin' out 'bout her and Naheem— 'cause the answer is gonna be Hell, muthafuckin' no, trick-ass bitch! I don't support or sponsor stupidity. And I damn sure ain't gonna ride with a bitch who had the dick of a nigga I was fuckin' with stuck down in her throat. Fuck what ya heard. Anyway, if a bitch gonna ride dirty, then a bitch better have her paper stacked and a legal team all lined up and ready to roll, in case her ass gets popped."

"I heard that," Chanel said, soundin' like she was deep in thought. She was probably feelin' sorry for the ho.

"Look, let me get off this phone. I'ma take a few hits off this blunt, then take it down. Call me tomorrow. Maybe we can do lunch or somethin' one day this week."

"Now that sounds like a plan," she said. I could almost see her greedy ass droolin'. "You treatin', right?"

"Damn, bitch," I replied, laughin'. "You always tryna get a handout. I need to start puttin' ya man-eatin' ass out on the stroll."

"Yeah, whatever," she said, laughin'.

As soon as I hung up from her the Kat line started ringin'. I rolled my eyes, takin' a deep breath.

"Yes, Cash," I answered.

"I got a day trip; you want it?"

"Where?" I asked, lightin' my blunt, takin' two long pulls, then blowin' the smoke out slowly.

"Baltimore. And I need for you to be able to get in and get out, not try to turn the shit into a week-long production."

I rolled my eyes. "Whatever, nigga."

"I'm serious, Kat. The nigga done fucked up some major paper and the cats he crossed want his ass fried, ASAP. He's down in B-more for some type of meeting."

"When you need it done?"

"Tomorrow night at the latest."

"Send me the paperwork with my money," I said, puffin' on the blunt. Damn this shit was good. I blew smoke outta the side of my mouth. Although I wasn't in the mood for fuckin, maybe I'd suck the nigga's dick, or just get my pussy ate out. I just hoped his grill wasn't wrecked and his body was on point. I hated them fat, nasty-lookin' muhfuckas with the big-ass titties, double-wide stomachs, and tiny link-sausage dicks. Humph. "I hope you not sendin' me no bullshit either."

He laughed.

"I'm not laughin', nigga. After that white man stunt, I gotta stay on ya black ass to make sure you don't try 'n clown me again."

"I got you, baby," he said, still laughin' all hysterical 'n shit.

I was startin' to get pissed. "Hahaha, hell, muhfucka."

"See, if ya freaky ass handled shit without all the extras it wouldn't be an issue."

"Whatever," I said, suckin' my teeth. I took two more pulls from my blunt, held the smoke in my lungs, then blew it out.

"Look," he said, gettin' all serious, "like I told you before, I don't care how you handle ya business. Do you. I just need this shit handled quickly. You the only one on the team I let turn down jobs 'cause you don't like how a muhfucka looks. Go figure."

I had to chuckle to myself. "Well, that's what happens when you got the hottest bitch on ya squad."

"Yeah, aiight," he said, laughin'. "You hot alright. Hot in that fat ass of yours. Now you gonna handle this shit or what?"

"Didn't I tell ya ass to send me the muhfucka's shit? Geesh."

"It'll be there later tonight. Get in and get out, Kat. No field trips until *after* you take care of this."

I rolled my eyes up in my head, frownin'. "Nigga, please... what the fuck I look like tryna make a field trip outta goin' down to Baltimore? Ain't shit down there I wanna see."

"Good, 'cause like I said, I need the shit handled."

"Alright, I heard you the first time. What the fuck?!"

"Kat, what I tell you 'bout your mouth?"

"You make sure you send my paper along with his shit, nigga."

"You'se a crazy bitch. You know that, right?"

"That's already been established," I answered. "Now beat it. I got shit to do."

"Aye, yo, Kat, keep poppin' shit, aiight."

"Cash," I said, lettin' out a deep breath, "kiss my fat ass."

"As long as I can slam this dick up in it when I'm finished," he said, laughin'.

I let out a disgusted sigh and hung up on his ass. *That nigga better be very careful what he asks for*, I thought, headin' upstairs to make my travel plans and pack an overnight bag. *The muhfucka might end up gettin' more than what he bargained for.*

Scary thing, the idea of fuckin' him, then puttin' a bullet in his skull, was startin' to get more and more appealin' to me.

TWENTY-THREE

Come on in from off the block...remove ya hoodie 'n Timbs...
drop ya boxers...lay back...relax...let's smoke some trees...
chill for a while...close ya eyes...free ya mind...listen to the
tick of the clock...while I drop to my knees...I'm here to give
ya what ya body needs...let a real bitch climb up on ya
dick...wet it nice 'n slow...lose ya'self in this pussy heat...call
my name, nigga...let Kat spill ya nuts...betta get it while ya
can...'cause I'm a 'bout to open ya guts...

It was almost seven-thirty p.m., and I had just turned left
onto Monument Street and was makin' my way toward the
Peabody Court Hotel in the Mount Vernon section of
Baltimore. Instead of takin' that borin'-ass three-hour drive, I
flew into the Baltimore–Washington International Airport, and
had the first flight outta there in the mornin'. I didn't even bother
tellin' Grant I was outta town since I was gonna be back in Jersey
long before he even realized I was ghost. Besides, it really wasn't
any of his fuckin' business. But, just in case the nigga called tryna
come through, I decided I was gonna tell 'im I was out chillin'
with my girls.

I pulled up in front of the hotel entrance in my rental, then got out and grabbed my overnight bag. I handed the keys to the valet, then made my way into the hotel lobby.

"Hello, welcome to the Peabody," the perky white chick said, greetin' me with a wide, toothy smile. She was a cute blonde chick with big-ass teeth. Humph. She reminded me of Mr. Ed 'round that mouthpiece.

"Hi," I said, givin' her a phony-ass grin. "I have a reservation." I gave her my name, slidin' my bogus ID to her.

She clicked the computer keys with her long fingas, pullin' up my information. "Ah, yes, Ms. Carmichael. Here you are." She clicked the keys a few more times, then waited for the room print-out. "There's a package here for you as well," she said, handin' me back my ID.

"Oh, good," I replied.

"Let me go get it for you," she said, handin' me my room key, and the printout to sign. "You're in room 302." I smiled to myself, knowin' my mark's room was right 'cross the hall from me. I never figured out how Cash always managed to know exactly what rooms these marks were in, but he did. The nigga had connects all over the country, in almost every type of industry. A muhfucka with that kinda power was not only dangerous, but it made my clit pulse, real talk. And I knew that the thing that kept me from fuckin' Cash was the fact that his ass was gorilla ugly. Otherwise I'd probably been had his dick in my throat. She came back with a small brown box. "Here you go," she said, handin' it to me.

"Thanks," I replied, gatherin' my things to bounce.

"Enjoy your stay."

"I'm sure I will." I walked off toward the elevator.

Once I was inside my room, I dropped my shit on the bed,

stripped off my wears, then headed to the bathroom to run the shower. I wanted to get showered and chill for a minute before it was time to tap on my mark's door to bring him room service—pussy and a bullet.

I decided to wait 'til 'round eleven to make my way 'cross the hall to his room. I had already changed up my look by skillfully puttin' in my Especially Yours light-auburn Bohemian clip-in extensions wig, then puttin' in a pair of contact lenses. The look was cute. Knowin' how to rock a wig and beat this face really helped to keep my look fresh, and keep muhfuckas from identifyin' me if shit got messy. I removed the hotel towel from 'round my body, then pulled out a handmade feathered flower from its satin pouch and dusted my body with Kama Sutra Honey Dust, Sweet Honeysuckle. Humph. I loved that shit. It conditioned the skin, leavin' it silky smooth and glowin'. And it kept a nigga wantin' to kiss all over ya body. Then I slipped into a breezy, multi-colored, abstract print Issa London kimono dress with plungin' V neckline. The shit was sexy as hell. And for the grand finale, I slipped my feet into a pair of four-inch Gucci Page pumps, then tossed my gun into my large white Michael Kors Beverly Python drawstring satchel. I peeked outta the door e'ery so often to make sure there was no one wanderin' the halls. When the coast was clear, I made my way to my mark's door and gently knocked.

My target for the night was a tall, thin but nicely chiseled, brown-skinned, B-ball-type nigga. He had a neatly trimmed mustache, goatee, and low-cut fade with thick eyebrows. He was thirty-one and recently married. Although I was 'bout to make his wife a widow, I was glad the nigga didn't have any children. I always hated havin' to body muhfuckas who had kids; I was robbin' them of havin' a father in their life. Oh well…life goes on!

For some reason, e'ery time I was 'bout to earth a nigga, I stressed 'bout havin' to go into plan B, in case a muhfucka wasn't beat for pussy, or I just couldn't get at 'im the way I wanted. The whole idea of havin' to squat somewhere in a tinted-out car, or be crouched down low, hidin' in bushes with a night-scope on my gun, waitin' to take a shot at a muhfucka, did not appeal to a freaky bitch like me. And I damn sure didn't wanna haveta flat-out shoot the nigga up without ridin' down on his dick first.

When there was no answer, I took a deep breath and knocked again. Although I heard the TV on, I knew that didn't mean his ass was in the room. I knocked again. And smiled when I heard a voice on the other side.

"Just a minute," the deep voice said. I heard the chain latch slidin', then the door opened. Humph, this nigga was fine. He stood in the doorway wearin' a white wife beater and some navy blue basketball shorts. "Can I help you?"

I scanned his body real slow and easy, startin' from his feet and calves, to his thighs, then the center of his crotch, to his chiseled chest and finally into his eyes. I smiled. "Oooh, I'm sorry," I said, standin' with my back straight, my chest out showin' cleavage for days, and my left leg forward, givin' him my best model stance while my satchel hung in the crook of my right arm. "I'm lookin' for Anthony."

My nipples were hard from the light brush of the fabric against 'em. And it was makin' me horny. He tried hard to keep his focus on my eyes and not my titties. I smiled to myself when he glanced at 'em. "Sorry, beautiful, no one by that name is here."

I acted like I was confused. "This is room 321, right?"

He looked at the room number on the door. "Sure is, but no Anthony is staying here."

I had already spent two minutes in the hallway with him and

was startin' to get antsy. I needed to get inside his room, and quick, before someone came out. I sucked my teeth, actin' like I was upset. "Oh, shit. I can't believe I done drove all the way down here, and this fool done gave me the wrong information. Well, I'm sorry for disturbin' you."

He smiled. "It's cool; you weren't disturbing me. I was just watching TV."

Okay, bitch, you need to hurry up and get into this nigga's room, I thought to myself, glancin' at my timepiece. "You mean to tell me a nice-lookin' brotha like you is all holed up in this room solo? Now, that's a crime."

He laughed. "Yeah, well, it is what it is. I'm outta this piece in the mornin' so it's all good."

"Well, let me get goin'. I guess I gotta go find out where this fool is. You enjoy the rest of ya night."

"You, too," he said, lickin' his lips. "Sorry I couldn't help you."

I smiled, preparin' to walk off. "If I can't track my friend down, who knows…maybe you can."

"Hell," he said, smilin', "if it makes you feel better, I can pretend to be him if you'd like."

"You know what," I said, turnin' around, "do you mind if I come in for a minute before I decide what I wanna do?"

He opened the door wider, and smiled, steppin' back. "Not at all." He spread his arm out, invitin' me into his space. I smiled as I lightly brushed past him, throwin' an extra shake in my ass. I silently blew out a sigh, relieved that I'd gotten up in his room. I glanced at my watch again. It took me four minutes to get in. "Here, have a seat," he said, removin' his clothes from outta one of the chairs. He had shit e'erywhere. Clothes, footwear, and newspapers were tossed all over the place.

"You mind if I use ya bathroom?"

"No, help ya'self."

I went into the bathroom and shut the door. This nigga was a damn slob. *Humph*, I thought, frownin'. *I'ma be doin' his wife a big-ass favor. Hell, if these niggas he fucked over wasn't tryna earth his nasty ass, it would only be a matter of time before his wife wanted him bodied.* He had wet towels on the floor, and the nasty muh-fucka had piss still in the toilet—and it was dark enough to look like he had pissed a few times without flushin'. I rolled my eyes, and flushed the toilet like I was gettin' ready to use it. I flipped open my cell and called Cash, whisperin' into the phone to let him know what was what, then I called my house and started spazzin' like I was really talkin' to somebody named Anthony. I talked loud enough so dude could hear bits 'n pieces of what I was sayin', if he was eavesdroppin', which I knew he probably was.

When I was finished, I flushed the toilet again, then ran the water and washed my hands and dried 'em with some tissue. I smiled at myself in the mirror, then walked back out into the room. Dude was sittin' on the edge of the bed, leanin' back on his forearms. I peeped the slight lump in his shorts as I walked by, and licked my lips.

"So where you from?" he asked.

"Jersey," I said.

"Oh, word? What part?"

"Jersey City," I lied.

"So, what brought you down this way?"

I tilted my head, twirlin' one of the wig's curls. "If I told you, you gonna think I'm crazy."

"No I won't. Try me."

"Dick," I said, eyein' him and taking a seat across from the bed. "That's what brought me down here."

He shut his legs together real tight, then opened them and

fanned a few times. I could see the happy lump in his lap start to thicken.

"Really," he said, noddin' his head and grinnin'. "So, this Anthony cat, is he ya man or something?"

I leaned back in my seat and crossed my legs, allowin' my dress to rise up over my thigh. He glanced at my smooth legs, but quickly shifted his eyes. I shook my head. "Nah, he's just this married dude I fuck from time to time."

"Damn, it's like that, huh?"

I decided to get up in his head and fuck with him a bit. I nodded. "Mmm-hmm. On some real shit, there's just somethin' 'bout fuckin' a married man that turns me on."

"Oh, is that right?" He started playin' with the string to his shorts, then slowly pullin' at the edge of his tee shirt, liftin' his shirt up enough for me to see the curly patch of hair 'round his navel. "So, what you gonna do? You gonna track dude down?"

"Nope," I said, uncrossin' my left leg, then shiftin' in my seat and crossin' my right leg. "I called him while I was in the bathroom, and cursed him out for havin' me waste my gas and money. So he won't be gettin' none of this tonight. I'm pissed I gotta turn 'round and take that long drive back to Jersey. I was really lookin' forward to somethin' real thick and chocolate tonight."

"Damn," he stated, shakin' his head. "That's f-d up. Well, you know…you can chill here if you want. As you can see it's just me up in here."

Bitch, shoot this nigga and be done with this shit. I glanced at the digital clock on his nightstand. It was 11:45 p.m. "Oh, no, I couldn't do that. It wouldn't be safe for me to chill up in here."

He laughed. "Nah, you safe, baby. I don't bite. Well, not unless you want me to."

I laughed. "Oh, it's not you I'm worried 'bout. It's me. As horny as I am, I'll be the one who might end up tryna bite you," I teased. "So bein' alone in a room with a fine man is definitely not a safe move."

"Oh, I'm a big boy," he said, spreadin' his legs open as wide as they would go. "I think I can handle a little bitin' if it got to that point."

"Be careful what you ask for," I said, eyein' him playfully. "I'ma chick in heat, and that makes me dangerous."

"Oh, yeah. Well, check this. I like livin' on the edge, baby." He stood up, proudly displayin' an imprint of a long, thick dick hangin' down the front of his shorts. I pressed my legs shut to pinch off the excitement stirrin' in the center of my pussy. "How 'bout I go hop in the shower, and then we can really chill?"

I smiled. "Sounds promisin'. I hope you can deliver."

"Give me a sec, and I'll show you what it is."

He went into the bathroom, leavin' the door cracked. I heard the shower go on, and the curtain slide back, then slide again. I waited a few more seconds to make sure he was in the shower, then got up and slid my gun up under the side of his mattress. I sat back down and waited for him to come back out.

Ten minutes later, he walked back into the bedroom with a towel wrapped 'round his waist and droplets of water still on his chest and arms. He dried the top half of his body with another towel. My God, this chiseled nigga's body was so fuckin' tight I wanted to throw him down on the bed and fuck him through tomorrow. I glanced at the clock, then returned my attention to him. I was ready to fuck. And ready to get this shit over with. I stared at him as he stood in the middle of the room, then a sly grin spread 'cross my face.

"Drop ya towel," I said, standin' up to remove my dress, "and stroke ya dick for me." I slowly slipped outta my wears, standin' in front of him in just my heels and black lace thong. He took my body in, starin' at my titties and huge dark nipples that were hard and achin' for his tongue on 'em. He kept his eyes on me as he started pullin' at his long dick, swingin' it, and cuppin' his smooth, fat balls. "Ooooh, you got a big dick," I moaned, pinchin' my nipples.

"You like that shit, baby?" he asked, strokin' his dick until it stiffened and got longer. "Damn, girl, you got a nice body. Turn 'round; let me see that ass." I slowly turned around, givin' him a full back view of my soft, fluffy ass. "Damn, girl," he said, pumpin' his dick in and outta his hand. "You gotta big ass. Bend over and open that shit up for me. Let me see the back of that pussy, and that pretty asshole." I smiled, lookin' over my shoulder at him dippin' at the knees while beatin' his dick. I removed my thong and bent all the way over, pullin' open my ass cheeks for him. "Oh, shit. Damn, that pussy looks good."

"And it tastes good, too," I said, makin' my ass clap 'n bounce for him. "Come over here and stick ya tongue up in it."

"You gonna suck this long dick, right?"

"Yeah, nigga, after you let me wet ya tongue up with some of this hot suga juice," I said, placin' my left foot up in the chair, then bendin' over and grabbin' my right ankle without bendin' my knee. He started walkin' toward me with his extra hard cock in his hand, then dropped down on his knees, pullin' open my ass. "Oh, yes," I moaned as he slowly lapped at my slit. He kept on lappin' and lappin, then dartin' his tongue in and outta my pussy until I felt a nut startin' to swell up in my belly.

"Oh, yeah," he said, lickin', kissin' and slurpin' my pussy, "I'ma tear this shit up."

"Humph," I grunted, slammin' my ass up against his mouth. "Stop all that talkin', nigga, and eat this pussy." He shut the fuck up and buried his face back up in between my ass cheeks, then stuffed his tongue deep into my wet slit, reachin' under me and playin' with my clit. I moaned and bucked back on his tongue. He had my ass pulled so far apart and his face so deep up in it, I thought I squirted my nut in his eyes when it started gushin' out. "Oh, yes…oh, yes…oh, yes…Uh, uh…Mmmph…" I kept cummin' and cummin' and cummin' until I almost toppled over. He kept his mouth on my hole, slurpin' up the last bit of my creamy nut.

"Damn, your pussy tastes good," he said, standin' up, lickin' his lips. He grinned. "I can't wait to ram this big-ass dick deep up in all that pretty, fat ass of yours."

I turned around to face him, then grabbed his brick-hard cock in one hand as I reached up and pulled him by the neck with my other hand to pull his face to my lips. I started suckin' my pussy juice offa his bottom lip, then his top lip. Then I shoved my tongue into his mouth and we tongue-kissed. I could taste and smell my pussy all over his lips and tongue and it was makin' me hornier than a muhfucka. A bitch was ready to ride some dick. I backed him up toward the bed, then pushed him down on it and crawled up on top of him.

"Damn, baby," he said, breathin' all heavy 'n shit. "I don't even know your name, and you got my head spinnin'."

I looked him dead in the eyes, then leaned in and whispered, "Don't worry 'bout that. Just know I'm here to fuck you to heaven, nigga." I slid down his body, leavin' a trail of wet kisses along his chest, his stomach, then over his dick. I lifted up his dick and started kissin' his balls nice 'n slow before puttin' 'em into my mouth, one at a time, then wettin' 'em up as I swirled my tongue 'round 'em. I gave the nigga an old-fashioned ball washin'. He let out a moan. "Ah, fuck..."

"You like that?" I asked, lookin' up at him as I slowly took the head of his dick into my mouth, then swallowed him down. His eyes were shut, and he was suckin' on his bottom lip.

"Hell yeah," he answered, lookin' down at me all lusty-eyed and whatnot. "Oh, shit...damn, baby, you know howta suck a dick. Ah, shit."

I greedily sucked him while softly yankin' and massagin' his balls. I sucked him slow, sucked him deep, sucked the nigga so good he started shiverin' and his toes opened all wide 'n shit, then closed real tight. "Oh, fuck...oh, fuck...Aaah...Damn, you gonna make me nut...Aaaaah, fuck..."

"I want you to put this big, muhfuckin' dick up in me," I said, pullin' his dick outta my throat and comin' up for air. "My pussy needs some dick. It's so fuckin' wet. You ready to fuck me?"

"Hell yeah," he moaned. Actually, the shit sounded more like a growl. "I'm ready to fuck, deep and slow, baby."

I slowly crawled up on top of him, then straddled him. I rested my throbbin', drippin' wet pussy along the shaft of his wide dick. We kissed while I ground down on him and he pushed up into me. "You feel that pussy heat?"

"Yeah, baby," he said, buckin' his hips up into me.

I leaned in and whispered in his ear, "I want you to fuck this hot pussy, nigga. Where ya condoms at?"

"Hold up," he said, tryna catch his breath. "Let me go get one." I rolled offa him, and he jumped up and started rummagin' through his suitcase, then his briefcase. I eyed him as he dumped shit out, tryna find a wrapper. And on some real shit, a bitch was startin' to get impatient. I glanced over at the clock. It was 12:38

a.m. *If this muhfucka don't hurry up, I'ma put a bullet dead in his ass, then blast his brains out.* I took a deep breath and started countin' in my head. I scooted to the center of the bed, then spread my legs wide, bendin' 'em at the knees, rubbin' my clit, preparin' to welcome him into the Kat Trap.

But the nigga was still fumblin' 'round the room lookin' for a goddamn condom. "Um, what the fuck is takin' you so long? This pussy is overheatin' and I'm ready for some dick."

"Give me a minute. I know I brought a box with me," he said, flippin' shit over, lookin' all desperate and whatnot. He went into the bathroom, then came back out—empty-handed of course! "I don't know where they are. Listen, baby, I don't have anything. What about you?"

No...this...nigga...didn't!

I twisted my face up, snappin' up in the bed. "'Scuse me?"

He climbed back into the bed and looked me in the eyes. He ran his warm hand up and down my back. "I'm negative, baby. Disease free. Are you?"

"Oh, sooo, you wanna hit this tight pussy raw?"

"I'll pull out. Just tell me where you want me to cum." This nigga had the audacity to look at me all serious 'n shit. He leaned back onto his forearms and looked down at his rock-hard cock. My mind was made up. I knew what I had to do. I looked him dead in his face, grabbed his dick and started jerkin' it, grinnin'. He smiled and winked. "Look how hard you got that dick."

"And you want me to wet it up for you, don't you?" I asked, jerkin' his dick faster.

"Oh, shit, yeah."

I let go of his dick and straddled him, then kissed him on the lips. "You want me to ride this"—I reached for his dick again, and started strokin' it—"and show you where I want this big dick to shoot that hot nut?"

"Yeah, baby," he moaned, holdin' his head back.

This no-good, retarded muhfucka would really fuck me raw, then go home to his wife.

"Lay all the way back," I said, stickin' my tongue back into his mouth and grindin' my pussy on his dick. I reached over and slid my hand under the side of his mattress and grabbed my gun. With my left hand, I reached under me and grabbed the base of his dick, then brushed it against the back of my pussy. I let the head of his dick press up against my slippery hole, and wet it up. "You wanna fuck this pussy? You wanna run ya dick raw up in this pussy?"

"Yeah, baby," he moaned. "Let me feel that wet pussy on this dick."

I pressed my lips down on his, and kissed him hard. I kept my eyes open, and waited for that moment—that window of opportunity—when he closed his. It came. And I pressed the silencer of my gun to his temple and pulled the trigger—*Theessrrpp!*—blowin' a hole in his skull. The bullet ripped through the other side of his head, splatterin' his brain all over the bed. Blood splashed on my face. I frowned. Then shot him again. *Theeerrrssp!*

"Next time, nigga, pack ya condoms," I snapped, climbin' offa him.

I went into his bathroom, grabbed a washcloth, then washed his blood off of me. I ran the water and wiped down e'erything, makin' sure I didn't leave any traces of blood or prints. Then I went into my bag and pulled out my cleanin' supplies, and got busy. Once I was done, I got dressed, grabbed my bag, and quietly slipped back into my room without anyone seein' me.

I called Cash, told him what was what, then stripped outta my wears and jumped in the shower. Twenty minutes later, I climbed into my hotel bed and fell into a deep sleep.

>>>

On the flight home the next mornin', I closed my eyes as soon as I buckled up. I was glad I was sittin' by the window so I wouldn't have to be bothered with someone tryna get in the seat next to me, or tryna crawl over me to get to the bathroom. I hated that shit.

The minute we hit the ground at Newark Airport, I flipped open my cell and called Chanel to see if she wanted to go out to Short Hills to shop, then do lunch. The ho almost jumped through the damn phone when I told her I would not only buy her lunch, but treat her to a pair of heels as well.

"Bitch, you tryna make me fall in love with ya fine, sexy ass or somethin'?"

I laughed. "Ho, please. What I tell you 'bout that lesbo shit? Don't get ya grill knocked." The white dude sittin' next to me looked over at me. And I looked right back at him, raisin' my brow like, "What muhfucka? Say somethin' and get ya pale face slapped." He turned his face the other way.

"Oooh, ma, I love it when you talk rough," she said, fallin' out laughin'. "What time you comin' through?"

"Yeah, I bet you do," I said, laughin' with her. "Annnywaaaay, freak, I'm still on the airplane waitin' for them to open the damn doors so I can get up outta here. I got muhfuckas all up in my damn face, ear-hustlin' 'n shit. I'ma go home, drop off this bag, and change my wears. I should be there to pick ya ho ass up 'round twelve-thirty or so."

"Bet," she said. We hung up. As soon as the plane door opened, e'eryone started scramblin' like roaches to get their shit and get off the plane. And I was right along with 'em.

The minute I walked through my door, I took a deep sigh. I was so glad to be home. Although I was only gone overnight, for some reason I was exhausted as hell. I jumped in the shower, dressed, then made my way back out the door to pick up Chanel.

Four hours later, Chanel and I had just finished our shoppin' spree, and now we were sittin' in Legal Sea Foods havin' lunch. We were loaded down with shoppin' bags. Of course the bitch ended up gettin' more than a pair of heels outta me. But it was all good.

"I love the food here," Chanel said as she bit into her lobster roll.

"Yeah, it's real cute," I agreed, takin' a sip of my drink. I covered my mouth and tried to stop from yawnin'. "Oh. Excuse me. I'm f-in' beat."

She yawned, coverin' her mouth. "Aah, now you got me doin' that shit. Divine's ass kept me up wantin' to talk and fuck all damn night. I swear I thought the nigga was skeed up the way he was actin'. It was like his ass was racin' a mile a minute."

I placed my elbows up on the table, and cupped my hands under my chin. "So, you think he's gettin' high or somethin'?"

She shook her head. "Nah, not at all. He was just bouncin' around like the damn Energizer bunny 'n shit." She leaned in and lowered her voice. "That nigga tore my pussy hole up last night. And then he had the nerve to say he wanted to crack this asshole open." I started laughin'. "That shit ain't funny. I wish the hell I would let some nigga run his dick up in my ass. I told that nigga I got three holes, but only two of 'em are for dick use, and one of 'em ain't my doo-doo hole."

I laughed, but I was thinkin' this ho needed to get with the program and make it do what it do. I noticed two white cats sittin' on our left tryna ear hustle. And they had the nerve to both be fine, tanned, well-groomed, and very fuckable. And both of 'em were clearly enjoyin' what they were hearin'. *Yeah, them freaky muhfuckas sittin' at their table with two hard cocks*, I thought, starin' at the one who was facin' my direction. I raised my eyebrow. He smiled, then quickly shifted his eyes.

"Girl, I thought you was a certified freak with yours," I said, makin' sure my voice was low enough for only her to hear. We stopped talkin' when the waitress came back to our table to see if we wanted anything else. "No, we're fine."

"I'll be right back with your check," she said, walkin' off.

"Hmmph, that's what Divine musta thought, too," she said, takin' a sip of her drink.

"Poor thing," I said, shakin' my head and laughin'. "Chanel, girl, you crack me the hell up."

"Well, I'm glad you find this all so humorous." She looked over at the white dude who was facin' her. He was dead in her grill. "Can I help you?" she asked with much 'tude. I lowered my head, knowin' she'd turn this spot out if he came at her wrong.

"I was just admiring you," he said. "We were just saying how beautiful the two of you were."

"Thank you," I said, lookin' over at 'em. Chanel grinned.

The waitress returned with our bill. I handed her my credit card. Chanel waited for her to walk off before leanin' over toward them and whisperin', "Ya'll want some chocolate pussy, hunh?"

I almost fell outta my seat. Dude's eyes popped open, and his face turned three shades red. His peoples almost choked on his drink.

"Oh my God, please don't pay her no mind," I said, shakin' my head. "She's on meds, and she gets nutty when she doesn't take 'em. Girl, get up and let's go before you get us tossed up outta here with ya mess."

She winked at 'em, then stood up. "Kat, I'm goin' to the bathroom. I'll be right back."

"And don't take all day in there," I said, watchin' her switch off toward the bathrooms. When the waitress returned, I signed the bill, slid my credit card back into my wallet, and waited for Chanel to get back.

When she came back to the table, we started grabbin' our bags to leave. She looked back over at the two dudes, and said, "Ya'll gentlemen enjoy the rest of ya meal."

They smiled, watchin' as she switched her ass out the door. I couldn't do shit but laugh. *That bitch is crazy*, I thought, followin' behind her.

TWENTY-FOUR

The whole summer was one big-ass blur to me. I couldn't believe the shit had just 'bout come and gone and, in another three weeks, Labor Day was gonna be here. Chanel and I were already talkin' 'bout maybe goin' to either Puerto Rico or St. Lucia to chill that weekend. Of course she wanted to invite Tamia's rotten ass, but I shut that shit down real quick. I told that ho I didn't want that dirty bitch nowhere in my space.

"Kat, that's fucked up," she said. "We 'posed to be girls 'n shit."

"Wrong answer," I replied. "You my girl. That ho was a bitch I chilled with on the strength of you. Yeah, okay, at first I thought we were cool 'n shit. And I ain't gonna front, I did try 'n embrace her and Iris…you know, show 'em mad love. But on some real shit, them bitches was always hatin' on us from gate. And you know it. You and I both know them sluts were ridin' on our styles to fit in. The only reason niggas was really fuckin' with 'em is 'cause they some greedy, dick-lovin', cum-guzzlin' hoes. But I ain't never judge they asses. I still fucked with 'em. But that was then, and this is now. And now, I'ma grown-ass woman tryna do grown-ass things. I ain't beat for none of that dirty shit she's into. That bitch can't even be real with hers, so hell no, that bitch can't roll no-muhfuckin'-where with me again!"

And there you have it. That was the end of that. And just like Iris's dumb ass got got, I knew Tamia's crusty ass was next. You don't go 'round fuckin' muhfukas when you know ya pussy is jacked, spreadin' shit. I don't give a fuck if a nigga ain't tryna use a condom or not. Yeah, the nigga gets what he gets, but fuck that. Bitch, be real with yours; that's all I'm sayin'. That shit is gonna eventually get ya ass beat, or a hole in ya skull. Whatever!

Anyway, so here it was a Friday night, and I was downstairs in the media room sittin' Indian-style in the middle of the floor in my panties, with my titties dancin' freely about, drinkin' Henny and blazin' trees in my own zone, mindin' my own damn business, when somebody started pressin' down on my doorbell like they had lost their f-in' mind. I started to ignore the shit, but when they started bangin' on my damn door, that did it. I got up and stomped up the stairs, then peeked outta the peephole. A bitch almost passed out. It was Juanita standin' on the other side of the door, with one hand on her hip and the other bangin' on my door. "Who the fuck is it?" I yelled, actin' like I had no clue she was out there.

"Kat, open this damn door," she slurred loudly. I could tell her mouth was still wired the way she sounded. It sounded like she had a dick stuck in her throat, or was talkin' with a mouthful of marbles. "It's your mother. You know. The one you don't seem to remember havin'."

I walked to the window to see who else was out there with her before I decided whether or not to let her ass in. I wasn't in the mood for gettin' jumped by her and my crazy-ass aunts. But I'd fight her ass one-on-one if I had to. I couldn't see anyone else, but that didn't mean they weren't hidin' in the bushes or still out in her car. I knew enough to know that it was unlikely for her ass to drive way out there solo.

"Hold on," I said, goin' to the hall closet to find somethin' to put on. I pulled a navy-blue silk robe off one of the wooden hangers, then put it on. I tied the belt 'round my waist, then started toward the door. *Unh-uh, this chick is a nut,* I thought. *Ain't no tellin' what she's gonna do.* I stopped in my tracks and turned back around and went into the kitchen. I dumped open my bag and grabbed what I needed along with my cordless phone, just in case. I walked back to the door and opened it. I kept the storm door locked and spoke to her through the glass. "Why you here?" I asked, frownin.' I leaned up against the door-frame, with one hand on my hip and the other behind my back.

"Are you gonna let me in or not?" she asked, slammin' her hands on both her hips. The right side of her face was still swollen, and her left eye had a patch over it. She was still tore-up so I knew she didn't come to put work in.

"For what?"

"What do you mean 'for what?'"

"Duh, just what I mean."

"Kat, don't be a bitch. Open ya damn door and let me in so we can talk."

I stood there in the doorway and looked at the woman who gave birth to me, the woman who practically abandoned me for the men in her life, and I felt nothin' for her. Not one damn thing. Not happiness. Not pity. Not sadness. Not contempt. Not a goddamn thing. I was empty toward her. And I realized that that emptiness was always there 'cause she never connected with me; she never embraced me long enough to fill my emotional cup. And it was fuckin' empty. And I was left to fill it up on my own.

I shook my head. "No. You wanna talk, then you talk outside 'cause you not welcome in my home. Besides, as far as I'm concerned, we have nothin' to talk about. I said all I'm gonna say to you the last time we spoke, and ain't nothin' changed."

She frowned. "I thought it was real fucked up that you didn't come to the hospital to see me. I'm still ya mother."

"Umm, and that surprised you, because...?" I said, openin' my hand and holdin' my arm out, pausin' for her to fill in the blanks. When she didn't, I continued, "I told you I was done with you. And I meant that."

Then outta nowhere, like I suspected, here comes Rosa talkin' shit. She musta been sittin' in the car, or squattin' on the side of the house. She came rushin' up to the door in a pair of faded blue jeans and a blue oversized 2006 *Essence* Festival shirt with a pair of crisp white Nikes. And the chick had her hair pulled back real tight into a ponty tail with it stuffed under her fitted base-ball cap like she was prepared to put some work in.

"Fuck all this back 'n forth shit, Juanita. Tell her ass we need to talk and to open up this motherfuckin' door," she said, talkin' with her hands, pointin' at me through the door. She stared at me. "Kat, open up this fuckin' door, or bring ya fresh ass outside so we can air it out. All that slick shit on the phone ain't forgot-ten, sweetie. I told you, I'ma put my foot in ya ass."

I laughed. "Oh, really? Well, I tell you what. Try it if you want. But what the both of you had better do is get the fuck up off my property."

"You fresh-ass bitch," Rosa screamed, slammin' her hand against the glass. "We ain't goin' no fuckin' where until I beat ya ass for disrespectin' ya mother, and me."

"What the fuck you think I look like, lettin' the two of you up in my spot? You think I'ma let ya'll up in here so you can try 'n toss my spot up. I don't think so." Then it hit me that maybe I should let 'em in. I mean, that way, when they got at me and I had to put a bullet in one of 'em, I could say they attacked me in my home and I was protectin' myself. Nah, fuck that! Them crazy bitches wasn't gettin' in.

Rosa kicked the bottom of the door. "Bring ya ass outside, then. 'Cause I'ma fuck you up, Kat. You came for the wrong bitch, sweetie."

"Rosa," my moms said through her clenched teeth. "Don't make a scene out here. I didn't drive all the way over here to get arrested. This ain't the projects."

"I don't give a fuck," Rosa replied loudly. "This bitch is too goddamn grown, Juanita. And it's time she gets her face cracked in. Kat, you got an ass whoopin' comin' so you might as well come outside and get it now while it's hot. And if I gotta stand out this bitch all motherfuckin' night, then that's what it is." She grabbed the door handle and started yankin' on it. "Bring ya ass outside, you fuckin' disrespectful bitch. You got me confused. I ain't ya Aunt Patrice. When I get my hands on you, you gonna wish ya ass was dead."

"Oh, really," I said, pullin' my nickel-plated 9mm from behind my back. Both of their eyes popped wide open in shock.

"Oh, my God," my moms said through clenched lips, slappin' her hand over her mouth.

Rosa let go of the door. "You'd pull a gun out on your own fuckin' mother? I done seen it all now," Rosa said, flingin' her hands up in the air. "*Dios mios!* I don't fuckin' believe this shit."

"I sure would. So believe it. And I'll fuckin' use it, too. Try me. Now both of you bitches get the fuck up off my property or you'll be leavin' up outta here in either handcuffs or body bags, take ya pick." Although I would never call five-oh on my own family—I don't care how serious shit got—I hoped one of the nosey-ass neighbors would. And I really didn't wanna put a bullet in either one of 'em, but I knew in my heart I would if they pressed me.

The porch light to the house on the left came on, then the lights to the house on the other side flicked on. My moms looked around. "Let's go, Rosa," she said, grabbin' Rosa by the arm.

She snatched her arm back. "No, Nita, your child needs a beat down first."

"I ain't a fuckin' child," I snapped. "I'm a grown-ass woman. Get it right."

"I knew this was a bad idea," my moms said. "I told you she wasn't gonna let us in."

"Then maybe you shoulda came by yourself," I said, keepin' my aim at them.

"And would that have made any difference?" she asked, starin' me in the eyes.

"Hell no," I said. "'Cause I want nothin' to do with you." For the first time in my life, I thought I saw hurt in her eyes. But that shit didn't matter. What about all the times she hurt me? Fuck her! The truth is what it is. "Um, I think you betta get goin' 'cause the cops are on their way. And since *neither* of you are invited here, it's called trespassin'. Now, like I said before, get the *fuck* off my property." I slammed the door in their faces.

I heard glass smash and knew Rosa punched or kicked, or threw somethin' at, the storm door. It took e'erything in me not to run outside and jump on that bitch's back, but I knew she'd have her razor spit out in her hand and would have me sliced from one end to the next before I knew what hit me. I already knew goin' out there meant I'd have to straight-up blast her head off. "Crazy bitch," I heard her yell. "The minute you step 'cross the bridge, bitch, I'ma see ya ass. I put that on ya grandfather's grave. Nita, I don't know where the fuck you got her from, but that bitch takes the grand prize for crazy. Can you believe she pulled a gun on us? A fuckin' gun! Oh, my God, wait 'til I tell everyone this shit!"

Rosa's nutty ass screamed at the top of her lungs all the way back to my mom's Benz. I flipped open my cell and called Chanel, watchin' them pull off outta the livin' room window.

"Hey, ho, what's good?"

"You not gonna fuckin' believe who came up over here tryna set shit off?"

"Who?" she asked, gettin' amped.

"My fuckin' moms and her nutty-ass sister, Rosa."

"Unh-uh, say it ain't so. I know you didn't let them in, did you?"

"Hell no, I didn't let them nuts in. I spoke to them hoes through the glass door; are you fuckin' kiddin'? I already knew what time it was. Please. They wasn't gettin' up in here fuckin' up my shit."

"So what happened?" she asked. I took a deep breath, then broke the story down to her from beginnin' to end. "Oh, my God, bitch, I can't believe you pulled a gun out on 'em. That shit is crazy."

"Well, believe it. I was gonna put some heat in that ass before they got up in here tryna serve me. Fuck that." I paused, openin' the front door. There was glass shattered all down between the doors. "This fuckin' bitch done kicked the glass outta my door, retarded ho," I said, slammin' the door shut. "Anyway, I don't think my moms was really tryna bring it, but Rosa's ass was ready to serve it for real, for real. You shoulda seen her ass foamin' at the mouth 'n shit, lookin' like Cujo. I was too through with them bitches, comin' here tryna fuck up my high."

She started laughin'. "Kat, ya crazy ass is going straight to hell. You do know that, right?"

"Well, there'll be a bunch of us down there then, 'cause I ain't the fuckin' one. I mean, on some real shit, I really didn't wanna haveta shoot my moms, or Rosa. But if push came to shove, they'd both get bodied. And I make no apologies for that. I was here mindin' my own fuckin' business. Them bitches came here—uninvited, mind you—tryna disrupt my groove. And my moms already knows Rosa's MO. She wanted to see that bitch bring it to me since her ass is still all broke up 'n shit. So, they both woulda caught a bullet."

"Humph. That shit is crazy, for real."

"Girl, trust, this shit was way over the top for even me. I mean, really. What the fuck made them think I was gonna let 'em up in here with open arms?"

"Your guess is as good as mine," she said, snappin' her fingas. "Oh, shit, girl, you not gonna believe this. Guess whose dumb ass done got arrested for stealin' prescription pads from her job?"

"I bet it was Tameka's porch-monkey ass," I said.

"Yep," she said, laughin'. "They came and snatched that ass up the other day. Now she's sittin' on Rikers, stressin' the fuck out 'cause ain't nobody tryna bail her ass out."

"That's what that baldheaded bitch gets for runnin' her fuckin' mouth. I'ma still see her ass, though."

"Well, you might have a long wait. 'Cause this mess with her stealin' prescription pads and shit has been goin' on for a minute. They were writin' all types of prescriptions, then sellin' them shits and whatnot. That ho may be goin' up the river.

These two other chicks were down with her, and they done put the shit all on her ass."

I laughed. "And that's exactly why I do my dirt solo."

"I hear you, girl. So, what's good for tonight?" she asked, changin' the subject. "You feel like rollin' out somewhere? There's this party at Mars 2112 tonight. And it should be packed with a lotta shakers 'n movers and big-dick ballers."

I rolled my eyes and sucked my teeth, glancin' at the clock. It was almost nine o'clock. I really didn't feel like goin' out, but it had been a minute since we dropped 'n popped. "What time ya ho ass wanna roll?"

"I'm ready when you are. All I gotta do is slip on my wears. I showered already, but you need to hurry up and scoop me before Divine comes up in here tryna get some pussy 'cause you know the nigga don't like me leavin' up outta here without him wettin' his dick up first."

"Awww, poor thing," I said, laughin'. "I'll be there to save you and your pussy in forty minutes."

"Please hurry," she said, laughin' with me. "The nigga done already texted me, talkin' 'bout he's gonna be home in like an hour. So make sure you get ya ass here before then."

"Aiight, trick. I'll see you shortly."

By the time me and Chanel got to Times Square, found parkin', and walked up to the line to get into the club, it was already eleven-thirty. We had smoked a blunt apiece on the ride over and we were both feelin' right. Chanel was lookin' all chic and whatnot in a fly-ass white-and-black print jersey dress that hung off the shoulders, and she rocked a pair of six-inch black strappy sandals with an oversized white Chanel bag. And I kept it cute—of course—in a black, red, and pink abstract dress with a draped front and bubble hem with a twisted cut-out racerback. And of course I had to serve them hoes my Jimmy Choo patent leather Riki Ring bag, and a bangin'-ass pair of Versace Mirror stilettos.

Chanel knew damn well I wasn't for standin' in no long-ass lines, and before I could open my mouth to say somethin' to her, my cell started ringin'. I looked at the number and flipped the phone open. "Hey," I said, followin' behind Chanel.

"What's good, baby?"

"You," I said.

"That's what it is. What you gettin' into tonight?"

"Me and Chanel are in the city gettin' ready to go up into this club."

"Oh word, which one?"

"Mars 2112."

"Oh, shit. That's where me and my mans are on our way to."

I laughed. "Yeah right, nigga."

"Nah, baby, real talk. Matter of fact, I'm rollin' through mid-town now." He started laughin'. "Yeah, I bet you thought you was gonna be bouncin' that ass up on them niggas tonight. Well, baby, big daddy's comin' through and I'm 'bout to shut shit down."

"Oh, puhleeeze," I said, grinnin'. "Ya ass tryna stalk me 'n shit."

"Yeah, aiight, if you say so. You make sure you got ya pretty ass somewhere where I can get at you."

"Yeah, yeah, yeah," I said, laughin'.

I spotted Chanel walkin' toward me. "Bitch, will you come on," she said, wavin' me forward. She apparently knew someone who got us in without havin' to play that long-ass line.

I sighed. "I gotta go," I said, followin' behind Chanel, "so hit me up when you get in."

"You already know," he said. "I'll get at you in a minute." And that's exactly what he did. We were up in the VIP section all night poppin' bottles and gettin' our throats wet lovely. Grant let me do me, but outta respect, I kept it cute. I let the nigga hug and kiss up on me, and I only danced with a few cats, but mostly danced with him. By the end of the night, I was lit and ready to go home and roll up on top of a hard dick. But of course, Grant had to take his mans back to wherever he had to be, and Chanel was gonna crash at my spot so that cancelled that out.

I had my arms folded 'cross my chest and my lip poked out like I was poutin' as we were walkin' outta the club. It was goin' on three-thirty in the mornin'. Grant and I stood outside waitin' for his peoples and Chanel's dick-hungry ass.

"Yo," he said, grabbin' me by the waist and pullin' me into him, "cut that shit out. You know what it is. I'ma see you later today. You make sure you take ya ass straight home."

I rolled my eyes, grinnin'. "Whatever, nigga."

He kissed me on the lips. "Yo, you know you got my dick hard, right?"

Chanel called me on my cell. "Bitch, where the fuck you at?" I asked, lookin' around for her.

"I'm on my way out now. I couldn't get to the bathroom without some nigga tryna get all up in my ear."

I sucked my teeth. "Bring ya ass on." I hung up when I spotted her comin' outta the door.

"So, I'ma see ya tomorrow, aiight," Grant said as Chanel was approachin' us.

"Yeah," I said.

Chanel walked up and spoke to him. "Hey, Grant."

"What's good, Chanel?"

"Not a thing," she said, smilin.' She looked over at me. "So, Grant...tell me. When you gonna bag this chick here?" she asked, flickin' her thumb over at me. "I told you her wild ass needs a nigga like you to tame her."

He laughed. "I don't know. You gotta ask her that. She act like she all scared 'n shit."

"Oh, please," I said. "Scared of what? And don't ya'll be talkin' like I ain't standin' here."

He smiled, lookin' down at his crotch. "You know what it is."

"Oh, whatever," I said, laughin'. "Don't gas ya'self."

Chanel chimed in, "You know she likes to get beat, right?"

"Oh, word?"

"Nigga, believe that shit if you want. Chanel's drunk ass'll have you catchin' a bullet."

"Oh, shit, you'd really shoot me, huh?" he asked, laughin'.

"Yep," I said. "Right after I finished wettin' ya dick up." Chanel and Grant started laughin' like they thought that was the funniest shit they heard all night. Humph. Little did they know, I was laughin' with 'em, but I was dead-ass.

"Yo, baby," he said, pullin' me into him. "You funny as hell." He kissed me again. "You ain't ever gotta worry 'bout me puttin' my hands on you; I ain't with that shit." He leaned into my ear, and whispered, "But I will spank that ass with this dick."

"Yeah, we'll see," I said, laughin'. "Chanel, let's get outta here."

He peeped his boy talkin' to some chick. "Yo, nigga, will you come on."

"Hold up, give me a minute," dude said, flippin' open his cell and handin' it to the chick so she could put her number in. I ain't gonna front, the nigga was fine; not as fine as Grant, but he could still get it.

Grant shook his head. "This nigga. Check it, meet me at the ride. I'ma walk my peoples to her ride." Dude nodded his head. Grant wrapped his arm 'round me while Chanel walked a few steps in back of us. Her cell rang.

"Hello?" we heard her say. "Nigga, where the hell you think I'm at?" I grinned, knowin' it was Divine. "I told you I was goin' out with Kat…Yes, I did…Whatever…No, I'm stayin' the night… Yes…No, Divine…I'ma be home sometime in the afternoon… Whatever, Divine…okay, aiight. I heard you…" She hung up. "Ugh, that nigga makes me sick."

I craned my neck, glancin' at her over my shoulder. "Yeah, right," I said. "You love that nigga."

"Whatever," she said, suckin' her teeth. "You worry 'bout gettin' some love in your life."

"Yo," Grant said, smilin'. "I'ma take care of that."

"Please do," Chanel said.

When we got to the parkin' garage, I unlocked the door for Chanel. Grant waited for her to get in, then pulled me into him, squeezin' my ass and kissin' me.

"Yo, make sure you take ya ass straight home," he said, kissin' me again. "I don't wanna haveta fuck nobody up."

"Whatever," I said. "You make sure you take ya ass home."

"You got that," he said, kissin' me again. He opened the car door for me and waited for me to get behind the wheel. He looked over at Chanel and was gettin' ready to speak, but her ass was already knocked out. "Get home safe."

"You, too," I said, startin' the engine, then backin' out. I tapped the horn as I drove by, then made my way back to Jersey with thoughts of Grant comin' through later on in the day. Yeah, this nigga was tryna have a bitch fall for 'im. I just hoped he was ready, 'cause I was tryna play for keeps. I took a deep breath, turned on the CD player, and listened to Aretha Franklin sing "The Tree of Life." And for some reason, after hearin' the *verse It's too late to cry...There ain't gonna be no next time...* I felt my chest tighten and an achin' in my heart. I clutched my chest and choked back tears as I headed toward the Holland Tunnel.

Erykah Badu's "Bag Lady" was playin' in the background and Grant and I had just finished blazin' our third blunt. He had come through earlier in the afternoon, like he said he would. And after diggin' my back out lovely, we were loungin' 'round chillin'. I couldn't front, things between us were really startin' to feel right 'n shit. But I didn't wanna jinx shit by gettin' all excited too quick. I was tryna play it cool and keep shit cute. I was really diggin' his ass. But the nigga wasn't my man, and I wasn't sure if that's what I really wanted. A part of me did, but then there was that part of me that was scared. Not of him, but of what I'd do if he turned out to be another nigga tryna play me. I really think a bitch would go postal for real. The nigga's dick game was so damn tight that I knew, without a doubt, that I could really get caught in him. And that shit had a bitch on edge; almost nervous. I'm not sure if it was my heart, my head, or my pussy talkin', but whichever it was, I knew if I gave in to the feelin's that were slowly startin' to stir inside of me and the nigga turned out to be on some other shit, it wouldn't be a pretty sight. My gut told me he was a good man, but what I couldn't figure out was if the nigga was a cheatin' man.

Anyway, as long as we kept shit the way it was, there was no stress and no pressure. I played my position, and allowed him to play his. If the nigga was fuckin' someone else, then so be it. He wasn't my man. So he could slay whoever he wanted. I wasn't beat 'cause I didn't see or hear 'bout it. He claimed he was just servin' me the dick, but I had heard that shit before so it didn't really hold much weight with me. Although I didn't have a reason not to trust him, I still kept my eyes and ears open for any signs of him tryna get slick. So far, there were none. But I was gonna give it more time. Most niggas showed they asses within the first three to six months. So I was gonna see how shit played out. But on some real shit, who was I to feel some kinda way 'bout him slayin' another bitch's pussy when I was still waxin' the muh-fuckas I was murkin'. I ain't gonna front, I was really startin' to fall for the nigga, and I could tell the nigga was diggin' me, too. But like I said, I didn't really wanna rush into nothin'. I was cool with how things were flowin' with us, and I didn't really wanna complicate shit; not yet anyway.

"So you still not lookin' for a man?" he asked, leanin' over and kissin' me lightly on the lips.

"Not today," I said, grinnin'. "Check back tomorrow."

"Yeah, aiight." He grinned back, pullin' me into his arms. He slid his tongue in my mouth. Damn, the nigga's tongue game was right. My pussy started gettin' wet. "Keep playin' with me." He kissed me a few more times, then pulled away. "Dig, one of my mans is gettin' married at the end of the month and I want you on my arm."

I smiled. "So you ready to show me off to ya peeps now, hunh?"

"No doubt," he said, leanin' over and peckin' me on the lips again. "You my baby; fuck all that shit you be talkin' 'bout you ain't ready for a man 'n shit."

"I wanna take it slow."

"I hear you," he said, rubbin' the side of my face. "There's no rush, baby. Big daddy got all the time ya pretty ass needs."

I smiled. "You sure 'bout that?"

"No doubt, baby."

"Well, I'd be honored to be on ya arm to let them hoes know what a real dime looks like."

He laughed. "That's what it is. His bachelor's party is this weekend so I'ma be outta town with my boys."

"Hmmm. When you leavin'?"

"Tomorrow."

"Oh, okay. You make sure you don't be lettin' none of them stripper hoes wet ya dick," I said, actin' like I was really pressed.

"Nah, baby. The only one I want wettin' this dick is you, real talk. You make sure you keep these niggas out here outta ya grill while I'm gone."

"Oh, please. I ain't thinkin' 'bout none of them whack-ass niggas."

"Yeah, aiight. Don't have me hurtin' nobody."

"It's all good," I said, shiftin' my body to face him. "I gotta go outta town overnight anyway."

"Damn," he said, eyein' me. "You do a lotta dippin'. On some real shit, you need to let me know now what's really good with you."

I raised my brow. "What ya mean?"

"I'm sayin'. If you fuckin' some other nigga, you need to let me know so I can fall back." *Oh my God*, I thought, *this nigga got the nerve to be soundin' all jealous*.

"Nigga, please. I ain't fuckin' with no one else," I lied, rollin' my eyes. Well, technically, I *wasn't* fuckin' with any other muhfuckas, so I wasn't really lyin', right? Besides a dead nigga really didn't count; well, that's what I kept tellin' myself.

He pulled me into him, then slid his tongue into my mouth. We kissed long and slow for a few minutes. He ran his hands along my back, over my hips, then grabbed my ass, starin' into my eyes. The way he was lookin' at me, I could tell he had somethin' on his mind.

"Why you lookin' at me like that?" I asked.

He shook his head.

"What?"

"Nah, it's nothin'."

Now, I started to leave it alone. And if someone asked me why I even pushed the shit, I couldn't tell you. I guess 'cause I dug the nigga and I really did wanna know what he was thinkin'. So I pushed the issue.

"'C'mon, don't try 'n play me for slow," I said, grabbin' at his dick. Mmmph. His dick was nice 'n thick, and slowly growin'. "I can tell you got somethin' on ya mind, so share." I held my breath, already knowin' where this was gonna go.

"I'm tryna figure you out," he stated, "that's all."

"And what are you tryna figure out?" I asked, bracin' myself.

"I've asked you several times how you made ya paper, and I still haven't gotten a real answer…any answer, for that matter." He sighed, sittin' up on his forearm, lookin' up. Now, in my head, I'm thinkin', *You need to curse this nigga out real quick for tryna clock ya flow. You don't ask him how he's collectin' his dough so he don't need to be askin' you shit 'bout how you movin'.* I had to bite down on my tongue to keep from comin' at him real slick. He pulled me into his arms. "Listen…I'm diggin' you. And I'm tryna make shit happen with you, but I need to know what's really good with you. You say you ain't fuckin' any other muhfuckas, but you always jettin' off somewhere. Please tell me you ain't pushin' weight for some nigga or somethin'."

I twisted my lips up. "Are you fuckin' serious? A bitch like me would never play herself and be some nigga's mule. I ain't that bitch."

"Okay, so how you livin', then? You stay dipped 'n shit in all the ill flavors, you pushin' hot whips, and ya spot is tight. Not that I'm tryna get in ya pockets or anything. I'm just tryna see where ya head is at; how you gettin' ya hustle on."

"I'm a consultant," I told him, hopin' that would keep him satisfied. The lie rolled off my tongue and outta my mouth so quick, I didn't have a chance to think it all the way through. *A consultant! What the fuck?!* I thought to myself, regrettin' I even said that shit. I decided to add a little extra. "And my moms came into some money and laced me 'bout two years ago so I was able to make some things happen."

"Hmm," he said, eyein' me. I could tell the nigga wasn't buyin' it. But he let it go—for the moment, anyway. "When you leavin'?"

"Tomorrow," I said.

"And when you comin' back?"

I didn't know what the fuck was up with all the damn questions, but I answered anyway. "Late tomorrow night."

He frowned. "And what type of consultin' you do again?"

I put muhfuckas outta they misery. But of course I couldn't tell his ass what I was thinkin'. Hell, I couldn't really tell him much of anything. I mean, on some real shit, how do you tell a nigga you tryna be fly with that you fuckin' niggas, then blowin' they brains out at point-blank range? That with a kiss on a nigga's lips and sweet whispers in his ear, you'll shoot him between the eyes while straddled on top of him, slammin' down on his dick? I mean, really. That'll fuck a nigga's head up; have him thinkin' ya ass is nuts or you some borderline psycho bitch. Fuck, I thought, takin' a deep breath, tryna figure out what I was gonna say to keep his ass from tryna sniff out more than what he needed to know. *I shoulda knew this nigga wasn't gonna just let this shit go.* I tried to think fast, but came up blank. So, a bitch did the next best thing. I pressed my lips against his, slid my tongue into his mouth, then grabbed at his dick. At first he sat there like he was in a trance, but I kept massagin' his dick and kissin' him. Slowly, his hands started roamin' all over my body. He started squeezin' my titties and pushin' himself up into me as I ground my ass onto his dick. I slowly sucked on his earlobe, lickin' 'round the edges, then dartin' my tongue in and out of his ear. Yeah, he knew I was tryna changin' the subject and it was workin'. I was smart enough to know that this wasn't gonna stop him from askin' me again how I stacked my paper but, for the moment, it was gonna keep him from askin' me anythin' else until I could figure out what I was gonna tell 'im. On some real shit, I knew there was no way I was gonna be able to dip outta town the way I do if I was gonna fuck with his ass on some serious-type shit without problems. Oh, well…I'd cross that bridge when I got to it. In the meantime, I'd keep it cute, and give him the bare minimum.

I whispered in his ear, "I wanna suck all over ya thick, black dick."

He lowered his voice. "Oh, word?"

I nodded, kissin' him on his lips and neck, then slitherin' my way down his body in between his legs, reachin' for his dick. "Can I suck daddy's big dick?" I asked, as if I was beggin' for it. I slowly licked my lips, pullin' his dick outta the slit of his boxers. I flicked my tongue across the head. "Oh, I need daddy's dick real bad." He lifted his arms up, then locked his fingers together, placing them under his head, spreadin' his legs wider apart. He lifted his hips and allowed me to remove his underwear all the way down to his ankles. His dick was brick. "Oh, yes," I said, grabbin' his dick at the base, lickin' the drool from the corners of my lips. "Look at all this big dick. Mmm…you got a pretty dick."

"Yeah, you love that dick, don't you?"

"Mmm-hmm," I moaned, kissin' the tip of his dick. "I"—kiss—"love"—kiss—"it."

He let out a soft moan as I nibbled and licked on his balls, then slid my tongue along the back of his dick. I slid my lips up and down it, from his balls back up to the tip of his dick, wettin' it up real nice, glidin' my tongue all over it. He moaned again. I smiled and wrapped my lips around the head of his cock, and slowly gulped it down one inch at a time until I had his entire dick down in my throat. "Oh, shit, baby," he groaned. "You tryna fuck a nigga's head up."

I increased the suction and neck bobbin', while massagin' and squeezin' his balls. He grabbed the sides of my head, slowly pumped his hips, then face-fucked me until he shot his thick, creamy load down into my throat. Humph. There was nothin' like lickin' and suckin' the nut outta a thick cock. Although I swallowed most of it, some still overflowed outta my mouth and dripped along the sides of his dick and down onto his balls. But a cum-hungry bitch like me never wastes a drop. I licked and slurped all around his balls and dick, then took him back into my mouth and sucked the remainin' drops of his nut until his body shook, and his eyes rolled up in his head. And for the rest of the night, I wet his dick and kept him fucked down to the bone, hopin' he wouldn't press me for answers I was never gonna be ready to give.

CHAPTER TWENTY-SIX

*Everything ain't always what it seems...Niggas frontin',
bitches stuntin'...at the end of the day, it's all a dream...so
you better watch ya step...there ain't no loyalty, there ain't no
love...just a bunch of niggas and bitches...grimy, ruthless,
rotten to the core...*

Biggie's "Niggas Bleed" was blarin' outta the Bose speakers of my sleek silver Jaguar XJ12 as I drove down the parkway, heading south toward Atlantic City. A bitch was feelin' sexy and real horny. It was close to midnight, and the ride was smooth as fuck until I almost hit a damn deer that raced across the highway. I swerved to the right, quickly brakin', then pressin' down on the gas pedal, pushin' one-ten. It takes a lot to shake a bitch like me, but the thought of havin' a damn deer flipped up on my fuckin' hood or comin' through my windshield with its hoof in my grill had a bitch shook. I ain't gonna front. But I sparked a blunt, took three deep pulls, and quickly pulled it together, thinkin' 'bout my mark for the night.

I was gonna fuck him real good, then splatter his brains out. I pressed my thighs together, tryna pinch the excitement stirrin' between my legs. Yes, I was gonna fuck this nigga to death, literally and figuratively. But then I felt guilty. Fuckin' with Grant had my groove all jacked up. Like I already told ya, I was diggin' the nigga. And I knew I wouldn't be able to live a double life if I wanted to be wifed-up by his ass. I was glad his ass was outta town doin' him for the weekend. Although fuckin' these marks was strictly a part of how I handled my business, it would be cheatin'. So I decided I'd have to stop fuckin' 'em if I was gonna rock with Grant. *Yep, this is the last mark I'm fuckin'*, I thought, veerin' off the ramp onto the toll road for AC. *From now on, I'll just kill 'em on the spot. No extras.*

I caught my reflection in my rearview mirror, pulled the front of my burgundy spiked, pixie-cut wig cap down a little, then made sure my self-made beauty mole over my lip was still in place. I adjusted my wire-framed Christian Dior glasses. I hated all these wigs and makeup 'n shit, but they were needed props. I pulled into the parkin' garage for the Borgata, then checked inside my Gucci duffle bag to make sure I had e'erything. It was show-time.

I entered the fly-ass hotel, strutted through the casino toward the elevators to my mark's suite. On the way up, somethin' didn't feel right. My gut told me to turn around and take my ass back home. I was startin' to feel real paranoid 'bout shit, but knew I couldn't back out. There was money to be made, and a body to be accounted for. *What the fuck!* I snapped in my head, steppin' outta the elevator. *I shoulda never smoked that shit.* The closer I got to my mark's room, the more shit didn't feel right. So, I decided to follow my gut. *I'm not fuckin' this nigga; not tonight.* In that split second, I decided I would just smoke his ass and bounce.

I reached his door, then looked around to make sure no witnesses were around. I knocked. A few minutes later, the door opened. There stood my mark in a pair of black jeans and black tee shirt. The nigga was fine. He had caramel-coated skin with thick lips, a big nose, and a bangin' body. "Yes?" he said, checkin' me out from head to toe. "How can I help you?"

Damn, this nigga looks like someone, I thought. "Somebody called for a massage," I said, takin' 'im in.

"Nah, baby, you got the wrong room."

I felt my nipples harden and licked my lips. "That's too bad," I said, eyein' him real slow and sexy-like. "I woulda loved roamin' ya body with my hands. Oh well. Enjoy ya night."

"Yo, hold up," he said. I stopped in my tracks, slowly turnin' around. *Gotcha!* "How much one of those massages run?"

"For you," I said, smilin'. "It'll be on the house. And I'll even give ya a nice release." I winked. He smiled. "I promise. You'll feel like ya floatin' on clouds when I'm done workin' ya body."

"I like that," he said, steppin' back and openin' the door with a big-ass grin on his face. "Come on in. After the night I've had, I can definitely use a little tension release."

I stepped into the spacious suite. It was just him there. "Okay, you'll need to remove all your clothes."

"Say what?"

"It's a nude massage, baby," I said. "You need to be butt-ass."

He chuckled. "Got ya. Uh, so this really does come with a happy ending?" He started laughin'. "Just kiddin'."

I smiled. "Actually, big daddy, it sure does. When I'm done with you, ya gonna be spillin' all over the place."

"Oh, word? That's wassup."

He removed his clothes, then lay across the king-sized bed. I tried not to look too hard at his muscled back and thighs. His ass was nice and firm. My mind started wanderin' and a bitch started wonderin' what it would feel like havin' my legs up over his shoulders and my nails diggin' in his muscular ass cheeks while he fucked me down. I shook away the thought before I changed my mind and gave him some pussy.

As soon as he turned his head, facin' the other way, I reached into my bag and pulled out my nickel-plated nine-millimeter with the silencer attached. I walked up on him. *Theessrrpp!* I blasted him in the back of his head. I hadn't touched shit so I was gonna be able to dip out real easy. I let out a deep breath, relieved that this went smoother than I had expected. Well, that's what I thought. But jas I was headed toward the door, it opened. And in stepped this fine-ass nigga. My eyes popped open. My face cracked. Keepin' shit real, a bitch almost passed the fuck out. It was Grant!

"Yo, who da fuck are you?" he asked, starin' me down. He squinted. The door closed behind him. I took a deep breath and backed up real slow, pullin' off my wig and removin' my glasses. I was caught and there was no need tryna talk my way outta it. "Yo, what the fuck you doin' up in here with my brotha?"

My mouth dropped. "Ya brotha?" I asked in disbelief as he walked up on me.

"Yeah, Kat, my brotha," he replied, soundin' heated. He glanced over at the bed and saw the mark sprawled on his stomach with blood oozin' outta a hole in the back of his head. He blacked. "Yo, what the fuck did you fuckin' do?" He ran over to the bed, shakin' the body. "Yo, Greg, man, you aiight? Wake up, man. Yo, Greg." He shook 'im, all frantic and whatnot, then looked up at me. "Why da fuck did you kill him, huh, bitch? Is you fuckin' crazy? That's my fam, bitch! You'se a dead ho. Word on my brotha's body." He jumped up and tried to come at me. But I had pulled my gun out and had it pointed at his head. He stopped in his tracks.

"Now put ya hands up and on the back of ya head, and don't move 'em," I said.

He did, turnin' his head back toward his brotha. When it finally hit him that his brotha was layin' there naked, he stared at him for a minute longer, then shot me a look. "Did you just fuck my fam, then turn around and kill 'im?"

"No, I didn't fuck him," I said, relieved I didn't. "You asked me several times how I made my paper," I said, starin' him in his eyes. "And I never answered you 'cause I hoped I wouldn't ever have to tell you. I hoped that I would be outta this shit. But, now it looks like it doesn't really matter." I knew the nigga was strapped so I tried to keep my eyes on his hands.

"I don't believe this shit!" he yelled, holdin' his head and walkin' in circles. "I don't fuckin' believe it! Why?"

"It's my job," I offered, avoidin' his eyes. It rattled a bitch's nerves to see the look on my man's face. Okay, the nigga wasn't officially my man, but he was the nigga I was fuckin' on a regular. And I was diggin' him. Anyway, knowin' I had caused the pained look in his eyes started fuckin' with me. *Keep shit cute, bitch*, I warned myself, tryin' fuckin' hard not to look at him. *Ain't no time for gettin' all soft up in this piece, ho.* He broke down cryin'. *Fuck! Fuck! Fuck!* E'erything was all fucked up. But there wasn't shit I could do 'bout it. It was too late. And what really fucked a bitch up the most was knowin' one of us wasn't gonna be walkin' up outta here. "I wish it didn't hafta go down like this," I said softly.

"Fuck you, bitch!" he spat. "Fuck you talkin' 'bout it's ya job? Fuck you wishin' for, bitch? You just bodied my brotha!"

"It's what I do," I said, keepin' my heat aimed at his head. But for the first time in years, my hands shook. On the inside a bitch was tremblin'. I took two deep breaths. "It's my hustle."

"Ya 'hustle'? Bitch, is you cracked out or what? How the fuck is killin' muhfuckas ya hustle? You killed my muhfuckin' fam."

My heart ached. *Fuck. Fuck. Fuck.* I took a deep breath. "Like with ya bruh," I tried to explain. "When somebody puts a hit out on a nigga, someone's paid to make that shit happen. Tonight, it was me. Trust me. If it wasn't me, it woulda been someone else slumpin' him. It was a done deal. Whoever he pissed on wanted him murked."

"Hits? Who the fuck ordered a hit out on him?"

"That's not my concern. Makin' it happen is. I don't get caught up in all the details. The less I know, the better. But had I known he was related to you, I woulda passed."

"But you woulda let someone else kill 'im? You fuckin' mean to tell me you wouldn't have warned me?"

I shrugged. "I don't know."

The nigga's eyes filled with hate. "That's some real foul shit," he said, shiftin' his weight from one leg to the other. He moved his hands from his head, then spread his arms open. "Now what? Am I next? You gonna smoke me, too?"

I looked in his eyes. I felt so fuckin' sick to my stomach. And for the first time in my life, regret crept up on me. *No time for regrets.*

"It's what I do," I said, shiftin' my eyes from his stare. The nigga had love and hate all wrapped up in his eyes. They were pleadin' with me. Even though he knew I was gonna blast him, he didn't blink. He was a real nigga. "I really dig you. Things with you coulda been great. But I can't let you live; not after walkin' in on this. I have a rule that I live by: No witnesses, no evidence. Killin' is my life, and I'm not goin' down on some soft shit."

"Just like that? You gonna shoot a nigga?" He tried to reach for his piece, but I was on him.

Theessrrp! "I'm a killa, baby," I said, shootin' him in the left shoulder. He stumbled backward, grabbin' the place where I shot him. Blood started runnin' down his shirt. He tried to reach for his gun again. *Theessssrrrp!*

"Aaaah, shit," he screeched, clutchin' his chest. "Whatchu gonna do, kill me? Is that it? I gave you my fuckin' heart! And you just gonna snake me." His breathin' was deep. It hurt me to see him cringin' from the two bullet wounds. *Shit! Shit! Shit! Why the fuck did he hafta come up in here? Why couldn't he stay where the fuck he was? Fuck!* The front of his shirt was soaked with blood and it was now runnin' down his thick fingas.

On the outside I was calm and collected, but on the inside I was straight fucked up. But this shit was much bigger than feelin's. It was a matter of life or prison—me sparin' his life versus me possibly goin' to prison. He lost. Prison wasn't an option.

"Grant, please don't make this any harder than it already is. And don't try my patience. If you move again, I'ma take ya head off. This shit ain't personal."

"Fuck you," he spat. "I wanted to make shit happen with you." He tried to reach for his gun again.

"I fuckin' warned you." *Theessrrp!* I shot him in the center of his forehead. He fell back onto the bed, next to his naked brotha.

I swallowed hard, watchin' blood spill outta his head and chest. "I wanted to give you my heart and make shit happen with you, too," I finally said, pressin' my eyes tightly closed, shuttin' off the pain that was startin' to burn in the center of my chest. I took in a deep breath, held it in for what seemed like forever, then slowly opened my eyes. His vacant brown eyes—the ones a bitch loved lookin' into when he was fuckin' her—were starin' up at the ceilin'. I looked at his lifeless body, grabbed his crotch area, and rubbed my hand all over the bulge of his big dick. I was gonna miss that good dick. I planted a soft kiss on his lips. "I'ma miss you, nigga," I said, almost whisperin'. My heart fuckin' ached. But there wasn't shit I could do 'bout it now. The nigga was dead, and a bitch had to keep pressin'. I slipped my gun back into my bag, put my wig back on, and headed for the door. I walked through the casino and outta the hotel to my car, realizin' that after tonight, a bitch's dreams would never come true. I got in my car, flipped open my cell, and choked back tears.

I took a deep breath. "I know why the caged bird sings."

"That's what it is. I'll hit you later."

"By the way, there was an extra birdie flyin' tonight."

"Did you catch it?" he asked. It was the code for an unexpected witness.

"Yeah, I snatched it by the wings."

"Bet."

"Uh, Cash."

"Yeah, what's up?"

"A bitch needs a break."

"Oh, word. How long you talkin'?"

"I'm not sure. I just know I gotta take some time and get away for a minute; maybe for good. I gotta do me."

"I can dig it," he said, pausin'. I'm sure he was thinkin' 'bout how he was gonna come at me. It wasn't like I was under contract or any shit like that, so I could bounce any time I wanted. But outta respect, I felt a sick obligation to let the nigga know. "Do what you gotta do," he finally said. "You know I'ma miss you, though."

I sighed, rollin' my eyes. "I'm sure a nigga like you will manage," I said, dismissin' his comment.

"So can a nigga finally get some of that pussy now?"

Yeah, muhfucka! And then I'ma put a bullet in ya head. I smiled, shakin' my head at the thought of two Hefty trash bags wrapped 'round his face, then one over his head and tied in a knot 'round his neck. 'Cause that was the only way a bitch would ever fuck his ass. "Maybe," I said, not sure at that moment if it was a lie, or half-truth.

"Oh word," he said, soundin' all excited 'n shit. "You already know what it is. Whenever you want it, me and this big, black dick are ready for ya fine ass."

"Whatever, nigga. Just get the rest of my paper to me."

He burst out laughin', then got all serious 'n shit with me. "Listen, Kat, on some real shit. No matter how hard you may want to, you can't run from this. It's in ya blood, baby. I knew that shit the moment I peeped you housin' that bitch on the floor at the Brooklyn Café; the minute you said you was gonna take it to her throat if she ever came at you again. I knew then. It was in ya eyes, Kat.

"It's twisted muhfuckas like you and me who can do this shit in our sleep. It takes a cold, vengeful, mean-streaked muhfucka to look a nigga dead in his eyes, then smoke his ass and never blink. Somewhere in our twisted minds, we think ain't shit wrong with takin' a muhfucka out. And what keeps us doin' this sick shit is the fact that we like takin' chances, livin' on the edge, thinkin' we'll never get caught. Killin' is ya callin', baby. You'll be back. And when you ready, I'ma be here waitin' for ya."

Crazy thing, the nigga was right. It was in my blood. The thrill of the kill turned a bitch on. It overshadowed the risks. But it cost me somethin.' It cost me what was startin' to feel like love, and the chance to finally be free.

I didn't say shit else. I hung up and drove in silence, sparkin' the half blunt that was in my ashtray. I took two long, deep pulls, then exhaled. I turned on the CD player, then pressed disc four. Lauryn Hill's "Peace of Mind" blared through the speakers. I smoked and listened, lettin' her words fill the car along with the weed smoke. Finally, a bitch broke down and cried—hard, clutchin' the steerin' wheel. Snot and spit was flyin' e'erywhere. I cried for all the shit I kept locked inside of me over the years. But most of all, I cried knowin' that no matter how much I might wanna walk away, in my heart, I knew a bitch like me would never have peace of mind. I knew the Kat Trap would be open again, and I'd fuck another nigga and smoke his ass with no hesitation; with no regret, and no fuckin' remorse. And with the promise of good pussy, a slow wet dick suck, and toe-curling orgasms, another muhfucka would be lured into his grave. 'Cause I was *that* bitch!

ABOUT THE AUTHOR

Cairo resides in New Jersey, where he is finishing up his next two literary creations, *The Man Handler*, and *Daddy Long Stroke*. His travels to Egypt are what inspired his pen name. You can email him at: cairo2u@verizon.net

IF YOU ENJOYED "THE KAT TRAP," CHECK THIS
SNEAK PREVIEW FROM CAIRO'S NEXT BOOK!

The Man Handler

BY CAIRO

COMING IN FALL 2009 FROM STREBOR BOOKS

CHAPTER ONE

Is it only me, or is there something primitively erotic, sexually enticing, about the scent of lust and musk that lingers beneath a man's balls, and clings to every strand of his dick hairs? Mmmm. I want to rub my face all up in it. Then inhale deeply, savoring the sweet, sweaty aroma. Mmmmmmmmm. The smell causes my nipples to harden, my clit to swell and pop out from under its hood, and my pussy lips to flare and flap open in anticipation…waiting, wanting, needing to be pierced by the hot spear of a dark, delicious man.

Oh, how I love the feel and the taste of a stiff, thick dick. Mmmm. I'm salivating from thinking about all the nasty, freaky things I can do with one right now. Suck it, slurp it, lick it, kiss it…Mmmmmmmm…gulp it down one inch at a time; nice, slow and very wet. Humph.

Umm, hold up. Before we go any further, let me officially introduce myself. My name is Bianca Rivers. And I LOVE to fuck. Oh my God, if that didn't sound like an introduction for an AA/NA meeting or something. Let me try again. Hello. My name is Bianca. I'm a thirty-year-old, five-foot, eight-inch, 125-pound, cocoa-brown beauty who is happily single with an insatiable sex drive and a penchant for being on the hunt for a stiff dick. It's too bad I haven't been successful at finding one man who can hold my interest longer than the time it takes for him to bust his nut. After the sex, I generally want nothing more to do with them until the next time I feel like riding down on their dicks. Stick and move. Stick and move. That's what I typically like to do. No need for anything else. I have no time to try and catch feelings for anyone. And I definitely don't want them catching any for me.

Now, just so we're clear. I have no intentions of bashing men, or having a pity party. 'Cause I'll be the first to tell you that I hate women who sit around like a bunch of hens, cackling and cawing about the woes of their lives, relentlessly complaining about their men, or men in general. So, no, I'm not going to spend my time dissing men. However, I will share my own personal experiences with them, and that will include the good, the bad and the ugly, as well as my thoughts, feelings, and views on women that definitely won't always be nice. So, if anyone can't handle that, then you might want to close up shop now, and excuse yourself.

Anyway, I'm not in a relationship (by choice). No children and never been pregnant. I've never contracted any STD's (thankfully!). I live in Jersey, and (again) I LOVE to fuck. And the best part about being single is that I can fuck who I want, when I want, how I want, where I want, and as many times I want, without answering to anyone about my actions. See. I'm what you might call a ride-a-dick-all-night-long type of chick. But, I consider myself more of a tri-sexual than anything else. Meaning, I'm into pretty much all kinds of nasty, freaky sex. As long as it doesn't involve animals, body wastes—being pissed and shitted on is a no-no—midgets, elderly, disabled, disfigured, or children, then I'm down for the get down. If I like it, I may do it again. And I'm typically turned on by men who are also tri-sexual. They tend to be less inhibited. And very secure in who they are as men. And that is very appealing to me. And when I first meet a man I want to know the following: How often do you have sex, or like to have sex? Do you masturbate? If so, how often? Can I watch? Are you into sex toys? If so, what type? Ever been handcuffed or blindfolded? When was your last HIV test?

Basically, if you really want me to break it down, I'm what you might call a certified freakologist. A term I use for peeps like me who specialize in freaking a man any way the wind blows until he slumps over. I'm also a skilled dicktologist who's dedicated to the fucking, sucking, and licking of fat, black dick. Yep, that's me. Okay, alright already. I'll say it for you…I'm a dick-loving ho. You already know. And? But don't get it twisted. I'm a responsible one. Hell, my motto is: If you're gonna fuck, be responsible. Wrap up and enjoy the damn ride!

And when it comes to fucking men, I have very few rules and restrictions. Don't be fat, nasty, and crusty. And in case someone is confused about what's fat to me: if you need a bumper jack or a 2 x 4 to lift up your gut, then dammit, you fat. If you look down and you can't see your dick or your toes, then, duh, fat. If you have more belly than dick, duh, fat! So buy a vowel, get a clue, and get your sloppy-ass on a diet before trying to get at me.

In addition, a man must have all of his teeth (that does not mean having a bunch of brown, yellow, or rotted ones either, or a row of gold or platinum fronts). He must wash his ass daily (there's nothing worse than sucking on a man's dick, then pulling up his balls and getting a whiff of ass funk, ugh!). He also must be drug-and-disease-free (that means no crack, no coke, no 420/weed/trees/collard greens, no dope/smack, no poppers, no damn pills and NOTHING that I can catch). He must be circumcised (a must! I have no time to pull back dick skin. That is an absolute no-no), and don't be busted in the face. I don't want anyone staring in my face hurting my eyes, or making my stomach turn. You don't have to be model-fine, but please, please, don't look like a damn manatee or a gorilla either.

I know, I know. Looks aren't everything. They can't get you an education, can't pay the bills, and definitely don't guarantee intellectual conversation, but dammit, if I want to see something out of Jurassic Park, then I'll go to the zoo! You can save that Wild Kingdom shit for those hard-pressed, ashy chicks with the black between their flabby legs, and titties flopping and sagging down over their nasty pussies. Those types of chicks are the kind to be happy someone is even willing to fuck 'em. So they'll be more than willing to spread their legs open and fuck a beast. But I'm not the one.

Oh, no, I'm not angry with men. Nor do I hate them. On the contrary, I have nothing but love for them. In my opinion, there's nothing sexier than a black man's swagger. There's something about his confidence, his aloofness, his unpredictability, his mysterious demeanor that makes my pussy drip with excitement, and keeps me wanting more. Give me a man with stamina, strength, a beautiful black dick, probing lips, magical hands, and a killer tongue and I'm in heaven. But loving him is not always an easy task. It requires too much damn work and is definitely not an option for me. They either have too much ego, too many women, or too little respect for relationships. And you never know what you're gonna get yourself into when dealing with their asses. Some are too bruised, broken, and beat down by life and fucked up relationships. Others don't know what the hell they want, and have no investment in a committed relationship. So, thanks, but no thanks! I think I'll wax his dick, and keep him fucked to the bone with no strings, no stress, and no damn mess.

Alrighty then. Now that we've gotten that all out the way, come closer. Let me whisper a little something in your ear: You see. I've come to understand that pleasing a man requires patience, and a desire to learn everything that turns him on. Ask him what he likes. And I can't stress it enough—be open-minded. Explore his body with your hands, your lips, your mouth, your tongue. Devour every inch of him. Trust me. All men love to be touched. They love it when you allow your hands to wander and roam all over their bodies when they're thrusting deep up in you. Grabbing and squeezing his ass, running your fingertips and hands down his back, along his spine, pulling him into you as he's stroking his dick in you. Men like to be encouraged, urged to serve the dick how you want it. Trust me.

Anyway, find out what excites him. I don't think a lot of women realize that men have erogenous zones like we do. But oftentimes his hot spots go untouched, or undiscovered. Personally, I liken a man's body to a playground. There's always something to swing on, slide down on, climb up on, bounce up and down on, and jump on.

And in my personal experience, one of the easiest ways to get a man's dick hard (besides talking dirty or showing him your pussy and ass) is to kiss him. A nice, slow, sensual, tongue-probing kiss will often get his mind wandering, and the juices flowing in no time. Before you know it, he'll start fantasizing about having his dick up in you.

See. When I'm with a man, I usually start off by massaging his outer ear in slow movements. I gently squeeze or nibble on his earlobes, explore the back of his ear with my lips and tongue, blowing lightly. Women don't realize how effective this can be. The sound of your breath and the soft moans alone will usually turn most men on. Now, of course this technique only works provided your breath doesn't smell like hot shit.

Anyway, then I travel to his neck, nibbling. Never sucking or biting. I have no interest in trying to mark someone else's territory since most—not all—of the men I fuck are already involved with somebody else. Now, don't go rolling your eyes or sucking your teeth. It's really so unnecessary. Anyway, as I was explaining, I use my lips and tongue to journey down and around his neck to his shoulders, planting soft kisses on them. Then I make my way to his chest. Massaging it with my hands, licking and nibbling, and twirling my tongue over and around his nipples until they become erect, and hard like miniature Skittles. Mmm. Plant wet kisses in the center of his chest, down to his navel, dipping my tongue in. Then I flick my tongue over the head of his throbbing dick before running my fingertips and tongue along the inside of his thighs; kissing, licking, and nibbling up and down them until my tongue reaches his balls. Mmm. I fondle them, lightly suck and lick on them, lapping up the scent of desire that clings beneath them. Finally, I place them in my mouth, and slowly start to hum, flicking them with my tongue. Then I increase the humming on his balls. Trust me. This little trick takes him to the edge every time, giving him an intense, mind-bending experience. You'll have him holding his head in his hands, biting on his bottom lip, grabbing the sheets, climbing walls.

Eventually, I give him what he wants most. What he aches for—my soft lips and hot tongue swirling around the head of his dick. I kiss and nibble on it, licking the excitement that seeps, and drizzles from its slit. Oooh, mmm. I can almost taste his sweet, sticky nectar. See. When I take him all the way in my mouth, I am swallowing him in, savoring the strength of his dick. And when I feel him about to explode, I massage the fleshy area between his balls and ass, pressing on his prostate, giving him a rush of pleasure that causes him to see stars. Yes, if you didn't know, now you do. I'm the Nut Cracker, aka the Man Handler. And this, my little darlings, is my official ho report. Welcome to my world, baaaaby!

Um, wait a minute. Before I let you get too deep into whom I am and what I do, I have some questions for you: Is it really as hard as most women say it is to find a good man? Are all the good men already taken? Is there really a shortage of good, decent men in the world? Is the black man really an endangered species? Or is there simply an abundance of lonely, miserable, sex-deprived women out here?

Now, before you respond, let me start off by saying I understand that no man is gonna respect any woman who drops her drawers, and throws up her legs to the first man who smiles her way. If you're an easy lay, that's all you're going to be seen as; a quick piece of ass. So, don't start getting all emotional when he starts dissing you, or acts like he doesn't know you after you've swallowed his nut. Take it for what it is, a fuck. If you a ho, say you a ho. And stop all the damn fronting. Chicks kill me, catching feelings when a man calls her out of her name, or tries to pass her off to one of his boys. Uh, newsflash: He nutted in your mouth, sweetie. No, he's not gonna kiss you. No, he's not gonna make you his girl. The minute you let a man run up in you, the minute you swallow his babies, you played yourself. So stop all the damn whining and begging. Do you. Get your fuck on, and keep it moving. Luckily for me I don't have that problem. 'Cause I don't give a fuck about a man's respect. Only what's hanging between his legs!

Between you and me—and yes, I'm an opinionated ho—I think the problem is that women have become so desperate to have someone in their lives, and in their beds, (out of fear of being alone) that they settle for a lot of unnecessary bullshit from men. As far as I'm concerned women are responsible for the shit they choose to put up with from men. There's no need complaining about their asses when (9 times out of 10) you already know, or at least have an idea, of what you're dealing with. That's not to say that there aren't some women who truly have no clue as to what their men are into, or capable of. But once the truth is revealed, they are responsible for their decision to leave or stay, or take their asses back. As far as I'm concerned, if they stay, then their dumb-asses deserve to get whatever heartache and grief the men's trifling asses continue to bring them. If they take the men back, they get what they get. So stop the damn tears, and take the shit and piss he throws in your face like a grown-ass woman.

I often wonder how many women buy into that, "It's better to have a piece of a man, than no man at all" mess. I bet there's hundreds of thousands, maybe even a few million women who embrace that distorted foolishness, causing them to shed tears, lose sleep, and fight to hold onto men they love more than they love themselves; women who sacrifice and lose pieces of themselves for the sake of having a man in their lives, no matter the cost, no matter the loss. A part of me wants to feel sorry for them, wants to be able to empathize with them; but because I've never been there, I can't bring myself to develop any level of understanding as to why any women would choose to keep a man in their lives that emotionally, mentally, physically, spiritually and (most times) financially drain them.

But, for the ones who do. Does this make these chicks stupid? Does it make these women victims of their own hearts? Does it mean they lack self-love? Are they bombarded with insecurities? Do they feel trapped?

I mean, really. Why in the hell would any sane, rational women put up with that shit? Hmmm...maybe, they're not sane. Perhaps that's the damn problem. Their asses are downright crazy for thinking they don't deserve better! Ugh! I need to go lie down. This shit has given me a damn splitting-ass headache. Later!